"I just loved how intriguing the mystery is but also the dynamics between a grandmother, a mother, and a teenage daughter."
—REESE WITH

"No novel has ever made family drama (or murder)
—KATY HAYS, *New York Times* bestselling author of *The Cloisters*

"How dare a debut be THIS GOOD!" —JESSE Q. SUTANTO, nationally bestselling author of *Vera Wong's Unsolicited Advice for Murderers*

Simon's wildly entertaining debut mystery... is an ode to strong women everywhere."
—ELI CRANOR, Edgar Award–winning author of *Don't Know Tough*

Equal parts charming and chilling: a fine mystery."
—BENJAMIN STEVENSON, nationally bestselling author of *Everyone in My Family Has Killed Someone*

"Simon mixes a light, breezy style with a harder-edge story with domestic suspense at its heart." —*SOUTH FLORIDA SUN SENTINEL*

"Simon's dazzling debut delivers everything a mystery fan could crave. . . . A cleverly crafted cozy crime novel." —*LIBRARY JOURNAL* (starred review)

PRAISE FOR
MOTHER-DAUGHTER MURDER NIGHT

"Simon's depiction of the difficult family dynamics is engrossing, but she also offers a riveting whodunit that will keep readers guessing to the end."

—*Washington Post*

"I loved the concept—three generations of the Rubicon family, all women, team up to solve a murder in their Northern California coastal town. But a novel can't succeed on concept alone, and I'm pleased to say that Simon crafted an endearing trio of fully-fleshed out characters."

—*New York Times*

"Simon's dazzling debut delivers everything a mystery fan could crave, including a realistically nuanced cast of characters, a vividly evoked coastal California setting, writing imbued with a deliciously desiccated sense of wit, and a perfectly plotted murder with enough red herrings deftly dropped in to confound the most experienced mystery reader. . . . Insightful and frequently funny analysis of family dynamics wrapped up in a cleverly crafted cozy crime novel."

—*Library Journal* (starred review)

"Clever. . . . An endearing tale about how something so unexpected can be the thing that repairs old family wounds and broken hearts."

—Shondaland

"With all the right touches of heart, humor and whodunit, *Mother-Daughter Murder Night* is the murder mystery that I didn't know I was longing for. Nina Simon combines compelling, easy-to-root-for characters with a cozy mystery, then amplifies and elevates both with complicated, tightly woven family dynamics and timely connections to real-world issues that will resonate with readers of all backgrounds."

—Bookreporter.com

"Three women bond while investigating a homicide in Simon's spirited debut. . . . Simon stocks her layered plot with plausibly motivated suspects and convincing red herrings, but it's her indomitable female characters and their nuanced relationships that give this mystery its spark. Readers will be delighted."

—*Publishers Weekly*

"Simon mixes a light, breezy style with a harder-edge story with domestic suspense at its heart. The plot . . . never lags as Simon also maintains the emotional growth of her strong characters. . . . *Mother-Daughter Murder Night* marks the advent of a new author to watch."

—*South Florida Sun Sentinel*

"Sleuthing is a family affair in this novel featuring strong women and even stronger motives for murder. . . . Simon knows how to build an intriguing plot with lots of suspects, plenty of red herrings, and a handful of jaw-clenching attacks on the Rubicons designed to stop their investigation. Nancy Drew meets Columbo in this feisty-female–driven whodunit."

—*Kirkus Reviews*

"Nina Simon's *Mother-Daughter Murder Night* is the rarest of novels: a lively and tender story of family that Simon deftly transforms into an edge-of-your-seat murder mystery set against the polarizing backdrop of land conservation. No novel has ever made family drama (or murder) this much fun. One part *The Maid* and one part family drama à la *The Nest, Mother-Daughter Murder Night* is a resounding and impressive triumph. I fell in love with Tiny, Lana, and Beth immediately, and so will you."

—Katy Hays, *New York Times* bestselling author of *The Cloisters*

"With a clear-eyed blend of family stresses and furtive schemes, the author produces a classic whodunit and embraces the strength that is often nurtured among multiple generations of women. Celebrate Simon's success."

—*Richmond Times-Dispatch*

"Simon's wildly entertaining debut mystery, *Mother-Daughter Murder Night,* is an ode to strong women everywhere. The coastal California setting, complete with a bootleg drive-in and the aptly named Kayak Shack, serves as the perfect proving grounds for the fiercely independent Rubicon women."

—Eli Cranor, Edgar Award–winning author of
Don't Know Tough and *Ozark Dogs*

"*Mother-Daughter Murder Night* is the perfect mix of family drama and murder mystery. Nina Simon's debut is a spot-on look at the complicated relationship between parents and their children. I can't wait to spend even more nights with her characters. Simon is a writer to watch."

—Kellye Garrett, award-winning author of *Like a Sister*

"As a reader, I inhaled this book hungrily, captivated by the truly delightful characters that Simon has created. The relationship between Lana and Beth is perfectly complex—hilarious, heartwarming, and frustrating because of how real it was. As an author, the writing made me clench my fists and shout, 'How dare a debut be THIS GOOD!'"

—Jesse Q. Sutanto, nationally bestselling author of *Dial A for Aunties*
and *Vera Wong's Unsolicited Advice for Murderers*

"As much a story about the complicated love between a mother and daughter as it is a sublime whodunit, Nina Simon's *Mother-Daughter Murder Night* is sure to enthrall any reader who likes their mystery with equal doses of humor, family intrigue, and surprises."

—Rob Osler, Mystery Writers of America's Robert L. Fish Memorial Award–winning author of *Devil's Chew Toy*

"On the cozy side, this debut mystery is woven around family rifts and redemption, and will leave readers with warm fuzzies."

—*Booklist*

"In the appealing *Mother-Daughter Murder Night,* first-time novelist Nina Simon integrates spirited family dynamics with the intricacies of a complex whodunit. . . . This skillfully crafted multigenerational study of disparate characters will keep mystery readers guessing with its surprising, immensely well-plotted crimes and clues."

—*Shelf Awareness*

MOTHER-DAUGHTER MURDER NIGHT

A Novel

NINA SIMON

wm

WILLIAM MORROW

An Imprint of HarperCollins*Publishers*

This is a work of fiction. Names, characters, places, and incidents are products of the author's imagination or are used fictitiously and are not to be construed as real. Any resemblance to actual events, locales, organizations, or persons, living or dead, is entirely coincidental.

HarperCollins books may be purchased for educational, business, or sales promotional use. For information, please email the Special Markets Department at SPsales@harpercollins.com.

A hardcover edition of this book was published in 2023 by William Morrow, an imprint of HarperCollins Publishers.

FIRST WILLIAM MORROW PAPERBACK EDITION PUBLISHED 2024.

Designed by Nancy Singer
Map by Beck Tench

The Library of Congress has catalogued a previous edition as follows:

Names: Simon, Nina, author.
Title: Mother-daughter murder night : a novel / Nina Simon.
Description: First edition. | New York, NY : William Morrow, [2023]
Identifiers: LCCN 2023002210 | ISBN 9780063315044 (hardcover) | ISBN 9780063315068 (ebook)
Subjects: LCGFT: Detective and mystery fiction. | Novels.
Classification: LCC PS3619.I56256 M68 2023 | DDC 813/.6—dc23/eng/20230522
LC record available at https://lccn.loc.gov/2023002210

ISBN 978-0-06-331505-1 (pbk.)

24 25 26 27 28 LBC 5 4 3 2 1

To my mother,
who reviewed every page of this book except this one.
Which allows her to stay humble while I tell you the truth:
she is simply the best.

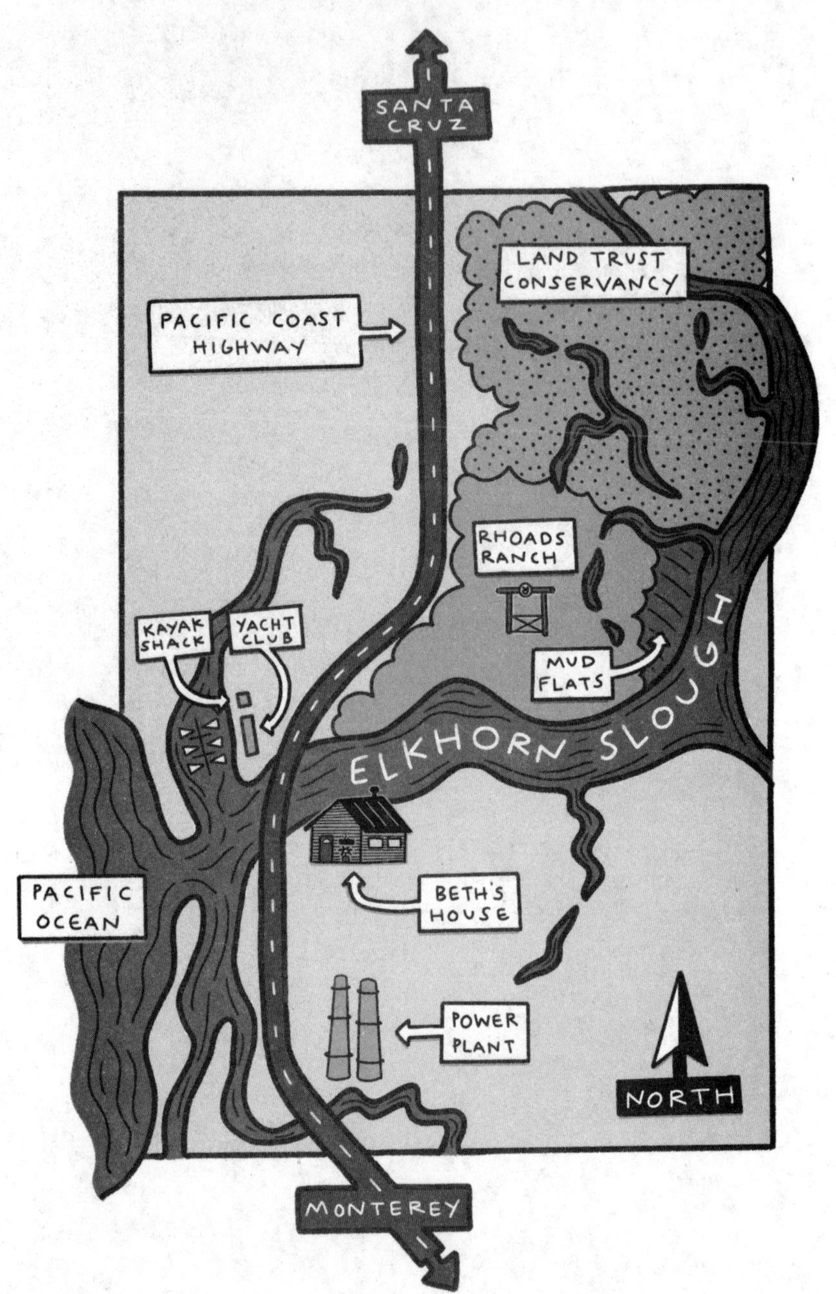
SANTA CRUZ
LAND TRUST CONSERVANCY
PACIFIC COAST HIGHWAY
RHOADS RANCH
KAYAK SHACK
YACHT CLUB
MUD FLATS
ELKHORN SLOUGH
PACIFIC OCEAN
BETH'S HOUSE
POWER PLANT
NORTH
MONTEREY

PROLOGUE

BETH KNEW SHE COULDN'T leave for work until she dealt with the dead body on the beach.

She gathered her breath and the supplies she'd need. Jacket. Boots. Rubber gloves from under the sink. She stepped outside, grabbed the shovel leaning up against her makeshift potting table, then looked down to the slough below. The salt marsh was choked in early-morning fog, and she could barely see anything. But Beth wasn't worried. She'd spent fifteen years picking her way down the steep, scraggly hillside to the water. And the stink of death told her exactly where she needed to go.

She clambered down to the bank by feel, and smell, letting the cool October mist wrap itself around her and tug her toward the dead body. Most carcasses that washed up were swept back into the water or eaten quickly by scavengers. But this harbor seal had been here almost a week. It was a big one, speckled brown, with a ragged hole in its side and pale patches where strips of skin were peeling away. Turkey vultures had pecked out its eyes and pulled a wet, maggoty trail of innards onto the beach. Beth grimaced. As a geriatric nurse, she'd seen her share of death, had seen it respected, welcomed even. Evisceration was another matter. She moved away from the seal and found a quiet spot by the underbrush. She began to dig.

Beth was still digging when Jack paddled up, her pink board carving a bright path through the fog. Her daughter was a cloud of dark hair and brown skin, her compact body swallowed in her red life jacket.

"Mom?"

Such a small word, but it never failed to warm her.

"I decided to bury it."

Jack wrinkled her nose at the smell. "Need help?"

"I don't think we have a tarp." Beth straightened up. She was taller than her daughter, and paler, her freckled arms strong from helping thousands of patients in and out of hospital beds. "But in the Prima box in the garage, there might be a tablecloth. Grab a trash bag too."

Jack nodded, then whipped her paddleboard on top of her head and carried it up the hillside.

Ten minutes later, she bounded back down to the narrow beach holding a shimmery white bundle in her arms.

"You sure you want to use this? It says it's from Italy." The fabric was thick and buttery, with an intricate pattern of silver vines snaking across it.

Beth snorted. "When exactly are we going to use a damask tablecloth?"

"I mean . . . Prima gave it to us—"

"Exactly." Beth's mother, Lana—or "Prima" to Jack—had never visited them in Elkhorn Slough. But every year for Chanukah, she shipped them ostentatious presents that belied her total lack of understanding of, or interest in, their lives. "Help me spread it out."

They unfurled the pristine tablecloth over the weeds and sand. Beth put on the rubber gloves and closed her eyes for a moment. Then, with sure, steady movements, she rolled the dead seal onto the fabric, folded it in, and dragged it to the hole she'd dug.

Jack stood there, hopping from foot to foot, while her mother buried the seal deep under the sand and brush, then shoved the now-putrid tablecloth into the trash bag.

"So, first Wednesday in October . . ." Jack said.

Beth held her breath. The day was coming when Jack wouldn't want to go out with her mother for a foot-long at the Hot Diggity and a movie at the bootleg drive-in a farmer in Salinas set up behind his barn. Jack was fifteen now. She had a job. Soon she'd have boyfriends and car loans and a life that didn't revolve around their little house by the slough. Beth knew how good it felt to break from your parents and make your own way. She just didn't want it for Jack. Not yet.

"It's sci-fi slasher night." Jack grinned. "You'll get home on time?"

"Of course." Beth had been pulling extra shifts at the nursing home, trying to save up for Jack's college tuition. But she wouldn't miss one of their drive-in nights.

Jack charged back up the hillside to gather her stuff and bike to school. But something held Beth to the spot on the beach. She looked down at the freshly piled sand beside her, then out to the fog blanketing the slough. She realized she was looking for a disturbance, a ripple in the water, someone to bear witness alongside her.

But that was foolish. With her jacket sleeve, Beth wiped a smudge of dried river mud off her face, then ran a hand through her short, sun-streaked hair. There were no mourners in Elkhorn Slough. No murderers either. Only death, natural and brutal, every minute of the day. Leopard sharks hunted flatfish in the muddy depths. Otters cracked open crabs. Even the algae, blooming green and full of life, sucked the pickle grass dry beneath the water's surface.

Beth picked up a moon-shaped piece of sea glass from the beach and placed it carefully on top of the mound. A pelican dive-bombed into the slough in front of her, resurfacing with a fish wriggling in its gullet. Beth was inexplicably reminded of her mother: Lana's sharp beauty, her biting tongue, her relentless hunger to swallow life whole, bones and all.

Her mother had never visited Elkhorn Slough. And no one had ever been murdered there.

But there was a first time for everything.

CHAPTER ONE

THREE HUNDRED MILES SOUTH, Lana Rubicon lay sprawled on the dark slate floor of her kitchen, wondering how she got there.

Her interest was not philosophical. She didn't want to know how she'd arrived on this planet or which of her Greek ancestors had blessed her with wrinkle-proof olive skin. She wanted to know why she'd collapsed, what was making her feel like a drunk at the carnival on a Wednesday at 7 A.M., and whether she could still make her 8 A.M. investor meeting.

She turned her head in small, careful increments, trying to get her bearings. Her briefcase and snakeskin heels were waiting for her in the front hallway to the left. To the right, the stainless steel door of the fridge was wide open, bottles of mineral water and premade salads lit from within as if they'd come from heaven instead of the Gelson's delivery boy. A gooey liquid streaked across the floor from the bottom of the refrigerator to the side of Lana's head. Lana put one hand to the matted hair at her temple and pulled it back for inspection. Her French-tipped fingernails were sticky and pink.

Not blood. Yogurt.

Lana decided it was a sign the day could only get better.

AFTER FIVE FAILED ATTEMPTS to lift herself off the floor, Lana slid her phone out of her jacket pocket. She wavered for a moment over who to call. Her daughter was a nurse. Could be useful. But Beth was five hours away, and Lana wasn't about to beg her own child for help.

She dialed the first number on her Favorites list instead.

Her assistant picked up on the first ring. "I know, I'm sorry, I'll be in the office at seven fifteen. Some idiot set fire to the hillside by the Getty again and the 405 is—"

"Janie, I need you to . . ." Lana squinted up at the ceiling. Needed her to what? Scrape her off the floor? Stop the world from spinning? "I need you to reschedule my morning meetings."

"But the Hacienda Lofts investors—"

"Tell them we're adding sixty more units. Very exciting. Have to rework the plans. Champagne for everyone."

"But—"

"Handle it. I'll check in later."

Lana closed her eyes for a moment, enjoying the feeling of cool tile against her cheek. Then she picked up her phone again and dialed 911.

LANA COUNTED HERSELF LUCKY that at fifty-seven years old this was her first time being wheeled into a hospital. Even lying on a gurney, Lana knew she looked worth saving. A tailored charcoal suit hugged her lithe frame. She hadn't yet twisted her hair into a chignon, and plum-brown waves flowed down her back, some of them now tinted in strawberry yogurt. She held eye contact with the nurse as he rolled her into a giant white tube, silently directing him to do his best work.

Once she blocked out the loud clunks from the machine, Lana found the MRI to be oddly relaxing. No emails from architects about why they couldn't get the drawings done in time. No calls from her friend Gloria about the most recent loser to break her heart. Lana figured this must be what being dead was like. No one asking her for anything.

After she emerged from the MRI scanner, Lana negotiated her way into a hospital room with no roommates, but also no windows. Her assistant messengered over three project files, two draft contracts, a red pen, a pair of black pumps, a smoked salmon salad, and a bottle of Sprite. Lana was about to send the girl a text about the importance of attention to detail—was it really too much to remember Diet Coke was the only soda she drank?—when she opened the offending plastic bottle and sniffed. Janie had filled it with Chardonnay. Lana took a sip. Not half-bad.

That afternoon, when they told her they were still waiting on test results and recommended she stay overnight for observation, Lana humored them. One bed was as good as another. Not exactly true, but she didn't relish the thought of wasting daytime hours in LA traffic shuttling herself back to the hospital the next morning to get a lecture from a doctor with mismatched socks about taking better care of herself. She figured she'd get the tests back early, pass with flying colors, run home to shower, and make her lunch meeting with the mortgage brokers.

Lana spent the evening in the hospital bed inking up development plans. When the nurses came to check on her, she smiled so she'd get better service, but she didn't chitchat. They sampled and poked her while Lana worked. She didn't tell any of her associates where she was. There was no reason for them to know.

THE NEXT DAY BROKE SOUR. Lana woke early, impatient, with a fog in her head and a rash on her neck from the cardboard hospital pillows. At 7:30 A.M., she rang the nurse and badgered her into getting someone more important. The doctor who showed up was tall and willowy and entirely unhelpful. The tests weren't completed yet. No, Lana couldn't leave and get the results later. No, they didn't have laptops for patients' use. Yes, she would just have to wait.

Lana counted the water stains on the ceiling and made lists of everything she'd have to do when she got to the office. She wanted a Diet Coke. She wanted her own bathroom. She wanted to get out of there.

After what felt like hours, a new doctor came in, a middle-aged man with unkempt hair and scuffed white sneakers. There was an angry squeak as he yanked a wobbly plastic cart clear of the hallway and into the room.

"Mrs. Rubicon?"

"Ms." Lana was perched on a visitor's chair in her blazer and pumps, tapping furiously on her phone. She didn't look up.

"I have some images from the MRI and PET scans we conducted yesterday of your head and neck."

"Can you just give me the highlights?" Lana gave him a brusque once-over, her fingers still moving across her phone. "I have somewhere I have to be. Had to be, three hours ago."

"Ma'am, you're going to want to see this."

The doctor wheeled the portable computer terminal over to Lana's chair. He clicked some windows into view. Then he angled the monitor and stepped aside.

It was strange to see her own head on someone else's computer screen. The images were black and gray, with thin white lines delineating Lana's skull and eye sockets and the top of her spinal cord. Lana rose to stand beside the doctor, getting as close to the screen as she could. He used the mouse to orient four different views into the four quadrants of the screen: from above, front, back, and in profile. Lana tried to follow his twisting motions, watching her gray blob of a brain rotate in the darkness, spinning in search of a solid foundation.

Once the doctor was satisfied, he hit a button. The gray blob went polychromatic. Clustered along the back of her skull were three bright smudges of orange with pink halos around them.

"What are those?" she asked.

"Those are the reason you're here," he said. "Have you been having headaches? Blurred vision? Any trouble finding words?"

A thin needle of fear pierced Lana's confidence. But there was nothing wrong with her. Lana was the fittest, most active woman in her loose gaggle of friends. All single. All professional. All surviving dickwad ex-husbands with bank accounts and dignity intact. Lana was stiletto sharp. Lana was thriving.

At least, she had been until yesterday morning.

"Those bright blotches are tumors," Dr. Scuffed Sneakers told her. "They're causing swelling and inadequate blood flow to the part of your brain that controls your balance and large motor functions. That's why you fell."

"Tumors?"

He nodded. "They have to come out. As soon as possible."

Lana lowered herself back into the stiff visitor's chair. She lined up the points of her shoes and held herself taut, muscles vibrating.

"I have brain cancer?"

"Maybe. Hopefully."

"Hopefully?" She fought to keep her voice from breaking.

"Sometimes, cancer originates elsewhere in your body and spreads to your brain. That would be worse, more advanced. We'll biopsy the brain tumors once they're removed to confirm the site of origin. And we'll do a full body scan now to see if there are any more."

She focused on his chapped lips, willing them to take back the words he'd just said. This couldn't be happening. When Lana had breast cancer ten years ago, it wasn't a big deal. Stage 0. Beth had come down for the initial surgery, but otherwise, she'd handled it on her own. After a few spins in the radiation chair and a reconstruction procedure she used to get a tad more lift, she was back to work.

Now this doctor was looking at her like she was an injured bird.

"Do you understand what I just said?"

"I've got to call my daughter," she said.

CHAPTER TWO

BETH TOOK A SWIG of tepid coffee and considered her cell phone. Three missed calls from her mother. One voicemail, short, asking for help. The content was alarming, and more so, Lana's voice. Was she drunk? Congested? Beth was used to her mom's staccato messages, a mix of crowing and indignation, with a slug of guilt thrown in for good measure. This was different. Unfamiliar. Lana's voice sounded lost, almost pitiful.

Beth left Amber in charge at the nursing station and walked out the side door of Bayshore Oaks. She gave a reassuring smile to the young man fidgeting by his car, clearly nervous about visiting the long-term care facility. Then she ducked around the corner, slipping into the grove of Monterey pines. She took a deep breath and dialed.

"Ma?"

"Beth, finally." Lana's voice came through in an urgent whisper. "Are you still working for the brain surgeon? The one with the big teeth?"

"The one with the Nobel Prize? You know I left two years ago to spend more time with—"

"Beth, listen to me. They're telling me I've got tumors. Lots of them. In my brain. That I need surgery, right away. But you should see the shoes this doctor is wearing. I mean, how can he expect anyone to take him seriously?"

Beth's face froze in a half smile. "Wait. Slow down. Where are you? Are you okay?"

"Besides being held hostage by a radiologist who can't be bothered to brush his own hair, I'm fine. I'm at City of Angels hospital. They say I can't check myself out. That someone has to take care of me. I need to get to a better facility. One with real doctors in decent suits. So . . ."

The non-question hung in the air.

If Lana had ever asked for Beth's help before, she couldn't remember it. Demanded her attention, sure. Assumed her acquiescence, constantly. But needed her help? Valued her expertise? If Beth weren't so worried, she'd mark the day on the calendar with a gold star.

"Ma, of course I'll come."

Silence. Lana was never silent. For a moment, Beth pictured her mother in a hospital bed, alone, maybe even afraid. It was hard to imagine.

Beth spoke in her most confident voice. "Dr. K retired. But I know the charge nurse in neurology at Stanford. It's one of the best neurosurgical facilities in the country. I'll make a call."

"Can't we do it at UCLA?"

There was the prima donna she'd grown up with. Beth knew it would be useless to remind her mother that she too had a life, a job, and a child. Instead, she responded in language Lana could understand.

"Ma, this is brain surgery. Let's get you the very best."

"Stanford?"

"Stanford. I'll take care of it."

"Hold on. Someone's coming in the room."

Beth scanned her schedule for the rest of the day. Two more patients, nothing complicated: vitals check, an infusion, a bath, and a chat. She could get Amber to cover her. Jack had already texted to ask permission to go to a soccer game after school and sleep over at her friend Kayla's house. Perfect. Beth could book it down to LA, scoop up her mother, and get her checked into Stanford the next morning.

Lana's voice shot back through the phone. "Stanford. Fine. But I'm staying in a hotel."

"Ma, you can't be alone when you're recovering from brain surgery."

"I hardly think I'll recover in a shack that's about to fall into a mud pit."

Beth closed her eyes and resisted the urge to throw the phone. "It's not your condo. It's not LA. But it's nice. I promise."

There was a long pause during which Beth presumed Lana was contemplating the many ways her daughter's shabby house and backwater town fell short of her minimum requirements.

"Can you ask what time you'll be released today?" Beth said.

"They want me to talk to an oncologist here, but then they said I'm free to leave."

"All right. Sit tight. Get as much information as you can. I'll be there in five hours."

BETH SPED DOWN the highway in her dented Camry, stopping only for gas, a caffeinated energy bar, and a supersize iced coffee. As she drove, her mind raced, punctuated by the intermittent buzz of text messages from her mother.

Tumors in brain, lung, maybe colon? Stage 4 at least. Not good.

DR picking his nose. GET ME OUT OF HERE.

Pls swing by the condo for my laptop, good jeans, black top (slimming).

Also if I die give my car to Gloria.

AFTER THE FIRST HOUR of texts, Beth decided she didn't need a car crash to go with the heart attack. She stuck her phone in the glove compartment and focused on the road and her spiraling thoughts.

Beth was used to medical emergencies. As a nurse, she'd called in more than one. But her clients were old, infirm, and for the most part, kind. They were in that stage of desperate hopefulness, counting days as good ones if there wasn't too much pain.

Lana was nothing like them. She didn't "do" sick. Beth assumed her mother would approach this cancer the way she approached everything else—as a series of hurdles to bulldoze. That's what she'd done when she had the breast cancer scare ten years before. That crisis had proved a kind of blessing in disguise, an external push that forced Lana and Beth back together after five years of not speaking. Since then, they'd built a tentative reconnection out of annual visits to LA for Passover and occasional, awkward phone calls, sticking to safe topics like Lana's work or Jack's grades.

But the news in these garbled texts sounded far from safe. And the fact that Lana had called her, had asked for help, had agreed to come to Elkhorn—that was downright terrifying.

FIVE OVERSTUFFED SUITCASES, one box of files and legal pads, and two triple-shot lattes later, the Rubicon women were heading north. As Beth drove, Lana made calls, dispatching her friend Gloria to water her plants, her neighbor Ervin to collect her mail, and her assistant, Janie, to do everything else.

"Think of it as a growth opportunity," Lana said, after dictating a long list of directives.

When Janie pressed her on what she should tell Lana's clients, the older woman looked down at her black satin peekaboo pumps for inspiration. Lana could see her chipped midnight-blue toenails peeking out.

"Tell them it's foot surgery. Very complicated. I need a specialist. Out of town. I'll be back in the office in six weeks."

Beth shot her mother a look.

"What?" Lana said. "They said there might be more tumors. Maybe there's one in my foot."

"Six weeks, Ma?"

"Seems like more than enough time to have the surgeries, get on a treatment plan, head back home, and forget about all this unpleasantness. Besides, it's not like we could survive living in the same house longer than that."

AFTER TWO HOURS CRAWLING through city traffic, they left the sprawl of Los Angeles. They wound up a mountain pass lined with citrus trees,

Beth's Camry chugging uphill as the stars came out. Lana shut her eyes at the first vineyards, and Beth drove on in silence, watching the rolling hills give way to the inky Monterey Bay. Even in the dark, the ocean made itself known, waves roaring onto rocks, spraying salt and mist over the bridge that separated sea from strawberry fields.

Beth's house was perched between ocean and farmland, on a tiny strip of gravel and sand above Elkhorn Slough. Beth loved the way the wetland shifted with the tides, rising and falling like a lover's breath below her house. When she'd first moved in fifteen years ago, she'd seen Elkhorn as a temporary refuge. But she'd grown to relish its foggy mornings and wild treasures, soft where Los Angeles was hard, scruffy where the city was slick. As Beth walked her mother to the door, she resisted the urge to point out the driftwood planters she'd carved and filled with succulents, the wreath of bracken fern she'd braided herself. She steered Lana to Jack's bedroom, bracing for her mother to pronounce her verdict on the secondhand furniture, the nicked floorboards, the peaty smell of the slough wafting up from outside.

That night, Lana didn't say anything about home decor or river mud. Lana didn't say anything at all. Her face was locked in grim determination, mouth shut tight. Beth opened the door to Jack's bedroom, waved Lana onto the bed, and helped her take off her shoes. It scared Beth to see her mother so compliant. It was easier too.

Once Lana was asleep, Beth started calling in favors. Her friend in neurology at Stanford had already connected her to their top brain surgeon, and he'd agreed to slot them in for a pre-op consultation the next day. Her old shift mate in oncology would find someone to cross-check the scans. Even the guy she'd dated last year, a bearded search-and-rescue paramedic from Big Sur, offered to be on standby. Beth was glad she'd spent so many years pulling long hours, covering for others, doing an extra house call for a doctor who asked. You only get one mother. Even if she was a pain in the butt like Lana.

CHAPTER THREE

February 4 (Seventeen Weeks Later)

LANA BOLTED UP at the sound of a scream outside her window. She'd been in Elkhorn Slough four months now: long enough to recognize the predatory snarls and howls that filled the night, not nearly long enough to sleep through them. She heard another shriek, then a rustle. There was a killer on the prowl again.

Lana turned on the light and pushed aside the mountain of pill bottles to get to her binoculars. It was 1:30 A.M. Another sleepless night courtesy of the wonders of modern medicine. Lana glared at the unfinished dinner smoothie on the dresser, her throat seizing as she caught a whiff of its chalky blueberry froth. No one had told her chemotherapy would wreak havoc on her senses. Lana could now smell a decaying deer from a mile away, but she couldn't taste anything. Everything she put in her mouth turned to damp wool, gummy and itching to get stuck in her throat.

There were lots of things about cancer she hadn't been prepared for. The brain surgeries had gone well. But then the Stanford doctors in their double-breasted suits informed her they could not slice out the small army of tumors flanking her left lung. This was not a brush with death to laugh about over cocktails. It was a long-term condition, which was decidedly less glamorous.

The chemotherapy stole her energy. Then her hair, sticking to her comb in terrifying clumps until she took an electric shaver to it on a tearstained, wine-spilled afternoon. And then she lost her work. Her two-hundred-unit condo project in Westchester went to a Beverly Hills airhead who carried a hairless dog in her purse. A thirty-year-old shark who wore mirrored sunglasses indoors stole the Hacienda Lofts account. She kept her health insurance, thankfully, but everything else dried up. At first her assistant, Janie, was indignant, relaying each new slight in breathless, high-pitched voicemails as if someone were personally nailing the girl's acrylic fingernails to a telephone pole. But Lana could hardly muster the energy to keep up the fiction of her imaginary foot condition, let alone raise the dead over another young buck who wanted to steal her perch on top of LA's commercial real estate market. The day before Thanksgiving, Janie called to tell her she'd found a growth opportunity somewhere else. Lana was surprised to find she didn't really care. She hung up the phone without saying goodbye.

Lana rang in the New Year with no hair, no business, and no clear answer on when it might all be over. "Too soon to tell," the doctors intoned, as if she were a crystal ball of maladies. After three months of chemotherapy, she was now just two weeks away from her first full set of scans since treatment had started. Soon she'd know if she was improving, or if she was stuck in the back bedroom of her daughter's shabby house forever.

A death sentence. That's what it felt like. Even on the good days, Lana had nothing to do and no one to do it with. Beth was at work. Jack was at school or out paddling on the water. Lana hadn't even opened the third care package from Gloria, which she knew would be stuffed with romance novels, crystals, and other worthless fantasies. All day, she watched life teem outside her window: egrets hunting along the banks, otters clutching their fuzzy babies to their chests, kayakers winding in and out of the shifting tides. She felt like a bystander, auditioning for a role that didn't interest her. No one asking her for sign-off. No one waiting for her opinion. A life of irrelevance. It was almost as depressing as the cancer.

TWO A.M. AND SHE was still awake. The shrieks had ended, but the beach was alive with a chittering, scuffling sound. Lana pulled up the window blinds and lifted the binoculars in search of its source.

The moon was full above the slough, and the whole world looked flattened out in grayscale: wispy clouds, grainy fields, fast-moving current. Glints of moonlight bounced off the water where harbor seals surfaced, hunting crabs along the mud flats that edged the slice of beach behind the house. *Beach* was an optimistic word for the narrow strip of grit, weeds, and long-dead jellyfish that stretched from Beth's scraggly neighborhood to an old power plant and the marina. Twice a day, the bank got swallowed up in a swirl of river and seawater, then spat out again at low tide, bearing tree branches, old tires, and whatever else the Pacific Ocean didn't want.

She scanned the beach with the binoculars. At the far end, she saw sand flying into the air beneath a set of furry paws and gleaming eyes. Her shrieking demon was a bobcat, digging frantically, a dead rodent flopping in its mouth. Was it hollowing out a den in which to enjoy its kill? Or did it plan to stash the carcass for later? Whatever its intent, she hoped it would stop making a racket soon.

Lana dropped her binoculars and stared across the water. Everything here was mud and vermin. She missed her condo in Santa Monica, where the only late-night sounds were automotive, the only wildlife hypoallergenic designer pets. Los Angeles was alive in a way she understood, a buzzing hive she'd wrestled her way to the center of, as a queen, or at least not a drone. But Elkhorn Slough belonged to someone else, to creatures dark and hidden.

A flicker on the far side of the slough pierced Lana's thoughts. It was a small circle of light, weak and yellowed, bouncing wildly through the scrub. Lana raised her binoculars and started scanning the murky hillside in slow horizontal passes. Finally she caught it. A person with a flashlight, stumbling down a faint deer path toward the north bank. The man—was it a man?—was pushing something. He was wearing an oversize coat, a hat, and gloves, bundled up against the February chill.

A wheelbarrow. That's what he was pushing. At two in the morning.

Lana frowned. She'd always been a city girl, but still. Surely there weren't farming tasks to be done in the middle of the night.

The man was moving fast, down toward the brackish water. The wheelbarrow dipped and surged in and out of view as he charged through the high grass. Either his cargo was heavy or the ground was uneven. Or both.

He stopped at a low point in the marsh Lana couldn't quite make out. He was down there for a couple minutes, spreading something out maybe, or arranging something in place. Lana found herself holding her breath, waiting for him to rise. Instead, there was a splash. The man shot back up, hat first, dark shoulders. Then he turned and stared straight across the slough at Lana.

Lana reared back, spooked. The man couldn't possibly see her from all that way in the dark. And yet. She could have sworn she felt the heat in his eyes.

It was impossible. Lana realized the warmth was coming from her own body, from her intense focus and shortened breath. She felt a sudden, fierce longing to be this man—not a farmer, but someone out in the world doing something, something physical and definitive and certain, while others slept. That was the life she was meant to live. To be the doer, not the watcher.

But here she was, clutching her binoculars. She envied the man, standing there on the north bank, breathing white puffs of air into the night. He stared out over the water for a full minute. Then he turned away.

Lana yanked the blinds shut and fell back onto her pillow. She felt suddenly spent, swollen and cracked, as if she'd wasted a day lying out at the beach in full sun. When she peered through the glass again, the man was gone. The shuffling labor of the bobcat had ended. The only sound was the great horned owls, coming home to roost.

CHAPTER FOUR

"TINY! HEY, TINY!"

Jacqueline Avital Santos Rubicon, aka Jack, aka Tiny, lifted her paddle out of the water and turned around. The eight-year-old in the front of kayak 12 was waving both hands in the air like he'd just found the lost city of Atlantis.

"You said to look out for jellyfish," he shouted. "I found the biggest one ever."

He leaned forward and pointed at a shimmering blob, the boat wobbling as his mother braced to keep it balanced.

"Great, buddy," Jack said. "Can you see it pulsing?"

The boy stared down, then nodded solemnly.

"That's awesome. Now remember, some birds and otters don't love it when we yell. We're in their home, right?"

He nodded again, eyes Boy Scout serious, mouth a wide smile.

She gave him a thumbs-up and glided past. She paused to watch an otter feed its baby, offering bits of crawdad to the tiny fluffball snuggled against its chest. Jack felt sure of herself, confident, in a way she rarely felt on land. On the water, a five-foot half-Jewish, half-Filipino teenager could be just as powerful as anyone else.

JACK HAD BEEN WORKING weekends as a kayak tour guide for almost two years, and by her calculations, she needed just nine more paychecks before she could afford a used sailboat. She'd started out saving up for a car, but the more time she spent paddling the sluggish water between the marina and the slough, the hungrier she was to go farther, wilder, into the open ocean. Not that she didn't love Elkhorn Slough. She just wasn't surprised by its secrets anymore.

Every Saturday, she barreled to the Kayak Shack on her bike at 8 A.M., arriving before most of the marina had woken up. This morning, she'd chained her ten-speed to the fence behind a fancy green road bike she didn't recognize. It wasn't locked, just sitting there waiting to be snapped up. Unbelievable. Some people trusted the universe to take care of them. And then there were people like Jack who took care of themselves.

The morning zoomed by in a flurry of life jackets, wet suits, and excited tourists. She guided a group of families into the slough at nine, and then a private tour, a pair of animal lovers who spent their hour watching a clutch of elderly otters gossip in a tight circle of sunshine. Jack pointed their camera lenses in the right direction, for which she was rewarded with a peaceful trip ending with a twenty-dollar bill she rolled from her hand to her pocket in a single motion.

She ran up to the office to wolf down some food before the sunset tour, waving at Travis, who was at the desk. She took her sandwich out the back door, rounding the corner just in time to see Paul Hanley step out of the outdoor shower, a pair of faded board shorts hanging from his hips. The Kayak Shack owner had to be at least forty, but he still dressed like a teenage surfer. Paul riffled his shaggy blond hair in his towel and bounded over to her.

"Tiny! Hey. Gotta question for you." Paul was committed to the use of nicknames for all the guides, for confidentiality, he said. He'd tried to dub her Moana, because she was small and brown and fearless with a paddle, but Jack had taken her grandma's advice and glared at him until he backed down and suggested Tiny instead.

"Can you close tonight?" Paul asked.

"I was the first one here," Jack said. "Can Travis?"

"He said he can stay for check-in, but then . . ." Paul gave her a hopeful, wide-eyed look.

"Yeah, okay," she said. "I'll lock up after the sunset tour."

"You're the best." Paul turned away to pull a ratty T-shirt over his head. "Hey, so I met this chick, this woman, at the yacht club today. She's in town for the weekend on that sweet seventy-footer by the fuel dock. She asked me about going fishing for marlin tonight, maybe tomorrow too. I'm gonna solo guide her."

Translation: Paul wanted to get laid, and Jack was on her own.

AFTER JACK GOT PAST her annoyance with herself for not asking Paul for overtime pay, she had an entertaining evening. Everyone else who worked at the Shack was male, and older, and while they were cool with her, it was nice to have a night off from being subtly treated like she didn't know what she was doing. The Saturday sunset tour was all adults: two athletic women, an older man with thick eyebrows and a bald head, and a bachelor party of eight young men in matching Hawaiian shirts. The bachelor party rolled in late, crashing the safety talk just as Jack assured the women there were no sharks in the slough this time of year.

"Except you, Brian," one of the young men said, slapping his buddy on the back. "You're the shark."

"Sharknado, baby."

"Nah, man, more like Brian SHARK do do do do, Brian SHARK do do . . ."

Jack rubbed her temple as more of them started singing off-key. Were these idiots going to cause trouble? Paul always said this business wasn't about seeing cute sea lions. It was about touching the wilderness, the jolt you get when you peek off the edge of your comfort zone. Jack's job wasn't to kill that buzz. Her job was to cultivate it. To indulge people's desire for adventure, while assuring their complete safety. As long as no one got hurt, a little looseness was fine.

And everyone else seemed to be enjoying it. The two women were wearing indulgent smiles and swaying their hips. The bald man was clapping along. When the singing died down, Jack cleared her throat.

"Right. No sharks this time of year." Jack gave the groom a small smile. "Except Brian, I guess. There are jellyfish, though, once we get out of the marina. Try not to fall in."

The group went through the paddling demonstration without any more singing outbursts. At the end, the men gave everyone high fives. Jack was surprised to find herself getting into it, grinning as she attempted a complicated hand-slapping sequence with one of them. Their energy was puppyish, infectious. There was no real danger here.

Once they were on the water, though, it got wilder. One man had stuffed a bottle of tequila into his life vest, and the guys toasted every otter sighting with a swig. They tossed the bottle from kayak to kayak, razzing each other when they missed. The other guests on the tour joined in on the fun, the bald guy chuckling, the women flirting.

When the air turned cold, Jack started to reconsider her "we're all friends here" approach. She was small, and young, and the bachelors were no longer listening to her. Neither was anyone else. At one point, Jack had to grab the bow of a woman's kayak to keep it from tipping over when the woman leaned way out to attempt a sloppy kiss with one of the young men. So much for worrying about sharks.

By the time the second bottle of tequila came out, Jack had had enough. She turned the group around early, leading them in a long, wobbly arc past the public fishing dock. Two of the guys were so blitzed they couldn't execute the turn and ended up drifting into the muddy drainage behind the rotted piers of the dock. Jack took three quick strokes toward them, snatched their paddles from them, and lashed their boat to hers. She did the same for the rest of the bachelor party. She towed them back, a line of troublesome ducklings following their long-suffering mother home.

Jack was just yards from the shore when one of the men behind her suggested a hermit-crab kissing contest. Jack heard a splash. Then another. She turned around and saw the four boats behind her abandoned, eight grown men hooting and shrieking in the oil-slick water.

Jack weighed her options. She was responsible for them. It was dark out, and the water was freezing. But in the marina, it was only knee-deep. They'd survive. Jack glided to the shore. The women had already headed up to change, but the bald man was still standing there, watching the silliness, his booming laugh chopping across the water. Jack pushed past him and hauled up the empty kayaks. She kept one eye on the bobbing life jackets in the shallow water. They'd be fine.

Jack had all the kayaks put away by the time the soaking men finally trudged out of the water. They shivered their way up to meet her at the edge of the parking lot in the twilight. The marina was silent, the boats racked, the other tourists long gone. The best man gave Jack a sheepish smile and pressed a hundred-dollar bill into her palm before hitching up his wet pants and stumbling into the parking lot. She looked at the money and smiled. Sailboats were born of tips like this.

• • •

In the time it took Jack to bike the three miles back to the house, Lana and Beth went to war. Beth was outside on the front porch shouting at her mother; Lana was inside, shouting back; and there were two increasingly uncomfortable-looking men holding Beth's old quilted sofa in the doorway between them.

Lana realized she had made a tactical error in not timing the new furniture to arrive when her daughter was at work. But Beth's schedule was always changing, and Lana couldn't keep living in a cottage decorated with mismatched cane chairs and palm frond lampshades. The house looked like Martha Stewart had been trapped on a desert island for a very long time. Recently, Beth had been lugging buckets of rocks up from the slough, and Lana worried they'd soon have a coffee table made of river stones.

"Beth, be reasonable." Lana tried to keep her tone even, while using one hand to urge the workmen to shimmy around her daughter with the threadbare sofa.

"We didn't talk about this," Beth said. "You should have asked."

"I'm not allowed to buy my granddaughter a decent fold-out? Don't you want her to get good sleep?"

"Ma, that's not the point."

"Your daughter gave me her room. She's been sleeping on that lumpy couch for months. This is literally the least I can do to thank her."

Beth looked over at Jack, who was taking a suspiciously long time removing her helmet. Then Beth exhaled and took a half step to the side. The two men hustled the patchwork couch down the front steps and into their waiting truck. Lana watched, triumphant, as they came back into the house with a brand-new, cream-colored sofa with spindly gold legs.

They came back outside and pulled a large cardboard box out of the truck.

Lana hurriedly answered the question in Beth's eyes. "A new mattress for me. European pillow-top. Lumbar support is crucial to my recovery."

"But—"

"Did you want a new mattress too? I can have it here in five days, no problem."

Beth's jaw was locked, her eyes fixed on the men hoisting the box up the steps. "I don't like having strangers in my house."

"Strangers? Please. This is Max. And Esteban." Lana beamed at them. "Next week, they're painting the interior."

While the men wrestled the mattress inside, Lana produced a stack of paint chips from the pocket of her robe and started laying them out on the porch swing. Jack came up behind her, smelling of salt and rubber, and put a finger on one of the samples.

"It's like French vanilla," the teenager said, crouching down to get a better look.

Lana nodded. "I was thinking that for the kitchen. Or it could be nice for my bedroom. I mean, yours."

"I don't think so," Beth said.

"You prefer the Arctic Gray?"

"I prefer the house we have now."

Lana gave Beth a wide-eyed look. "I'll make sure they do it all while you're at work. You don't even have to see them. That textured fern pattern in the kitchen, it's practically sliding off the walls—"

"Ma, that's not what I mean. You don't get to replace my furniture. You don't get to redecorate my house."

"I just want to make it comfortable—"

"It *is* comfortable. Jack and I have been making it comfortable for fifteen years. Right?"

Lana looked at Jack. She expected her granddaughter to speak up for herself, for what she wanted. But the girl just nodded, looking uncertainly at her flustered mother.

"We're happy to have you here, Ma," Beth said in a more conciliatory tone. "We can keep the new couch. And your mattress. But please. Give it a rest."

"I'll rest when I'm dead."

"We're doing everything we can to make sure that's a long, long time from now."

"Not if that textured paint kills me first." Lana swept up the paint chips, shoved them into her pocket, and shuffled back into the house.

CHAPTER FIVE

JACK PROMISED HERSELF her shift on Sunday would be different. By the book. Calm. The early-morning fog matched her mood, wrapping a silvery blanket of stillness around her as she pedaled to the marina. She arrived to a silent shop. The green road bike had disappeared, either reclaimed by its owner or taken by someone else. No one was around. Apparently Paul's private guiding gig was still going strong.

Jack opened up the Kayak Shack on her own, securing waivers onto clipboards and hauling boats down to the shore. Jorge, one of the older guides, rolled in and took the 9 A.M. group out—six people, quiet and manageable—while Jack ran the shop. Before Jack knew it, it was time for her 11 A.M. tour.

None of them looked like trouble. There was a German family of five, a father and son, a young couple, and a serene older woman with a deep tan. By 11:05, Jack had the group lined up at the beach, repeating after her as Jack ran through the safety and wildlife protection procedures in her most responsible voice. There were no shark songs. No booze. By 11:10, they were in the water.

The tour was just what Jack needed. The kids liked her nickname, the adults appreciated her knowledge about the migratory patterns of herons, and even the otters seemed to be on their best behavior. Jack's gaggle of kayaks traveled quickly upriver, most of them pausing at the narrow beach by Kirby Park, where harbor seals clustered to sleep the day away. The boy and his dad in kayak 33 went farther, exploring the mouth of one of the fingers of the slough. The couple in kayak 9 was obsessed with sardines, taking picture after picture of the shimmering schools swarming the kelp beneath their hull.

The wind picked up, and Jack corralled everyone into the bright line of smooth water that would take them back to the marina. She got all her boats moving west, except 33. The father and son. Jack looked around and frowned. Where were they?

Shifting her weight to a crouch, Jack squinted across the water. She saw their kayak over in the mud flats, bobbing in place. Were they stuck? Jack signaled to the rest of the group to wait and started paddling across the slough.

The dad was out of the kayak, down in the shallow muck. The kid was looking over the side, rocking the boat. Had they lost a paddle?

"TINY!"

The kid was yelling.

Jack took sharp, decisive strokes to close the distance between them. They looked okay, not bleeding or anything, but anchored in place. Maybe they got too curious and a jellyfish stung one of them. Jack moved faster, using her feet to nudge the first aid kit out from between her legs as she windmilled her paddle forward.

"TINY! TINY!!"

The kid was screaming something awful now, like a high-strung foghorn. Jack came right up alongside them, the kid's voice unrelenting, the sound of it drowning out the chatter of the birds overhead.

"Tiny." The dad's voice cut through his son's screams. "Look."

There, floating in the muck where the culvert hit the slough, was a person. A mud-covered balloon of a person. Facedown in the water. Not moving. Kelp-ruffled pullover, dark pants, hiking boots. And a red Kayak Shack life jacket.

Jack dropped into the frigid mud and charged forward, one hand on her kayak, one reaching out in front of her, as if to steady herself in the water.

"Hello?" she yelled. Even in her wet suit and booties, she felt numb. "Are you okay?"

No response. Closer up, she saw long brown hair swirling around the head.

Jack took a deep breath, reached forward, and grabbed one of the straps on the life jacket to flip the person faceup. It was a man. She didn't recognize him. Or maybe she did. Was he on her tour? When had he fallen in?

She told herself to breathe, to push aside the questions and focus on what was in front of her. The man needed her help. Jack tried to attempt resuscitation right there in the marsh, but as she started to unclip his life jacket, she realized there was no way she could manage chest compressions with everything bobbing around. She had to get him to the bank.

She squelched through the mud, dragging him with her, running through the CPR steps in her head as she did so. But as she got closer to the bank, she started to notice how still the man was. His skin looked wrong, slippery and taut, and a thin film of silt coated his entire body.

Jack hauled him up onto the shore. She grabbed his wrist. No pulse. The man's eyes were bulging out, his dark, dilated pupils swimming in a yellowed, leaking sea. His skin, which looked like it ought to be amber-brown like hers, was mottled greenish-white. The side of his head looked caved in, and there was something gummed up under his hair. The pieces clicked together. And the whole horrible fact of it became clear.

Jack let go of the man's wrist and twisted her head away. She doubled over in the mud, trying not to retch. Then she splashed her way back to her kayak, filling her eyes with the calming sight of its orange hull, plunging her hands into the freezing water to wipe away the feeling of his slick, clammy skin.

Before she got back in her boat, Jack looked one more time at the dead man lying on the bank. His eyes were wide open, as if he couldn't believe how far the clouds stretched today.

For the first time ever, Jack wished she was far from the water, anywhere but the slough.

CHAPTER SIX

AFTER A STUNNED MOMENT in her boat with her head between her knees, Jack snapped into efficiency mode. She had responsibilities. She radioed the coast guard, and then wrangled the father and son to rejoin the group. She did a count. Everyone on her tour was there. And they were going back to dry land now. The dead guy was on the bank, and he wasn't going anywhere. The father looked nauseous, the son a spinning top of adrenaline and fear. But Jack kept her voice calm and firm, and they followed her directions.

Jack led the group back to the Kayak Shack in a ragged line, her paddle churning through the water like a quiet, determined dishwasher. The tour group passed under the highway and across the chopped-up ocean. The news spread from boat to boat in whispers and heads whipping around to look back, as if to accuse the slough of ruining their day.

The boats approached the shore. Travis was on the boat launch ramp, waving his arms like a girl at a drag race, too smiley by a mile, and Jack realized she hadn't called Paul or told anyone at the Shack what had happened. As far as everyone at the marina was concerned, this was just another group of tourists to unload. She shot a glare at Travis, who was trying to tease a smile from the older woman along with her paddle. He didn't get it. Jack hauled her kayak up and stomped over to him.

"Travis. You're not going to believe this."

"What's up?"

"We found a body. A dead person. In the slough. Can you get Paul on the phone and tell him to come down here? I'll close the group out."

"Whoa. Are you—"

"Just go. Now. Please."

Jack's grandma had told her it was always good to give men simple instructions in complicated situations.

WHEN TRAVIS CAME BACK ten minutes later, Jack had the tour group lined up on the picnic tables by the launch, heavy towels draped over their shoulders. Cops were starting to arrive. Sheriffs, it seemed like. And the coast guard. They appeared to be consulting each other, maybe arguing about who was in charge, pausing from time to time to glance at the group of petrified tourists.

Travis came up next to Jack. "I couldn't get Paul on the phone," he said. "Left a voicemail."

Jack felt tired, cold, and not at all surprised.

"But I did bring hot chocolate," Travis said, pointing to a large metal thermos and a stack of paper cups. "Want some?"

The warmth sounded good, but Jack didn't trust herself to keep anything in her stomach right now. She gave him a weak smile, and they walked over to the guests at the picnic tables.

"Who's in charge here?" a coast guard officer asked. It seemed the jurisdictional pissing match had reached some kind of conclusion and the officers were ready to begin.

The tourists looked at Jack. Jack and Travis looked at each other.

"Our boss is away," Travis said.

"Who's in charge of this group?"

"I am," Jack said.

She knew how ridiculous it sounded. A fifteen-year-old girl, barely a hundred pounds, in a red life jacket and booties, leaning on a paddle.

The officer gave her a hard look. "Where's the body?"

"On the north bank of the slough. About two miles past the bridge. In the mud flats across from Kirby Park."

"Is there anybody there now?"

"No. I was leading the tour alone. I thought I should bring the group back here safe first."

"The dead man was on your tour?"

"No."

"You sure about that?"

"Yes. Everyone who was on the tour is here at these two tables. I was guiding, and Travis"—she pointed at the other teenager—"was taking care of the shop."

"And where's the owner? Your boss?"

Jack looked over at Travis. He shrugged.

"His name is Paul Hanley," Travis said. "I tried calling him, but it went to voicemail. He should show up here before it gets totally dark."

The officer turned back to Jack. "Can you take us to the body?"

"Right now?"

"Yes, ma'am."

JACK CLIMBED SILENTLY onto the coast guard motorboat. It felt cramped, with a pilot, two Coasties, and three sheriff's deputies occupying the bench seats. She stood by the rail and folded herself into her sweatshirt, hunching her shoulders against the wind. The harbormaster was already out on the water with a bullhorn, directing all remaining kayakers and paddleboarders to return to the shore.

Once they got to the mud flats, Jack pointed but didn't look. She kept her eyes trained on a snowy egret grooming itself on the bank. The pilot re-angled the boat for peak viewing and minimal disturbance of the scene, and the deputies swarmed port side.

Jack traded places with them. She wedged herself on the starboard side and looked south across the slough, searching for the window in the back bedroom at her house. She could just barely see the wedge of mirrored black, glinting between the cypress and eucalyptus trees. She wouldn't wave. The house was too far away for her to look like anything more than a bug on a boat, even if Lana was sitting in bed with her binoculars like usual. But it calmed Jack's nerves a bit, knowing her grandma was there.

Jack's thoughts were cut through by the voices of the deputies behind her.

"Maybe a giant octopus got him."

"Or rabid otters."

Jack shook her head. They weren't marine biologists, but still. Soon these cops would be suggesting a swamp monster had killed the man.

She heard sirens by the bridge and saw another coast guard boat headed their way. Its deck was less crowded. A man and a woman wearing suits, a couple more Coasties, and maybe that old guy who ran the land trust—she'd seen him at the marina sometimes, but couldn't be sure. All those grizzled enviro-fishermen types looked the same.

The second boat sidled up next to the skiff, and the men started talking to each other across the gap. The woman in the suit took a cautious step from the second boat to the first and approached Jack.

"You found the body?" She was a curvy woman with a warm voice and golden skin, her hair in a tight blond twist that yanked the skin back from her eyes. She reached out a hand to shake Jack's, revealing bejeweled purple fingernails that looked killer but wouldn't survive a single day with a paddle.

"Yes. No. I mean, two people on my eleven A.M. tour did. I'm the tour guide. My name's Tiny. I mean, Jack. Jacqueline. We use nicknames when we do the tours."

Great. She was babbling.

The woman didn't seem to notice. "I'm Detective Ramirez, and this is Detective Nicoletti." She gestured to an older white man standing on the other boat. "Can you tell us what happened?"

Jack went through the story of the father and son, the facedown body, dragging it to the shore, and her attempt at first aid.

"When you first approached the body, you thought he might still be alive?"

"I saw the life jacket. It's one of ours. And I guess I just immediately assumed it was someone on the tour."

"You flipped the body over?"

"Yes."

"Did you touch it in any other way?"

"I pulled him to the bank and checked his pulse. His wrist. I was going to start CPR, but . . ."

Jack shuddered.

"You recognized the life jacket. Did you recognize the person?"

Jack thought back on what she'd seen. A mess of long hair. Dark pants. The bright red life jacket, the words "Kayak Shack" in faded spray paint across the back. Could she remember his face? Was she even sure he had a face? Jack saw her own arms, reaching out to the body, pulling away. She shook her head and tucked her hands all the way inside the sleeves of her sweatshirt.

"No. I mean, I didn't take too long of a look. But I don't think so."

The detective nodded.

"How many people were on the eleven A.M. tour?"

"Ten. They're all back at the marina." Trying to hold down their hot chocolate, probably.

"And you were guiding them on your own?"

"Yes. I'm fully certified. I can take up to twelve on my own."

"How old are you?"

"Fifteen, almost sixteen. I'm fully certified."

"You're sure this man wasn't on one of your tours?"

Jack was feeling more confident now. These questions were safe. She was safe. She was Paul's most reliable guide.

"No, Detective. Not one of my tours. This group was my first today. Moondog, I mean Jorge, Jorge Savila, he did the nine A.M. tour. I was supposed to do the two P.M. And Travis Whalen has the sunset today."

"Those will have to be canceled."

Jack nodded dully. The prospect of phone calls to angry tourists made her feel tired all over again. Hopefully Travis would handle it.

"We'll take you back in the other boat. Follow me." Ramirez nodded to her partner and took small steps to the starboard edge, lining herself up with the bigger boat. Nicoletti reached out and yanked Ramirez toward him. Jack ignored the man's outstretched hand and leaped aboard on her own. The older detective stared at Jack for a long moment. Then he turned to the pilot and gave the nod to depart.

Jack and the detectives chugged back to the marina in silence. Jack kept her eyes on the water, resisting the urge to point out the baby seals, the pulsing jellyfish, the schools of anchovy swimming laps in the glittering midday light. They crossed under the highway bridge, cut the engine, and cruised up to the dock.

When they got back to the Shack, the sheriff's deputies were talking to the tourists from Jack's group. Paul was still nowhere to be seen. Ramirez wrote down Jack's address and phone number and promised to be in touch. Then she told Jack she could go home. And to be safe out there.

Jack unlocked the shop and tried Paul one more time from the office phone. Nothing. She debated calling home. Prima would be there. Maybe her mom by now too. Jack stared at the phone receiver in her hand until it turned into a foreign object, something alien and forbidding. She realized she was not yet ready to talk, not ready to be bombarded with questions and concern. She put down the phone, locked the door, and headed outside.

Her bike was waiting for her at the fence, as if nothing had happened. She clipped on her helmet and took the back way around the yacht club, avoiding the people clustered at the picnic tables. She turned out of the marina and pedaled across the bridge. She didn't look out at the slough to see what was happening at the motorboat. She didn't care to see anything alive. No seals. No jellyfish. No bodies. She kept her eyes on the cracked gray asphalt, letting the thin winter sun bounce off and blind her to everything but the road and the wind.

CHAPTER SEVEN

BETH GOT HOME LATE AGAIN. Gigi Montero had an allergic reaction to the soup at lunch, and she'd insisted on Beth accompanying her in the ambulance to the hospital. By the time they got back to Bayshore Oaks, Rosa was on duty, Miss Gigi was asleep, and Beth had missed her chance to make it home in time for dinner.

She tossed the greasy foil from her burrito into the trash can on her way into the house. Beth opened the front door, expecting to see Jack on the couch with her head in her phone, texting with friends. But the kitchen and living room were dark. No sound anywhere in the house.

Beth slipped into her moccasins and glanced at the family calendar of school holidays, Kayak Shack tours, overnight shifts, and chemo appointments affixed to the fridge. Nada. Maybe Jack was at Kayla's?

Beth popped open a beer and rolled out her shoulders. She headed to the back bedroom to ask Lana about Jack's whereabouts, steeling herself for another ambush from her mother about remodeling the house. Instead, she walked into an improbable portrait of grandmotherly care. Lana was reading a book in her robe, which was normal enough. But Jack was curled up next to her on the comforter. And Lana was stroking Jack's hair.

Neither of them noticed when Beth entered. Jack had her eyes open, but she didn't seem to be looking at anything. She was turned away from her grandma, staring at the blank wall above the desk.

Beth watched for a moment, transfixed by the hypnotic, gentle motion of her mother's hand over her daughter's tangled hair. She didn't recognize either of the women on the bed as hers. She felt like a clumsy interloper, as if she had stumbled into someone else's family by mistake.

Lana looked up from her book. She spoke in a soft voice Beth had never heard before. "It's been a long day. Can you get us some crackers and cheese?"

Strange feelings of confusion and jealousy rose in Beth's stomach. Back in the kitchen, she took another swig of beer. Then she set out a box of Wheat Thins, some Swiss cheese slices, a Diet Coke for Lana, a real one for Jack. She put out place mats, seagrass hexagons she'd woven with Jack years ago. And waited.

"Can you two come to the table?" Beth called, feeling slightly ridiculous.

Jack slouched her way to a chair, the sleeves of her sweatshirt pulled down over her hands. Beth watched her daughter insert crackers into her mouth. There was definitely something strange going on. Lana wasn't dominating the table with her opinions and pronouncements. She was sitting across from her girls, sipping a Diet Coke, eyes shifting from one to the other.

Beth tested the water, watching Jack out of the corner of her eye as she spoke.

"Well, I had a hard day. My patients get wound up this time of year. It's cold outside and in their bones. The holidays are long gone, and family isn't showing up with babies and presents anymore."

No reaction from Jack. She was looking down at the table, eyes locked on the slice of cheese she was tearing into strips.

"February is tough," Beth continued. "Some of them start misplacing pills or not taking such good care of themselves in the shower. I had one guy today who had a rash on his—well, you're eating. Anyway. Mr. Rhoads, the gentleman from up here, with the ranch across the slough? He's not doing well. He's got one of those coughs that sounds like he's pulling a rake up his throat. And I can tell he's not getting enough—"

"Mom?"

"Yes?" Beth tried not to sound too eager.

"Do we have any cherry tomatoes maybe?" The girl's head was still down, her hair forming a thick curtain Beth longed to pull away from her face.

Beth kept her hands to herself. She walked to the fridge, using the trip as an excuse to shoot a look at Lana, searching for a hint as to what was going on. Lana bugged her eyes at Beth in a way that meant either "Keep pushing her" or "Get the damn tomatoes."

Beth placed the tomatoes gently in front of Jack. "Honey, how was your day?"

Nothing.

"Jack?"

Lana coughed. "Jack had a challenging day. There was a dead body found in the slough."

Jack rocked her head back and forth, in assent or recognition. Lana continued in a whisper. "She had some tourists who came upon it over by the north bank. She had to take charge and report it and everything."

Beth reached out to touch Jack's shoulder, slow and tentative at first. When she felt Jack press into her hand, she scooched her chair closer and swept Jack into a tight sideways hug.

"Honey. That must have been awful."

Jack leaned into the hug and ate a tomato.

"It's terrible seeing a dead body. It still gets to me every time when a patient's life ends. It must have been scary to come upon him in the water like that."

"He was young," Jack mumbled. "At first I couldn't tell if it was a boy or a girl because of the long hair. For a minute it felt like it could have been me."

"Jack, you know that would never happen to you. You're so careful. You're a great swimmer. And strong. The slough is your second home."

Beth remembered their earliest days together, just the two of them, Beth collecting rocks on hikes through the high grass, Jack cooing at the sea lions from the front of the baby carrier. By seven, Jack was picking her way down the scree behind the house on her own, wading into the muck to build tiny forts where she imagined otters might like to sleep at night. When she was twelve, Jack begged Beth for a paddleboard for Chanukah. After a tense negotiation in which the girl just kept repeating, "I am very responsible," Beth gave in. And got used to watching Jack shuffle down the hillside, the board affixed to the top of her head like a helicopter blade.

Now that same pink board was leaning against the wall by the back door, a towel draped over it like a shroud.

Beth pulled back to look at her daughter, her hands holding up Jack's shoulders.

"What happened after you . . . ?"

"The coast guard came. And some sheriff's deputies. A couple detectives from Monterey. There were a lot of uniforms."

"Jack, you were very brave."

"No, not really, I mean, I just took care of my group and showed the officers where the body was in the mud."

"Did they say anything about who it was that died?"

"Not while I was there."

Lana coughed. "I looked it up on my phone. So far, they're just reporting that the slough is shut down until further notice. The last time someone died in the slough was two years ago. A fisherman had a heart attack and fell out of his boat. They found the boat, and then they found him a couple days later."

They all turned to the window, as if the dark could tell them something.

"I don't know what could have happened." Jack's voice was low, uncertain. "The guy was wearing one of our life jackets, but he wasn't on my tour. He didn't have an empty boat or a paddleboard or anything that I could see. He was dressed in normal clothes, jeans. Heavy boots. Like a fisherman. But not one of the regulars. I think."

"Did Paul know who he was?"

"Paul wasn't there."

Beth put her arms around Jack again and gave her a long, slow squeeze.

"I'm so sorry this happened, honey. You can sleep in my room tonight if you want."

Jack closed her eyes and gave a grateful nod. She pressed her head into Beth's soft shoulder, breathing in her mom's steady scent of eucalyptus trees and salt.

Lana coughed again. "I'll call the school and tell them you won't be in tomorrow. You can stay home with me."

Jack raised her head in surprise.

"What? No, Prima. I mean, thank you, but I should go to school. I'll feel better that way."

"We'll all feel better in the morning," Beth said. "Go get your pillow. And your blanket. It's too cold tonight for you to steal mine."

Lana watched them get up from the table and fingered the pills in the pocket of her robe. She was six days away from chemo, which meant a bad week was starting. She felt short of breath, her lungs laboring to push out a hacking cough that made her eyes water. Not that her girls noticed. They were focused on each other now, shuffling to Beth's bedroom in a tight huddle of hugs and whispers. No "You okay, Ma?" Not even a "good night." Lana felt the energy drain out of the room, the tide of love receding.

CHAPTER EIGHT

JACK FLOATED THROUGH North Monterey County High on Monday in a fog. On one level, she felt comforted by the normalcy around her—the shouting kids, the smell of chalk, the ritual passing of papers from desk to desk—but each time the bell rang, Jack realized she had no memory of what the teacher had talked about all period. Presidents, maybe. Or covalent bonds. She headed home with a backpack stuffed with indecipherable notes and arrived to a quiet house. There was a note on the counter that her mom had gone to Gilroy to visit a former patient. She peeked into her old room and saw her grandma, snoring in bed. She grabbed some grapes from the fridge and settled on the couch to try to do her homework.

At six o'clock, there was a knock on the door.

Jack ignored it and kept plodding through Spanish verb conjugations. She figured it was one of Lana's deliveries of new appliances or fancy face serums. But then the knock came again, louder.

Jack followed her mom's rules. Walk to the door. Ask "Who is it?" without unlocking. Wait.

"We're here from the Monterey sheriff's department."

Jack squeezed her eyes shut, hard. Her mind flashed back to the mud flats. The glint of sun on the dead man's long hair, the water pooling in his jacket. Jack wanted to run into her old room and crawl under the covers. She wanted to grab her board and charge down the gravel hill to the water, to paddle back in time somehow to before yesterday ever happened, before the water darkened.

She opened the door.

It was the man and the woman from the day before, him in a dark brown suit, her in a shiny purple jacket that matched her nails.

"Jacqueline Rubicon?" the woman said. "We met yesterday?"

Jack stared at her, a mess of hair and discomfort.

"Is there an adult home with you?"

"Uh . . . hold on." Jack shut the door, ran to the back bedroom, and woke up her grandma.

When the door opened the second time, Lana stood in front of Jack, wearing a headscarf and her thick, satiny bathrobe like a shield.

The man spoke. "I'm Detective Nicoletti. And my partner, Detective Ramirez. From the Monterey sheriff's department. May we come in?"

Lana swept out her arm, directing them to the kitchen table.

Nicoletti seemed to be the one in charge. "We're glad you're both at home," he said. "We were hoping to talk with you, Jacqueline, about what happened at the slough. Of course, if that's all right with your mother."

This last word earned the detective a full-wattage smile from Lana and an offer of something to drink.

"She's my grandmother," Jack said.

"You didn't have to tell him that," Lana hissed, her back to the detectives as she scrounged in the cabinet for matching water glasses.

The detectives lined up with their notebooks on one side of the table, Lana and Jack on the other. Before anyone else could speak, Lana leaned forward.

"Have you determined what happened?"

"We've identified the person who died," Nicoletti said. "On Jacqueline's tour yesterday."

"He wasn't on my tour."

Nicoletti kept talking as if he hadn't heard Jack speak. "We'd like to show you a picture of him. Not from when he was in the water. From before."

The detective slid a photograph across the table. His thick fingers stuck to it for a moment. Then he looked up.

"Do you recognize this man?"

Jack and Lana both stared at the picture. The man was handsome, slim, with dark brown hair hanging past his shoulders. Thick eyebrows, big bright eyes, clean-shaven. He was wearing a fancy backpack with neon straps and clips, standing in a forest and smiling wide for the camera. He looked like he was ready to charge up a mountain.

Jack shook her head. "No. I don't think so."

"Are you sure?"

She looked up at the detectives and started ticking off reasons why. "He's too old to go to my school. He doesn't work at the Kayak Shack or any of the other places at the marina. I haven't seen him on the slough. He doesn't really look like a water guy, unless maybe he has a dad or an uncle he goes fishing with. And I know most of them."

The detectives looked at Lana. This time, the woman, Ramirez, spoke.

"Ma'am, do you recognize him?"

Lana shook her head. "Cute kid," she muttered.

"His name is Ricardo Cruz. He was twenty-nine years old. Resident of Santa Cruz. A naturalist, working for the land trust up there. And here's the thing, Jacqueline: he was on the sunset tour you ran on Saturday."

A flicker of surprise ran across Jack's face. "Saturday? Not Sunday?"

"Saturday."

Ramirez pulled out the logbook from the Kayak Shack, the one they used to manage reservations. Seeing a piece of the Shack in her kitchen felt impossible and a little dirty, like seeing your chemistry teacher at the beach in her swimsuit.

The detective opened to the pages from the weekend and turned the book around so Jack could see. Ramirez tapped a bejeweled fingernail halfway down. Ricardo Cruz, Saturday sunset tour, with a phone number and the word "PAID," scrawled in Paul's handwriting. Despite Paul's supposedly glorious past career in technology, the Kayak Shack was strictly a phone and walk-in operation—no apps or online booking systems.

Jack pulled the logbook toward her. Holding it made her feel more confident. "He booked it Friday afternoon. But there's no checkmark by his name. He must not have shown up Saturday. That night I had a group of eleven: eight guys from Fresno, a bachelor party. And two women. One older man. There wasn't anyone else on the tour."

"What do you do when there's a no-show?" Ramirez asked.

"If we have a phone number, we call. But I wasn't in the office. I was out hauling boats. I don't know if Travis called him. When I'm guiding, I just go when I get the signal that we're all good."

"But what if Mr. Cruz just didn't get checked off? He could have met you down by the water, right? Maybe even jumped in your boat with you?"

"No. I had seven boats at sunset, nine men, two women. No one else."

The two detectives shared a look. Nicoletti leaned forward, putting his massive forearms on the table.

"Here's the thing, Jack—can I call you Jack?" His voice was soft, but the false kind, the kind that's hiding something hard behind it.

Jack gave him a tight nod and looked nervously toward Ramirez.

"Don't look at her. Look at me," Nicoletti said. "Here's the problem, Jack. We talked to Carl Willis."

Jack said nothing.

"Don't remember him, Jack? From your Saturday sunset tour."

"The bald guy?" Jack asked.

"So you do remember him," Nicoletti said.

"I . . . uh, I don't always learn their names." Jack was watching the detective very closely now.

"Mr. Willis said you were having a real party out there on Saturday night, *Tiny.*" Nicoletti said the nickname sarcastically, in a way that implied she'd done something wrong. "He said you were drinking. Flirting. He said y'all splashed around in the dark, had yourself a good old time. He thought this Ricardo was there."

"He's wrong. Did you ask the women? Or the bachelor party? They'll tell you."

"As far as we've heard, Mr. Willis was the only guest on that tour who wasn't drunk."

This suddenly sounded bad. Very bad. Jack had seen enough cop shows to know that a bald, middle-aged white guy trumped a brown teenage girl every time. Jack could feel her heart thumping, her body tense.

"Is drinking something you do on a lot of tours, Jack?"

"No, I never—"

"You like to play it loose with your clients?"

Jack felt Lana's cool hand cover her sweaty fist on the table. "Detective, my granddaughter just told you—"

"I'm not lying," Jack said. It came out hoarse. She took a breath and tried again. "I never saw Ricardo Cruz before. You don't underst—"

"Oh, I understand plenty. You like older men? Like *Señor* Cruz?" Nicoletti waved the photo in Jack's face. Jack looked toward Ramirez, hoping for sympathy, or solidarity, or something. Maybe they were running some kind of good cop/racist cop routine. But the female detective's eyes were dark, mouth sealed shut. And Nicoletti kept coming at her. "I know about girls like you, you—"

"Enough!"

Lana's voice shot across the table. She was standing now, glaring down at them, her hands clenched on the back of Jack's chair. She looked frail, but her voice was regal, leaking fury. She glared down at Nicoletti, dropping her voice from a roar to a low, slow warning.

"We don't care for your tone, Detective," Lana said. "A man drowned. Jack found him. It was a tragic accident. That's what happened."

Jack breathed in her grandma's precise, steady words. She hoped it was enough.

The detective matched Lana in tone, speaking slowly, as if to a child.

"All due respect, ma'am." He made the word sound like an insult. "What happened to Ricardo Cruz was no accident."

CHAPTER NINE

LANA CLOSED HER EYES, her hands held firm around the back of Jack's chair. She didn't care if the detectives thought she had fallen asleep. She needed time to recalibrate. And to resist the urge to drop her eyes to Jack's with any kind of question in them.

There was no way her granddaughter was involved. But Lana now saw this conversation in a different light. They weren't here to confirm the timeline of an accidental death. They were questioning Jack, aggressively, about someone who had been murdered. Which meant they had to be much more careful going forward.

"Someone killed him?" Jack said. "How do you know?"

Now Lana looked at Jack, trying to beg the girl with her eyes to be quiet. But Lana had never been any good at begging. And Jack kept talking.

"I mean, if he drowned, how do you know someone killed him? Like, wouldn't it look the same?"

Lana sank down in the chair next to Jack. It was a good question. And a terrible question. As if Jack were trying to check her work. Everyone's eyes were on the girl now.

"There's more than one way to kill someone," Nicoletti said.

"So he wasn't drowned?" Jack said. "How did he—"

"You go out on the water a lot, Jack?" Ramirez's voice cut in, but it didn't sound harsh. She sounded curious. Warm. Jack turned gratefully toward her.

"Well, yeah," Jack said. "It's my job, guiding kayak tours. And I like to go out most mornings before school. On my paddleboard." She waved to the ten-foot board by the door, its leash dangling, a lonely dog waiting for someone to take it out for a walk.

"Do you ever go out with anyone else? A friend, maybe?"

"You don't have to answer that," Lana said.

"No, it's okay." Jack gave Ramirez a tiny smile. "I don't. I haven't. None of my friends from school are into it."

"And the people you work with at the Kayak Shack? Jorge Savila? Travis Whalen? Paul Hanley?"

Jack cursed herself for blushing. "Paul's the boss. He's older than my mom. And Travis and Jorge are in college. I wouldn't say we're friends."

Nicoletti leered. "More than friends?"

This time, Jack kept her mouth shut. She pulled her hands into her sweatshirt sleeves, picking at the cuffs under the table.

When Jack had counted to fifteen, Detective Ramirez spoke again, leaving her partner's question hanging in the air like a bad smell. "You're younger than everyone there, right? Tiny, they call you?"

Jack nodded cautiously.

"Well, Tiny, here's our problem." Ramirez's voice was smooth. "A young man paid for a tour Saturday night with you. You say he wasn't there. Mr. Willis says maybe he was. Regardless, we all agree that you didn't run that tour by the book."

"I—"

Ramirez raised a hand and started ticking points on her purple fingernails. "You were responsible for their safety, but you let them drink. You let them get in the water. That's against the rules, right?"

If there was a way to nod miserably, Jack pulled it off.

Ramirez nodded back.

"And then, the next day, Ricardo Cruz is found in one of your life jackets, dead, floating in your slough."

"But—"

"Maybe you saw something. A weapon. Or a fight. Maybe you let Ricardo get in the water and his kayak flipped and he slammed his head. Whatever happened, let me give you some advice. Things will go much better for you if you tell us. Now. Because from where we sit, you're a scared kid who made a mistake, and you're trying to cover it up."

Lana saw Jack's eye twitch. She couldn't let this continue.

"*I* saw something," Lana said. She pulled herself up straight, drawing her robe tight around her.

"Ma'am?" Ramirez looked confused. So did Jack.

"But it wasn't Saturday night," Lana continued. "It was Saturday morning. Early. Two A.M. A person with a wheelbarrow. On the far side of the slough."

"You were out on a hike at two in the morning?"

"No. I was here. Out the back window. No one's supposed to be on the slough at night. But someone was there. Suspicious." Lana remembered his jerky movements, his furious gaze.

Nicoletti leaned forward. "You spend a lot of time looking out the window?"

"Well, I—"

"Lady, you probably saw a farmer dumping something he couldn't be bothered to take to the recycling plant. There's all kinds of junk in the slough. Ricardo Cruz died at least a mile north of here, two maybe. I doubt you can see that far out your window."

"No. Ricardo Cruz was *found* two miles north of here. Do you have evidence that proves he was *killed* there?"

The man leaned back and fixed Lana with a cruel gaze. "I don't discuss evidence in open cases with grandmothers."

"Saturday. Two A.M. Write it down."

"Ma'am—"

"If you're going to harass my granddaughter based on the claims of one tourist on a kayak cruise, you can at least follow up on the information I'm providing you."

Lana locked eyes with Nicoletti, fixing him with an imperious stare. She sat up very straight, puffing her chest out in her blue-and-gold robe in her best imitation of an irate peacock.

Internally, she debated whether to start talking again, to insist the man she'd seen was suspicious and that the detectives should give her the respect she deserved. But she decided silence was a more powerful weapon. It was already doing its job. The energy in the room felt scattered, no longer driving toward a climax. Ramirez's pen scratched against her notebook. Jack's leg bounced under the table. Nicoletti looked from Lana to Jack and back again, his eyes hard.

Finally, he stood up. "I see this is as far as we're going to get today. You"—he pointed one meaty finger at Jack—"don't go anywhere. If we discover you knew Mr. Cruz, or that you're covering up—"

"You are welcome to return another time, Detectives," Lana said. Her voice was crisp. "We're happy to entertain your questions. But not your unfounded threats."

Nicoletti glared at Lana. She glared back.

"We'll do that," Nicoletti said. "You girls think about telling us the truth next time. The whole truth." He stood and shook his head. "Ramirez, let's go."

• • •

It took a full five minutes after Lana locked the door before Jack's heart stopped racing.

"That was messed up," Jack said. "Like, really messed up. What are we going to do?"

"Jack." Her grandma's eyes weren't cruel, but they were firm. "You're absolutely sure he wasn't on your tour?"

"I—I am." She stumbled over the simple words.

"Speak up, Jack. Winners never mumble." Her grandma's gaze stayed steady. "Is there anything else, anything you haven't told me?"

Jack swallowed. She debated whether to mention it.

"It's possible I met Ricardo once." Jack ducked away from her grandma's searing gaze. "Not on a tour. I didn't recognize him at first, but when they said he worked for the land trust . . . I think maybe I waved to him early one morning, a couple months ago, when I was out paddling."

Lana closed her eyes for a moment. Jack couldn't tell if her grandma was angry or disappointed or something else.

"Did you talk to him?"

"Just a few words. He was collecting water samples by the north bank, way upriver, a mile or two past the mud flats."

"Was anyone else around?"

"I don't think so. It was just, like, a quick hello on a foggy morning. Do you think I should tell the detectives?"

There was a brief pause, and then Lana gave her a curt shake of the head. "No. Not yet. Is there anything else?"

"Nothing, Prima. I swear." Jack was surprised how forceful her voice sounded, how the volume masked her fear.

Lana's eyes softened. It almost looked like she was going to offer Jack a hug. Instead, Lana gave her a single, tight nod.

"Right. I'm going to call your mother. You're going to heat up a pizza. We're going to figure this out."

• • •

Beth charged into the house thirty minutes later, swooping Jack into a hug that lifted the teenager off the floor.

"Honey. I'm so sorry I wasn't here."

"S'okay. Prima was pretty great, actually."

Lana looked over from the counter, where she was working a corkscrew into a dusty bottle of cabernet she'd found under the sink.

"The cops here are idiots," Lana said. She pulled out the cork with a satisfied pop. "Trying to threaten Jack into admitting some part in that poor man's death. I mean, honestly."

"This isn't a joke, Ma. They must be coming after Jack for a reason."

"The reason is they're lazy. Scared, probably."

"I'm sure they loved it when you pointed that out to them."

"Beth, please. They have an unsolved murder on their hands. Of course they're looking for someone to blame. Jack found the body, she ran the tour the guy was supposed to be on. I don't think these sheriffs have the capacity to connect more than two dots."

"Wait, back up. Which tour?"

Jack explained what the detectives had said about the Saturday sunset tour and the bachelor party and Mr. Willis. Then she realized something. "That Saturday tour didn't even get within a mile of where Ricardo's body was found. Even if that guy Willis was right—which he wasn't—we never got there. Just like the detective told you about your wheelbarrow man. We were nowhere near the mud flats."

"So it's your word against this Mr. Willis?"

Lana waved it off. "They can't build a whole case around one tourist who thinks maybe he saw Ricardo Cruz."

"But if they're as lazy as you say, they might try." Beth could feel the fear rising in her throat.

"I know this is stressful, Beth." But it didn't look like Lana felt worried. If anything, Lana looked excited, her eyes glittering in a way Beth hadn't seen since before the cancer. "But we can fix it. They're sheep. They go where they're told, so all we have to do is point them in a new direction."

Beth shook her head. "You don't know the sheriffs around here. They'll make something up, try to stick it on her. They see someone like Jack, a girl with brown skin and no daddy, and they assume the worst."

Lana sniffed at the wine. "Please," she said. "Not everything is about racism or discrimination. This is just good old-fashioned incompetence."

Beth frowned at her mother. Lana hadn't been there when other parents asked too loudly about Jack's heritage, or when Beth pushed Jack around in a stroller and heard strangers' coos turn cold when they saw the baby with the dark skin. In the Salinas Valley, people came in two colors, and everything was organized to put one on top of the other.

"I can see you're concerned," Lana said. "But I'm going to help. Don't worry."

"You'll find a good lawyer?" For a moment, Beth hoped Lana might do something useful. Her own network of nurses and single moms wasn't exactly a great source of legal contacts.

"I can make a call. But Jack isn't going to need that." Lana waved her hand loftily, as if a lawyer were an option for lesser people to consider. "All we need to do is explain it was impossible for Jack to have done it. Like she said. She wasn't anywhere near there Saturday night. Jack, is there anyone who could have—"

"Ma. Stop." Beth felt a sudden need to be outside in the fresh air, where she could think. She took a deep breath and faced her mother. "You can find a lawyer. But that's it."

Before Lana could respond, Beth turned away from her and stretched an arm out to Jack. "I'm going for a walk, to hunt for rocks. You want to join me?" Beth tried to soften her voice, but her frustration was still trickling out.

Apparently, Jack could hear it too. "Thanks. But I'm good."

"We're going to get help, Jack. We'll figure this out." Beth walked to the back door and stood there, trying to believe her own words. "I promise."

• • •

Lana sat at the table with what was left of the wine, staring blankly out the window. The slough was dark, a thick blanket of clouds spread low over the water. She flashed again to the man she'd seen moving down the hillside in the dark, the harsh shadows of his face. Whoever it was, he wasn't out there now.

This place was supposed to be calm. Boring. A slice of nothingness where Lana could rest and receive care. Instead, she was getting tangled up, slapped down, treated like she was a joke. Like she didn't matter.

"Do you think I'm going to get arrested?" Jack's voice floated over from the couch, low and sudden.

"What? No. No way." Lana was surprised by the determination in her own voice. "We won't let them."

Jack stared back at her. She looked small, anxious.

"But somebody killed that man," she said. "Do you think . . . do you think it's dangerous for me to go out there now?"

"On the slough? That's for you and your mom to figure out." Lana took a swallow of cabernet. "Wouldn't be surprised if she didn't want you to, you know?"

"Yeah. It's scary. But it's also life, right? Chances are it's just a weird place for some person to die."

Lana looked around the dingy room. She heard the egrets croaking on the water. Just a weird place for some person to die. Not if she could help it.

CHAPTER TEN

BETH WOKE UP EARLY Tuesday morning, her mind still buzzing. She slipped out the back door and over to the pile of treasures she'd collected. She started organizing them mechanically: pale green sea glass, yellowed sandstone, russet clay, lining them up in a sinuous curve along the side of the house. As she placed the rocks, she sorted through her thoughts. There was no way she'd trust Lana to talk their way out of this without a professional by their side. Beth had dealt with the courts only once, when she was eighteen and petitioning for full custody of Jack. That time, it had been a sure thing—Manny didn't even show up. But it was still terrifying.

Lana was right about one thing: the evidence against Jack was slim. If the sheriffs did their job, they should find out quickly that Jack had nothing to do with this. By the time the rocks formed a large, messy spiral, Beth was resolved. They needed a lawyer who could hold the detectives' feet to the fire. If her mother could find one, great. If not, she'd figure it out.

THE FRONT DOORS of the nursing home were blocked by an ambulance. It sat quiet, engine cold, doors shut, as if someone had scrubbed the emergency from the vehicle. Beth stepped around it and braced for the blast of recycled air that hit as the glass doors swished open. The entrance to Bayshore Oaks bore an unfortunate resemblance to a grocery store:

the reverse rubber kiss of the doors separating, the sense that something might spoil if it stayed there too long.

Beth swiped her badge and went down the hall to the nursing station. She slowed to watch the EMTs wheeling a gurney toward her. She couldn't tell what room they'd come from. Was it Sal Castillo in 8B? He was over a hundred and woke up every morning a little smaller, more winded. Or Sylvie Mendelson, who'd fractured her hip and gotten a nasty infection from the surgery? Beth approached Rosa, the night nurse, who was doing paperwork behind the desk.

"Who?" she asked, gesturing down the hall.

Rosa looked up, her brown eyes worn from a long night. "Mr. Rhoads," she said. "He took a nap yesterday afternoon. Never woke up."

The news hit Beth like a punch to the chest. She didn't like to play favorites with patients, but if she did, Hal Rhoads would be at the top of her list. Mr. Rhoads had calm eyes and a soft voice. His sunbaked skin was crisscrossed with deep wrinkles, like grooves cut in leather. He'd arrived two months earlier, after his third stroke, which brought with it labored breath and the threat of congestive heart failure. He had a chronic cough about which he never complained. Mr. Rhoads treated Bayshore Oaks and its staff as a tribulation to be endured, like weevils or kidney stones. He was polite, always. But never a joiner, never a smiler, never giving one inch of himself to the place. He wore a stiff-brimmed hat every day, even when the fog hung low and the sun was miles away, blazing down on the ranch he'd had to leave, the one he'd hated to leave, where his cows and strawberry vines wandered aimlessly without him.

It was the ranch that had brought them together. That, and the slough.

One day, a week into his stay, Mr. Rhoads was marching laps down the hallway in his hat and flannel jacket, strong hands clenched to his walker, when he passed a conflagration.

Gigi Montero was at the nursing station, stretched to her full four-foot-ten height in gold lamé leggings, wagging her neon-pink press-on nails at Beth.

"Your daughter, she is a precious gem! You cannot let her dirty herself in that filthy ditch."

Beth cast a placating smile. "Miss Gigi, Jack and I have been hiking around Elkhorn Slough all her life. And she's been paddling out for years. She's careful. We're fine."

The smaller woman stepped back, cutting off Mr. Rhoads's path of travel. "Beth, you do not know what is in that water."

Beth's smile sharpened. "Well, there are the jellyfish, and I've heard some stories about sharks . . . but they haven't taken any teenage girls yet."

Miss Gigi clutched at the rhinestone heart on her sweater. "Ay, Beth. You are killing me."

Mr. Rhoads decided his best way past was through. He spoke up. "She's telling you Elkhorn Slough's a fine place for a young person to be."

The two women turned, Beth grateful, Miss Gigi annoyed. Mr. Rhoads looked calm. He was a man who could stay still for a long time.

"You are Mr. Rhoads," Miss Gigi said, appraising him. "I met your son. Tall. Very clean. But I have not met you." She held out one pink-taloned hand to him.

Mr. Rhoads looked at Beth. "Your daughter a sculler?"

"Paddleboard. And she leads kayak tours."

Mr. Rhoads nodded in satisfaction.

Miss Gigi did not. She flung her Day-Glo hands in the air. "That girl should be working somewhere respectable. Like 7-Eleven. You say the word, I call my regional manager. Cesar will get her out of that stinky water and into a good store in Salinas." She whirled down the hallway and disappeared into the TV room, the door banging closed behind her.

Beth and Mr. Rhoads looked at each other. Their mouths were set, but their eyes were smiling.

"What's your daughter's name?" he asked.

"Jack. Short for Jacqueline."

He nodded. "Good name. How long has she been going out on the slough?"

"We've been walking it for fifteen years. She's been paddling for three. We live right alongside it."

"North bank?" he asked. "Only I don't remember you."

"South. I don't think we've met."

"I lived on the north side for eighty-four years, on the old Roadhouse ranch. Raised my kids there. Wish I was there right now."

The Roadhouse ranch was right across the water from Beth's house, on the rolling hills that sloped up and away from the slough to the north. Beth imagined what it must have been like to grow up there, to have a parent like this, someone who listened.

"Maybe you can tell me about it sometime," she said.

His filmy eyes lit up. "Anytime. You know where to find me." He looked up, as if he could spot pelicans flying above the popcorn ceiling. Then he shook his head and continued his walk.

NOW, BETH STOOD SILENT on a cold Tuesday morning as the EMTs rolled Mr. Rhoads to the double doors. She turned back to the desk.

"Has the family been informed?"

Rosa nodded. "I called his daughter. She was scheduled to visit today. And I left a message for his son. The poor man. He was just here on Saturday."

Most patients' families visited in groups, as if there was safety in numbers. But Hal Rhoads's children never came at the same time. His son, Martin, was a weekend visitor, a clean-cut Silicon Valley techie in his early forties who drove down each Friday afternoon from San Francisco to receive a long list of weekend ranch chores Hal had assigned him. Martin was friendly, stopping by the nursing station most Fridays before he left to chat about his father, the ranch, and his start-up that was going to revolutionize nanotechnology.

Hal's daughter, Diana, on the other hand, had no interest in conversation. Diana was older than Martin, a frosty Carmel matron who approached the nurses each Tuesday and Thursday morning with a faint but unshakable look of disapproval. She fell into the camp of visitors who held themselves distant from the nursing home staff, out of either haughtiness or, more likely, fear. If they didn't build relationships with the staff, they could hold on to the fantasy that their loved one's stay was temporary.

When she entered his room, Beth saw the extent to which Hal Rhoads had cooperated with his daughter's delusion. Despite two months at Bayshore Oaks, it still looked like he had yet to fully move in. Some residents could fill suitcases with photo albums and tchotchkes, but packing up Mr. Rhoads required only one small cardboard box. He had a half-empty dresser, a couple spy novels, an almanac, a stack of papers, a wall calendar with each day slashed through, and two photographs in heavy silver frames.

Beth picked up the larger picture. A family shot. Mr. Rhoads was in his fifties, strong and sunburned, with his pretty, proper daughter and his dark-haired teenage son, squinting into the sun. The three of them stood amid a crowd of cattle, calves maybe, with an upside-down *R* branded on their back left flanks. Diana stood apart from the two men, in spotless riding clothes, the English kind. There was no wife to be seen.

The wife was in the other picture, the smaller frame. It was a formal photograph of a young couple, black-and-white, him in a naval uniform, her in dark lipstick and tight pin curls. They were sitting close, her almost on his lap, his hand gently claiming her waist. They were smiling, him broadly at the camera, her slighter, facing toward him, as if she hoped he'd go out in the world and make a name for them both.

Beth wondered what had happened between the two photographs. Mr. Rhoads had told her he'd been on his own for a long time, but she didn't know the particulars. Had his wife died? Run off with a farmhand? Gotten tired of the strong, stoic type?

She looked back at the family photograph. Martin Rhoads couldn't have been much older than Jack was now. Beth knew what it was like to raise a kid alone, to have people constantly ask about the parent who wasn't in the picture. When Jack was little, it was especially brutal.

Pushing her in the shopping cart, debating whether to answer when the cashier asked about "daddy" or throw a box of Cheerios in his face.

Beth took one last look at the family photo before she flipped the picture frame over to place it in the box. And paused. There was something wedged into the cardboard backing, a corner of waxy paper peeking out. For a moment, Beth told herself it wasn't her place to investigate. But then the emptied room reminded her. Mr. Rhoads was dead. There was no more harm that could be caused.

The cardboard slid easily from the frame under Beth's fingers. Behind it, she found another snapshot, a thin piece of tissue paper separating it from the family photograph.

The picture was a funny shape, a narrow vertical slice, as if someone had cut it out from a larger photo. Hal Rhoads was standing stiffly next to a short, dark-skinned woman with a toddler in her arms. They were outside, at the edge of a patch of dead grass that spread behind them like a shadow. Mr. Rhoads looked about the same age as in the family photo. The woman was young, early twenties. She looked tired, her eyes dull, hands maintaining a tight grip on the wriggling boy. They were posed in front of the open doorway of a smart wooden building, but the woman hunched away from it, as if she didn't want to acknowledge its existence. The back of the snapshot had the words "new barn" in Hal Rhoads's spidery script. No identification of the woman or the child.

Beth frowned at the snapshot. What kind of story did it tell? Had Hal Rhoads traded in his first wife for a younger model? Beth didn't want to believe it. But maybe Mr. Rhoads was no different from her own father, chasing younger and younger women the older he got. The last time Beth had heard from her dad, he'd been in Bermuda with a twenty-five-year-old dental hygienist.

Beth tucked the snapshot back into its frame, trapping the mystery between cardboard and tissue. She put both picture frames in the box with Mr. Rhoads's books and papers and layered his clothes on top, folding his faded flannel jacket with care. Whatever his past, Mr. Rhoads had meant something to Beth. When things felt upside down the past couple months, with Lana sick and driving her up the wall, Mr. Rhoads was someone she could rely on, someone solid.

And Beth could use some solid ground right now. She realized, half-guilty, half-glad, that Mr. Rhoads's death had made her temporarily forget Jack's predicament. But now the fear rose up again, a wave crashing at the back of her throat. Mr. Rhoads would have known how to handle the detectives the night before, how to garner their respect. He could have calmed them down instead of riling them up like Lana probably had. Beth checked her phone for the fifteenth time that morning. Still no callbacks from any of the lawyers. There was a text from Lana telling Beth "Don't worry!!!" But that only made Beth more stressed-out.

The masking tape made a smooth, crisp seal over Mr. Rhoads's old clothes and secrets. Beth carried the box to the nursing station and called the front office to let the family know. Hal Rhoads's children could decide what to do with the women in their father's life. Beth had her hands full with the women in her own.

The rest of Beth's shift passed in a fog. Her phone stayed silent, her thoughts dark. Even Miss Gigi couldn't get a smile out of her with the latest gift she'd received from her son—a stuffed mini poodle with blue glass eyes that Miss Gigi had enhanced with long, stick-on eyelashes.

By the time all the IVs had been replenished and the medications checked, Beth was exhausted. She looked longingly at the couch in the nurses' break room, but she knew if she lay down, she might not get up. She refilled her thermos with bitter coffee from the communal pot, checked her phone one more time, and trudged out to her car to head home.

CHAPTER ELEVEN

BEFORE BETH COULD TOUCH the handle, the screen door flew open.

"Mom, hi, Mom. I have something I need to ask you." Jack's face was flushed, her words coming out in an urgent jumble.

"Hey, honey. Just give me a sec." Beth stepped around her daughter and into the kitchen, dumping her bag on the counter. She headed to the fridge and waved a box of frozen waffles at Jack, who shook her head.

"We already ate dinner."

Beth moved methodically from freezer to toaster to sofa, while Jack circled her double-time, chewing her nails and doing her best impression of a volcano about to erupt. Lana watched from the table, where she nursed a Diet Coke and a small pile of oyster crackers.

"I need to talk to you," Jack said.

"Did the detectives come back?"

"No. Not that."

Beth closed her eyes. Maybe the sheriffs had found another suspect to harass. Or maybe they were busy gathering evidence against Jack, conjuring up a story that she was an unreliable teenager who let a tourist die on her watch. Beth wondered what they might dig up. Would someone at the Kayak Shack talk about the time Jack marooned a group of tourists in the flood zone at king tide? Or would they find out she lied about meeting Ricardo? When Beth opened her eyes again, Jack was right up in her face.

"Mom, listen. They're going to open the slough tomorrow. I want to go out there. In the morning, before school. Is that okay? I mean, they haven't figured out yet what happened, but it must be safe if they're opening it, right?"

Beth looked at her daughter, a 105-pound tangle of nerves and hair. "Honey, those detectives still have questions about you. Our priority has to be keeping you safe. What if something else happens?"

"Like what if someone else dies?"

The toaster dinged, and Beth flinched. She'd been so focused on her fears about the detectives that she hadn't even considered the possibility the murderer could still be out there. Hearing it out loud made it an even scarier prospect.

"I just want you far from trouble," she said, retrieving her waffles and returning to the sofa.

"Why am I being punished if I didn't do anything?"

"I know you didn't. But they don't." Beth wondered if her mother had made any headway yet on finding them a good lawyer.

"Mom, don't I look even more guilty if I stop going out there? Isn't it, like, a sign? If I change my routine?"

"The only thing it's a sign of is that you listen to your mother."

Jack's eyes went dark. "It's not like I'm some scared bunny rabbit."

"I didn't say that."

"I know how to take care of myself."

"Honey, I'm not saying you don't. But this is serious. Can we just take this one step at a time?"

"Please, Mom. I need to get back in the water. Remember when I fell off my bike and you told me to get on it again? And the first time it was weird, but then after six times it felt totally normal? I think that's what I need to do now or—"

Jack's voice broke, and she collapsed into her mother's shoulder. "Every time I close my eyes, I see him. I see the mud and the pickleweed and his red life jacket. It's like the slough isn't my place anymore."

Beth stroked her daughter's hair. Jack's head rose and fell with Beth's even breaths. "It's awful when someone dies. Even someone you didn't know very well."

"I only met him once." Jack's voice was muffled against Beth's sweater.

Then, the girl looked up. "How do you deal with it? Seeing death every day?"

"It isn't every day. And it usually isn't shocking, like what happened to that young man." In a soft voice, Beth told her daughter about the patient who had passed away the night before. A gentle rancher who'd lived across the slough with his cows and his vegetable garden, a man who was pleased to hear about Jack going out to paddle every day. A man who lived long and died without pain. Beth's words formed a monotone lullaby, softening death into something both far away and ordinary, with no hard edges, no surprises.

• • •

Lana sat at the table, stone-faced and silent. She couldn't buy the fairy tale Beth was spinning. Every ragged breath she took reminded her of the tumors attacking her lungs, death rattling its alarm clock against her rib cage. Half of her wished she could escape to Los Angeles, to toast a real estate deal with cut crystal in a restaurant that would never dream of serving waffles for dinner. The other half of her wished she could slide onto the couch, join the embrace, maybe even offer something heartfelt to her girls.

But heartfelt wasn't going to make this go away. Beth was right. The detectives were going to come back, and Lana wanted to be prepared. Nicoletti's dismissive words still rattled in her ears, most of all that horrible, nasal *ma'am*, flattening her into something used up and worthless.

Lana hated being invisible. It was only slightly less terrifying than being dead.

She wasn't going to just sit there waiting for the detectives to move along. She might be sick, but she wasn't incapable. She was going to find a way to clear Jack.

She just needed to figure out how.

CHAPTER TWELVE

LANA'S FIRST DAY as an amateur detective began with a whimper. She woke up late. Groggy. After a coughing fit that left her heaving over the bathroom sink, she pulled on her robe, dumped honey into her tea, took her morning pills, and got back into bed.

But Lana was a woman who had renegotiated a contract during her daughter's bat mitzvah. If she knew how to do anything, it was how to work. She downed her tea, got back up, and hauled out her neglected boxes of files and office supplies from under the bed. She wiped the dust off her chamber of commerce award for "fearless real estate mogul" and put it on the desk, alongside a stack of favorite books that used to line the shelves of her office. Then she pulled out a pen and a legal pad to take notes. She resisted the impulse to write a header across the top announcing her intention to find the true murderer and clear Jack's name. She settled for neatly inking the date into the corner.

Lana wrote down what she knew. It wasn't much. Ricardo Cruz was murdered. He died sometime between Friday evening, when he made a kayak tour booking for Saturday, and Sunday midday, when Jack found his body in the slough.

She racked her brain for more. There was the strange man with the wheelbarrow. Lana heard the detective's voice in her head telling her she was a day early and a mile off. But she didn't care. She'd seen him on the north bank of the slough, the same side where Ricardo was found. It was something to write down.

She looked at the legal pad in frustration. Half of what she'd written down was common knowledge, and the other half probably wasn't relevant. She turned to a fresh page and made a list of important questions. Murder questions. The detective had said there was more than one way for someone to die in the slough. If Ricardo hadn't drowned, how was he killed? Was there a weapon involved? Who exactly was Ricardo Cruz? Was his death related to the water sample testing he'd been doing a couple months ago? How did he get to the slough the day he died? Was his car still nearby? Had he been out with a girlfriend or a wife or a buddy who killed him?

By mid-afternoon, Lana's page was full of questions and her head was cooperating. She got a fresh Diet Coke and, as she'd promised Beth, called a criminal defense attorney, an ex of hers who had retired in San Francisco. He offered to put her in touch with a good lawyer in Monterey. Lana ignored the follow-up texts he sent, providing names, numbers, and an awkward string of winking and kissy-face emojis. She could deal with all of that later. She had other calls to make.

Lana dialed the Central Coast Land Trust, where Ricardo had worked. A perky young woman answered the phone. She expressed a feathery desire to help and an iron unwillingness to do so. No, the director wasn't available. No, she didn't know when he would be back in the office. No, she couldn't discuss the terrible thing that had happened to Ricardo. No, she couldn't give Lana anyone else's number. Yes, she could take a message . . . but by then Lana was so exasperated she just hung up.

The sheriff's office was no better. The number on Detective Ramirez's business card just rang and rang. The same was true for Nicoletti. Lana tried the main line and reached a clearinghouse of operators who passed her from extension to extension, each voice more doubtful she had useful information to offer. She ended up listening to a prerecorded, gruff-sounding man inviting her to leave a detailed message on the tip line, and if she was playing a prank to PLEASE HANG UP NOW before she did something she would regret because providing false information to police officers was a SERIOUS CRIME for which one could be SEVERELY PUNISHED. When the signal came, Lana politely asked the detectives in the Ricardo Cruz case to please call her back as soon as they could.

They didn't.

CHAPTER THIRTEEN

THE NEXT MORNING, Lana caught a break.

Beth had to be the only person under seventy with a landline. Lana couldn't understand it. Her daughter refused to pay to get her eyebrows waxed, but she'd drop fifty dollars a month for the privilege of a direct connection to every robocaller on the West Coast.

Lana shuffled to the kitchen and snatched up the receiver.

"Hello?" she said.

"Is Tiny there?" It was a man's voice.

"Who's calling?"

"It's Paul, from the Kayak Shack."

Lana felt a flicker of excitement. If anyone had the ability to clear Jack—or make things worse for her—it was her boss.

"Hello, Paul. As you may be aware, it's ten thirty on a Wednesday morning, so . . ."

Nothing. His brain must be waterlogged.

"She's in school," Lana said, enunciating each word.

"Oh. Right. Sorry, who's this?"

"I'm Jacqueline's grandmother. Lana Rubicon. From Los Angeles. Are you calling about Ricardo Cruz?"

"What? No. I mean . . . can you just have Tiny call me?" He sounded stressed. Maybe the detectives had squeezed him too, about Jack, or his own involvement. Either way, Lana wanted to know more.

"Paul, you're asking me to ask a fifteen-year-old girl to call you about a dead body she found wearing your life jacket while working for your kayak hut. I think I'm owed some assurance before I—"

"It's not a hut."

"Excuse me?"

"It's not a kayak *hut*. It's a kayak *shack*."

Lana rolled her eyes at the decoupaged cupboards.

"Paul, I don't care if it's a kayak jetport. Why do you want to speak with my granddaughter?"

"I don't wanna talk about it with a stranger over the phone."

"Then let's change that." Lana lowered her voice, her words padding softly over the line. "Let's have a drink."

"At ten thirty in the morning?"

"I don't accept same-day invitations." There was silence on the line, and Lana caught a whiff of the familiar scent of a man aroused by his own confusion.

"But I can tell you feel some urgency, Paul." Her voice held his name and stroked a lower part of his brain. "And I'd like to help. Let's meet in a few hours. For lunch."

"Uh . . . okay. I'll meet you at the yacht club." He paused. "How will I know what you look like?"

"You won't have to guess."

Lana didn't have to see the man to know he was smiling.

"All righty then. Yacht club. One o'clock."

"Twelve forty-five. Here, at the house. I assume you have the address. You're picking me up. Until then, Paul."

Lana fell into the couch, spent but satisfied, the way she used to feel after she landed a big client or crushed the competition at Pilates class. She jotted down a few questions for Paul about Jack, the murder, and how power flowed through Elkhorn Slough. Then she closed her eyes, just for a few minutes. Maybe she could swing this detective stuff after all.

CHAPTER FOURTEEN

LANA PREPARED FOR HER LUNCH with Paul in the usual way. She pulled out a close-fitting skirt suit, one that made her look like a shark crossed with a kitten. She did her makeup with a subtle, smoky eye, smoothing out ten years without letting anyone think she was trying too hard. She fished out a jet-black wig she'd bought online and spritzed it with perfume. Then she downed her midday pills and grabbed her purse.

When Paul rounded the corner in his battered Mazda, Lana was sitting on the salt-bleached porch swing, back straight, legs crossed, black heels dangling just so.

Paul parked in front of the house. He sat in the car waiting, engine running, staring at her.

Lana didn't move. She watched as he looked at the faded numbers on the mailbox, then up at her on the porch. She sat serene, a can of Diet Coke in her hand, perched between Beth's succulent towers as if she were queen of the aloe plants.

Paul rolled down the passenger side window and leaned out to yell. "Hello? Lana Rubicon?"

She took a sip of soda and ignored him.

She could see Paul weighing his options. His hands fluttered in agitation, pausing over the steering wheel, the horn, his phone. Then he sighed and did exactly what Lana expected of him.

He got out of the car.

He looked halfway decent for a man with an overgrown mullet. Paul was tall and lanky, with bronzed, freckled skin and shaggy blond-gray hair. Lana took in his unshaven scruff, hemp-twine necklace, and cargo pants with a pocket missing on the left side. Some women probably found the lost-puppy look adorable.

As soon as his feet touched the property line, Lana turned on the charm. She hit Paul with a megawatt smile and rose slowly in her four-inch heels. By the time he was up the step, her hand was reaching out to greet him.

"Paul. It's a pleasure to meet you." She caught him in a handshake that spun him around 180 degrees, sending him back down the stairs with Lana lightly holding his forearm.

"Ms. Rubicon."

"Call me Lana." She dropped her voice into a husky register, leaning forward so he could catch a whiff of the perfume she'd applied to her collarbone.

Paul stood up straighter in his flip-flops.

Lana rode his arm down the path like a princess, her jacket crisp, high heels floating over the cracks in the pavement. They did a clumsy dance at the car, her waiting for him to open her door, him opening her door, her looking in the car, her looking at him, him looking in the car, him gathering up beer cans and fast food containers and finding a beach towel to toss over the stains on the seat. Once he'd unfurled the towel and tucked it under the headrest, she threw him another generous smile and lowered herself into the car. As he walked around the hood, Paul spat into his hand and ran it through his hair.

A brief thunderclap of heavy metal shook the car when Paul turned it on. He shut off the radio, and Lana rolled her window down to air out the stench of sweat socks dipped in pine sap. They traveled to the marina in silence, Lana looking out the salt-streaked windshield, Paul sneaking glances at her between stop signs.

"Is there something you'd like to ask me?" Lana said.

"You're Jack's grandmother?"

"That's correct."

"And she's fifteen?"

Lana could almost see the wheels turning in his head. She used one manicured finger to smooth down the hem of her skirt where it rode up her thigh.

"Women in my family, Paul," she said, brushing a speck of nothing off her sheer black stockings, "we have children early. It leaves time for more . . . fulfilling pursuits."

They arrived at the marina before she had the chance to elaborate.

PAUL PARKED BEHIND the Kayak Shack, in the gravel lot that spanned the short distance between his business and the South Spit Yacht Club. The patio outside the yacht club was flooded in sunshine, packed with sunburned tourists tossing french fries to a crowd of barking harbor seals. Lana ignored the busy picnic tables and swept inside the club, letting Paul hold the door for her and admire her calves as she passed by.

Inside, the dining room was quiet and cool, all dark wood and brocade curtains. Lana took a slow lap around, her eyes adjusting to the faded light, the black-and-white portraits of high-waisted bathing beauties smiling down on her from behind the bar. She could smell the memory of salt in the air. Three long-retired fishmongers sat on bar stools, swaying to Sinatra, their wrinkled hands mirroring the grooves in the mahogany bar.

After a brief conference with the bartender, Lana pointed Paul toward a worn velvet booth in the corner. She slid into the bench with the more flattering light. Paul scrambled to keep up, tripping on his way into his seat. But once he was there, something shifted. He lounged in the middle of the bench, legs spread wide, his arms draped across the table. It was as if Paul had just remembered that he was the local, Lana the interloper.

"Scotty," he called out, his voice booming across the room. "Heyo. Can we get some service over here?"

The bartender straightened his apron, turned his 49ers cap backward, and stepped out from behind the bar. Where Paul was blond and lean, Scotty was dark-haired and muscular, with thick, curly hair covering his tattooed forearms.

Scotty dropped two menus on the table and handed Paul an already-opened Corona. "Who's your friend, bro?"

Paul took a long pull from the beer and winked at Lana.

"We're just getting to know each other. Lana Rubicon, this is Scotty O'Dell."

"A pleasure," Lana said. She made a mental note to examine her plate before eating.

"Want a beer?"

"Gin martini," Lana purred. "Straight up."

LANA'S SHRIMP SALAD was halfway decent. Not that she could enjoy it. Chemotherapy had stripped her tastebuds and clenched her stomach, so she could smell everything and taste none of it. But Lana had never been a foodie. She'd picked her way through LA power lunches, feasting on the power, barely touching her plate. Yogurt for breakfast, salad for dinner, Chardonnay for dessert: the Lana Rubicon wonder diet. It had kept her lithe and active and making a killing in size 2 Chanel for three decades.

By the time Paul finished attacking his fried snapper sandwich, his mouth was loose and unguarded. It took only the gentlest of prodding for him to spill a story of Silicon Valley exploits, followed by an ayahuasca-induced awakening that spurred him to renounce the fast lane and switch to rowboats when he turned forty. He'd been running the Kayak Shack for five years now and claimed he had never been happier. As he boasted about the billion-dollar deals he'd turned down, Lana felt a rare pang of desire. She flexed her feet in her heels, imagining herself back in her old corner office towering above West Los Angeles. She could almost smell the real estate developers, their Italian cologne laced with sweat, lining up to ask her to fill their high-rises.

A spray of tartar sauce hit Lana's hand and brought her back to reality. "Now the only board I answer to is my paddleboard," Paul said, beaming across the table. "I've got the water, and the Shack, and that's all I need."

Lana put her hands in her lap, out of spitting range, and gave Paul a wan smile. "I'm so glad you found such"—Lana hunted for a vaguely flattering option—"clarity."

Paul nodded, pumping his smile.

"And that you've been able to provide employment for young people like my granddaughter."

"She's a good kid, Tiny. Great kid. Course, when I met her, she didn't know much about kayaks. You'd think a girl who grew up next to—"

"I have to ask you, Paul." Lana's voice cut in low, forcing him to lean in. "Why are we here?"

His neck went pink. "Uh . . . I'm gonna need something stronger than a beer to answer that one. Maybe later we could head out on one of my boats and—"

"Paul." She stayed just on the purring edge of a growl. "Why are *we*"—Lana used her hand to draw an imaginary line between them—"here?"

He tried again. "The yacht club? Unless you want to go to the Shack?" Paul started to shift in his seat.

Lana stayed still, her eyes locked on Paul. It was a trick she'd learned from a land-use attorney in Malibu, André Medina, whose first career had been in the FBI. When you want someone to go somewhere they don't want to go, introduce confusion. Maybe even a little pain. And then make your destination the solution, the alleviation of that pain.

"Paul, we are here because of the man who was killed."

Paul smiled with relief. Nodded. Lana made a mental note to send André a bottle of cognac.

"I'm worried for my granddaughter."

Paul nodded again. He squared his shoulders in his best imitation of someone dependable.

Lana rewarded him with a cautious smile. "Can you please tell me what you know about what happened?"

"I wasn't there," he mumbled. His eyes skittered around the room. Scotty O'Dell was watching them. One of the regulars at the bar gave them a thumbs-up. Another shot a gesture she chose not to follow to completion.

"So Jacqueline tells me."

Paul snapped back to attention. "What did she say? Did she tell the cops?"

"Is there something you'd prefer the sheriffs not know?"

"Look, I already told them, it's none of their business. I wasn't there. So what? I'm the owner. I don't have to be there every second . . ." Paul's eyes were growing wider, his hands juggling imaginary balls in the air.

Lana put her hand lightly on his forearm and brought him back to the table. "Paul, they didn't even bring it up. When the detectives came to our house, they focused completely on Jacqueline."

"Really? That's good." Lana's eyes narrowed, and Paul quickly changed his tone. "I mean, not good. But I guess they know what they're doing."

"Hardly," Lana said. "Seems to me they don't know squat."

Paul shot her a smile. "You want another drink?"

TWO MARTINIS, SIX CORONAS, and a basket of fried calamari later, Paul and Lana were old friends. Paul extolled his business acumen—beers two and three—and then expounded—beer four—on the incompetence of the local authorities. The harbormaster was a watered-down, sauced-up version of the three previous harbormasters, all of whom were related. The coast guard cared more if their uniform pants were creased than if the waterways were in order. The sheriff wanted total control of the marina, except when anyone who'd donated to his reelection campaign got in trouble. The jurisdictions crisscrossed in dizzying permutations, leaving parking tickets double-charged, boat fires uninvestigated, and enterprising businessmen like Paul completely on their own.

Which was apparently the way he liked it. Paul described the marina as a kind of Wild West, himself and his buddy Scotty O'Dell the heroic duo working together to keep the peace. Lana squinted up at a grainy photo of bristly fishermen in a gilt frame above Paul's head, trying to imagine Gary Cooper among the crabbers lined up in their rubber waders. It was a stretch.

Lana shuddered and gave Paul her widest eyes.

"It sounds lawless. Do you really think it's safe for Jacqueline to be out there?"

"Tiny's my best guide. I'm gonna need her back at work this weekend, now that the slough's reopened. And she'll be safe with me."

"You mean, when you're there. Which is when, exactly?"

"Look, Lana, I'm not gonna lie. What happened to that guy was terrible. But whoever hit that dude over the head knew him. A crime of passion, they said. Committed by someone who was seriously pissed off. So unless your granddaughter was close with Ricardo Cruz—"

"She wasn't."

"Then I can't imagine anyone wanting to hurt her."

"He was hit in the head by an acquaintance? How do you know that?"

Paul's hands went still on the table, as if he was surprised to hear his own words spoken back to him. His eyes darted around the room. "Uh . . . that's what Fredo told me." Paul pointed to a shriveled man in dungarees at the bar. "His great-nephew is the harbormaster."

"With what?"

"What what?"

"With what did he get hit in the head?"

"I'm not sure," he finally said. "Something heavy. Metal, I heard."

"That's even worse." And interesting. As far as she knew, there weren't any heavy, metal objects just lying around the slough. Lana looked at the fork in her hand, willing herself to remember to jot down a note about the weapon later. Then she looked up at Paul, who was eyeing her with discomfort, as if his sandals were suddenly too tight for his feet. Which warranted one more push.

She shook her head. "A young man. On one of your tours. Violently attacked."

"He wasn't on a tour."

"Oh, and you'd know. Because you were there. Except, you weren't."

Paul's face flashed fierce for a moment, like an angry rodent flushed from its den.

Lana leaned back. She should have known better than to use sarcasm with a man. She gave him a weak smile and shifted her tone.

"Paul, I'm sorry. I'm just worried. I want to believe you, but until we know more about what happened or even who this Ricardo was . . ."

His face softened from concrete to clay. She kept going.

"So far, all I've heard is that he was a young man from Santa Cruz, some kind of naturalist, booked on one of your tours."

"A naturalist?" Paul looked at her. "What kind of naturalist?"

"The detectives just said he worked for the Central Coast Land Trust."

"Huh." Paul shoved the last of the calamari into his mouth and squinted out the window, where a seagull was eviscerating a tray of half-eaten hamburgers. "I don't like those guys."

"The detectives?"

"The land trust. I know it's supposed to be good, land trusts, saving trees and otters and all that, but around here all they do is make rules and stick their pollution monitors where they don't belong. If it were up to them, no one would ever go out on the slough. Let alone make a living off it."

Paul motioned to Scotty for the bill. "I've kept you out way past lunchtime, Miss Lana," he said. "Tide's coming in. Time to head home."

CHAPTER FIFTEEN

LANA AND PAUL STEPPED out of the yacht club and stumbled across the parking lot toward his car. Lana held Paul's arm and counted out slow, careful steps. The martinis and the blazing sun hit her in rapid succession, two sharp jabs warning of a massive headache to come. She just had to make it to his car. Then she could go home and lie down. Possibly forever.

At step fourteen, Paul dropped her arm. Lana wobbled, then looked up to see a Buick double-parked on the gravel. Beyond it, a man and a woman were peering into Paul's car.

Paul stomped toward them. "What do you think you're doing?"

"Mr. Hanley." Detective Nicoletti straightened up and adjusted his tie. "It's nice to see you again. We're here from the Monterey sheriff's department . . ."

"I know who you are. When are you going to stop harassing me?"

Detective Ramirez stepped in. She was wearing a jacquard blazer with a pattern so loud it ticked Lana's headache up a notch.

"Mr. Hanley, this is a murder investigation. When we visited you on Monday, you assured us you would give us your full cooperation. Has something changed?"

Paul looked peevish. "No."

"Well, unfortunately, nothing has changed on our end either. We can't figure out how the deceased signed up for one of your kayak tours and then showed up dead in the water two days later. It seems no one saw or heard from him between the time he registered Friday night and the time his body was found on Sunday."

Lana stepped around the cop car and forced herself to speak. She could deal with her pounding head later. This was an opportunity she had to take.

"No one at the Kayak Shack?" Lana asked. "Or no one at all?"

Nicoletti turned to her. "And you are . . ." His eyes scanned down from her perfectly bobbed hair to the hemline of her skirt.

"We've met." She gave him half a smile and subtly angled her left hip in his direction. "Only last time, I was wearing a bathrobe."

Ramirez cut in. "Ms. Rubicon. What a surprise. How is Jack?"

"She's getting her feet back under her. No thanks to you." Lana glared at Nicoletti. "I left a message, you know."

"We've been busy, ma'am. Trying to catch a murderer."

"Does this mean Jacqueline is no longer a suspect?"

"Your granddaughter is still a person of interest. As is Mr. Hanley here. Sir?"

"What do you want?" Paul asked. His eyes were cautious.

"Perhaps we could talk in private? In your office?"

"I'm not letting you snoop around in there. I've got rights, you know."

"This is a voluntary interview, Mr. Hanley. Would you prefer to sit down at our station?"

Paul looked around wildly, as if he were casting for a better option. "Fine. We can talk at the Kayak Shack. Just let me clean it up first, so we all have a place to sit."

Nicoletti stepped between Paul and the most direct path to his shop. "I'll come with you."

Lana could see the panic on Paul's face. Maybe he did have something to hide. She considered what Paul had said at lunch, plus the three beers he'd had for each martini she'd put down. Murderer or not, the guy was in a bind.

Lana took a single step forward, letting her hip bump gently into Paul's.

He looked down at her, perplexed. Then grateful.

"Fine," Paul said. "But I want Lana to be there with me."

She nudged him one more time.

"Otherwise, I have to take her home before I can talk with you."

Lana smiled up at him. Despite his obvious deficiencies, Paul Hanley was a fast learner.

"Ms. Rubicon?" Ramirez looked at Lana doubtfully. "Are you two . . . related?"

Lana frowned back at her, willing her throbbing head into submission. "You said this is a voluntary interview. My friend Paul here has volunteered his interest in my presence. Are you going to grant his request?"

The two detectives looked at each other, then at Paul, who had placed a proprietary hand on Lana's shoulder.

"Fine. Let's go."

Lana let the fresh burst of adrenaline carry her to the Kayak Shack. When they reached the door, she hung back to dig into her purse for a pill bottle and a bobby pin. She dry-swallowed two aspirin as she jabbed the hairpin into her wig, shoving aside her headache, her doubts, and a misplaced strand of synthetic hair in one brusque motion.

THE SHOP WAS WORN, with whitewashed wood floors, bright blue walls, and plexiglass displays of stuffed otters, sunglasses, and keychains. Hanging above their heads, high-end kayaks and paddleboards formed an undulating ceiling, as if they were sitting underwater.

Lana insisted on the one real chair, a designer knockoff mesh office number with squeaky wheels. She sat a full six inches above the others, her forearms resting on the desk where tourists signed their waivers. The two detectives and Paul slumped in front of the desk in orange canvas camping chairs, trying not to bump into towers of water bottles and eco-friendly sunblock.

Nicoletti scooted forward on his chair as far as he could go, giving

Lana a view of the sweat pricking the back of his cheap dress shirt. He narrowed his eyes at Paul, ignoring both Lana and his partner.

"Let me get this straight. Last Friday evening, you get a call from Ricardo Cruz booking himself on the Saturday sunset tour. You write it down"—he gestured at the logbook on the table—"here."

Nicoletti pressed his finger to the words "RICARDO CRUZ 831-555-4923 PAID," underlining them with his fingernail. "That's your handwriting?"

Paul nodded.

"Saturday comes, it's time for the tour, and Ricardo isn't here. You aren't here. One of your employees . . ." He snapped his fingers at his partner.

"Travis Whalen," Ramirez said.

Nicoletti nodded. "Travis is working in the office. He checks in all these other people for the sunset tour." The detective ran his finger down a series of eleven checkmarks in blue ink.

"But no Ricardo." He dug his fingernail into the logbook again. "And the procedure would be, if someone doesn't show up for a tour, Travis would call, see if they're running late."

Paul nodded.

"So when we get Ricardo's phone records, we should see this cancellation call, right? From this office number to his phone, Saturday around four P.M.?"

Paul looked nervous. "I mean, I can't guarantee it. That might not even be Ricardo's number, for all I know. I never met the guy."

"But it's the number he used when he made the booking on Friday."

"I guess."

"And he gave you a credit card number when he booked the tour." Nicoletti's fingernail outlined a circle around the word "PAID" in red next to Ricardo's name. "Did you run the card?"

"If it says 'paid,' I ran the card. And it went through."

"On Friday Ricardo paid, on Saturday he didn't show, and if Travis was following procedure, he called to check on him."

"Did you ask Travis?"

"We did."

"And?"

"He says he called him. Says it went to voicemail, and that Kayak Shack policy is not to leave voicemails."

Paul nodded. "If they don't pick up when they see us on their caller ID, we figure they aren't rushing to get here. If they decided to go hit golf balls instead of kayaking, we call it good. We don't want to get into a game of phone tag about a refund."

Ramirez scooted forward, her chair tipping precariously. "So Travis calls Ricardo," she said. "And Jacqueline, your granddaughter"—she pointed her chin across the desk at Lana—"she runs the Saturday sunset tour. Eleven people. Two women. Nine men. No Ricardo."

Lana was listening carefully from behind the desk. No Ricardo. They believed Jack about that. Good. She wished she had her legal pad.

Ramirez continued talking. "Sunday morning, Jacqueline comes back to work. You still aren't there. She sets up the nine A.M. tour, works the office, and then leads the eleven A.M. tour. The group goes out farther than usual, all the way east to Kirby Park. And in the mud flats across the slough from the park, two tourists find Ricardo's body. Wearing a Kayak Shack life jacket."

"We talked about all this when you were here on Monday."

"I'm aware of that, Paul. And I'm sure you're aware there are two questions we asked you Monday that we still don't have answers to."

Ramirez ticked them off on her sparkly purple fingernails. "One. Where were you Saturday night? Two. Why was Ricardo Cruz wearing your life jacket?"

Lana watched as Paul tried to cross his legs, almost tipped over, and settled for a low crouch on the edge of his chair. Everyone was staring at him. Ramirez looked eager. Nicoletti looked annoyed. And Lana was evaluating, finding him wanting.

Paul waded in. "I don't know *why* he had a Kayak Shack life jacket.

But I might have a guess on how he got it. Someone could have loaned it to him."

"Someone?" Ramirez asked. "An employee?"

"Not necessarily." Paul stood up and started pacing as he talked. "I have two hundred and fifty or so life jackets here at the shop. It's not like they're some precious resource under lock and key. When they get faded, or the fabric gets a tear, I throw 'em in the storeroom. If a buddy needs one for a boat trip, I give him an old one. Technically, I can't resell used life jackets—there's too much liability with safety equipment. But I can loan them out as long as they're functional. And I'm not banging down anyone's door to get them back."

"How many would you say you've given out?" Ramirez asked.

"Over the five years I've owned this place?" Paul stopped and looked up at a stuffed harbor seal above his head. "Maybe fifty."

Lana rubbed her temple. "So that life jacket could have come from anywhere." She leaned across the desk. "Paul, where were you last weekend?"

Nicoletti twisted around in his camping chair. "Ma'am, this really isn't any of your business."

Paul kept his eyes fixed on Lana. "I already told the detectives," he said softly. "It's private."

Lana leaned toward him and matched his tone. "Someone is dead, Paul. I don't think that's an acceptable answer at this stage." They were almost whispering. It was as if she had cast a line in his direction, dragging his words out.

Nicoletti was about to barge in, but Ramirez knocked him back with a stare. The detective sank into his camping chair, his torso trapped in orange canvas.

"Jack told me you were with a woman, Paul." Lana let a small pout cross her lips. "Who was she?"

Paul flushed. His hand shot up and back through his shaggy hair. "Just a sailor. Passing through."

"You took her out? To the yacht club?"

"We went out on her boat. Saturday. I gave her a moonlight tour."

"And a sunrise tour Sunday as well?"

Paul let out a low chuckle.

"Who was she, Paul?"

He looked over Lana's left shoulder toward the tide chart on the wall, his eyes unfocused. "Tatiana," he said dreamily.

Ramirez swallowed a snort. Nicoletti's voice broke the spell. "Do you have contact information for this Tatiana?" he demanded.

Paul blinked and turned toward the older man. "I . . . uh, it was just a onetime deal."

Nicoletti insisted. "Last name?"

Paul shook his head.

"She had a boat docked at the marina?"

"A seventy-footer. She was anchored out in the ocean, over by the old fuel dock they decommissioned last year."

Ramirez grimaced. "Shit."

Nicoletti looked at her.

"They don't require registration for boats that drop anchor out there."

Nicoletti turned back to Paul. "Did anyone see you with this Tatiana?"

"Sorry, man. It was just us, the dolphins, and the deep blue forever."

Paul's unkempt hair flopped over one eye. He struck Lana as a man-child, someone who could flash hot or cold but preferred to spend his time floating in a warm bath. What kind of secrets could he be hiding?

Before she had enough time to seriously contemplate the possibilities, the detectives ended their interview. They'd extracted a promise from Paul that he'd stay in the area, that he wouldn't go out on any more strange boats with strange women without at least getting their phone number, and that he'd stop handing out old life jackets like candy. They told him he was cleared to reopen for business that Sunday, as long as he agreed to let Detective Ramirez come that day to observe the Kayak Shack in action.

Ramirez looked less than thrilled when her partner volunteered her for this assignment. She eyed the boats hanging overhead, patting her tight bun as if the wind had already started wreaking havoc on her hair.

"What if you accompany Jacqueline on her tours on Sunday?" Lana suggested. She curled a strand of wig behind her ear. "She's Paul's best guide. You'll see how safe she is, how responsible. And I'm sure she'd feel more comfortable with an officer like you in her boat."

"If you want, I can hook you up with a sweet discount on a new wet suit," Paul said, motioning to a rack of hot-pink neoprene.

Ramirez pulled her blazer tight around her waist. "I'm good, thank you. See you Sunday."

The detectives extracted themselves from their camping chairs, Nicoletti leaving his flipped on its side like a wounded animal.

"Wait," Lana said, when they got to the door. "I'm sorry to impose, but could you give me a ride home?"

Everyone looked at her, the detectives in surprise, Paul in cool assessment.

"Only if you're leaving now; I thought it might be easier for everyone." Lana turned to Paul. "I'm sure you have work to do." He nodded, saying nothing.

Ramirez gave her jacket a tug. "Fine. But no more questions about the case."

"Of course." All Lana wanted was a safe place to think about what had happened. And getting into Paul's car alone no longer felt like the best option.

CHAPTER SIXTEEN

"WHERE WERE YOU?"

Lana walked in exhausted from the ordeal with Paul and the cops, ready to yank off her wig and flop into bed like a dead fish. Instead, she was accosted by a raging woman with a grocery bag who bore an uncanny resemblance to her daughter.

But it couldn't be Beth. Her daughter was like a hermit crab: able to defend herself if provoked, but lacking a killer instinct. Lana ticked through her mental Rolodex of past fights—the big ones—full of operatic shouts, thrown chairs, and door-slamming accusations. Plenty started by her ex-husband. A few launched by fiery boyfriends and business associates. None by Beth.

"*Ma?* Where have you been?" Beth repeated.

Lana smiled lazily and kicked off her heels. "I'm not your daughter."

Beth banged a case of Diet Coke down onto the counter. "I know that. My daughter is out on the back porch, doing her chemistry homework. My daughter came home from school on time. And when my daughter noticed you weren't here, weren't answering your phone, she called me. And I raced home early from work to find that my mother with cancer was indeed missing. So I went to get groceries and look for you in ditches along the road while my daughter waited here, wondering what the heck had happened to her grandma."

Beth started shot-putting cheese sticks into the fridge. Lana cautiously stepped past her to the table.

"And what the hell are you wearing?"

Lana turned and threw back her shoulders. "This, my dear, is Armani."

Beth snorted. "You had a board meeting?"

"Of course not. I was at lunch."

"With a lawyer?"

"No. Someone better. Jack's employer. Paul Hanley."

Beth said nothing.

"And I talked with the detectives. The Kayak Shack is reopening this Sunday. I've arranged for Jack to have a police escort that day, to keep her safe. The female detective. Ramirez. It'll give Jack a chance to prove she wasn't involved."

It was at this moment Beth snapped.

She stormed over to Lana, Diet Coke in hand. For one terrifying moment, it appeared that Beth might swing the soda can directly into her mother's perfect right cheekbone. Instead, Beth slammed it onto the table. Foam spilled over, lapping at her clenched fist. Beth didn't seem to notice.

"Ma. What the hell were you thinking?"

"I—"

"First you take off on a ridiculous date without telling anyone. With a guy who is at best unreliable, at worst some kind of mud flat murderer."

"I'm sure he's harmless."

"You're sure, huh? Did the detectives tell you not to worry about sweet little Paul and his killer life jackets?"

"No, of course not. Those detectives are idiots."

"Idiots. Right." Beth took a sip of soda, gathering energy from inside the can. "Have those idiots cleared Jack yet?"

"They say she's still a person of interest, but I think—"

"You think? You didn't think. You volunteered my daughter to take a detective out in a kayak on Sunday, before they've even figured out what happened to the dead guy, before they've stopped looking at Jack like she's a teen assassin, before I've even given Jack permission to go back out there."

"You're being ridiculous. You should have seen how they went after Paul Hanley. They're grasping at straws, giving everyone the third degree, and we're just sitting here waiting for them to make a move. This is *our* move. A smart one. It gets the detectives to see Jack as an asset, not a suspect. And she'll be safe with them."

"Oh sure, she'll be safe. Right up to the moment they get her in a trap. And then—"

"Jack has nothing to hide," Lana said. "So there's nothing to trap her in."

"Are you really that naive? You think you can just order the sheriffs to do the right thing? They aren't your employees. You don't have power here."

Lana refused to back down. "Jack wants to get back out there. You said yourself the slough is her second home. She needs it to be okay. She needs it to be safe. And if she gets to know the detective better, she might be able to help me solve the case."

Beth put her soda back on the counter. Her voice went heavy like a heated cast-iron skillet, flames licking at the edges.

"You. Are going to solve the case."

Lana gazed back, steady.

"You. Who can barely get out of bed. Who can't even finish a crossword puzzle. Who is afraid to drive."

"You said I could help," Lana said.

"I said you could get her a lawyer."

"And I can. But this is different. Better."

"The only thing different is that the world no longer revolves around you, Ma. You know why Jack calls you Prima, right? Well, you aren't the star of this show. This is my house. Jack is my daughter. And—"

"Why won't you let me help you, Beth?"

"You think that's what you're doing? *Helping me?* Like how you helped me move up here on my own when I was pregnant? Like when you sent gold-plated baby shoes instead of showing up yourself to give me a hand with Jack? Or maybe the way you've spent the last four months helping me see how far every single thing I've accomplished is from your impossible standards? If you want to help me, Ma, just stop. Just lie down on your European mattress and take your damn medicine."

Lana couldn't decide if it was the harshness of Beth's words or her headache that made her want to sit down. But she stayed standing, staring at Beth, refusing to look away or give in to the part of her that did want to curl up in bed, take a pill, and go to sleep. She could feel her real self, her strong, hard self, grasping for a weapon she could use. Lana's eyes swept the room, from the messy table to the new couch. And then to the back door, behind which Jack could probably hear their shouting.

"You're scared, aren't you?" Lana moved toward Beth and dropped her voice to a whisper. "Not of the sheriffs—it's more than that. You've got this fantasy that you're this perfect little team here, you and her against the world. You're terrified of anything screwing that up. You're afraid you're going to lose your precious baby when she goes out and for once in her life does something you don't want her to do. You're scared that when she does that, she's going to decide she *likes* being out in the world, she doesn't want to hide in this dead-end town, she wants to be big and powerful and wholly on her own."

"Don't tell me what my daughter wants." Beth's hazel eyes were dark, her voice a low warning.

"I don't have to! She's telling you, if you'd take half a second to stop and listen."

"You're talking about you, Ma, what *you* want. But Jack isn't like you. She's a good girl."

"That doesn't mean you can control her." Lana set her feet steady beneath her. "I had a good girl once too, you know. Before she ruined her life by getting pregnant."

Beth blinked. She took one step back, then another. "Jack didn't ruin my life, Ma," she said, her voice filling the room. "She saved it. She got me out from under you."

Beth grabbed her soda, turned, and speed walked to the front door. The latch clicked behind her.

Lana ran after her in stocking feet. She made it out to the front porch just in time to see Beth hurl the half-empty Diet Coke into the recycling bin, miss, then slam her car door and drive away.

Jack inched out from around the side of the house, keeping one hand on the stucco, as if it were helping hold her up. Lana saw her, but she didn't say anything. She wrapped her thin arms around her torso and watched the soda bubble out over dry dirt, shriveling to nothing.

THAT NIGHT, LANA COULDN'T SLEEP. She kept straining her neck to hear Beth come in, falling back into the pillow each time a creak revealed itself to just be the wind. Around midnight, Lana finally heard the front door open. She shut her eyes, feigning sleep in case Beth came in to check on her. But the back bedroom door stayed closed.

Shit. She may not have been a contender for one of those tacky "Mother of the Year" mugs, but Beth had to see Lana was trying. They both just wanted what was best for Jack. Even if they defined that differently.

Though she had to admit that Beth wasn't entirely wrong in pointing out Lana had her own reasons for pursuing the investigation. The last two days, Lana had almost felt like she was back at work, not in her prime, but in the early days after Ari left, when she was a nobody, the only woman in the room, the tiny divorcée with big hair and sharp elbows. She could still remember her first win, at a meeting about a Culver City condo complex, when she smiled sweetly at the investors and explained how they could get another 2 percent of profitability by replacing the phallic tower the architect had insisted on with another floor of units. She felt the warmth of the nods from the bankers, but she only had eyes for the architect. She saw the exact moment his assessment of her shifted, his furious gaze upgrading her from arm candy to adversary.

She lived for that shift. She'd felt it earlier at the Kayak Shack, with Paul and the detectives. She didn't like being underestimated. But it rallied her to fight, and fighting made her feel alive.

It also kept her awake. The steroids she took didn't help, stirring her agitation into a lather. By 1 A.M. Lana had fallen into the itchy, overheated half sleep of the uncomfortably medicated. By two she was up again to open the window, deciding she'd rather get bitten by a river bat than sweat through another set of sheets. But when she pulled up the blinds, she saw movement on the water. It was a kayak, moving east, away from the marina and into the slough.

Lana grabbed her binoculars and strained her eyes. She could see the thin glow of a flashlight illuminating a wavering halo ahead of the kayak, a blot of silver in the blue-black water.

There was one person in the kayak, bundled in a jacket and a knit cap pulled down to their eyes. A duffel bag rose toward the bow from between their legs, as if the kayaker were riding an enormous cigar through the water. It was impossible to tell if it was the person she'd seen with the wheelbarrow the week before.

Whoever it was, they weren't out for a casual cruise. This person clearly knew where they were going. She could just barely make out the slow, deliberate strokes, the water breaking and re-forming each time the paddle entered it. The kayaker was moving steadily upriver, melting into the shadows.

Once the boat was no longer visible, Lana dropped the blinds, switched on the bedside light, found her cell phone, and groped for the detectives' business cards. Then she remembered Nicoletti's reaction to her last tip. She wasn't ready to be another 2 A.M. voicemail on the sheriff's phone tree for the overnight cops to laugh at. She put down her phone and got out her legal pad. She printed the date and time carefully across the top and wrote down what she'd seen. And then tried, impossibly, to get some rest.

CHAPTER SEVENTEEN

BETH AVOIDED HER MOTHER all day Friday, knowing better than to hope for an apology and not yet ready to offer one of her own. But when she stumbled out of her bedroom Saturday morning in search of coffee, Lana surprised her. Her mother was standing next to the table in a burgundy dress, a silk scarf with horses galloping across it, and a dark pageboy wig with an attached beret. She wore an assured smile on her face.

"Going to Paris?" Beth asked.

"I'm coming with you to the rancher's wake."

"You should be in bed."

"Tell that to my steroids," Lana replied, taking a sip of coffee. "I'm stuck all day in this stupid house. You don't want me to disappear on you or redecorate. Fine. Take me with you. I want to meet the neighbors."

"This isn't exactly a plus-one situation, Ma."

"Nonsense. It's a wake. The Rhoadses aren't counting chicken dinners. And Ricardo Cruz might have died near there. Maybe I'll find some critical information about the case."

"There is no case, Ma. Not as far as we're concerned." Beth turned to the counter, channeling her annoyance into the electric coffee grinder Lana had insisted on buying. Beth let the noise of tiny coffee chain saws fill the room, holding her finger on the button longer than was factory-recommended.

Lana waited.

Beth poured fresh black dust into the filter. "Jack, honey? What are your plans for today?" Beth looked over at Jack, who was sitting on the couch inhaling a bowl of cereal.

"Uh . . . nothing this morning. Kayla and I are maybe hanging out at her place tonight, but—"

"Okay, then. Get dressed. Everyone can pay their respects to the Rhoads family." Beth pulled out a mug and started pouring. "We're leaving in twenty minutes."

THE DRIVE TO THE RHOADS RANCH was bumpy, dusty, and quiet. Beth and Lana barely spoke, with the exception of a mutual expression of disapproval for each other's footwear.

After the bridge and the marina, Beth swung the wheel toward the unmarked road that flanked the north bank of the slough. They chugged up the hill past No Trespassing signs and electric cattle fencing that lined both sides of the private road. The car slowed as the potholes proliferated, crunching up the gravel past gnarled Monterey cypress trees and fallow strawberry fields waiting to be planted in the spring.

A mile up the road, they passed through two massive redwood pillars that held an open gate and a cracked, wooden sign with an upside-down *R* burned into it. Beth pulled off into a churned-up pasture alongside a line of fancy sedans and old pickups. The guests resembled their vehicles, some wearing suits, others in worn flannel and coveralls. Lana opened her door and pursed her lips at the dirt clods between her velvet high heels and the paved driveway.

"Still sure you wore the right shoes, Ma?" Beth asked.

"I've run across four lanes of traffic on Santa Monica Boulevard in these heels. I can get through a patch of dirt." Lana squared her shoulders, plucked a tissue from her handbag, and marched to the driveway. Her pumps were wiped clean and standing pretty before anyone at the wake even said hello.

The event was set up outside, in a wide span of asphalt that linked the ranch house, a barn, and two old greenhouses. Workers in starched white shirts rushed in and out of a large, stately house of flagstone and redwood, carrying plastic-wrapped trays of sandwiches and fruit salad to a line of tables alongside the barn. Folding chairs were set out in rows, facing a dark-haired man in a suit who was wrestling a microphone onto its stand.

A somber family stood in a line at the edge of the asphalt receiving guests.

"That's the daughter," Beth whispered. "They call her Lady Di."

Lana cast an assessing eye on the graceful blonde ahead of her. Diana Whitacre stood ramrod straight, like a grieving general, in a high-waisted pantsuit and a small pillbox hat with a veil. She was flanked by a balding husband and two pale college-aged children, a matched set in tailored black wool. Diana clutched her husband's hand firmly. Lana had the sense that she was holding him on a tight leash rather than relying on him for support.

"Ah, Daddy's nurse," Diana pronounced, as Beth approached. "And I see you've brought guests." The woman gave her son a pointed look, and he thrust three programs toward them.

"Mrs. Whitacre, I want to offer you my sincere condolences," Beth said. "Your father was very special to me. I know you meant so much to him."

Diana gave Beth a slow nod, scanning her from top to bottom. "Thank you, dear. You must be coming straight from work. You are welcome to use the powder room at the house to change before the ceremony if you like."

Beth's face flushed red. She gave Diana a fumbly thank-you and backed away.

"What did I tell you about wearing jeans to a funeral?" Lana hissed as they headed for their seats.

The program consisted of a series of speeches from Hal Rhoads's family and closest associates. His son, Martin, played master of ceremonies, introducing speakers and gently removing the ones who broke down crying on the dais. Diana offered a host of generic platitudes in an affected English accent. A gruff-looking cousin from Houston proved too torn up to speak. A dreadlocked niece who lived on an ashram in Jackson Hole said a prayer that suggested her great-uncle was now a red-shouldered hawk, or a sycamore, or possibly a hawk nested in a sycamore.

It got more interesting when friends came up to the microphone. Scotty O'Dell, the manager of the yacht club, told a story about how Hal had taken a chance and staked him as a professional windsurfer, the only guy on the racing circuit with a cattle rancher for a sponsor. Beth's boss at Bayshore Oaks, Cecelia, talked about the meticulous notes Mr. Rhoads had given her regarding how she might improve the productivity of the small herb garden that lined the exercise yard. Victor Morales, a distinguished-looking man with salt-and-pepper hair, spoke at length about Señor Rhoads's generosity to the Central Coast Land Trust, his support for small farmers, and his vision that old ranches might find new ways to exist in harmony with nature.

Victor gestured to Martin and Diana and beamed. "The whole Rhoads family, we are lucky to have them in our community. I look forward to working together to protect this precious land for many generations to come."

There was a smattering of applause, which Martin cut short by stepping to the microphone. Martin was a tall, slender man, the kind who retained a boyish awkwardness into adulthood. The local men seated behind Lana whispered about how he'd made a killing in tech but couldn't shoe a horse to save his life.

"Thank you all for coming," Martin said. "My father was not a religious man, but he was a dreamer, and we have all been touched by his dreams." He looked over his right shoulder and gestured to an ancient oak tree on a hill beyond the cow pasture. "After today's remembrance, my father will be laid to rest in the family plot. So he can keep dreaming on this land that he loved."

Once the speeches were over, the Rubicon women stood up from their uncomfortable chairs, intent on different directions: Beth to pay her respects, Lana to look for clues, Jack to explore.

"Try not to get into trouble," Beth said.

Lana flicked her wig behind her beret and headed toward the refreshments.

• • •

At the wine table, Lana found a local sauvignon blanc and Victor Morales.

"It was lovely, what you said about Mr. Rhoads."

Victor smiled and tipped a bottle of wine in her direction. She nodded and he poured. Lana had never had reason or desire to learn the finer points of land trusts and the do-gooder side of real estate. But Victor Morales was worth studying. He was about sixty, one of those men who aged into their attractiveness, with broad shoulders and warm, crinkling eyes. Lana bet he was aware of the effect the combination might have on women.

With a flourish, Victor presented her with a glass of wine and winked. Well aware.

"Señor Rhoads was a prince among men."

Lana caught a sliver of accent in his speech. "Are you from Oaxaca?"

"How did you know?"

"I developed a resort there. A long time ago."

Victor regarded Lana with increased interest, his eyes holding hers as they migrated together away from the wine table.

"And how did you know Señor Rhoads?"

"I didn't. My daughter, Beth, is a nurse at the facility where he died. They were close. Talked about the slough. She lives across the water from here." Lana offered her hand. "I'm Lana. Lana Rubicon."

"Lana Rubicon." He turned the name over in his mouth, savoring it.

From where they stood at the edge of the ranch's driveway, Lana could see 270 degrees around, with the slough and Beth's little house to the south, the ocean glinting to the west, and farmland stretching east. The marsh below them was a no-man's-land of pickleweed and sludge cut through with tiny creeks, spiraling and crisscrossing from the grassy hills of the ranch to the slow-moving slough. Lana spotted a few patches of solid ground, but mostly, the bottom of the hill was a mess of muck and stagnant water, a perfect feeding ground for the birds that punctuated the marsh in little crowds.

"You should see it at king tide." Victor was standing at her left shoulder. "Twice a year, the whole marsh floods. The cows have to swim back to the ranch. When the water recedes, there are new streams, new ponds, new valleys. It reshapes everything." He looked at her. "Do you live nearby?"

Lana paused, unsure which version of her saga she wanted to share. "I've spent my whole life in Los Angeles. Working in real estate. But for now I'm here, with my daughter and granddaughter."

"Real estate? Then we are in the same business!" A mischievous smile lit up his face.

"To be honest, I'm not precisely clear on how a land trust operates." Lana had yet to meet a man who could resist the opportunity to explain himself.

"It is our ambition to ensure that all of this"—Victor swept his arms out wide—"persists. We work with property owners who share this vision."

"Preserving all land for nature? What about people? What about progress?"

Victor locked eyes with her. "We are not so simpleminded as that. Just like the marsh, the land will keep evolving. We are here to balance it in harmony with the changing of the world."

He told her about some of their current projects. The heiress of a timber empire had donated a ten-thousand-acre forest to the land trust, and they were now converting it from a clear-cut operation to one that could be logged sustainably. Two property owners on either side of a forest highway had formed an easement to build a wildlife tunnel, so animals could cross the busy road without becoming roadkill. And near the slough, just beyond the Rhoads ranch, the land trust managed nearly a thousand acres on the north bank, converting the land from bedraggled vegetable farms into a world-class refuge for coastal wildlife.

"And what were you cooking up with Mr. Rhoads?"

Victor glanced back to the main house. "It is so sad," he sighed. "This is a terrible week. First, to lose Ricardo, and now Señor Rhoads . . ." He remembered himself. "My colleague Ricardo Cruz, he was working with Señor Rhoads on a big dream. This ranch, this one property, will enable us to make the entire northern bank of the slough a wildlife protective zone. Señor Rhoads and I agreed to form a partnership years ago, and Ricardo was working with him to finalize the details. It will be the largest conserved wetland in the western US, saved forever from development and extractive practices."

"Sounds like quite the undertaking." Lana's mind raced. She wanted to ask more about Ricardo Cruz, but it felt awkward to do so at someone else's funeral.

"It is what dreams are made of. This project will mean international recognition, federal funds . . ."

"And a home for the animals."

Victor looked at her, his eyes shining. "Of course, it is all for the animals."

Then he blinked, and his thick eyelashes erased the glorious vision he'd been erecting. "But now, with Señor Rhoads and Ricardo gone, it is hard to imagine the project without them."

"I'm so sorry. How did Ricardo die, may I ask?"

She decided to play dumb, hoping he'd have additional information to add to what she'd already learned. But Victor's face clouded over, and he shook his head. "They do not yet know what happened."

He turned toward the house, his voice hardening. "This is our one chance to protect the bank, all the way from the ocean to the hills. This is generations of possibilities. Thousands of species. This was Señor Rhoads's vision. The project must go on."

"Do you have a relationship with Mr. Rhoads's children?"

"We are still getting to know each other. They came to my office together two months ago, after Señor Rhoads moved to Bayshore Oaks, to learn about the nature of his commitments. I am hopeful they will honor their father's intentions for the ranch." He looked over Lana's shoulder and smiled. "And its glorious potential."

Lana turned and saw Mr. Rhoads's daughter gliding toward them with a determined look on her face. Diana Whitacre was in her early fifties, with porcelain skin that splintered into faint lines at the corners of her chilly slate-blue eyes. Her mouth held a smile that was equally cold.

"Señor Morales," she murmured, leaning away as he moved to kiss her cheek, "you aren't signing up new donors at my father's wake, are you?"

"Señora Di. I would never—"

"I'm very glad to hear it. If you might excuse us?"

Victor raised an eyebrow at Lana. Then he turned to Diana and tipped his hat. "I hope you will allow me to take you and your brother to lunch soon, Señora Di. We have much to discuss."

"We're quite occupied at the moment," Diana said.

"I only want to honor your father—"

"Another time. Please." She waved him off with a tiny flick of her hand.

"Charming man," Lana said, watching him walk away.

"I suppose that depends on your definition of charm." Diana's voice was low, clipped. "Are you a patient of that nurse?"

Lana felt a prickle of heat under her silk scarf. Had something given away her condition? Was it the new wig?

"No, I . . . she's my daughter."

"I see," Diana said. "Visiting?"

"From Los Angeles. I'm here temporarily. Lana Rubicon. My condolences."

The blond woman dipped her head in acknowledgment. Apparently she was too polite to ask why precisely Lana had decided to crash her father's wake. But not too polite to keep her hands to herself. Diana reached a well-manicured finger out to stroke a dancing horse on the scarf around Lana's neck.

"Forgive me. I saw you earlier and I had to ask. Is this—"

"Dior," Lana said. She resisted the urge to step back.

"The dressage collection," Diana said. "Only one hundred were made."

"It was a gift," Lana said. "I thought it might be appropriate for this occasion."

"Quite. My father and I shared a deep love of horses." Diana looked off across the fields, then focused back on the scarf. "A gift from a friend?"

"Business partner. We developed the Zuniga Spa and Ranch together, down in Malibu."

"Zuniga." Diana repeated the word under her breath, like an incantation. "I've stayed there. Very impressive." She paused and looked at Lana uncertainly. "Are you . . . working on a project up here?"

"In a way," Lana said. Diana was fishing for something, but Lana couldn't figure out what. So she decided to do her own digging. If Ricardo was working with Hal Rhoads, perhaps he was connected with others here as well. "I've been learning about the slough. And that young man who died."

"Ricardo Cruz?"

"Did you know him?"

The blond woman looked off over the rolling fields that led down to the water. She straightened her shoulders and adjusted the veil over her hair. When she turned back to Lana, her cool, thin smile was again in place.

"Hardly, my dear. I'd heard that he was back, working for the land trust. I only saw him once, walking the fields up here with Daddy."

"Back?"

"His parents worked for Daddy decades ago. Ricardo was one of the ranch kids, always underfoot, taunting cows and making mud pies. It's a terrible shame, of course."

"My granddaughter was the one who found him." Lana was watching Diana carefully now.

"Is that so?" Diana glanced over to the fields once more. Then she fished an embossed card out of her tiny black purse and pressed it into Lana's hand. "Ms. Rubicon, I hope you might call me. Perhaps on Monday? I'd like to talk . . . business. Now, if you'll excuse me—I see my brother is making a fool of himself again."

CHAPTER EIGHTEEN

BETH BACKED AWAY from the buzzing clusters of people until she found herself on the edge of a grassy field, face-to-face with a large, doe-eyed cow. Behind it, she could see two fallen fence posts and a strand of twisted wire sagging down onto the ground.

She stood very still, daring the cow to come closer. It was orangey-brown and huge, with long eyelashes and an upside-down *R* branded onto the left side of its rump. Beth had dated a rodeo manager once who'd explained to her how brands worked. There was a whole system for registering brands, like trademarks, so you knew whose cows were whose. One rancher might own a brand that looked like an upside-down *L*—a "crazy *L*" they called it—on the left back flank of the animal, and another cattleman might own the same design on the right. Her ex-boyfriend had talked about reading the brands, "calling" them, like it was an art form, the farmer's version of interpreting graffiti on train cars. Beth thought it was barbaric and capitalist and beautiful all at once.

It suddenly hit her that she was standing in the same field she'd seen in that photograph of Mr. Rhoads with his kids and cattle, so many years ago. She squinted at a cloud of flies dancing above the cow's tail, wondering how many generations, how many creatures, had been raised under Mr. Rhoads's care. And what would happen to them now that he was gone.

"Hey! Cow!"

Beth spun around at the man's voice. It was Mr. Rhoads's son, Martin. The sun was directly behind him, forming a corona around his dark suit that made him almost glow. He stepped onto the grass in his shiny dress shoes, pointing sternly at the animal. The cow seemed unimpressed.

"Does that ever work?" Beth asked.

"For my dad, sure," Martin said. "I never got the knack for it."

Mr. Rhoads had told Beth once about how cows don't have much depth perception. She positioned herself squarely in front of the animal, waving her arms like an air traffic controller. It felt a little ridiculous, but then the cow looked at her, gave a deep sigh, and started to move.

"Wow. So you're a nurse *and* a cow whisperer."

Was he making fun of her? Beth looked carefully at the tall, well-groomed man standing beside her. Martin's watch alone was probably worth more than her car. But his deep-set brown eyes were tired, and there were threads of silver running through his dark hair. She decided today, of all days, he deserved the benefit of the doubt.

"Your father told me a lot of stories about this place," she said. "I'm so sorry that he's gone."

They stood together, watching the cow shuffle back through the broken fence.

"Do you go to all your patients' funerals?"

"Only my favorites."

"Dad told me he liked you. Having you show up today, it's even more clear why."

"What do you mean?"

Martin smiled. "Your jeans. Dad was never much for fancy clothes or parties. All this hoopla. He'd have said we might as well make ourselves useful and castrate the calves or raise a barn."

"Or fix the fence."

"I never had the knack for that either. Dad would always ask what all my fancy engineering degrees were worth if I couldn't maintain a cow fence."

Beth heard the sadness in his voice, as if somehow his father had died because Martin hadn't lived up to his standards. She watched him fidget with his silk tie.

"Just because you're different from your father doesn't mean he didn't love you."

He looked at her for a long moment, and Beth wondered if he was going to cry. Instead, he swallowed hard.

"I know you deal with this at work all day, but I'm wondering . . ." He shook his head. "Would you be willing to get coffee one morning? To talk about my dad? I'll be here at the ranch for a while, working with my sister to iron things out. I'd love to hear a little more about the man you knew."

"My work schedule is pretty tight—"

"A beer then? Maybe Dad told you some stories I haven't heard. I'd love to have something to look forward to after long days arguing with my sister over who gets his favorite saddle."

It didn't sound half-bad to Beth to have a night off from Lana either. "I'll think about it."

He grinned, and Beth caught a flash of the gawky kid he must have been, before the tailored suits and high-priced haircuts.

"Martin." A sharp, cultured voice summoned him from the edge of the crowd.

"Duty calls," he said. "I'll be in touch. Thanks."

He turned and walked into the line of fire of Diana Whitacre. Beth faded into the crowd, watching the blond woman retie Martin's Windsor knot.

• • •

Jack wandered around the ranch, relishing a moment away from the cold war between her mom and grandma. It was sunnier on the north bank of the slough. It felt closer to the sky than the water. She imagined Mr. Rhoads's kids growing up on the ranch, mucking out stalls in the morning, then jumping on horses in the afternoon to gallop out into the tall grass.

She reached the barn and poked her head inside, cautious at first, then stepping in all the way once she realized no one was around. It took a minute for her eyes to adjust to the dim light, the cool quiet in contrast to the crowd and sun bouncing off the asphalt outside. She could smell the memory of horses in the air, a mix of grass and sweat and cedar.

There weren't any animals in the barn anymore. Just junk. Lots of it. Other than a shiny red fire extinguisher at the door, everything was gray, grubby, and stale. One stall was packed with horse blankets, saddles, bridles, and branding irons. Another was dusty with hay bales and pitchforks. Jack could see remnants of a plant nursery, peeling boxes of pesticides stacked at odd angles threatening to topple to the ground.

At the back, there was a stall full of old sports equipment and toys. Kid stuff. Dad stuff. Jack picked up a weathered bow missing its arrows and thumbed the string, imagining for a moment what it would be like to have a dad instead of a mom. She'd met her father only once, when she was seven and they ran into each other at a mini-mall while she and her mom were in Los Angeles visiting Lana for Passover. All she could remember was a wispy mustache over skin as dark as hers, her mom clutching her hand tight as they exchanged a few stilted sentences.

Jack put the bow down, balancing it on an old electronics set. She turned and headed back toward the open barn doors. Before she reached them, she pulled up short. There, lofted in the corner, was a kayak. It was a two-seater with an ombré design, yellow on the bottom turning cherry red on the sides, with the words "Kayak Shack" stenciled in purple spray paint on its hull. There was a paddle propped against the wall. And hanging on a hook next to it, a life jacket. The kayak didn't have a number on it, so it wasn't used for tours. But it was one of theirs.

What was Paul's kayak doing in this barn? Boats were expensive, and while Paul was loose with a lot of things, he was a hawk when it came to keeping his kayaks in order. Last year, he'd taken two out of rotation, for personal use, he'd said. Was this boat one of them? If it was, what kind of personal use was it fulfilling hanging here?

Even if someone up here was going to have a kayak, this barn seemed like a weird place to keep it. Access to the slough had to be half a mile down the hill, through a maze of boggy marshland. You'd probably sink knee-deep in the mud multiple times before you got to the water. You could drive the kayak down to the marina, but at that point, why not just rent one or get a boat locker at the docks? It didn't make sense.

Jack took one last look at the lofted boat before she left. She'd overheard her mom and grandma's argument the night before about her going back to work at the Kayak Shack tomorrow and giving Detective Ramirez a tour. Even if it was risky, she wanted to do it. She had to do it. That boat hanging in the barn looked innocuous, all bright colors and plastic, but it wasn't kayaks she had to pay attention to. It was the people in them. Especially that detective.

• • •

Lana spotted Jack first, emerging from the barn and blinking in the sunshine.

"Jack!" Beth called. "There you are. Time to go."

By the time Jack slid into the back of the Camry, Lana was already buckled in the front, seat angled back, eyes half-closed. The earlier tension seemed to have thawed a bit with the sunshine and the wine. Beth started down the dirt road back to the highway, trying to avoid the ribbon of dust peeling off the pickup truck in front of them.

Once they got moving, Lana turned to Beth. "That wasn't so bad, was it? Bringing me along?"

"You tell me, Ma. Meet any murderers today?"

Lana chose to ignore the sarcasm in Beth's voice. "Perhaps. Your rancher's daughter, Lady Di, she knew Ricardo Cruz. I think she's got something to hide. And I got good information from the land trust director, Victor Morales. I'm going to set up a time to visit his office this week, see what I can find."

Beth shook her head. "I must have missed the one where Nancy Drew flirted her way to a solution."

"Oh really? And what exactly were you doing with that rancher's son?"

"I was just talking with him. Consoling him. You may have heard of it."

"Are you planning to console him again sometime?"

"Ma, you're making this something it's most definitely not."

"Whatever it is, it's perfect." Lana braced herself as they sailed over another pothole. "You've got an in with someone who, like Diana, might have known Ricardo. You can grill him for me."

Beth blinked. Shook it off. "What about you, Jack? Did you have an okay time?"

Jack shrugged. "They have a kayak in the barn."

"Surely lots of people have kayaks around here," Lana said. Her eyes were mostly closed now. She could almost see the names of suspects lining her legal pad, fresh possibilities to dangle in front of the sheriffs to shift their attention off of Jack. "There's not much else in the way of entertainment."

"Yeah, but this was a Kayak Shack kayak. And one of our life jackets. I don't know how they got it. But maybe when I go back to work tomorrow, I could find out."

"Jack, we still have to discuss—"

"It's my job, Mom."

"I know, but—"

"I want to do my job."

The car went quiet. Lana ignored the battle of wills between her daughter and granddaughter and tried to remember exactly what Paul had said at the shop about loaning out Kayak Shack equipment to friends. He'd mentioned life jackets. But not boats. Why would he have given one to Hal Rhoads? Paul hadn't been at the wake, so he probably wasn't a close friend of the rancher. She couldn't picture him hobnobbing with Martin either. Did he have some other connection to the Rhoads family? Maybe a fling? Lana could see Paul with the grandniece, the hippie, reeling her in with some nonsense about free love. Or was it possible a socialite like Lady Di was slumming it with Paul Hanley? She'd add that to her notes to look into when she spoke to Rhoads's daughter on Monday.

"Fine." Beth jerked the car to an abrupt stop before the bridge. "Everyone can do what they want. Everyone can take care of themselves. That's your philosophy, right, Ma?"

Lana opened her eyes and gave her daughter an uncertain nod.

"Independence is a gift."

"Sure, Ma. I'll keep that in mind while I drive you home."

CHAPTER NINETEEN

AT SIX THIRTY SUNDAY MORNING, Jack tiptoed outside onto the tiny wedge of concrete behind the house where she stowed her bike.

"Mom?"

Beth was bent over in sweats and a beanie, meticulously rearranging her rock garden. It seemed to have expanded along the whole side of the house, lining the top of the gravel hillside that led down to the slough. The rocks formed a maze, a feathery, intricate spiral.

Jack nudged her.

"Mom? Everything okay?"

"I couldn't sleep. Decided to work on the labyrinth."

"It's nice," Jack said tentatively. The closer she looked, the more complicated the stone pattern appeared to be. Jack wondered if her mother had slept at all.

Beth reached out for a quick hug, and Jack felt the familiar warmth of her mother's concern. But today it felt too hot, smothering. Jack knew what she needed to do. She pulled back and looked her mom in the face.

"I'm going to the marina. You may not be ready yet. But I am."

Beth nodded slowly. Her eyes had dark circles under them. "She uses people, you know. Your Prima. When I was little, she'd pinch me so I'd cry and we could skip the line at the airport. Everyone's just an employee to her, in service to her goals."

"I'm not doing this for Prima."

"Just because she enlisted you doesn't mean you have to join her crusade."

Jack felt herself stand up straighter, her hands clenching the handlebars of her bike. "This is what I want to do."

Her mother swallowed. Her voice was gentle, tired. "Okay. I trust you. Go."

JACK PEDALED HARD past the old dairy and the power plant, the wind racing her thoughts down the road. It had only been a week, but she'd almost forgotten how much she loved the scent of the marina, the sweet blend of motor oil and salt rising toward her. One day, she'd have a boat that smelled like that. She didn't think her mom would let her solo navigate around the world like some of the teenagers she followed on Instagram, but even a few nights on the open ocean, a trip down to Catalina or up to Seattle, would be magic. Freedom. Her sweatshirt billowed in the wind, and she let herself imagine for a moment the fabric was a sail.

When she crossed the bridge, she stopped daydreaming and focused on the big day ahead of her. She wasn't going to get rattled. If the detective had questions, she'd show up with answers. She ran through where she'd been, what she'd been doing, who was there. As long as the conversation stayed focused on last weekend, she could handle it.

Jack flew into the marina, turning her wheels into a skid in the parking lot outside the Kayak Shack.

"Early today, Tiny," Paul said, ambling toward her and rubbing a towel through his hair.

Jack shrugged.

"Well, it's gonna be a weird one," Paul said, "with the cops and all. Better get everything all buttoned up for the big show."

Jack smiled. This, she could do.

• • •

Lana woke three hours later to the rattle of a pill bottle.

"Ma." Beth was standing over her. "Time to get up. Chemo day."

Lana rolled over and groaned.

"Let's go," Beth said. "Get dressed."

Beth left the room, closing the door harder than she needed to. Lana pushed herself up and into the cashmere sweater, wide-legged slacks, and fleece infinity scarf she wore every third week for her chemotherapy treatment. This was not Stanford Hospital with its attractive doctors and orderlies dashing around. Chemo was five mind-numbing hours in a glorified hallway on the second floor of a strip mall, sitting in a cross between a BarcaLounger and a dentist's chair getting poison pumped into her veins. The treatment room was freezing, and the knockoff boutique on the ground floor of the shopping center did a brisk business in wool jackets and fuzzy socks for the underprepared. Lana made sure her shoes were cute—today, black-and-white Italian leather booties—but other than that, she focused on staying warm.

Beth was silent on the drive. Each time Lana attempted to start a conversation, Beth turned up the radio. By the time they'd reached the clinic, the weatherman was practically shouting at them about the chance of rain.

Beth pulled in between the nail salon and the math tutoring center and idled.

"Aren't you coming in?" Lana asked.

"Can't," Beth responded. "Too busy."

Lana paused for a moment, considering whether to pout. She decided to go on the offensive instead. "So, it's Jack's big day back at the Kayak Shack?" She smiled at Beth.

Beth stared straight ahead, hands clamped to the steering wheel. "I'll pick you up at four."

Sensing the distinct possibility that her daughter was about to shove her out of the car, Lana picked up her purse, swung herself out of the passenger seat, and sashayed to the elevator. She didn't look back.

• • •

Jack's thorough examination of the boat locker left it in better shape than it had been in years. Eighty-five kayaks and seventeen paddleboards crack-free and accounted for. Sixty paddles standing at attention. Two hundred thirty-seven life jackets hanging on rods in long rows labeled by size. She still didn't know why there was a double kayak in Mr. Rhoads's barn, but it wasn't part of the tour inventory. At least for today, it wasn't worth worrying about.

She had a momentary hitch while inspecting kayak 33. As she adjusted the foot pegs, Jack remembered the ragged O the boy's mouth had formed when he made his horrible discovery the Sunday before. But then she moved on to kayak 4, which was caked in muck for no good reason, and her attention shifted to hauling it outside and untangling the hose to spray it down.

By 8:45 A.M., the entire Kayak Shack shone with dingy pride. Two life-size stuffed otters flanked the entrance. A fresh logbook was out on the counter. Paul had even rustled up a collared polo shirt from somewhere deep in his office. When Detective Ramirez pulled up, he was outside, grinning like a golf caddie who cut his own hair.

Jack was wary when Teresa Ramirez emerged from her car. But the detective looked even less comfortable. She launched out of the Buick, propelled by an enormous pair of neon-green waders over a tight black turtleneck. She had cinched her sheriff's duty belt around the outside of the fishing bib, causing the nylon to pool over her waist, revealing glimpses of radio, handcuffs, and holster as she squeaked her way toward the Shack. Her frosted hair was in a high, stiff braid, waterfalling away from the top of her head without making contact with her neck.

After a perfunctory tour of the Shack, Ramirez strapped herself into a life jacket and shuffled down to the docks to join the 9 A.M. tour. She chose to sit with Jack in a two-seater instead of getting the full tourist experience in her own kayak. She waved off the paddle Jack offered her and braced herself as Jack hopped into the rear seat.

Jack wasn't used to having someone in her boat while guiding, but thankfully the group was big enough to merit two guides. Jorge was in the lead boat, telling guests about the five major differences between sea lions and harbor seals. All Jack had to do was hold up the rear and make sure no one got lost or stranded. And answer any questions from the nice green detective with the gun.

In the first ten minutes, Ramirez asked Jack only two questions: what were the chances the boat would tip over, and what do you do if a jellyfish stings you. After that she fell silent. They spent the two-hour tour in a quiet trance, Jack keeping them moving steadily forward, watching the detective's braid swing back and forth and hoping she wasn't feeling seasick. Out of habit, Jack pointed out the wildlife along their path. The otter who seemed to wave at them from under the bridge. Hawks and plovers launching off of Bird Island, diving for anchovies. The detective said nothing. Her head twisted back and forth from the boats to the north bank. What she was looking for, Jack didn't know.

When they got back to the marina at the end of the tour, Jack offered the detective a hand getting out of the kayak. Ramirez paused, eyeing a seagull on the dock. "It's pretty out here," she said. She stepped out of the boat. "Too bad about all the bird poop."

Ramirez spent the next few hours in the office, watching Paul sweat his way through a dozen bookings and paperwork for two more group tours. She rejoined Jack in the double kayak for the 4 P.M. sunset tour, the same one Ricardo Cruz had signed up for the Saturday before.

There were sixteen guests, and once again, Jorge took the lead boat, with Jack and Ramirez minding the stragglers in the back. This time Ramirez accepted a paddle. She even attempted a few shallow strokes before dropping the paddle back in the cockpit next to the first aid kit.

The wind was favorable, and they made it farther than they had on the morning tour. Just before they turned to head back in for the evening,

Ramirez pointed port side, to the north bank. "The body was found up there, right?"

Jack leaned forward, and Ramirez grabbed the hull to keep from tipping. "More like over there."

Jack crouched just behind the detective, pointing to the mud flats glinting in the quick-setting sun. Jack could smell the detective's perfume mixed with sweat and swamp grass. When she glanced down, she could see Ramirez's snub-nosed gun in its holster.

"How did someone on your tour get all the way out there?"

Jack grimaced. "I told you. He wasn't. On. My. Tour."

The detective swung around in her seat, forgetting the water for a moment. "Jacqueline, that's not what I meant. I wasn't asking about Mr. Cruz. I meant the Baldwin family, that poor man and his son who found the body." She carefully turned back to the bow. "I don't see anyone out that far today."

Jack sat back in her seat. "The tides control everything out here."

"So?" Ramirez's braid cocked to one side.

"When the tide is coming in, ocean water rushes into the slough. It's like pouring from a big bucket into a funnel. When the tide is going out, it's the opposite. The water flows from the slough back out to the ocean."

"How does that affect how far people go on your tours?"

"The tides don't just impact how high the water is. They also affect the currents. At low tide, it's like the kayaks just get swept up into the slough. It's easy for boats to go too far, even past those mud flats. Sometimes we have to use a motorboat to haul them back. In high tide, like now, it's the opposite. The boats swirl around closer to the river mouth. And the wind makes a difference too."

Ramirez was silent. Jack couldn't tell if she was boring her or if the detective was just thinking.

Thinking. "The tides are different every week, right? Because of the phases of the moon?"

Jack was impressed. Most people didn't know anything about how the world worked. "That's right. Tides are diurnal, which means they happen twice a day. Two high tides, two low tides. But since the moon isn't on an exactly twenty-four-hour schedule, the tides shift by about an hour a day. That means a week ago, the tides were seven hours earlier than they are now. It's confusing at first, but also totally predictable. Like today, there was a high tide at four forty-five A.M., and another one at four P.M. Low tide's at eleven thirty A.M. and eleven tonight."

Ramirez turned her head from left to right. "Right now is high tide. This morning was low," she mumbled. "I guess the water does look different than it did this morning."

Jack nodded. "The high tide makes the slough look more like a river and less like a swamp."

The detective looked north. "So, over there, where Mr. Cruz was found, sometimes the mud is covered up?"

"Yup. Even right now, if you got close, there'd be a lot more water and less mud than there was this morning. The Baldwins might not even have found him there if the tide wasn't shifting low during their tour."

"But he was wearing a life jacket."

"Yeah." Jack closed her eyes and a flash of red fabric shot across her eyelids. "I guess we would have found him somewhere."

"How far could something float in the slough in a day?"

"A day? Does that mean you know exactly when Ricardo Cruz was killed?"

The detective made a careful quarter turn to look at Jack. It seemed like she was deciding whether to answer.

"Ricardo Cruz was killed on February third," Ramirez said carefully.

Jack counted in her head. "Last Friday? But . . ."

The detective nodded. "You found him Sunday. I know."

"Then you also know he wasn't on any of my tours." Jack gave Ramirez a pained look, remembering the way Detective Nicoletti had yelled at her at the house.

Ramirez either forgot or wasn't going to acknowledge it. "According to the coroner, Mr. Cruz was killed Friday between ten A.M. and four.P.M. And then he was in the water for twenty-four to forty hours."

Jack did the math in her head. "So he was already in the slough when I did that Saturday sunset tour. We didn't make it anywhere close to the mud flats that afternoon. Those guys were way too blitzed to paddle much beyond the bridge. Ugh. I hate thinking he was floating out there Saturday and we didn't even know."

"Did any Saturday tours go all the way to the mud flats?"

Jack considered. "None of mine did. But there are always people on the slough on a nice day like that. Somebody would have gone out that far. Farther. Even if it wasn't one of ours. Is the coroner sure—"

"He's sure Mr. Cruz was in the water at least twenty-four hours. And it was slough water. It wasn't like he could have been dunked in a bathtub and then transferred here later."

Jack suddenly felt her lunch knocking against the top of her stomach. A real-life person had been killed and dumped in her slough. It didn't make sense that Ramirez was giving her all these details. Jack remembered her mom's fear that the cops might set some kind of trap. Maybe she'd been stupid to say as much as she already had.

"Why are you telling me this?" Jack asked in a small voice. "I don't want to—"

"Jack, I'm not in charge of this investigation. I don't call the shots." Ramirez's eyes were tired. "But I think you have the right to know you're no longer a serious suspect. As you said, Mr. Cruz died before your shifts even started. You went to school that Friday, right?"

"I was there all day."

"Did you go out on the water afterward?"

"No. I went out in the early morning." This time of year, it was too dark after school to get in a good paddle.

The detective nodded. "We're doing a full survey of everyone who was on the slough starting at ten A.M. the day Ricardo died. If you weren't here, you'll be cleared."

Jack felt a rush of relief. Then, just as quickly, the photograph of Ricardo Cruz flooded her brain, his bright eyes and wide smile. He didn't deserve what happened to him.

Ramirez's voice interrupted her thoughts. "If Ricardo Cruz was in the slough all day Saturday and no one saw him, where was he?"

"If he had thirty hours to float?" Jack thought about it. "He could have gone a long way. Or gotten stuck somewhere. There's all these little creeks that let out into the slough on the north side. They go for miles. He could have gotten stuck in a dead end in the pickleweed, or one of the branches upriver. It all depends which way the water's moving, and how fast."

Ramirez gave a quick, involuntary shiver. The sun was down, and the temperature was dropping as well.

"We done here?"

Jack nodded. She dropped her paddle in the water, using it like a rudder to spin the boat around in one long swipe. The detective shimmied her paddle out from between her feet and started turning over cautious strokes. The water moved under their paddles like breath, emptying and filling in a steady rhythm, taking them back to the marina in silence.

CHAPTER TWENTY

BETH MET JACK at the back door before she'd even locked her bike.

"How did it go?"

Jack leaned the bike against the house and accepted a one-armed squeeze from her mother. Then she made a beeline for the kitchen.

"It was okay. Good, I guess."

"The detective?"

"She was cool, actually. She wasn't excited at first about being in nature. But then she got into it." Jack sat down at the table with a bag of tortilla chips and a bowl of salsa. She glanced at her mother. "And Prima was right."

Lana's voice floated over from the couch. "Right about what?"

Beth raised an eyebrow. "Go back to sleep, Ma."

Lana pulled herself up out of the couch and staggered over. The toxins never hit Lana smack on the day of chemotherapy—Beth knew the steroids kept her wired for at least a couple more days—but it still looked like an ordeal for her to shuffle over to the table.

Jack looked from her mother to her grandmother. "She told me I'm not a suspect anymore. I got downgraded, I guess."

Hope surged in Beth's throat. "What do you mean?"

Lana rewarded her with a wink. "See, Beth? I told you Jack didn't need a lawyer."

There was no way Beth was going to get sucked into that argument again. "What made them change their mind about your innocence?"

"I think it had nothing to do with me. It turns out Ricardo Cruz died on Friday, before my tours ever happened."

"Friday?" Lana asked. "Do they know when?"

"During the day. And then he was in the water twenty-four to forty hours before I found him."

"If he died in the daytime, and you found him midday on Sunday . . . isn't that more like forty-eight hours? In which case—"

"Jack, this is fantastic," Beth said. She pulled Jack in for another hug, a big one this time. She didn't need to know how many hours Ricardo Cruz had been in the water. Her daughter was cleared, and that was all that mattered. "Now we can just put this whole thing behind us."

Lana was still muttering to herself. "Maybe he was killed, and then put in the water later. Or maybe . . ."

Beth watched, annoyed, as Jack broke off their hug and looked at Lana.

"What is it, Prima?"

"Did she tell you anything else? Do anything detectivey?"

"Ma, Jack's out of the woods. We're safe. I don't think—"

"There was one weird thing," Jack said. "She made us unpack the first aid kits, and she took all the Maglites. Paul was pretty ticked off about that. She said they might be evidence."

"Hold on." Lana walked to the couch and returned with her legal pad and a pen in hand. "Tell me about the Maglites."

Beth stared at her mother scrawling furiously across the yellow notebook. This was supposed to be a happy moment. A peaceful moment. But Lana wasn't going to give her that.

Beth turned to her daughter. "Jack, you don't have to . . ."

"I want to know too, Mom. The slough's important to me. I want it to be safe. For everyone."

Beth sighed. Then she got up from the table and started banging plates from the dishwasher to the cupboard.

• • •

"So. Maglites?" Lana asked. She was exhausted, and just taking notes felt like an ordeal, but she'd felt a flare of panic when Beth had proclaimed the problem solved. Like something had been taken from her, like she was in danger of losing the only source of energy she had. She wasn't ready to give up her investigation, her small flicker of agency. Not yet.

"Every guide boat has a first aid kit in it," Jack said. "Basic stuff, like Band-Aids and drinking water, and a big honking flashlight. In case we get stuck out late. The only time I used it was when someone lost their ring in the water."

"Did you find it?"

"No. The lady wanted to dive in and look for it, but then she saw a jellyfish and changed her mind. She said she'd get her boyfriend to buy her a better one."

"What do the Maglites look like?"

"Like normal flashlights, but beefy. They take like six of the big-size batteries. And they have an American flag design all over them. Paul got them on sale at Army Surplus."

"Detective Ramirez took all of them?"

"I think so."

"What do you mean?"

"We have six guide boats, so six first aid kits. But only five of them had flashlights in them. Paul said the other one got lost a while ago. It's probably true. I don't check inventory on the first aid kits." Jack frowned. "I probably should."

Lana looked down at her notes. Maybe the missing Maglite was the murder weapon. If Paul had killed Ricardo with it, he might have dumped the flashlight or hidden it somewhere. Or he really had lost it. Which wouldn't surprise her either.

Beth walked by, lugging the old vacuum from the hall closet to her bedroom. She slammed the door and they heard what sounded like a small airplane taking off.

Lana ripped out a page from her pad and made a note to buy a new vacuum. "Was there anything else the detective asked about?"

Jack told her grandmother about the tides and the timing of it all. Lana narrowed her eyes, trying to follow Jack's explanation about the water and the moon and Ricardo Cruz floating in the slough.

"Twenty-four to forty hours," Lana said. "So he was killed Friday, and then, at some point that night, or on Saturday, he went into the water. Which means he probably didn't die where you found him."

Jack nodded. "I should have realized it sooner. It would be super weird for anyone to get in a fight in those mud flats or get hurt right there. Half the time they're flooded, and the other half they're too shallow for a boat to approach. And if he was there all day Saturday, someone would have seen him."

"If he floated to that spot from somewhere else . . ." Lana started scribbling. "Where? How far could he have come?"

"Depends if he was traveling through open water or along a side creek."

Lana pushed herself back from the table. "Can you show me?"

"Like on a map?"

"No." Lana headed to the back door. "Outside."

JACK AND LANA STOOD at the top of the hill that led down to the slough from the back of the house. Lana looked around, surprised she hadn't been out here before. They were standing right under the bedside window Lana looked out of every day, but it felt different without a pane of glass in the way. There was a rock garden out there, a maze of stones weaving in and out of each other in mesmerizing swirls.

"Did you make this?" Lana asked.

"Mom did. She started working on it a couple weeks ago. Says it's healing. She was out here this morning when I got up."

"Huh."

Lana wasn't sure how to square this delicate labyrinth with the Beth who'd shoved her out of the car at the chemo clinic earlier. She wrapped her robe tight across her chest against the chill. The slough felt more alive out here, more demanding. The smell of overripe marsh rose up the steep embankment. Hawks ripped sharp lines across the sky. Lana could see little switchbacks in the hillside dug in from all the times Jack took her paddleboard down to the water.

Lana clenched her freezing toes in her slippers and looked out to the slough. "If I dropped a leaf or a paddleboard in the water right here, where would it go?"

"When the tide is coming in, it would go east, upriver, to Kirby Park. When the tide goes out, it might just swirl around or maybe go west to the marina. It could float for miles, maybe, all the way out to open ocean."

"Could it cross over to the other side of the slough? Like, from where we are here to Bird Island?" Lana pointed at the shit-splattered rock on the northern bank of the slough where a group of pelicans was holding court.

Jack considered it. "I doubt it. The water moves fastest in the middle, west to east, ocean to farmland. When the wind comes up, kayakers hug the banks so they don't have to fight the current as much. It would have to be totally stagnant or swirling weird for something to cut across in either direction."

Lana watched a pelican choke down a fish, anchovy probably, shaking silver in the dusky light.

"And besides, if there was a body floating right in the middle of the slough, someone would see it before twenty-four hours had passed," Jack said. She sat down on the concrete pad that pretended to be a back porch. "Ricardo must have gotten stuck in a creek, or snagged on something. He had a life jacket, but he was wearing shoes, and jeans, which would weigh him down. He could have gotten caught underwater, on a rock or one of those old shark-hunting blinds, and spun around."

"Especially at low tide? When the water is lower in the channels, right?"

"Right."

Lana sat beside her granddaughter and squinted across the water, searching out places a man could get trapped. The Rhoads ranch was over there. And the land trust property beyond it. "Could he get stuck, and then break loose again?"

"I guess," Jack said. "Yeah. In twenty-four hours he'd hit multiple high and low tides. But it would have to be somewhere people wouldn't see. A creek or a drainage ditch. There's hundreds of those. He could travel down a creek at high tide, get stuck at low, and then get moving again."

"Always staying on one side of the slough?"

"Right. None of the creeks cross over."

According to Jack, Ricardo couldn't have floated to the mud flats from just anywhere. He must have been traveling somewhere along the north side of the slough. He could have been killed along a creek that let out into the slough, or maybe an irrigation ditch. But the path of travel was all along the far bank.

Lana was comforted to learn he hadn't died on their side of the slough. It put the murder farther from her window, past the weeds and fast-moving water. She gazed out to the far shore, wondering where Ricardo's life had ended.

"Can I ask you something?" Jack's voice was thin, uncertain. "Why don't you and my mom get along?"

Lana tilted her face to the sky, her eyes tracking a pair of white-tailed kites circling the marsh for their dinner. She wondered how much Jack had heard of their argument on Thursday night.

"You know how you call me Prima?" Lana finally said.

Jack nodded, too fast. "If it hurts your feelings, I could call you something else—"

"No. I like it. In opera, prima donnas are the stars. Leading ladies. Some people say they're demanding, but that's just another way of describing women who have power, women who know their own worth."

"I never thought of it that way."

With Beth as her mother, of course she didn't.

"Your mother is always supporting others, Jack. It's a good thing. Noble, even. She loves you more than she loves herself." Lana turned to look at Jack. "But you have to love yourself the most. No one else can do that for you."

They stayed there on the freezing step for a long time.

"But do you—don't you—?" Jack didn't have the words to ask, or didn't want to find them.

"Of course I love you. Your mom too. But I don't think for a second you're what makes me strong. I'm strong because I go after what I want. A Prima. Like you."

Jack let out an involuntary smile, the compliment washing over her like warm milk. But then she shook her head.

"My mom might not be a Prima. But she did all this"—she waved her hands wide, taking in the house, the labyrinth, herself—"on her own. I think you're more alike than different."

Lana looked up one more time. The birds were gone now, the sky darkening like a bruise. Whatever pain was floating there, whatever wisps of forgiveness, the night swallowed it all.

CHAPTER TWENTY-ONE

"DO YOU ALWAYS HUM in the morning?"

Beth jumped at the sound of her mother's voice. Seven thirty A.M. on Monday, and Lana was already sitting at the table, laptop open, legal pad covered in notes. It was the earliest she'd been up since she came to Elkhorn.

"I'm allowed to make noise in my own house, Ma." Beth turned away and smiled at the coffeemaker. "Nice to see you've got some energy."

"It's my last day of the steroids this month. I might as well get some use out of them."

Jack walked over to the table, waffle in hand. "What're you working on, Prima?"

"I'm trying to make a map of the slough. The jurisdictions. Who owns what. Did you know the Rhoads ranch is two hundred and fifty acres?"

"Massive, huh?" Beth said.

"I've developed bigger."

Jack leaned over her grandma's mess of arrows and jagged lines, punctuated by question marks. "I met this grad student at the marina last month who does ocean cartography. She goes out with this sonar machine and measures how the seafloor is changing. She offered to take me out on her boat sometime. If it's okay with you, maybe I could ask—"

"Did Ricardo Cruz die in the ocean?" Beth asked.

“Probably not,” Lana said. “Maybe in one of those creeks.”

Beth looked at the mess of squiggles. “Looks like spaghetti.”

“It’s a first draft.” Lana yanked the pad closer. “You don’t usually work Mondays. What time will you be home?”

Beth looked at her. There was an edge to her mother’s words, as if she needed something. Maybe the chemo was hitting her harder than usual. “I picked up a half shift to cover for the time at the wake. I should be home by four.”

“Me too,” Jack said. “Maybe we could all watch a movie tonight or something?”

“Or you could help me fix this map.”

Beth looked one more time at her mother. Lana’s hair was a patchwork of chick fuzz and wiry moss, and she looked anxious, as if she didn’t want to be left alone in the house. Then she lifted the map and waved it at them.

“Have a good day, girls.”

• • •

The door closed, and the house went quiet. Too quiet. While part of Lana relished having the house to herself after the packed weekend, another part of her hated the silence, the ugly reminder that she was stuck here while others went out into the world.

It was time to do something about that.

At nine on the dot, she called the land trust. To her surprise, Victor Morales picked up right away. He was happy to hear from her, and yes, he’d love to give her a tour on Wednesday afternoon.

Then she called Diana Whitacre. Despite the urgency with which Diana had requested to talk to her, it took eight minutes of stilted pleasantries before the woman would get to the point.

“Ms. Rubicon, I’ve looked you up. Your projects, your work, it’s impressive. I don’t know exactly why you’ve come to our little hamlet, but it’s a godsend as far as I’m concerned.”

In Lana's experience, unexpected compliments were usually followed by unreasonable requests.

"I'm hoping we might be able to meet. Soon. My children are in town until Wednesday, but after that, I'd like your counsel. Regarding the future of the ranch."

"Surely there's plenty of time to consider that." The woman's father was barely in the ground. Lana assumed Diana had at least ten designer black veils to go through before she turned her attention to anything as crude as real estate.

"I wish that were the case. But there are sharks circling, and I need to speak to someone disinterested, someone with discretion."

"Sharks?" Lana said.

"I'll tell you when we meet. Of course, I'd be happy to pay for your consultation." Diana coughed, as if the very idea of talking about money had to be cleared from her throat.

While Lana was discreet, she wasn't exactly disinterested. And there was no way she wanted Diana to think of her as an employee. "That won't be necessary."

"Much appreciated." Diana's voice shifted back into its clipped accent. "Might you be able to squeeze me in? Wednesday?"

"I have a meeting in Santa Cruz that afternoon . . ." Lana couldn't decide if it would be efficient or exhausting to do two meetings back-to-back.

But Diana chose for her. "Perfect. I have to drop my daughter off at the airport early in the morning. Then I was going to take a ride. The little stable where my horses board is on your way. Could you pop by before your meeting?"

LANA TOOK A LONG NAP that afternoon. By the time she padded into the kitchen, dinner was over. Beth was bent over the table, surrounded by succulents, using hot glue to line a rusted-out teapot with sphagnum moss.

"I was thinking about what you said this morning," Lana said. "You were right."

A handful of moss flew into the air. "Ma! Can you not sneak up on me in my own house?"

Lana brushed a bright green tendril off her cheek without comment.

"Right about what?" Beth asked.

"The Rhoads ranch. It is massive. Valuable. And now it's in play."

"Is this your way of apologizing for the other night?"

"What? This has nothing to do with that. We were upset. We had a chat. It's over. What's there for us to apologize for?"

"Whatever." Beth resumed dotting the inner rim of the teapot with tiny beads of glue.

"Beth, listen. Jack says Ricardo probably died on the north side of the slough. Mr. Rhoads's ranch is over there. And the land trust, where Ricardo worked, it owns the land just east of the ranch. The two men died just a couple days apart. So I got wondering—what if their deaths were connected?"

Beth stared at her mother. "Hal Rhoads died in his sleep."

"Was there an autopsy?"

"Doctors don't order autopsies for deaths by natural causes, Ma. Not unless the family requests it." Beth put the glue gun down on the table. "Look, I'll give you this. Ricardo worked for the land trust. Maybe he died on land trust property and drifted down into the mud. Maybe there's a big torrid mystery there with your new friend Victor and his tree-hugger buddies. But I'm not seeing any connection to Mr. Rhoads."

"What if the connection is the ranch? There may be a battle brewing over control of the property. Lady Di and Martin are involved. Victor as well. It's possible Ricardo might have been too."

"Leave it to you to turn this into a real estate drama," Beth said.

The comment stung, but only for a moment. Lana considered whether it was possible she was projecting, forcing the world she knew onto this small-town tragedy. She didn't think so. The Rhoads ranch was substantial. That many acres, that much money—Lana knew plenty of developers who would kill for less.

Lana cleared the far end of the kitchen table and sat down with her legal pad to make a list. Who was connected to both Ricardo Cruz and Hal Rhoads? Victor Morales, of course. He'd worked with both Ricardo and Hal, one as an employee, the other as a donor. He seemed intent on turning the ranch into a conservation showpiece, a golden feather in his cap. She put Victor's name in big block letters at the top of a page.

Next on her list were Hal Rhoads's family. Diana Whitacre. Her husband, Frank. The son, Martin Rhoads. The cousin from Houston, Caleb something? And the hippie niece from Jackson Hole.

Lana looked at the list. It felt too short. Was there anyone else who knew both Hal Rhoads and Ricardo Cruz?

"Jack?" Lana called over to the couch. "Do you think it's possible your boss, Paul, knew Mr. Rhoads or Ricardo Cruz?"

Jack looked up from her homework in confusion.

"I'm making a list of everyone who knew both the men who died," Lana said.

Jack walked over to the table to look. "I don't know," she said slowly. "I mean, Scotty talked at the funeral, and he and Paul are tight, so maybe Paul knew Mr. Rhoads? And there was that kayak hanging there . . ."

It was good enough to put him on the list. There were already plenty of suspicious connections between Paul and Ricardo Cruz. Paul had taken the tour booking. Ricardo was found wearing one of Paul's life jackets. And then there was the missing Maglite.

"Are you going to tell the cops about this, Prima? I mean, they might not even know about Mr. Rhoads's death."

More likely they wouldn't care. "They won't listen to me. I need to find evidence that links the two deaths, something real, to get them to pay attention."

"Can I help?" Jack asked. "I mean, I already met the detectives. And now that I'm not a suspect . . ."

Jack seemed eager, her pupils dilated with excitement. But then Lana looked past Jack, to Beth, who was aggressively snipping leaves off a tiger-tooth aloe plant with a pair of shears.

"You've already done a lot, Jack," Lana said. "We don't want to draw attention. You can help me stay organized here."

Jack's eyes lost a bit of their sparkle. But she quickly recovered. "What are you going to do next?"

"I'm visiting Victor Morales at the land trust on Wednesday. And Lady Di, at her stables. You can tell me if you hear anything from Paul or anyone at the Shack about what the detectives are asking."

There was another suspect on Lana's list who wasn't spoken for. Lana looked up at Beth.

"Is your date with Martin Rhoads happening?"

Beth decapitated another succulent. "It's not a date."

"Why not?"

Jack coughed. "Mom only goes out with lumberjacks."

"Jack! What are you talking about?" Beth's tone was annoyed, but she was smiling.

"There was that park ranger who only wore flannel. The paramedic with the beard. And that musician who—"

"I date laid-back, capable men . . ."

"Who all happen to look like lumberjacks."

It was one of those moments that would have been sweet if Lana didn't feel so left out. She told herself she didn't want what Beth and Jack had: the casual banter, kitchen-table craft projects, or questionable standards for male company. But she wanted them to see her. To listen to her.

"I'm not asking you to date Martin," Lana said. "But can you spend some time with him?"

Beth's smile faded. She looked down at the garden shears in her hand.

"This is important, Beth. You can ask if he knows anything about the murder."

"If it's so important, maybe you should get a beer with him."

Lana took a step back. She needed this. "Beth. Please."

Lana and Jack both looked at Beth. Her face was a mottled mess of irritation at the request and pleasure at their interest. Lana knew if she'd asked Beth when they were alone, Beth would have stormed out or snapped back at her. But Jack had softened her up. Jack was Lana's trump card.

Beth put down the clippers. "I can't make any promises."

"But maybe you'll try?" Jack said.

Beth gave a curt nod and picked up the freshly planted teapot. A ribbon of moss dangled from her sleeve, following her out the front door.

• • •

By the time Beth had all her cuttings potted, Jack and Lana were on the couch, a giant bowl of popcorn nestled between them.

"Hey, Mom, you want to watch with us? They already showed the murder, but Columbo hasn't figured out yet how he did it."

"Can't. Too busy." Beth dragged a rag across the table, wiping away little bits of aloe and moss.

"It wouldn't kill you to take a break." Lana took a single kernel of popcorn from the bowl and turned to Jack. "When your mom was a kid, Columbo was her favorite. She even dressed up as him one year for Halloween."

"Did you give her a cigar?"

"I made a fake one out of a toilet paper roll." Beth plopped down on the end of the couch and wiped her hands on her jeans.

"I didn't know you were into detective shows."

"It was a long time ago." Beth reached across Jack and pulled the bowl of popcorn toward her. "It started after Dad left, before Ma became a big shot. We'd melt cheese on bialys and watch in her bed. Mother-daughter murder night, we used to call it. It was our little ritual."

Lana remembered the stress of that time, barely covering the rent on their tiny apartment, pushing herself day and night to build a career out of nothing. Trying to be strong, willing herself strong, for Beth. For both of them.

"Columbo's kind of a dope," Jack said.

"That was his genius," Beth said. "Everyone underestimated him. They didn't see what he knew, what he was capable of, until it was too late."

Lana looked over at her daughter. Beth's nails were bare and half-bitten, her hair sticking out from under a hand-crocheted beanie. She had one hand in the popcorn bowl, the other arm around Jack.

"No more talking," Lana said. "We're just about to get to the good part."

CHAPTER TWENTY-TWO

BETH HAD JUST ENOUGH TIME after work on Tuesday to race home, swipe on deodorant, and head back out to meet up with Martin. She'd agreed to get a beer and an arepa with him at the food truck in the marina parking lot. For a minute, she debated whether she should dress up. She didn't want to give Martin the impression this was a date. On the other hand, she could hear her mother's voice in her head telling her it was always worth making men want more than they could get. She grabbed her bomber jacket and a pair of ankle boots from the closet, inspected the shoes for spiders, and slid her feet in. She looked at herself in the mirror, combed her fingers through her short, wavy hair, and shrugged. This was as good as it was gonna get.

Beth drove down to the marina and parked behind the Kayak Shack. She gave a half wave to Paul Hanley and Scotty O'Dell, who were hauling Styrofoam coolers of something—sand dabs, maybe—into the yacht club.

A silver Maserati pulled into the marina in a long arc, avoiding the fisherman spraying mud off the eighteen-footer by the boat launch. Martin swept out of the convertible in the winter uniform of Silicon Valley males: a shiny blue puffy vest, crisp button-down, gray chinos, and complicated sneakers.

"Beth," he called, a bit too jovial for the grimy parking lot.

She was still staring at his car. Even in the cold air, he had the top down.

"I know it's ridiculous," he said, following her gaze, "but my life is all work, all hustle. And I just . . . I love it."

His honesty surprised her. It blunted the obscene ostentation of the convertible, turning it into a simple pleasure. The car was ridiculous, and it was beautiful. Beth found herself smiling back at him.

The two of them walked over to the arepa truck, arriving just in time to see the owner, Flora, flip the sign in the window from "Open" to "Closed."

"Sorry, Beth," Flora said. "We got cleaned out by a corporate retreat group. Those guys." She pointed at a pack of men in matching fleece jackets headed into the yacht club. "They even bought all the vegetarian ones."

She really did look sorry. Flora was one of the first friends Beth had made in Elkhorn, another single mom with two sons of her own, and they'd babysat and looked out for each other for years. But that didn't change the fact that she was out of arepas.

"What about the yacht club?" Martin asked.

Beth shook her head. She wasn't ready for a deep-fried sit-down dinner among a crowd of drunken tech workers.

"Let me think." Nothing else in the marina was open at this hour, and most of the nearby restaurants were overpriced tourist traps. Then she had an idea.

"I'll take us to a real local's place," Beth said, looking back at the Maserati. "On one condition."

"What?"

"Let me drive your car."

He hesitated. Beth knew it was possible the night was about to come to an abrupt end. There were plenty of jerks who didn't think women were capable of driving any car, least of all theirs. Especially if it cost more than she made in a year.

Then Martin spoke. "You drive stick?"

"You like burritos?"

They both nodded.

He put his keys into her open hand, closing it in his.

THE MASERATI WASN'T NEARLY as obnoxious once Beth was in the driver's seat. She zipped up her bomber jacket against the wind and took the back roads through the lettuce fields, the car dipping and purring around the curves.

Martin spent the drive telling Beth about his childhood, regaling her with stories about growing up on the ranch, chasing cows and runaway hay bales that flopped end over end down the hillside to settle in the creek. Beth was content to listen, and drive, her heart thrilling each time she pushed the sports car into a higher gear.

But when she turned inland, his farm-boy fairy tale turned darker. When Martin was fifteen, his mother, Cora, died, trapped in a burning barn with some workers. It sounded awful. After Cora's death, the family unraveled. His dad was distracted. Diana disappeared to live abroad. Martin spent two long years in the ranch house with his father, alone with their ghosts.

"It didn't get better when my sister came back," Martin said. "I was seventeen then. She was twenty-four. Things didn't work out for Di in England, and all she wanted to do was take her disappointment out on me. It got claustrophobic. I couldn't wait to go to college."

Beth slowed as they approached the outskirts of Salinas, fields giving way to a long line of blank-faced buildings. Martin stared out at the warehouses.

"But even that was hard." Martin's voice caught on the wind, dipping and wavering as it reached Beth's ears. "When I left for MIT, it was like the last thread had snapped. Dad wanted me to stay on the ranch, go to community college, work with him. He wouldn't even come east for graduation. Said it was calving season and he couldn't get away. Implied I was neglecting my duties, that I should be with him pulling heifers out of some cow's ass instead of walking across the stage."

"But you did come back," Beth said.

"To Silicon Valley. Now San Francisco. I've built three nanotech businesses. I have a restored loft with eighteen-foot-high ceilings and a guest room with a world-class view of the bridge. Not that my dad would ever come visit. It's only a ninety-minute drive, but as far as he was concerned, it might as well be the moon."

He gave her a quick, hopeful glance. Beth could see a request for validation, redemption maybe, in his eyes. She stopped at a red light and touched his forearm. "I know what it's like to defy your parents' expectations."

"Big disappointment when you left home too, huh?"

Beth looked up into the rearview mirror and saw her mother sixteen years ago, doing her eye makeup in the front hallway of the house in Beverly Hills. Beth stood behind Lana, looking past her own unwashed face to her mother's perfect reflection in the mirror. She tried to stand up straight, to speak calmly. But she was only seventeen, and there was no easy way to say this.

"Ma. I'm pregnant." The word died in her mouth before it fully got out.

"Winners don't mumble, Elizabeth."

So she said it again.

Lana drew the eyebrow wand down from her face and stared at her daughter in the mirror.

"Is this some kind of joke?" Lana said. "Did you take that psychologist's advice and join an improv group to boost your confidence?"

Beth kept her voice steady. "I'm not joking."

"Say it again."

"Ma."

"Again," Lana demanded.

"I'm pregnant."

The dam broke. Her mother's voice picked up speed and heat, calling her stupid, selfish, saying she'd ruined everything for the both of them. She didn't ask how Beth was feeling (frightened), whether it was that baseball player Manny (it was), or what he thought (that it was her problem). Lana insisted on an abortion, in Palmdale maybe, somewhere fast and anonymous so Beth could go back to being the perfect Stanford-bound daughter to her perfect business-mogul mother.

Lana raged, and Beth kept her mouth shut. She knew she couldn't win an argument with her mother. She couldn't even compete. Lana was always on attack, never truly listening to or caring for another human being, even her own flesh and blood. Silence was the one form of power Beth had at her disposal. Silence, and her own intuition. Beth was scared, and angry, and there were tears sticking to her cheeks. But down in her belly, she felt a kind of tautness, a pressure building. Like she was pregnant with a storm.

And just like that, Beth knew what she wanted.

"I'm keeping the baby."

Lana's makeup bag fell to the floor with a clatter, sending compacts, mascaras, and lipsticks rolling across the buffed hardwood.

"So you're going to ruin your life, is that it?" Lana was talking to her shoes, to the makeup strewn across the floor, looking anywhere but at Beth. "You're going to throw away college and med school and your goals for what—a squawking pile of poop and need? Where are you and this baby going to live? Not here with me. Not with your father in Costa Rica or wherever the hell he is. What are you going to do?"

Beth had not considered this. But she did now. She took a deep breath and wiped her face with the back of her sleeve. Beth decided to behave as if this were a calm, normal question from her mother. She waited until the storm settled inside her before she spoke.

"I was thinking I could move to the beach house," Beth said.

Lana snorted. "What beach house?"

"The foreclosure up the coast. The one that client dumped on you."

Lana stared through her daughter.

"That bungalow is a disaster." Lana's voice cooled to its clipped, businesslike baseline. "I never should have accepted it. It's probably slid down into the marsh by now. No one's even been in there in ten years."

Beth didn't hear a no.

"I'll clean it up," Beth said. "I'll pay rent if you need me to. Once I get a job."

Beth bit down hard on the inside of her lower lip to keep herself from bursting into tears again. Her head was swimming. But her body felt sturdy. Beth held Lana's dry gaze until her mother was the one to break eye contact.

"Rent won't be necessary," Lana said. "You'll have your hands full as it is."

And just like that, she went back to doing her makeup.

"Beth?" Now it was Martin's hand on her forearm, bringing her back to the Maserati, idling at the traffic light. "You there?"

It had only been a flash, a moment lost to the past. She wasn't the same person anymore. Neither, maybe, was her mother. Beth tore her eyes away from the rearview mirror to look at Martin, to wonder about the years he'd spent away from his father. And whether they'd been able to close the distance between them before the end, when it mattered.

When the light turned green, she gunned it.

SHE NAVIGATED THEM into downtown Salinas, to a quiet parking spot on a wide, dusty street. As they exited the car, Beth gave Martin back his keys, feeling a twinge of loss as she handed them over.

He looked around at the darkened storefronts, seemingly reluctant to leave his car.

"Where are we?"

"You'll see."

Beth walked up to a rough rectangular cutout in the restored adobe wall, between a check-cashing place and a thrift store. There was no maître d'. No sign.

She turned to Martin. "You like spicy?"

He nodded.

She gave him a quick smile and stuck her head into the opening in the wall. "Dos burritos de camarones a la diabla, por favor. Y dos Modelos."

A battered service door beside the window swung open, and Beth grabbed the proffered bag of food and beer. She led Martin down a narrow, dingy hallway to another door and opened it onto a hidden miracle: a cozy courtyard, crisscrossed with colorful flags and strings of lights. It was cool outside, but the bustle of families and couples crowding the picnic tables made it feel warm. Beth and Martin sat at the end of one table, side by side.

"I had no idea this was here," he murmured.

"A lot has changed since you lived around here," Beth said.

"Has it?" Martin smiled. "When I was a teenager, some drunk guy drove his tractor across the highway and barreled into the marina. People were still talking about it the last time I took my dad to a grange hall meeting."

"It's a quiet place. One of the things I love about it. That, and the food."

She unwrapped her burrito, rolling back the top layer of foil into a barrier to keep the sauce from spilling out. Martin attempted to do the same. Beth took a bite, relishing the snap of the fresh shrimp, the oozing cheese, the crisp fine-diced onions. Smoky anchos and chiles de arbol filled her mouth with warmth. There were few things in life that couldn't be improved with a shrimp burrito.

When Beth looked up, Martin was staring at her. "You look the way my dad looked when he bought a new horse."

She grinned. "This is cheaper." Beth tried to imagine Mr. Rhoads somewhere like this. He'd be out of place, but not uncomfortable. Sort of like his son looked now. Martin's sleeves were rolled up, and he was attacking his burrito with gusto.

Again she wondered about the distance between father and son.

"Did things get better between you?" she asked. "After the strokes? I know it's a terrible thing to ask, but I've seen—"

He nodded slowly. "I know what you mean. Yes and no. We spent more time together, sure. I think both of us wanted to try to make it work. Every Friday, I'd knock off work early and drive down to help out on the ranch. I took over the business operations without a problem. But outside the office, I could never do things to his specifications. I milked the cows crooked, or I put the wrong herbicide on his marionberries. After his third stroke, we had to make a change. Di arranged it all."

"Was he comfortable at Bayshore Oaks?" She had to ask.

"He liked you, if that's what you mean. Said you were the only one there with a good head on your shoulders. It was hard for him to be away from the ranch. But it seemed like he was doing better at Bayshore Oaks. At least, I thought he was."

Beth was surprised to hear it. The Hal Rhoads she knew had been strong, but suffering. She'd watched him grow dimmer, eat less, cough more, every day until the end. She wondered if Martin had avoided seeing his father's pain. Or if Hal had kept it hidden, maintaining a proud distance even when his son came home to him. Either way, Beth didn't know Martin well enough to challenge the way he'd seen it.

"Your father struck me as so grounded," Beth said. "Like an oak tree." She could almost see him, standing sentinel behind his walker in the long hallway of Bayshore Oaks amid the daily churn of wheelchairs and IV carts.

A smear of diabla sauce had stained Martin's bottom lip bright red. "It's funny, you know? We were both entrepreneurs. We both had big ideas. He dreamed of mite-resistant lettuce. I dreamed of microscopic robots. But he never got interested in my work. I'd invite him to check out the lab, or come to a presentation. He never did. For Dad, everything had to revolve around the ranch. He gave a loan or an acre for 'experimental purposes' to every wild-eyed huckster in the region. He even leased a slice of marsh to that loser who owns the Kayak Shack. He took one of his boats as a down payment. Meanwhile, I've funded every one of my tech start-ups on my own."

She could see it was eating at him. "I'm sorry, Martin. He may not have had an easy time showing it. But I know he loved you."

Martin winced. "That last visit. We argued. It was stupid. I got stuck in the city late on Friday at this investor pitch event. I couldn't get down to Bayshore Oaks to see him until Saturday. I wish . . ."

Beth touched his forearm. "Every family has its rough moments."

"I know." His eyes were wet, shining. "I just hate that it was our last one."

She told Martin what she remembered, how Mr. Rhoads told her about his boy who came home after many years away. Maybe he'd been too proud to say it directly to Martin's face.

"He called me that? His boy?"

"He did."

As a geriatric nurse, Beth had often been in the delicate position of watching a man battle with the question of whether to cry in front of a woman he hardly knew. She looked away, took a swallow of beer, and gave him room to compose himself while she figured out how to change the subject. She considered what he'd said about Paul Hanley and his lease, and her ridiculous promise to help with the investigation.

"So you've had dealings with Paul Hanley?"

Martin looked at her quizzically. Then he nodded.

"My daughter works at his Kayak Shack," Beth said. "As a tour guide. She saw one of his kayaks in the barn at your father's wake."

"You don't seem old enough to have a daughter who is employed."

"She's fifteen. Mature for her age." Beth started picking at the empty foil wrapper in front of her, rolling it into a ball. "What's your impression of Paul?"

"He seems like the kind of guy who always has a hustle going."

"What's he doing on the land he leases from you?"

"He says he's growing strawberries." It was clear from Martin's tone that he didn't entirely believe this.

Neither did Beth. The Paul Hanley she knew definitely wasn't a berry farmer. "I'm surprised to hear he has another business besides the

Kayak Shack. It must be quite the juggling act, especially now, with everything going on."

"What do you mean?"

"The slough . . . it was shut down by the sheriffs last week. Two tourists on a kayak tour found a dead body. My daughter, Jack, was the one guiding them."

"What? That's terrible!" Concern flooded Martin's eyes. "My sister mentioned someone had died nearby, but I had no idea . . ."

"It was the Sunday before last. Just nine days ago." Beth suddenly realized Ricardo Cruz had been found the day before Mr. Rhoads passed away. No wonder Martin hadn't gotten the full story.

"What happened?"

"The body of a young man was found up by the mud flats on one of Jack's kayak tours. She thought he was a guest who'd fallen in. But when she rolled him over . . ." Beth squeezed the tinfoil ball tight in her hand.

"Heart attack?"

"That's what I thought too. But no. Worse. They say he was murdered. And Paul Hanley might be a suspect."

"Whoa."

Beth looked down. She hadn't meant to turn the conversation toward gruesome gossip. "I'm sorry," she said. "We're here to talk about your father. Not this."

"It's okay. Dad would have wanted to know about everything going on around the ranch. I guess I should too."

It took Beth a minute to understand what he meant. "The ranch is yours now, isn't it?"

"And my sister's."

"Are you planning to keep it?"

"I don't think so. Di has her life in Carmel, and mine is up in the city. Dad's memories I want. His land, not so much." He took a swig of beer. "And it wouldn't hurt for my start-up to have a fresh source of capital without investor strings attached. I've actually already heard from a potential buyer. I just have to get on the same page with Di about it. And Victor Morales."

"The land trust director?"

"He's been calling the house, claiming Dad intended to donate the development rights to the land trust."

"It is a beautiful place," Beth said.

"True. One I've spent my whole life trying to get away from."

Beth tried to imagine Martin in a cowboy hat and a worn pair of chaps, his smooth skin growing leathery grooves like his father's. It was a stretch.

"Well," she said, "if Victor Morales is up to something, my mother will probably sniff it out."

"Your mother?"

"She met Victor at your father's wake and strong-armed him into giving her a tour tomorrow."

"Is she a . . . conservationist?"

"Not exactly." Beth considered whether there was any sensible way to explain what Lana was doing. But there wasn't. So she just stuck with the truth.

"When my daughter found the dead man, the sheriffs started pressuring her about it. Treating her like a suspect. That prompted my mother to decide to swoop in and solve the case."

"So your mother's a detective."

"Well . . ." Beth glanced over at the makeshift bar in the corner. "You want another beer?"

OVER SWEATY MODELOS and hot churros, Beth told Martin all about her glamorous mother. Her real estate career. The collapse. The rushed occupation of Beth's back bedroom. And Lana's insistence on driving her completely up the wall.

"She can't accept that she isn't the center of the universe anymore, sending up skyscrapers with the flick of her pen. She can't pay a demolition crew to pummel her cancer into submission, so she's put all that energy into bulldozing my life instead. Roping my daughter into her fantasies. And figuring out who killed the dead man in the slough."

"And she's doing it because . . . ?"

Beth rolled her eyes. "She wants to help, supposedly. To feel important, more likely."

"Sounds like it's bringing her closer to your daughter."

Beth considered, for a moment, what Lana might not be telling her about her motivations. But she knew her mother. It was all about the hunt, all about herself.

"The sheriffs have gotten interested in Paul Hanley as a suspect. But she's hot on the trail of that land trust director."

"Why?"

"The man who died was working for him as a naturalist."

"Victor Morales." Martin repeated the name slowly, rolling it around in his mouth like a slug. "I don't trust him. Sweet-talking old people into giving away their land."

"He tried that with your father?"

"A couple months ago, Victor showed me and my sister a document Dad signed about possibly donating our development rights to the land trust. But it's meaningless. It isn't binding. Dad never even mentioned it to us. He probably signed it just to get Victor off his back."

"He'd do that?" Beth always thought of Hal Rhoads as the kind of man who lived and died by his word.

"Dad was a pretty wily businessman when he wanted to be. He said sometimes you gotta get close to your enemy to get rid of him." Martin smiled. "I saw him catch a rattler once. He scooped it up and slammed its head in the dirt in one continuous motion, all before I even got a good look at it. Three months later, he had a new hatband. Dad knew how to handle a snake."

"I'll tell my mom to avoid getting bit." Beth smiled back at him.

"You know, she'll probably grill me about any juicy clues you might have to offer."

"I did see an otter signaling suspiciously at a harbor seal yesterday." He raised the stub of his churro into the air. "To maddening parents!"

Beth lifted her last bite in his direction. "Amen to that."

CHAPTER TWENTY-THREE

LATE AT NIGHT, the bungalow's kitchen bore an unfortunate resemblance to an interrogation room. Beth had never registered the similarity until she walked in and found her mother at the table in her bathrobe, back straight, dark shadows under her eyes accentuated by the glow of the single light bulb. Lana had removed Beth's homemade lampshade two weeks earlier, when it dumped a palm frond in one of her protein shakes.

"How was your date?" Lana asked. She had Beth's glue gun in one hand, twirling it around her finger. Beth hoped it wasn't plugged in.

"It wasn't a date."

"Fine. How was it?" Lana was sipping something, jet fuel probably, and speaking in a familiar clipped tone.

"Good."

"How good?"

"About as good as you can expect when you're having burritos with a guy whose father just died." Beth stared at her mother. "Shouldn't you be in bed?"

Jack stood up from the couch. "Prima, tell her."

Lana put the glue gun on the table. She ran a hand through her patchy, close-cropped hair. "I'm concerned Martin might be involved in the murder. Murders."

"Really." Beth felt her frustration building. "You're concerned that a man whose father just died, who wasn't even in town when Ricardo died, may have killed them both?"

"Did he know Ricardo?"

"I didn't ask. It didn't matter. He was in San Francisco the Friday Ricardo died. He didn't get here until Saturday. He'd barely even heard about it. It was awkward to bring it up, and I didn't want to get too weird. But I did it. For you."

"Where exactly was he?"

"Where was he when?"

"That Friday."

Beth stared at her mother. "He was at a nanotech pitch event. For investors. His start-up builds robots that assemble circuit boards. Microscopic ones." She frowned. "I think I have that right."

"Where was this tiny pitch conference?"

"Next time I'll tap his phone, Ma." Beth shook her head. "Seriously. He's a good guy. Smart. No ax-murderer vibes. We had more in common than I expected."

"Anything I should know before I see his sister tomorrow?"

"There was one thing." Beth paused for a moment, relishing the naked interest on her mother's face. "Apparently Victor Morales is harassing them about donating the ranch to the land trust."

"From what Victor said at the wake, it was what Hal Rhoads wanted."

Beth shrugged. "Not according to Martin. He says whatever his father signed was just for show."

"Are you going to see him again?" Jack asked.

Something was hiding in Jack's question, and Beth couldn't tell if it was hope or concern. Her voice softened. "It wasn't a date, honey."

"But could it be?" Lana said.

"Excuse me?"

"Could you turn it into a date?"

Beth wasn't sure what her mother meant. She wasn't ready to get into a discussion about how rich tech guys weren't her idea of boyfriend material.

"I know he's not a lumberjack," Lana continued. "But if we needed more information from Martin, could you put on a skirt and . . . ?"

"Ma!"

"You're right. A tank top and jeans are probably better. You have good shoulders."

"Ma, you're not pimping me out for your investigation."

"You just said yourself he's not a murderer."

"You know what?" Beth leaned across the table, swallowing up the light in her bomber jacket. "If you want to manipulate people, that's your business. You've got a big day tomorrow, right? Seeing Martin's sister *and* Victor Morales?"

Lana nodded.

"If anyone's going on a date with a murderer, Ma, it might be you."

CHAPTER TWENTY-FOUR

THE THIRD DAY AFTER CHEMO was always Lana's worst. She felt a century older than she had a week ago, when she'd first ventured out for her investigation to meet up with Paul. She was exhausted. Her scalp itched all over. And she had mysterious aches. This morning she woke up with a dead left arm, as if a raccoon had slept on it. She couldn't raise her hand above the shoulder without piercing pain. But she had meetings to attend, and a job is a job. Even if you aren't getting paid.

Lana downed two aspirin and got dressed one-handed. The pale blue skirt suit hung loose on her frame, and she was starting to look more stick than figure. For the first time in her life, she was trying to gain weight. It wasn't easy. Anything she forced down stuck in her throat like a mouse trying to burrow through a drinking straw. Today, she'd managed half a protein shake, a banana, and coffee before the mouse came sniffing. Her doctor had warned her off caffeine, but there were only so many concessions a woman could make. She slid into her sling-back stilettos, the ones with the metal heels, stuffed her legal pad in her leather tote, and opened the garage.

Her gold Lexus rested quietly on the concrete. Lana hadn't driven since the collapse. It took two months to convince Beth to clean out the garage so she could have it shipped north, then another two for Lana to get over her fear of having another fainting spell behind the wheel. It didn't help that getting to Stanford Hospital required driving over a twisty mountain highway behind clattering trucks packed with boxes of lettuce and strawberries. Easier to rely on her daughter than risk ending up splattered jam salad.

But today was the day. She wasn't going to overthink it. Lana strode up to the driver's side door and felt the satisfying clunk of the latch disengaging, the door opening smoothly against her thumb. She felt the engine purr to life beneath her foot on the brake. After a flash of pain when her left arm gave out and she had to twist and pull the door closed with her right, she got moving. It was only after she crossed the bridge over the slough that she realized she'd been holding her breath.

THE TURNOFF FOR THE EQUESTRIAN CENTER where Lady Di trained was marked by a small, tasteful sign set into a wall of sculpted hedges. A security guard buzzed Lana through the gate and onto a private road lined with blocks of polished granite and gnarled Monterey cypress trees. The effect was something between a secure CIA facility and an ancient coastal forest. Lana parked and gave her name to a severe-looking woman with an earpiece by the front door of a stately, hulking building. Less than a minute later, a clean-shaven young man dressed entirely in white emerged from behind the heavy oak door.

"Mrs. Whitacre is still in session," he said. His tone was half-apologetic, half-proud, as if Lady Di was to be admired for her dedication. "She called ahead and asked for you to come meet her at the arena. If you'll follow me?"

The young man waved her into an electric golf cart and chauffeured her along a curving cobblestone pathway. There were women and horses everywhere. Young women in skintight pants leaping over fences. Older women in crisp jackets, turning dizzying circles around a ring. A group of eight- and nine-year-olds, their hair pouring like wheat from under their helmets, learning the proper way to mount. It was everything Lana had always imagined the Christian girls doing while she was stuck at Hebrew school.

The golf cart pulled up alongside a rectangular ring, in which a black horse with a plaited mane was prancing. It hopped sideways, then trotted in place, like a small child with a desperate need for the bathroom. Diana Whitacre sat astride the horse, wearing spotless ivory breeches, a black blazer, and tall black boots. As far as Lana could tell, the silvery whip Diana held in her white-gloved hand was just for show. The woman was controlling the horse with some kind of witchcraft.

After an impressive and confusing display of goose steps and pirouettes, Diana walked the horse in a slow promenade around the ring. When she reached the gate, she swung herself off the saddle and handed her helmet to a groom without looking at him.

"Lana!" she called out. Diana's perfectly white skin was flushed, her blond hair pressed sweatily to her head. Lana gave her a smile and a curt wave, keeping a respectful distance from the heaving horse.

"I appreciate you coming to our little stable," Diana said. She clipped a lead rope on her horse and started walking toward a large tent. The golf cart had disappeared, so Lana had no choice but to follow her. The tent was noisy and moist, with overhead fans drowning out all other sound. Lana realized the droplets hitting her jacket were coming from giant misters placed above each stall.

"A car wash for horses," Lana mused.

"A cooldown station," Diana corrected her. "Dressage training can be strenuous."

"How often do you come here?"

"It used to be almost every day." She sighed. "Since Daddy got sick, I've been in Elkhorn all the time. But I sneak up here when I can."

"I see." Lana stepped back to make way for a well-built groom leading a brown, foaming horse into the tent.

"Daddy and I both loved horses," Diana said. She was watching the horse's muscular backside, or perhaps the groom's. "I do believe they are the best cure for heartache in the world."

"From what I've heard, your father was quite a gentleman."

"Daddy insisted Western riding was superior to English. Other than that, he was perfect." Diana pulled her eyes away from the mist-filled tent, removed a glove, and patted her hair back into place. "Come," she said. "We can talk in the saddlery."

LANA FOLLOWED LADY DI into a small, immaculate workshop, which thankfully smelled of leather instead of horse. Diana closed the door, trapping them inside. Lana sat on an uncomfortable bench, hoping this would not be a long conversation.

"Thank you for coming." Diana was standing, stroking a saddle laid on top of a mahogany sawhorse. "I appreciate your time, truly."

Lana nodded, then shifted on the bench. "Of course. I have to admit, I'm curious. What do you want to discuss?"

"My brother and I have a difference of opinion about the future of the ranch."

Lana stayed silent. She could see Diana gathering her energy, readying herself for some kind of prickly disclosure. Something she didn't want to tell a stranger but was prepared to do regardless. All Lana had to do was wait.

"He wants to sell it right away. He says he's getting an all-cash offer, from some real estate jackal who sent flowers to the wake."

The former jackal on the bench gave Diana an encouraging smile, prodding her to continue. Was this it? Diana wanted her help negotiating the sale? Cash offers typically came with tight deadlines. Lana wondered how long ago Martin had put the property on the market. It would be aggressive to have offers just a week after the owner's death.

"Is Martin in some kind of hurry?"

"I think he needs the money." Diana flicked a speck of nothing off her sleeve, as if the very idea of it had dirtied her jacket. "Something about investors who didn't come through for a crucial round of funding for his nanotech start-up. These little robots of his are very complicated."

Lana nodded. "As are these real estate deals. If I can be of help—"

"I don't want to sell," Diana interrupted.

Then it was something else.

"What do you want?"

"I've always dreamed . . ." Diana suddenly looked younger, her hair a wispy halo around her face. She took a deep breath. "I'd like to turn the property into a wellness ranch. With horses. Equine therapy, trail rides, mineral baths. Healing retreats for a select clientele. Now that my children are grown, I need something to care for. I've been researching high-end spas and wellness centers, reviewing business models. I think it could work."

"Have you shared your dream with your brother? Or your father?"

Diana's fingers tightened on the skirt of the saddle. "Not fully. Not yet. I started talking with Daddy about it at Bayshore Oaks, just a bit. He seemed interested, but I wanted to wait until he was feeling better to fully explore it. I hoped we could get aligned and then talk to Martin about it together. Of course, we never got that far."

"So you've told no one your full plans?"

"Only my husband."

"And?"

"He thinks it's ridiculous. Says we might as well throw money into the slough. But I've stood by him through his own . . . indulgences, and quite frankly, he owes me."

Diana looked Lana straight in the eye and continued. "I'm not a professional developer. But I'm serious about this. I have a plan. I even picked out a manager. I was getting ready to present it all to Daddy. And then he—" Diana's voice twisted and fell, her eyes dropping to the dark leather under her hand.

For a moment, Lana wondered if Diana was going to break down. It was disappointing when a powerful woman showed weakness. But when Lady Di looked up, her cool blue eyes were dry.

"This is my chance," she said. "I may not like the way it has come to me. But I'd be a fool not to take it."

Lana asked for specifics about the project, and Diana kept talking. Her vision was comprehensive, her passion clear. She knew the market, and she had a good handle on how wellness ranches made money and where they spent it. The project sounded ambitious. Expensive. Maybe even good.

After ten minutes, Lana had heard enough. "So you want to buy your brother out?"

Diana gave Lana a wry smile. "That, my dear, would require filling two sloughs with money. My husband has obligations to me, but there are limits to his capacity. No. I've got to find a way for Martin to see things my way."

"Or else what?"

"What do you mean?"

"If you and Martin can't agree on the future of the ranch, what happens?"

A crease deepened between Lady Di's perfectly sculpted eyebrows. "Victor Morales."

Lana waited.

"He has a signed letter of intent from my father indicating his plans to donate the ranch to the land trust."

This must be the document Beth had mentioned. "You have a copy of it?"

Diana shook her head. "The lawyers do. The original's at the land trust. Martin thinks it's meaningless, but . . ."

"What do you think?"

"I think more than anything, Daddy wanted us to hold on to the ranch. He was old-fashioned. He would have loved for Martin to keep running cattle and leasing out strawberry fields. But clearly Martin has other interests." Diana's hand started stroking the leather again. "I could never be his son. But I understood what mattered most to Daddy. Family. Legacy. Progress. I like to believe he'd have supported the equine spa if he'd fully had the chance to hear about it."

"And the letter at the land trust?"

"Maybe it was Daddy's backup plan. Or he felt pressured. Victor

Morales has been after our ranch for years, like a rat terrier. He'd do anything to get the land."

"Does Victor have some kind of leverage over your family?"

Diana stared at her for a long moment. It seemed as if she was about to say something. Then, instead, she shook her head.

"I don't know what he's capable of." Diana looked up toward a wall of heavy metal stamps and carving tools, as if she were deciding which she'd like to use to fend off the director of the land trust.

"Diana, I want to be honest with you." Lana kept her voice calm. "My meeting in Santa Cruz this afternoon is at the land trust, with Victor. I don't intend to talk about any of this. Our conversation—everything you've told me here—I'll keep confidential."

Diana's hand wrapped tightly around a metal stirrup. "If you find something, will you let me know?"

It was an impossible question. If Lana said yes, it would shift the balance of power in Diana's direction. But saying no would close the door to any further information from her.

"I will."

Diana gave her a brief nod. When she spoke again, her voice was low and hot. "This isn't just about my family or what Daddy wanted. If Victor gets control of our ranch, the entire slough will become a national sanctuary. It would regulate every farm in the region out of business. Everything our neighbors and tenants worked for, handed over to the hawks and swamp grass."

She broke off her tirade to reach down and pull a buzzing cell phone from the side pocket of her tight breeches. Her angry countenance fell away, her face softening to reveal a calm, almost warm smile.

"My daughter. A freshman in college, which means she's far too busy to text me back most days. But she still sends me a picture every time the plane takes off."

Diana raised the phone to show Lana. "It's awful when they move away, isn't it?"

Lana pretended to look at the phone. But she didn't see the preppy, well-kept girl on the screen. Instead, she saw Beth at seventeen, her frizzy hair and oversize sweats, standing in the hall of her old house. Pregnant.

Lana remembered her makeup bag crashing to the floor, the panic rising inside her like a steam engine cranking itself to life, firing out accusations and threats before she fully knew what she was saying. And Beth had just stood there, solid as a concrete wall, not responding. Maybe not even listening. Lana remembered speaking faster, louder, trying to get through to her, to help her see reason, to do anything she could to get her daughter back, and failing.

Lana could still feel the white-hot pain of Beth's departure, could still see her toss her duffel bag with the broken zipper onto the back seat of her car and slam the door. Beth drove away from the house without saying goodbye. Not that Lana had said it either.

"Sorry." Diana pulled back the now-ringing phone. "My daughter, she's calling. That never happens. Excuse me."

Diana pushed open the door, and daylight flooded the workshop. Lana sat alone on the terrible bench, seeing and not seeing, letting the sunshine blast away her memories of the past.

CHAPTER TWENTY-FIVE

THIRTY MINUTES LATER, Lana pulled up in front of the Central Coast Land Trust offices. She had been to Santa Cruz only once, in December, for an ill-advised consultation with a nutritionist who extolled the healing powers of bee pollen and raw turmeric. The town struck her as defiantly dirty, with women who didn't shave and grown men strolling around in sandals and tie-dyed socks. But at least it had ample free street parking.

Lana sandwiched her Lexus between a late-model BMW and a dusty pickup truck. Her mind wasn't done sifting through what Diana had told her. But she had to focus. Her left arm still felt limp, so she used her right to straighten her wig and take a swig of water. After a coughing fit followed by thirty seconds of slow breathing into her tote bag, she was ready to go.

The woman at the front desk was Lana's least favorite kind: young and beautiful. In Lana's experience, women like this receptionist—perky breasts, French-tipped fingernails—were hostile toward older women, using wanton cruelty to mask the fear that they too might someday become undesirable. But this one was all smiles. Her name was Gabriella-call-me-Gaby, and her voice was even breathier in person than it had been on the phone. She beamed at Lana, then cranked it up another notch when Lana told her she was there to see the director. Gaby placed a quick call to the back, then offered Lana an armchair, a water, a coffee, a tissue, and a magazine. Lana suspected the girl might offer her a pony if Victor Morales didn't get to the front soon.

A few minutes later, Victor was holding Lana's hands and kissing both her cheeks.

"It's a pleasure to see you again," he said. Victor had on the same silver belt buckle as at the wake and a different pair of cowboy boots, black with golden lions pawing at the sides.

"Gaby, this is Lana Rubicon." He rolled the *r* slightly, lifting it to the light. "She is in the commercial real estate business in Los Angeles. But she wants to learn about our work. Thinking of joining us on the side of the angels, no?" He winked at Lana. "Shall we?"

The land trust may have been a nonprofit, but they'd spared no expense on their offices. Behind Gaby's desk was a large, sun-filled room with bamboo flooring and exposed redwood beams overhead. The windows at the far end framed a small grove of spindly eucalyptus trees and coyote brush behind the building. Everything was tasteful and well lit, including the taxidermic eagle in mid-flight above their heads. "It was electrocuted on a power line over a property we manage," Victor explained. "They are endangered, of course, but when one dies . . ."

He walked Lana past a herd of attractive twenty-somethings on ergonomic chairs, hard at work in ironed canvas shirts. The reward for giving away your land, apparently, was a naturalist with good hair and an amber bracelet handing you a cappuccino.

They reached a solid oak door on the left side of the office, and he ushered her in. "Our library," he announced. "Also our only meeting room. The architect was obsessed with open plan."

It was an elegant den of cushy chairs and low light, the kind of room where you could cement a clandestine arms deal or sign away the deed to grandma's orchard. Two walls held floor-to-ceiling bookshelves, a third was covered with hand-drawn maps, and the fourth had a low window looking out at a parking lot.

Victor whipped a curtain across the window to hide a single rusted Toyota Corolla on the concrete. "I tried to convince the neighbors to let us plant a garden," he said. "I wanted to do heritage native crops, rare ones we've been reintroducing in the field. But no luck." He shrugged. "They say they need the parking."

Once settled at the table—sustainably logged teak, Victor assured her—Lana took out her legal pad and water bottle, and palmed an extra-strength aspirin for easy access.

"Thank you for seeing me today," she cooed. It came out with more croak than she'd hoped for. "It must be a distressing time, and I'm hoping I can be of service."

His left eyebrow lifted. "What were you imagining?"

Despite her interest in the arguments over the Rhoads ranch, Lana decided to focus on what was most important. "I've been looking into the events that led to Ricardo Cruz's passing."

Now his right eyebrow joined the left. "You are assisting the police?"

"More of a personal service opportunity. I don't think the detectives are doing a very good job." This opinion was solely based on their unwillingness to return her calls, but heck, they were terrible at that.

"They came here," Victor said. His eyes were grim. "Early last week. The older one, the man, he was more interested in Ricardo's immigration status than anything else. And insisting this must be our fault."

"Why?"

"The land neighboring Señor Rhoads's ranch to the east belongs to the land trust. The shore closest to where Ricardo was found, we manage it. They took half our property management tools for testing. Shovels. Sledgehammers. Potential weapons." He shook his head. "They threatened one of my naturalists, a colleague of Ricardo's, implied he might have been the one to hurt him. When I tried to protect him, they turned their ridiculous accusations on me."

Lana nodded in commiseration. "It's a kind of abuse, the way they're jumping to conclusions. I want to find a real suspect, to refocus the detectives away from innocent people like your naturalist. Like you. I've come here hoping to get a more complete picture about Ricardo. What he did, who he spent time with. That sort of thing."

Victor held her gaze, his eyes calculating. He rose from the table and turned to the wall. "Do you know what this is?" he asked, pointing at a large, framed map with ornate lettering at the top.

Lana reluctantly left her armchair and joined him for a closer look. She recognized the coastline and the shape of the western United States. But the words and symbols portrayed a different place. There were lakes where there should be deserts and mountains where there should be valleys. The words "ALTA CALIFORNIA" stretched from the Pacific across the Colorado River. Lana picked out a few names along the coast she recognized—Puebla de los Angeles, San Diego, Monte Rey—and many more she did not.

"This map was made by John Frémont in 1848," Victor said. "The year California became a US state. Before that, this was part of Mexico, New Spain. And before that, Native land. Every time an individual makes a claim on a piece of land, there is someone standing behind him who was there first. Land is fought over. Land is sold. Land is stolen."

Lana rubbed her right temple. Either Victor was going to get to the point soon or she was going to ask Gaby to get her a Diet Coke.

Victor waved his hand across the map. "Here at the land trust, we believe there is another way to hold space together. To hold it in trust. For everyone, past, present, and future."

"And Ricardo?"

"Ricardo was a true believer. More than a believer. The boy was a prophet."

Lana remembered the photograph of the long-haired, bright-eyed young man in hiking sandals. "What do you mean?"

Victor looked back at the map. "It takes most people many years to learn this business. Conservation science, land use technicalities, legal paperwork, and of course the delicate relationships with our land stewards, our donors. For Ricardo, it was instinctual, like he was choreographing a dance between land, owners, and lawyers."

"What made him so good at it?"

"It's in his blood. His grandparents came to the Pajaro Valley in the

1950s as braceros, and his father carried on as a farmer. When Ricardo was small, he and his mother left to live with her sister inland because of some kind of difficulty, but he came back as an adult. Farmers here know the Cruz name. They trust it. Ricardo was able to accomplish more in two years than others here have achieved in ten. Sometimes he played it a bit loose. But he got results." Victor fixed his eyes on Lana. "He helped donors see what it might be for land to be truly public. To be not owned by any of us, but stewarded and cared for, honored and preserved."

"This is what he was helping Mr. Rhoads with? Donating the ranch to the public?"

"We were on the path to making that vision real."

"May I see what he was working on? Before he . . ."

A sudden grimace twisted Victor's face into a rush of emotion, red-hot and pained. Then, as quickly as it had come, the storm passed. His eyes settled, and he was back again. Lana had to blink to convince herself the look hadn't been a mirage.

"One moment," he said.

Lana walked to the door and watched as Victor approached a long glass cabinet lining the rear wall of the open office. He made a careful selection and walked back toward her carrying two thick hardback binders.

They settled at the table in the library, the binders between them.

"These were Ricardo's projects," he said. "Masterpieces, every one." He slid them toward Lana with a sad smile.

"I miss him," he said.

Lana was always suspicious of a man with tears in his eyes. She placed the binders side by side, running her hand over the textured canvas cover of the one on the right.

"He sounds very special," she said. "Did you know much about his life outside of work?"

Victor hesitated for a moment before answering. "Ricardo was devoted to his work. And a handsome young man. I imagine he had girlfriends, but I wasn't familiar with his romantic life."

Lana wondered if the detectives had found any angry exes worth investigating. For now she focused on the information at hand. She looked down at the binders. “May I take a closer look at these? I might find something that can send the detectives in a more appropriate direction. So you can have peace, and justice, for Ricardo.”

“Justice would be welcomed.” Victor took one last, longing look at the binders. For a moment Lana thought he was going to grab them back from her and whisk them away. But then he nodded. “Take all the time you need.”

He rose, turned, and tipped an imaginary hat. Then he walked out, closing the library door firmly behind him so she would not be disturbed.

Perfect.

CHAPTER TWENTY-SIX

THE FIRST THING LANA did was take the aspirin. And another one. Her head was throbbing in time with her left arm, and Victor's history lesson hadn't helped.

She shoved aside the pain and started working her way through Saint Ricardo's land conquests. He certainly had been busy. Lana counted seventeen projects in the binders, hundreds of pages of correspondence, site maps, and contracts. Some projects were small, like a single-acre lot inhabited by endangered salamanders. Others were complex, involving multiple parties and pages of legalese. Each project file ended with a letter of agreement between the property owner and the land trust and a handwritten thank-you note. The flowery signatures on monogrammed notecards spoke of an earlier time, when penmanship and stewardship were drilled into would-be land barons.

But not every project file was complete. The file on Hal Rhoads's property appeared midway through the second binder, one of three projects in progress when Ricardo died. The thin file contained mostly printed emails and a calendar of meetings stretching back six months. Ricardo visited Hal weekly, at first with Victor, then later, on his own. The men toured the ranch. Ate picnics. It looked less like a business transaction than a multigenerational bromance, complete with horse rides over the hillside.

And, strangely, medical appointments. The Rhoads project calendar showed some listings for an unspecified doctor on Wednesdays. It seemed Ricardo had been accompanying Hal to a regular checkup, presumably one trivial enough that a non-relative could take him. Blood tests, maybe. Lana thought of her own datebook, the business meetings replaced with DR this and DR that. She hated having her daughter chauffeur her like a child, to appointments she wouldn't have chosen, days drained of her own control.

The rest of the Rhoads file focused on the ranch—parcel descriptions, maps, lists of active leases. There were grainy black-and-white photographs and historical documents that had been photocopied several times, not always at right angles. Before she flipped each page, Lana took a photograph with her phone, figuring she could make better sense of it on a day when the words weren't vibrating off the page. She imagined Beth rolling her eyes at her with every click.

She was almost surprised to see the letter of intent just sitting there, sandwiched between copies of the subleases Mr. Rhoads maintained with his tenants. For a moment, she debated whether to take it. But she decided a simple photograph would suffice. Nothing about the letter screamed coercion or foul play to her, but it was strange. It was short, just a page, and didn't say anything about transferring ownership of the ranch. Instead, the LOI described the potential to form some kind of easement. Even stranger, none of Ricardo and Hal's correspondence appeared to acknowledge or build on it. The emails between the two men spoke in lofty tones about unprecedented opportunities. There were no specifics. No contracts.

It was time for a bathroom break and a more pointed conversation with Victor about the future of the ranch. But when she moved to stand up, Lana discovered her left leg had gone numb. Great. Now she had a limp arm and a dead leg. She was a pirate joke in the making.

She wheeled her chair back from the table and grabbed under her left hamstring with both hands, shaking her leg to jolt it awake. She used one of the binders to massage her thigh, pressing the hard spine into her muscle to squeeze it back to life.

As pins and needles started moving down her leg, a piece of paper slid out of the binder and floated to the floor.

Lana picked up the sheet of thin-lined paper. It looked like a rough draft, with words scribbled and crossed out in blue block writing.

> Dear Victor,
>
> Thank you for all the ~~inspiration~~ guidance you have provided to me. I truly feel honored to have worked with you. But I must ~~take the next~~ move forward on my own. Someone close to my heart has approached me with a bold vision for a project too ~~significa~~ big to live at the land trust. Thank you for setting me on this path.

Lana flipped back through the two binders, looking for something she could use to identify who had written the note. But the block print didn't match any of the flowery thank-you cards from past donors. Was it from Ricardo? Was he planning to leave the land trust to pursue some other project—a project that got him killed? Or was it from Mr. Rhoads? Could Diana's intentions have gotten through to her father more than she'd imagined, causing him to change course? Lana got out her phone to take a photograph of the note. Then she glanced at the closed library door and made a decision. She slid the note into her legal pad, stuffed the pad into her tote, and clasped it shut.

Now to find that bathroom. Lana got up from the table, wobbling a bit before distributing her weight across both legs.

The first thing Lana noticed was that she felt much worse than she had before the first aspirin. The second thing she noticed was the door back to the main office was locked. She jiggled the handle. Nothing. She pressed her shoulder against the door. It pressed right back at her: sturdy, implacable, uninterested in her plight.

She heard the pop of a car backfiring outside. The high-pitched whine of an airplane. Everyone was going places except her.

She banged on the door with her right hand. The heavy door absorbed her fist, deadening her thumps and crushing her hopes of being heard. And then a blaring siren erupted all around her.

Lana jumped back from the door, slipped, and fell to the floor. Had she tripped some sort of spy wire? What kind of operation was Victor running?

She used the closest armchair to hoist herself up to standing. All was well. No broken bones. No eco-warrior SWAT team. But still the screeching wail continued, pounding at her skull, making it impossible to think.

Above her, she spotted a red light flashing from a plastic disk tucked into a crossbeam overhead. Fire alarm. Terrific.

She shuffled back to the door and tried to make sense of the situation. Was the door locked or just jammed? There was a keyhole in the door handle, but Lana couldn't see a bolt in the frame. Not that it mattered. She couldn't get out. She tried yelling, but she couldn't even hear herself over the damn alarm.

Lana decided her best option was to return to her chair, press her left ear to the cover of one of Ricardo's binders, clamp her right hand over her other ear, and wait for someone to make the shrieking stop.

The alarm scattered Lana's thoughts, shooting off sparks in different directions. Did someone intentionally lock her in? Wait, was that a fire engine?

Lana unclamped her right ear. She could now hear two sirens, the initial screech and a lower tone, overlapping in an earsplitting cacophony. Lana crossed to the window and pulled back the curtain. The air smelled acrid, like a hair straightener left on too long. She couldn't see any people, but when she craned her neck toward the street, she saw a huge fire truck blocking the driveway to the parking lot next door. When she turned her head the other way, she saw something worse: a bright orange eucalyptus tree behind the building, flames racing up its papery bark.

She needed to get out of there. She could try calling 911. But the fire truck was already outside. Why hadn't they come to get her? Presumably the firefighters would do a sweep of the building. But if no one alerted them that she was inside, they might not come looking until the fire was out. And that might be too late.

For the first time, Lana found herself wishing she'd said yes when Beth tried to foist one of those "I've fallen and I can't get up" emergency responder buttons on her when she first got sick last fall. But even thinking about that sent a surge of adrenaline through Lana. She wasn't going to die of cancer. And she sure as hell wasn't going to burn to death in an office of evacuated environmentalists.

It was definitely getting warmer now. Lana inspected the window in front of her. She was on the ground floor, which was good. But the window didn't open. Which was bad.

She rapped her knuckles against the glass. It didn't seem to be that thick, but she wasn't exactly a karate master. She scanned the room for something she could use to break the glass—a brick, or a ceremonial ax hanging on the wall to commemorate the last tree ever felled in an old-growth forest. No luck. All she saw were maps, books, and binders. She tried to lift one of the armchairs, but the best she could do was flip it over on its side. It fell on the floor with a loud clunk, knocking five books off the wall and half the wind out of her lungs. Dizzy with effort, she bent over her knees and sucked in oxygen. Her forehead dripped with sweat from the exertion. Or was that the fire getting closer?

After one more desperate glance around the room, Lana had a flash of inspiration. She bent down and took off her shoes. She picked up one in her right hand, running her fingers over the metallic spike heel, remembering when Jimmy Choo himself had kissed her hand at Nobu one glittery night. She fished her sunglasses out of her tote bag. She slid on the shades and wrapped her fingers around the stiletto. She pulled her arm back, took a deep breath, and swung with all her might.

Crack. A tiny spiderweb fractured the glass where she'd hit it. She slammed it again, and a second set of cracks bloomed, as big around as a fist. She did it again, and again, plunging the metal spike heel into the shuddering glass until it splintered and rained down around her.

Jackpot.

She didn't have time to admire her work. Thick, gray smoke poured in through the now-open window, and she had to keep moving. After stuffing her shoes in her bag, she leaned toward the bookshelf with her right hand, reaching for a heavy hardcover book. "THE BARK BEETLE BIBLE," it said on the worn leather cover. She hoped it wasn't a rare first edition. She used it to clear as much glass as she could from the window, until she had a crude opening the size of a trash chute in front of her. Then she ripped out fistfuls of pages and used them to line the sides of the ragged hole in the window so she wouldn't slice herself on the way out.

Lana looked at her handiwork, panting. She'd done it. She had chiseled her own escape route. Now all she had to do was use it.

In theory it should be simple: put one paper-wrapped hand on the crumbly windowsill, then the other. Swing one leg over. Then the other leg. The bottom of the window was only a few feet from the ground, three at most. No problem.

Reality, however, was riddled with problems. Lana's left leg was still tingling, and her left arm was doing its best impression of a wet noodle. She figured she'd have only one shot to lift each bare foot clear of the glass-strewn floor and out the window, and she didn't trust her balance, let alone her ability to hurdle a jagged windowsill. It was entirely possible she'd crash back down onto the shards tiling the library floor and bleed to death in a blazing inferno next to an open window.

Lana shuffled back, away from the broken glass. She dragged one of the armchairs to the window, crawled onto the seat, and peered out. The fire was coming around the building from the back, licking its way toward her. Over the screaming alarm, the cracks and rumbles of the fire echoed around her, trapping her in a storm of heat and fear. Her feet were bleeding, and pain shot like sparks up her legs. She could feel the fire filling her nose, pounding at her heart.

It was now or never.

Lana placed her tote bag on the windowsill, creating a buffer between her and the broken glass. She rose from the chair, sat on the bag, tucked her knees to her chest, and started sliding toward the parking lot.

Midway through her slow-motion slide over the broken windowsill, Lana remembered she still hadn't canceled her membership at Body by Pilates Beverly Hills. For four months now, Fritz had been charging her to lie in bed three hundred miles north of the studio while he yelled at other women to raise their pelvic floors. But maybe Pilates worked through osmosis, because she could feel her obliques flexing, her abdominal muscles straining in synchrony with her hamstrings. In her head, she heard Fritz demand one more thrust, and she toppled all the way out the window.

She landed with a curse and a thud on the asphalt.

Freedom; it hurt like hell. She could already feel the bruise forming on her right butt cheek. Her hands were scraped, her face bleeding. And her wig was missing. She glanced up and saw it hanging like a hostage from the broken window. But the fire was just a few feet from the window now. She had to get out of there.

In all the commotion, it seemed that no one had seen her heroic drop into the parking lot. Firefighters rushed past her with hoses aimed at the building. A cluster of office building refugees flowed the other way, into the street. Part of her was relieved no one saw her. Part of her was disappointed. But most of her was hot, in pain, and wishing for her European mattress.

"Lana! Lana!" She heard Victor's voice before she saw him, red-faced, eyes wild, running toward her from the throng in the street. "Dios mío! Let me help you!"

Lana remembered him smiling down at her and closing the library door. A cocktail of fear and fury flooded her brain. She forgot everything she'd taught herself about interacting with men. She scowled. She may have even barked.

When Victor didn't slow, Lana fished one of her shoes out of her tote and brandished it at him, metal spike out.

"Don't come any closer," she growled.

Lana started crawling as fast as she could in the other direction, right into the shins of a burly firefighter. Her eyes made it from the tips of his steel-toed boots up to the base of his suspenders before she collapsed.

"Thank you," she whispered, and fell into unconsciousness.

CHAPTER TWENTY-SEVEN

JACK WAS IN THE SCHOOL LIBRARY, trying to craft the perfect response to an online ad for a used twenty-two-foot single-hull Catalina for sale in San Luis Obispo, when her mom called to tell her Lana was in the hospital for injuries related to a fire. Jack had about eighty-five different questions, but Beth cut her off.

"I'll pick you up in twenty minutes," Beth said. "Meet me in the parking lot."

As they sped north, toward a black tornado of smoke hovering over the freeway, Beth told Jack what she knew.

"Holy shit," Jack whispered. "Is Prima going to be okay?"

Beth clutched the steering wheel tighter. Nothing made sense right now. Ever since Lana's brain surgery back in the fall, a part of Beth had been holding her breath, waiting for the call that confirmed the worst—that the tumors had spread, or treatment had failed. Now Beth saw those fears as pedestrian lightweights compared to the monstrous nightmare of the truth. An hour ago she'd received the call, an angry swarm of phrases like *structure fire* and *embedded glass* and *bleeding unconscious* that still buzzed in her head, making it difficult to drive. She prayed for the nightmare to end, to right itself, for her mother to rise like a phoenix as she always had. Someone who burned as bright as Lana couldn't just turn to ash.

At least, that's what Beth was hoping. "I don't know, honey. The hospital, they didn't tell me much. But your Prima's a fighter. We'll see."

Beth had never worked at London Nelson Memorial Hospital. She signed in like a civilian, scanning the reception area in hopes she might see a former colleague, a friendly face. There was no one. Once they were finally admitted, Beth hurried through the maze of hallways, Jack jogging to keep up. They found Lana in a single room near the OR, lying still and shrunken on a bed in a pink-striped hospital gown.

Beth flagged down the attending physician, a wiry, bald man with glasses and pursed lips.

"I'm looking for information on a patient," she said. "Lana Rubicon."

The doctor looked Beth up and down. "Just coming on shift?"

"No. I'm her daughter." Beth stood a little taller in her scrubs, attempting to project competence. "How is she?"

"Your mother is breathing on her own. Her heart rate is normal."

Beth could hear what he hadn't said. "But she hasn't woken up?"

The doctor shook his head. "Not yet."

"My mother has lung cancer. Do you think there's a possibility of lung collapse or breathing impairment? If she inhaled too much smoke from the fire . . ."

"Her airway is clear, and so far, we haven't identified any breathing issues."

Beth was relieved. Then she remembered something. "What about bleeding? She's on blood thinners because of a blockage in her carotid artery, and . . ."

"It's taken care of." He patted her arm. "Your mother will be fine. I need you to do the most difficult thing."

Beth knew what was coming next.

"I need you to wait."

By seven that evening, Beth had talked to Detective Ramirez, a fireman, and every nurse on the ward about her mother. But that didn't bring Lana back to consciousness. After a soggy grilled cheese sandwich in the cafeteria, Beth turned to Jack. "We should head home for the night."

"What if Prima wakes up?"

"She probably won't. Not tonight."

"But what if she does?" Jack twisted a greasy napkin between her fingers.

"You have school in the morning."

"You have work." They stared at each other in the fluorescent light.

"Fine. We'll stay. C'mon."

Beth and Jack set up makeshift bedrolls out of towels and pillows, one on each side of Lana's narrow hospital bed. They stayed up late, Beth reading studies about the impact of fire exposure on patients with lung tumors, Jack pretending to do homework. They took turns sneaking glances at Lana whenever the other one wasn't looking.

By midnight, Jack had finally fallen asleep. Beth rose to close the curtain over the tiny window and check on her mother one more time. No change. In her pocket, she turned over a heart-shaped rock she'd found that morning in the spindly grass. It was pumice, rough and speckled, its surface pockmarked like a tiny moon. Evidence of the life she'd chosen, the home she'd built, as far from her mother's sleek, hard-edged world as possible. For the first time, Beth considered everything Lana had lost when she came to Elkhorn: the power she wielded, the energy that fueled her battles, the freedom to make her own path. Beth put the stone on the nightstand next to her mother and prayed Lana would keep fighting.

BETH AND JACK WOKE UP Thursday morning cramped and disappointed. Lana was still asleep. The hope they'd clung to the night before felt foolish in the sunshine, a cheap and flimsy dream. They folded their towels in silence and each gave Lana one more look, one more chance to save them from a day of clock watching, then dragged themselves out of the room.

Jack went to school. Beth went to work.

At 6 P.M., the two younger Rubicon women stumbled back into the hospital, less hopeful but more prepared, with clean pajamas for Lana, and burritos for themselves.

After an unsatisfying check-in with the doctor in the patient waiting area, Beth sent Jack to get hot chocolate and entered Lana's room on her own. The only noticeable change was a large bouquet of wildflowers on the bedside table next to the heart-shaped rock. The card read, "I am so sorry. Please call me. I want to know everything you saw, everything that happened, so I can make it right. Wishing you every recovery. V."

Beth didn't understand it. But the flowers were the least of the things that didn't make sense about the situation. Just a few days ago Lana had been strong-arming Beth to help with the investigation. And now here she was, prone on a hospital bed, a bundle of ragged breath and unanswered questions.

Lana looked even smaller than she had the day before, fragile, as if the aura of invincibility that usually surrounded her had cracked and torn. Beth had always seen Lana as one of the strongest women on the planet. That didn't exactly qualify her as a good parent, but Beth had gotten over that a long time ago. Lana was someone impressive. Someone, she realized, she was proud to know.

The woman in the hospital bed before her had dark bruises, sunken eyes. There was a butterfly bandage over the tiny stitches on her cheekbone. Beth bent down and gently ran her hand over her mother's patchy hair, picking a tiny black pebble from her scalp.

"What were you doing?" Beth whispered. "Come back to me."

CHAPTER TWENTY-EIGHT

ON FRIDAY MORNING, after a fitful sleep at home, Beth and Jack arrived at Lana's room to find an empty bed.

Beth's heart raced. "Ma?" She knocked on the pocket door of the tiny bathroom. "Are you in there?"

The door slid open. Lana shuffled out of the bathroom and stumbled toward her daughter. Beth flung her arms wide, and Lana fell into them. Jack came over and wrapped herself in from the side. For a long minute never to be spoken of again, the three women hugged.

They resettled around Lana's bed, Lana propped up against a stack of crinkly pillows, Jack curled on the mattress around her feet, Beth on a plastic visitor's chair.

"Is one of those for me?" Lana asked, eyeing the Styrofoam cups of coffee.

Beth handed her a bottle of water, twisting the cap half-open. "How are you feeling?"

"I'd be better with coffee."

"Let's take it slow, Ma. You've been out for almost two days."

"Not quite. I woke up late last night with a terrible crick in my neck. I would have called you, but I couldn't find my phone."

"I have it. And your tote bag."

Lana took a long sip of the water. "Did my wig make it?"

"I don't think so. I have your suit, but it's in pieces. The ICU nurses had to cut it off you because of all the glass embedded in the back. How are you feeling?"

"Sore. But I'll survive. The doctor came by this morning. He said he expects I'll make a full recovery." Lana's voice was rough, as if she'd swallowed a lump of charcoal.

Jack squeezed Lana's hand.

"You were so brave, Prima."

"Not really, Jack. I just don't want to miss your high school graduation."

"Don't start getting modest now," Beth said. "I talked with the firefighter, Chase Tucker, who brought you in. He said you practically leaped out of a burning building and kept going. He said if he hadn't run into you, you would have crawled all the way here yourself."

"Mmm. Chase. I had a dream about his . . . suspenders." Lana looked over at the bedside table. "Are the flowers from him?"

Beth handed Lana the card.

Lana read it, looked at the bouquet, and jammed the card back into its envelope, her mouth set in a tight line.

"Victor. Hmpf. He probably set the damn fire," she said.

"The man who runs the land trust? Why would he do that?"

Lana glared at a calla lily. "Maybe he wanted to scare me off. I think he was involved in Ricardo's murder."

Jack rested her hand on her grandmother's ankle. "What did you find?"

"Victor and Ricardo were doing a brisk business in that little do-gooder office. Lots of contracts, lots of money. The fire started right when I was getting to the good stuff."

Beth shook her head. "I don't think you'll be able to go back anytime soon. The rear of the building is apparently a crater, and the rest of it's covered in water and soot. You got out of there just in time."

"It was arson, right?"

Beth rubbed at the dark circles under her eyes. "I don't know, Ma. But Detective Ramirez came by. Apparently the Santa Cruz police towed your car. Evidence, the detective said. She wants to meet with you."

"Now she's willing to talk to me." Lana's smile broke into a hacking cough.

Beth handed her mother the bottle of water. "We can call her when we get home."

"Once I get my list of questions together."

"Sure, Ma."

Lana put down the water bottle and motioned with her chin to the Styrofoam coffee cups. "You aren't going to tell me this is a stupid endeavor? Trying to crack the case? Chasing down a murderer?"

"No. I'm not." Beth passed Lana a cup of coffee. "I can see this is important to you—"

"It is."

"Can you tell me why?"

Lana sniffed the coffee before taking a sip. It smelled of stale almonds, like the kitchen in her first house in Los Angeles, the one Ari bought for them. She saw her twenty-six-year-old self there, bustling and humming to herself as she arranged new knives in the new butcher block. She'd quit law school to have the baby, but life was good, Beth was manageable, and Ari was passionate as ever. She hadn't listened when her brother suggested it was dangerous, marrying a divorce lawyer. She loved Ari's heat, the way he charged through life, fighting everyone—waiters, cab drivers, opposing counsel—to get exactly what he wanted. Their love language was war, and they were champion arguers, both of them, throwing barbs so sharp they sometimes paused midstream to appreciate each other's virtuosity.

And then, one Saturday, while Beth was down for a nap, Ari bombed their battlefield. Lana stood there in that bright housewife's kitchen, surrounded by new appliances, as Ari calmly announced that the life they'd built, the family Lana was building for them, no longer suited him. When she tried to argue, he brushed her aside. He looked at Lana like she was a soft, embarrassing wound. And then he walked away.

She had never forgotten that moment, the way it rendered her both disposable and desperate, a stock whose value had plummeted to zero. She ran from it as fast as she could, remedied first with wine and tears, then, more successfully, with work. She would never put herself in a position to be at someone else's mercy again. She would provide for Beth and protect herself. It wasn't about status or vanity. It was about survival.

Lana scrapped her way into real estate and kept building skyward, gladly sacrificing her softest parts to make herself hard, building a reputation as someone who never trusted but always delivered. Every deal cemented her safety. Every fallen adversary buttressed her strength. She kept herself impeccably tailored and toned, relentless in battle against the forces that turned other women invisible as they aged, stepped on and stepped over.

But now cancer was tearing down the iron defenses she'd built. She could see her impending irrelevance reflected in the faces of arrogant oncologists and overworked nurses. Even her daughter. People who thought they could shove her into a smaller life and expect her to be grateful for it. The only times she didn't feel threatened these days were when she was working on the investigation, when she was asking questions instead of answering them.

Lana fingered the hospital bracelet around her wrist, the plasticky edges sharp against her skin. Heat swirled in her body. Agitation. Fear, even, fear of being prone, in a hospital bed, stranded there forever.

Of course, Lana didn't say any of that.

"I . . . I just want to help."

"Uh-huh."

She tried again. "This matters to me. Doing something, working, it matters. I want to help."

Lana looked up at Beth. She knew her words sounded hollow, but she hoped that behind them, Beth could hear her trying. To say something honest. To show her something real.

Beth gazed back at her and swallowed. When she spoke, her voice was soft. "Okay. Then I want to help too."

"You? Miss don't-touch-that-magnifying-glass?" The words were out of Lana's mouth before she had a chance to reconsider them.

But Beth didn't take the bait. "I might not get it," she said. "I might not love it. But if it's important to you, it's important to me. I'm not going to throw someone out for doing something I don't understand."

Lana flinched, turning her head to see if Jack was listening. The girl was following every word.

"If tracking down murderers is what you want to do, I'm not going to stop you," Beth said. "And frankly, I don't imagine anyone else could either."

Beth held her hand out to her mother. Lana placed the empty Styrofoam cup back in her daughter's hand, gently brushing her fingers as she did so.

"Let's get out of here," Lana said. "If we're going to make progress, we need decent coffee."

CHAPTER TWENTY-NINE

AFTER GETTING CLEARED by the hospital with a stern directive to rest, change her bandages daily, and return if she had trouble breathing, Lana and her girls went home. She slept most of the weekend, rousing only to return Detective Ramirez's call and request a meeting as soon as possible to discuss the fire.

Early Monday morning, she woke to hear Beth on the phone in the kitchen, wavering over a request to cover another nurse's shift at Bayshore Oaks. Lana pulled herself up to standing and shuffled out of the back bedroom, ignoring the flickering pain that accompanied the movement.

"I'll be fine," she said. "Go to work. Go to school. I can take care of myself."

As soon as her girls left, Lana took her pills and crashed back into bed.

Three hours later, armed in a cream-colored suit, heavy makeup, and a wig with bangs to cover the worst of her bruises, Lana opened the door for the detectives.

As soon as she saw them, Lana was glad she'd dressed up. Instead of her dour older partner, Detective Ramirez was accompanied by a young, well-built man with teeth so white they glowed.

"Ms. Rubicon." Ramirez nodded. "How are you doing? When I came to the hospital, your daughter told me about your ordeal, and the lung cancer, and—"

"I'm fine," Lana snapped. She tried to sound as strong as possible.

Ramirez pulled back at her sharp tone. "Well . . . good. This is Detective Choi, from Santa Cruz PD. He's leading the investigation into the fire at the land trust."

"Investigation? So it was arson?"

"We're looking into it." His white shirt was crisp, his tie well knotted. "I hear you had quite the adventure in our city."

"You have my Lexus," Lana said.

"It's safe in our lot."

"Safe from what?"

The detective flashed his perfect teeth instead of answering. "Can you tell me what happened?"

Lana sat down at the table and walked the detectives through her experience. Choi interrupted her several times, asking where she had parked her car, who she had seen in the building, and when she first detected the fire. Throughout her retelling, he took careful notes. Ramirez hung back, leaning against the kitchen counter with a travel mug in hand. She didn't say a word.

"The first thing you saw on fire was a tree behind the building?"

Lana looked to the window. But the slough was invisible to her. Instead, she saw the burning eucalyptus, dropping a fountain of sparks onto the building.

"That's correct."

Choi sighed. "Thank you, Ms. Rubicon." He looked disappointed.

"Have you talked to everyone who was there?" Lana asked.

"You were the last one. I hoped you might have something new to tell me."

Lana felt very sorry she didn't.

Then a thought occurred to her. "Detective, was the fire set inside the building?"

Choi looked up, interested. "Is that why you exited via the window? Did you think the main office wasn't safe?"

"No. I couldn't get to the office. The door was locked. Or stuck. I don't know which. And then when no one came to get me . . ."

Both detectives were looking at her now.

"Don't you think that's suspicious? That I was trapped in that room during the fire?" Lana tried not to let too much indignation creep into her voice.

Choi checked his notes. "No."

She frowned. "No?"

"Ms. Rubicon, about how long would you say that you were trapped? From when you first heard the alarm to when you got out?"

Lana considered. There was the alarm. The locked door. And then the convoluted work of smashing her way to freedom. It had felt like forever.

"Half an hour?" she guessed.

"According to the fire captain, less than two minutes passed between when the alarm went off and when you busted out of the window. I think it's reasonable, in an emergency, that no one was able to reach you in that span. Unfortunate, of course. But reasonable."

Lana looked at him, incredulous. She couldn't decide if it was more surprising that she hadn't been forgotten or that she'd escaped so quickly.

Choi was moving on. "The fire started outside," he said. "We found remnants of a remote-activated incendiary device in the brush behind the building." He pulled out a photograph and passed it across the table. "Does anything here look familiar to you?"

The picture was a mess of blackened dirt, splintered wood, and broken glass. The central focus was a puckered exterior wall with a gaping hole in it. The hole looked like it was puking out the guts of the building, a mixture of drywall, curled brown paper, and metal rings.

"This is behind the building?"

"That's correct."

Lana closed her eyes and recalled the floor plan. "There was a back door, and a long glass cabinet along the back wall of the building. It held all their records in heavy binders."

She opened her eyes and pointed to the twisted metal rings in the picture. "That's probably what's left of them."

She thought of everything in Ricardo's binders, the papers that were now destroyed. Thank God she'd taken pictures. She wondered what, if anything, she might have missed.

"What are those?" she asked, pointing to a few specks of yellow and red in the photograph peeking out from under a charred brown blob.

"We think that's what was used to set the fire."

"Dynamite?"

Choi suppressed a smile. "You'd be half-deaf if that was the case."

"I heard a noise that sounded like a car backfiring—"

He made a note. "That could have been it. It was a black powder device, probably stuffed in a cardboard box with rags and accelerant. We believe it may have been one of those shell crackers orchardists use to scare away birds."

"Shell crackers?"

Choi nodded. "They look like this." He showed her a picture of a small, plasticky black-and-orange gun. It looked like a toy. Lana wondered whether the land trust had trouble with birds on any of the reclaimed farms they managed, and, if so, what they used to flush them out.

Choi was still explaining. "But bird bombs can also be in the form of cartridges that are activated remotely. Which is what we believe happened in this case."

"Is that complicated?" Lana thought of Martin and his tiny robots.

The detective shrugged. "Not particularly. Lots of farmers have remote systems for pest control."

"Could it be triggered from inside the building?"

"Sure. Or a vehicle parked nearby."

"Like my Lexus?" A spike of pain flashed across Lana's forehead. "Are you kidding me? First you go after my granddaughter, and now this?"

"Ms. Rubicon"—Choi put his hands up in a conciliatory gesture—"your car was processed. It's clean. No black powder. No remote control."

Lana said a silent thanks that Beth never had given her a clicker for the garage. Then she remembered something. "There was a rusted Toyota in the parking lot . . ."

Choi nodded. "We checked it."

"And the BMW parked on the street?"

"It belongs to Mr. Morales."

"Was it clean?"

"Do you have a concern about Mr. Morales?"

"Detective, do you know why I was visiting the land trust?"

"Mr. Morales told us you were inquiring about Ricardo Cruz. He was quite eager to hear about your recovery."

"I've been looking into Ricardo's work on a property near the slough. Near where his body was found." Lana attempted a small smile in Ramirez's direction. "Not to step on your toes, of course. Just, my granddaughter, well . . . I want her to be safe."

"So you threw yourself out of a burning building," Ramirez said. The detective's eyes were firm.

"I told you, I was trapped. And I'm just wondering—what if I was the intended victim of the fire? Because of my . . . investigation?"

Ramirez raised her hand to her mouth and covered a strangled cough. Lana had the impression she was trying to hide a snort of laughter, or disdain. She couldn't tell which.

Choi reached over and put a reassuring hand on Lana's forearm. "If that's the case, ma'am, I'd say they failed miserably."

Lana straightened up. "When will you know who did this?"

"Arson investigations take time. It might be a few weeks before we have anything concrete."

"A few weeks? Do you need my car for all that time?"

"No, ma'am." Choi put a xeroxed flyer on the table. "You can retrieve your car anytime at the impound lot in Santa Cruz. Call this number. They can give you the specifics."

"That's fifteen miles from here. How am I supposed to—"

Ramirez stepped forward. "Ms. Rubicon, I'll take you there."

Lana craned her neck around. "Couldn't Detective Choi drive me?"

"He's busy," Ramirez said flatly.

Lana made a point of taking her time getting up from the table, shaking Choi's hand, and putting on her jacket. She left a note on the counter before following Ramirez out the door.

RAMIREZ OPENED the passenger door of the Buick and gestured to Lana.

"You don't want me in back?" Lana asked.

"Would you prefer that?" Ramirez's politeness sounded strained. Lana decided not to push it.

They drove the first few miles in silence, Lana squirming in the sunken seat. She could feel the broken springs poking the bruise on her right hip. She pushed herself forward and touched a finger to a colorful, lumpy string of beads hanging from the rearview mirror.

"Rosary?" Lana said. "I always wished Jewish women had a wearable accessory. Smart of the Catholics to think of the whole necklace thing."

Ramirez kept her eyes forward. "It's an art project," she said. "My niece made it at preschool."

They drove in silence for another minute, Lana idly fingering the lumpy beads, Ramirez watching the traffic. Then the detective erupted.

"What do you think you're doing?"

Lana pulled her hand back from the beads. "I'm sorry, I didn't mean to—"

"What are you doing sniffing around my case?"

Lana straightened up in the seat as best she could. "I'm just trying to protect my family," she said.

"By inserting yourself? Getting trapped in a burning building? Do you have some kind of death wish?"

Lana wondered for a moment how much her daughter had told Ramirez about her medical condition. "I'm just curious. And persistent. Traits I'd imagine someone like you might appreciate."

"Someone like me?"

"A detective."

"Right." Ramirez's hands were clenched tight around the steering wheel. "*I'm* the detective here. The first woman, the first Latina, to work a murder in Monterey County. It's hard enough for me to get taken seriously by my colleagues. I don't need someone's grandma getting in my way."

Heat rushed to the bruise under Lana's stitches on her cheek. She could feel it throb, as if all her frustration, her hot, congealing blood, was trapped in there.

"In my experience," Lana said, articulating each word with precision, "women who blame other women for their problems have their own deficiencies to deal with."

It was a risk, saying this in a moving vehicle. But Ramirez just shook her head.

"That's what you think this is? You think I'm threatened by you? More like exasperated by you. Worried about you. That I'm going to be on the brink of cracking this case and I'll have to come rescue you from some hole you've dug yourself into."

"You don't have to worry about me."

"I do have to worry about you. I went to bat for your granddaughter, and this is how you repay me? Sneaking behind my back to meddle in my case?"

"Please. You sat there while your partner practically called Jack a whore."

"Not every battle is fought in the open," Ramirez said as she pulled into the impound lot. Her voice came in low and fast. "You're a smart woman. You know that. If it weren't for me, Nicoletti would still be breathing down Jacqueline's neck."

Lana locked her eyes on the front windshield. "Are you telling me I can't look into this case anymore?"

"You have a right as a private citizen to do whatever you want, Ms. Rubicon. I just wish you'd do it farther away from me."

Ramirez walked up to the entry kiosk at the impound lot on her own. Lana sat in the Buick like a surly teenager while the detective talked to an officer with a clipboard and a lollipop sticking out from under his mustache.

Ramirez returned to the car with Lana's keys. The two women drove silently through the lot, winding past smashed sports cars and ash-speckled minivans with the windows blacked out.

"Mobile meth labs," Ramirez said, when she saw Lana looking. "They steal 'em from soccer moms, rip the seats out, and start cooking. I found one last week in Royal Oaks."

Lana knew a peace offering when she heard it. It might be wise to reciprocate.

"You know, I've been thinking about that kayak tour booking," Lana said.

The detective looked at Lana, her eyes wary.

"Ricardo signed up for my granddaughter's Saturday sunset tour," Lana said. "You showed us the registration book. Paul took the call. It said 'paid' and everything. But that call happened on Friday afternoon."

"So?"

"So did Ricardo even make that call?"

Ramirez smiled. "Good one. Nicoletti didn't spot it right away. You're correct. The booking was made at five P.M., when Ricardo Cruz was already dead."

Lana was disappointed she hadn't given the detective new information. But at least they were talking again.

"Was it Ricardo's phone that made the booking?"

"Yes."

"Someone murdered him, took his phone, and booked a tour?"

"That's right. We're still waiting on the historical cell location data, so we can find out where the call was placed. Hopefully there's something useful there."

Lana wondered who might have been close enough to Ricardo to know the passcode to unlock his phone. She resisted the urge to ask more questions. "Sounds like you've got it covered," she said.

"I like to think so."

Both women got out of the Buick and stood in front of Lana's Lexus, facing each other.

"I want you to be successful," Lana said. "If there's any way I can help . . ."

"The best thing you can do is to stay out of it."

"We both want the same thing," Lana insisted. "Justice for Ricardo Cruz."

Lana felt the younger woman's eyes sweep over her. It had been a long afternoon. Her wig itched, her bruises ached, and she could feel the liquid foundation she'd slathered over her stitches sliding down her face.

"Are you sure justice is what you want, Ms. Rubicon?"

Lana stood and watched in silence as Teresa Ramirez adjusted her badge, got back in the Buick, and drove away.

CHAPTER THIRTY

"BETH! QUICK!" LANA SHOUTED as the front door slammed. "Can you help us with something?"

Beth dropped the Chinese food on the counter and rushed into the back bedroom. "Are you okay?"

"Is this straight?"

Jack was standing on top of her old desk, holding an enormous corkboard up against the wall. Lana was watching from the doorway. She had one of Beth's hand-knitted beanies on her head, a lavender one with a fluffy pom-pom. There were nails in Lana's mouth and a hammer in her hand. The stitches on her cheek were covered by a Wonder Woman Band-Aid. If she didn't look so deranged, it would be kind of cute.

"What are you—"

"Is it straight?" Lana demanded.

Beth could see Jack's shoulders trembling. "It's fine."

"Good!" Lana bounced forward with the hammer, Jack ducked out of its path, and the corkboard clattered to the floor.

"Shit. Well. Third time's a charm." Lana gave Jack an upward nod, and the teenager climbed back onto the desk.

Beth looked around the bedroom. The desk was stacked with Lana's books: *The Art of War*, *The Emperor's Handbook*, and one featuring a woman with big hair and shoulder pads under the title *They Can Kill You but They Can't Eat You*. The bedspread was buried under a pile of printouts: contracts, maps, and blurry photographs. It was clear they'd been at it—whatever it was—for a while.

"What's going on here?"

"Prima found a lot of good stuff at the land trust."

Beth looked back at the papers on the bed. "You *stole* all these?"

"Of course not." Lana was lining up an army of pushpins on the corkboard. "I took photographs with my phone."

"I see."

"And I used the printer at the library after school," Jack added.

"Uh-huh."

"We've been going through it, and Mom? It's pretty interesting." Jack held her breath and prayed this wouldn't turn into a fight.

"Well . . . good. I brought dinner. Maybe you and the Zodiac hunter can tell me about it over fried rice."

"I'VE DECIDED TO RECALIBRATE my approach," Lana said. "To focus on finding evidence. Not apprehending the murderer."

"Seems wise," Beth said. She looked apprehensively at the hammer, which was now sitting on the table next to Lana's plate.

"The woman detective, Ramirez, she's the one who should get the solve."

"Very generous of you, Ma."

Lana nodded. "But no one involved in the investigation is more qualified than I am to review these real estate documents."

Lana held forth about the land trust, sharing what she'd learned from her visit. The land to the west of the Rhoads ranch was public. The land to the east was managed by the land trust. The ranch was a linchpin. For what, she didn't quite know yet. But she was sure she'd figure it out.

"You still think there's a connection between Mr. Rhoads's ranch and Ricardo's death?" Beth tried to keep the skepticism out of her voice.

"There's more than one. Jack, can you get the list?"

Jack picked up an old Spanish test and flipped it over. The back was covered in neat lines of purple ink. "One," she read. "Ricardo talking with Mr. Rhoads about the future of the ranch."

Lana nodded to her to continue.

"Two. Suspicious note about taking a big project away from the land trust. Three. Mr. Rhoads's daughter, Diana Whitacre, squirrelly about Ricardo at the wake."

"She seems . . . complicated," Beth said.

"Strong women often are. I like her. We're having lunch later this week."

Beth looked at her. "If you're up to it."

"Please. I got more sleep in that hospital than I have in months. If I have enough energy to get strapped in a box for my MRI and PET scans Thursday morning, I think I deserve a little reward afterward. Now, Jack"—Lana brandished a chopstick at the girl—"back to our list."

Jack's eyes darted from Lana to her mother and then back down to the sheet of paper. Lana kept waggling the chopstick until Jack finally spoke. "Four," she said. "I thought of this one. Ricardo's body may have been dumped on the ranch."

Beth looked confused. "I thought you found him in the mud flats?"

Jack nodded. "The mud flats, the slough, that isn't technically owned by anyone. But Prima and I were looking at the property above the flats, and—hold on. I'll show you." Jack got up and disappeared into the back bedroom.

"You sure this is a good idea?" Beth asked Lana.

Lana's eyes were shining.

Jack returned with a large map in her hands. She moved aside the container of fried rice and spread out the map on the table. "Here's the ranch. And here's the land trust property, right next door. See?"

Jack's thumb left a smudge of grease across the farmland north of the slough. The land trust property snaked along the water for miles before taking a sharp left turn up into the hills to the east. Beth could see small creeks crisscrossing the land, ignoring property lines. She'd explored the north bank a few times, bushwhacking past No Trespassing signs, her boots kissing mud every fifth step. Some creeks were former irrigation ditches, shooting in straight lines across what had once been fertile fields. Others wound and turned and curled in on themselves, dead-ending in marshy bogs. Only a couple creeks linked back to the slough. You'd have to be a real expert to know which were shortcuts and which went nowhere.

"I found his body here." Jack made another oily mark on the map, this time in the water, about a mile up past the land trust boundary.

"He could have floated in from anywhere," Beth said.

"Not anywhere." Lana's voice was sharp, teacherly. "Jack showed me. It had to be from somewhere on the northern bank. Probably one of the creeks that lead to the slough. Or an irrigation ditch. It could be one that links up to the ranch."

"Couldn't it have come in from the open ocean? Or somewhere up by the lettuce fields?"

"We don't think so," Jack said. "He was in the water for twenty-four to forty hours. On a weekend. Someone would notice if a body was floating in the open slough. We think he had to be in one of the side creeks. On private property. Like these."

Jack pointed at the maze of blue lines between the ranch, the land trust, and the mud flats.

Beth pushed her plate to the side. "Some of those creeks don't cross onto the ranch."

Lana nodded. "True. Victor Morales is high on my list of suspects right now."

"In which case this would have nothing to do with Mr. Rhoads," Beth said. "It could be all about the land trust, some kind of power grab there."

Lana regarded Beth coolly. "Why the sudden interest, Beth? Anything to do with that nanotechnologist you've been consoling?"

"Please, Ma. I'm just trying to help you explore all the possibilities. And Martin and your new friend Lady Di just lost their father. I don't love you pulling an innocent family like the Rhoadses into this"—Beth waved her hands at the papers on the table—"whatever this is."

Lana arched one eyebrow. "No more murder night for you?"

"Ma, this isn't—"

Lana stood up and rolled out her neck. "Jack, I know you have school tomorrow, but after that, I was hoping . . ."

"I'd love to help," Jack said quickly, before her mother could interject.

"Tomorrow, then." Lana gathered up the papers and patted them into a messy stack. "We'll see what these have to say about who's innocent."

CHAPTER THIRTY-ONE

BY THE FOLLOWING AFTERNOON, Lana's bedroom looked like the headquarters of a secret crime-solving squad. Which Jack supposed it was. Sort of. The corkboard was covered with the list of suspects, the greasy map of the slough, the handwritten note, and a sketch of the Rhoads ranch showing its many leases and subdivisions. The most recent addition to the board was a grainy blown-up photograph of Martin Rhoads standing on a stage in a gaggle of men at the nanotechnology pitch contest on February 3, which apparently was a real thing. All the men were wearing logo T-shirts from their various start-ups. Most of them looked about twenty-five, scrawny and spiky-haired. Martin looked like their nerdy uncle trying to fit in.

Lana had all the printed papers she'd photographed at the land trust on the bed, organized in piles. Jack sat down and started leafing through the messiest stack.

"That's the historical stuff," Lana said. "I haven't gone through it yet. But let me show you this first."

They walked over to the bulletin board. "I was thinking about what your mom said about the body and where it could have floated from."

Jack figured this was the closest Lana might come to admitting she might be wrong.

"We don't know where Ricardo died yet," Lana continued, "but I thought it might be a good idea to really understand what happens where the land trust and the ranch hit the water. Creeks don't obey property lines, and we know Mr. Rhoads leased out ranch land to other businesses. I found the details about the leases in the papers at the land trust, and here's what that looks like."

Lana pointed to the sketch on the board. It looked like a toddler's rendition of a checkerboard, the land carved into blocks of different shapes and sizes.

"You want me to take notes?"

"Never volunteer to be a secretary," Lana said, handing over her legal pad. "Now write this down. Mr. Rhoads and his family have always run the fifty acres at the top of the hill, where the main house and the barn are."

"Where we went for the wake."

"Right. The Rhoads family manages the fields on the hillside east of the house. The south hundred acres, closer to the slough, those are leased out to an organic strawberry farmer. Over here"—Lana circled an area north of the house—"there's another hundred acres, leased to a salmon hatchery, cauliflower hybrids, one that just says Mrs. Pickle, and an outfit called Splatterball. I looked it up. Sounds terrible, all those young people in camouflage running around with guns."

Lana paused. "Do you think a man like Ricardo Cruz could have been into paintball?" She made the word sound like a degrading sexual act. "I don't see it."

Her cell phone started buzzing on the comforter. Lana looked at it and shook her head. "Victor Morales. The man has called every day to apologize."

"Have you talked to him?"

"Not yet. It's always good to make a man sweat, Jack. At least until you have something you want from him."

Lana ignored the call and turned back to the sketch, pointing to the southeastern corner of the ranch by the water and the boundary with the land trust property. "The interesting bit is over here. Last year, Mr. Rhoads leased this little slice of land to Paul. Your boss."

Jack looked closer. "Mom mentioned something about that to me."

"Your mother?"

"Yeah . . . I guess it came up when she got burritos with Martin. She told me she might have figured out why Mr. Rhoads had that double kayak in his barn. I guess he leased Paul some land and Paul gave him a kayak in exchange. That's all I know."

Lana wanted to ask more, but she turned to the board instead. "Well. Here it is. Technically it's leased to something called Fruitful LLC, but Paul's name is on the lease. Do you have any idea what he might be doing there?"

Jack shook her head. "I've never heard of it. It's not like we have a snack stand or keep boats up there. Does it go all the way to the water?"

Jack and Lana looked at the skinny wedge. Paul's land was small, less than an acre, a tiny Pac-Man mouth opening toward the slough from the vastness of the ranch. Lana wondered for a moment if it could be the seed of the kind of big, bold project referenced in the handwritten note she'd found.

"Judging from satellite images, it's a field," Lana said. "Close to the bank, but not right up to it. Probably a lot of those standing pools that fill with salt water too."

Jack's eyes darted between the sketch, the map of the slough, and her notes. "I think I know that area. There's kind of a valley. And a fence. You can't see much of what's up there."

"It's pretty close to the mud flats."

"Do you think . . ." Jack wasn't sure if she wanted to ask. "Do you think I should stop working for him?"

Lana looked at her granddaughter. She wasn't chewing her pen or ripping tiny holes in her sweatshirt cuffs. She looked calm, steady. Like her mother. "Let's not rush to any conclusions." Lana gestured to the piles of paper from the land trust on the bed. "Let's see what else we can find."

Jack took the historical documents, and Lana tackled the contracts. She paused again on the letter of intent, carefully reading its brief paragraphs about a wetlands conservation easement. She thought she understood it, though she'd never dealt with a document exactly like it before. And clearly Martin, Diana, and Victor all had different opinions on what it meant. She took out her phone and shot a text to an old friend who would know definitively how to interpret it. But André didn't get right back to her like he used to. After all this time away, maybe he'd forgotten about her.

At the two-hour mark, Jack got up and left. Lana wondered if the girl was done humoring her. Perhaps Jack had realized this was not a glorious game but an itchy, tiresome hunt through bales of bupkis. Then Jack returned with a Diet Coke for Lana and a big bowl of tortilla chips and salsa. Jack smiled and grabbed a fresh genealogical report from her stack.

It took half the chips and all of the salsa before they found something.

"Finally!" Lana said. She was waving a piece of paper in her hand.

"What is it?"

"An email from Ricardo Cruz to Hal Rhoads about the mystery project they were working on. From the week before he died. Before they both died. Listen to this."

> Dear Hal, The hawks are circling high today. The architect's office just called. The first sketches for Verdadera Libertad are ready. The architects will mail a set to you, and I'll bring mine when I come see you Friday. I won't peek—I want you to have the first view of them. Until then, Ricardo.

Lana looked triumphantly at Jack. "See the date? Ricardo was visiting Mr. Rhoads on February third, the same day he was killed. You found Ricardo's body two days later, that Sunday."

"Okay . . ."

"It links them together. Not just in general. But the weekend they both died."

Jack scanned the document. "This phrase, Verdadera Libertad. It means true liberty. Freedom."

"I'm glad you're learning something at high school."

"No, I saw something about that . . ." Jack started digging through the pile of paper in front of her. "Here. I thought this was kind of nuts when I read it. There's this history of the ranch from the perspective of one of the descendants of the original owners. I guess this would be Mr. Rhoads's great-great-great-uncle or something. The name is a little different, but it's the same ranch. There's this part about when they were first building it in 1853," she said, pointing with her finger.

The typewritten history had been xeroxed several times over, tilting the text to the right in a dark, grainy font.

One day as the men were working on the buildings, a band of Mexicans approached to drive them off the land they still considered their own. Mr. Roadhouse, upon seeing their approach in the distance, was known to say, "It looks as if we will have to fight. I wish we had an American flag!" Whereas his father-in-law replied, "I do have one and a big one! It's in my trunk on the wagon."

They quickly brought it out and nailed it to a pole, which they pushed through and above a large oak tree. The Mexicans, seeing the flag of the new government and evidently thinking it a US Army installation, changed their minds and went away. Thereafter that particular oak tree came to be known to the family as the "Liberty Tree."

Lana looked up. "You think the project that Ricardo and Hal were working on has to do with this Liberty Tree?"

"Liberty Tree, True Liberty . . . I don't know." Jack shrugged. "Seems kinda weird given the history that they would name it that in Spanish. Maybe it's just a coincidence?"

"Or a reference we don't understand yet."

Jack leaned back against the headboard. "American history is so messed up," she said. "The white people straight up stole that ranch from Mexicans."

"The Mexicans likely stole it from the Native people too."

"Why does land have to belong to anybody?"

"Land is the most precious form of power on this planet. There's only so much of it. When you buy it—"

"—or steal it—"

Lana nodded. "You stake a claim on its future. If you own the land, you can do what you want. You can plant trees, build skyscrapers, or plan a whole new city. You can shape the future you want for yourself and your family."

"Sounds like just another way for some people to hoard power over others."

Lana smiled, thinking of the gleaming white lacquer desk in her old West LA office. "Sometimes that's true. But owning land isn't always about power. It's about rootedness. Stewardship. Like how Mr. Rhoads felt about his ranch. Or how the land trust people feel about the places they care for."

Jack looked skeptical.

"Think about this place," Lana continued. "How does it make you feel to know your mom owns this house?"

Jack thought for a moment. "It makes me feel safe. Like no matter what happens, I can come home."

"Exactly. When you own something, it's there for you. And in a way, it even owns a bit of you. From the first day you own a piece of property, it gets its hooks into you. You walk around and it whispers to you what it wants to be, who it wants you to be. You feel the need to take care of it, nurture it. I've seen it happen again and again with my clients."

"I still think it isn't fair."

Lana snorted. "Real estate never is."

BETH TEXTED THAT SHE'D had a hell of a shift and could they please figure out dinner. While Jack called in an order to Pizza My Heart for a large sausage and onions with extra olives, Lana texted André again. The pizza arrived just after Beth did. Thankfully, Lana's phone rang before she had to entertain the idea of eating it.

Lana rushed into the back bedroom and shut the door. Beth raised an eyebrow at Jack, but the girl was too busy redistributing toppings for maximum flavor variety per bite to notice.

"Thank you for calling me back so quickly, André." Lana sat down on the bed facing the window with the slough and pulled the letter of intent onto her lap.

"Darling, of course! Where are you? Your assistant told me something about an out-of-town medical procedure, and then you never responded to my texts, and when I called her again, she was working for some kind of lifestyle influencer in Ojai."

Lana hadn't realized how good—and painful—it would be to hear her old friend's voice. It was like ripping off a Band-Aid she'd forgotten she had on.

"André, I'm fine. Things up here have just gotten more complicated than I anticipated."

"Where are you?"

"Monterey Bay, near Carmel." Near enough.

André let out a long exhale. "Thank God. Here I was thinking you were stuck somewhere awful, like a Siberian prison, or Bakersfield." He paused. "Wait. Are you getting one of those EscarGlow treatments? You beast! I hear the snail slime smell is awful but the wrinkles positively melt away."

"Please. You know I don't have wrinkles."

"You're not going to tell me, are you? So what's up?"

"I was hoping you could tell me a bit about conservation easements."

"You haven't gone Green Party on me, have you?"

"No, nothing like that. I'm looking into a few contracts with a land trust up here, and I had some questions. I've never gotten my hands dirty in nonprofits before, and I knew you'd be the right one to ask," Lana said.

He chuckled. "That's my girl. All business. Fire away."

"I'm looking at a signed letter of intent from five years ago for a conservation easement between a rancher and a land trust. Just to be clear, an easement like this, it's a transfer of development rights, not a transfer of land, correct?"

"That's right. The owner holds the land, relinquishes the rights to do anything on it, and gets a tax write-off for doing it. In a way, it's like the easements we've negotiated in the past to put new roads through private land. But instead of building, it's blocking—the easement creates a no-development zone."

"So if no one is actually buying or selling land, what role does the land trust play? What's in it for them?"

"Control. The land trust is a kind of nonprofit nanny to the process. They strip the property of all meaningful paths to progress and profit. They get the papers signed and new deed restrictions recorded. And then they monitor the properties under their care, to make sure no one puts up a lemonade stand or a house or God forbid a factory on the premises."

"How does the land trust make money in that scenario?"

"They don't. Hence the non to their profit."

"That doesn't make sense."

"Not to you, it wouldn't. Not to me either, darling. But different strokes . . . and I suppose land trusts do often get large gifts of cash for their efforts. Kind of like making a donation to the hospital where dear old mother gave it up."

Lana tried to ignore that last analogy.

"What if a land trust had enough land under conservation easement to get some kind of federal status as a wildlife protection zone?"

"What kind of wildlife?"

Lana looked out the window. "Seals. Otters. Waterfowl."

"Charismatic megafauna," André said. His voice betrayed a combination of respect and disgust. "The cuter the animal, the bigger the prize. Very popular with Sierra Club billionaires. And the feds. If the land trust could prove such animals were unique or endangered, it could trigger a federal designation. It could mean lots of funding, and power to call the shots for miles around."

So Diana hadn't been exaggerating. Lana imagined Victor Morales, conservation king, reclaiming Elkhorn from the ranchers who'd controlled the area for generations. She could see him up on the grassy hillside of the ranch, astride a horse, in custom boots, surveying his eco-empire. He'd enjoy it. He wouldn't look half-bad doing it either.

But there was one unresolved question between him and that dream.

"In my experience, a letter of intent isn't binding," Lana said. "There isn't some special exception for conservation projects, is there?"

"Nope. An LOI is just a promise. And you know how easy it is for a real estate project to change or fall apart between the promise and the finish line."

"No contract, no deal." It was one of her mantras. "Thank you, André. This is exactly what I needed."

"Not at all. You've given me the pleasure of being the one person who has actually talked to you in months. Everyone will be jealous." He paused. "It's less fun here without you. Chat is nice, but I miss watching you carve up apartment buildings."

"You miss getting my business."

"Well, that too. But, darling, there's this maddening little show on right now in West Hollywood where all the men's roles are played by pigs and everyone is talking about it. Are you coming back soon?"

Lana felt a sharp pang of longing for her old life, the intoxicating drumbeat of commerce, clinking glasses with friends and enemies alike.

She missed restaurants that seated you based on how much power you wielded in the city. She missed valet parking. But she wondered how much of her old world would be open to her if she came back now, with sunken eyes and stitches. There was a reason she hadn't told anyone but Gloria about the cancer. Powerhouses like André avoided weakness like it was contagious. Before she got sick, Lana had too.

She looked around the cocoon she'd made of her daughter's back bedroom in Elkhorn. Chipped furniture. Papers everywhere. Not a place she'd chosen, but a place where she could be herself, a fragile, incomplete self: Lana-with-cancer. In two days, on Thursday, she'd take the tests that would tell her when she could go back to being Lana, full stop. It could be soon. It could be never. She couldn't let go of the hope that the tumors would shrink and she could go back home, become dazzling and diamond-hard once again, and put all of this behind her.

Until then she had new ways to occupy her time.

"I'm not sure when I'll be back, André." Out the window, Lana could see the slough waking up for the evening, terns and harbor seals slipping into the water to hunt for dinner. "Something up here has piqued my interest."

"A hundred acres of opportunity? A silver fox? Knowing you, it's probably both."

Lana smiled. "I'll tell you all about it when I'm back, André. Omakase. My treat."

"Darling, I can't wait. And bring him with you."

CHAPTER THIRTY-TWO

WHEN LANA STUMBLED into the kitchen at nine thirty the next morning, the landline was ringing.

"Mrs. Rubicon?"

Lana was too tired to correct her.

"I'm calling from the office at North Monterey County High School."

"Yes?" Lana yawned.

"Is Jacqueline out of school today for an illness? We don't have a note on file that she would be absent."

"What? Hold on." Lana looked over at the sofa bed. Jack's pillow was stacked on top of her folded comforter, like usual. Through the window she saw Beth's car in the driveway. Lana tried to stretch the phone cord far enough to knock on Beth's bedroom door but couldn't reach. "We'll have to call you back."

"This will be marked down as unexcused."

"I said we'll call you back!" Lana snapped at the phone, which flipped to a dial tone before she could finish.

"Beth?" Lana gingerly opened the door to her daughter's room.

"Uhn." Beth's face was squashed into her pillow, her body swallowed by a mound of blankets. "Day off. Lemme sleep."

"Beth. The school just called." Lana tried to keep the panic out of her voice. "Jack isn't there. She isn't here either."

Beth shot up into a sitting position. "What? How long has she been gone?"

"I don't know. The phone woke me up."

"Is her backpack on the table?"

"What?" Lana turned and looked behind her. There were some books and papers on the table, but no backpack. She shook her head.

"Back door," Beth ordered, pulling on a pair of jeans.

The two women went outside and surveyed the scene behind the kitchen. Jack's bike was there, leaning up against the house, along with a jacket and her neon helmet. But no Jack.

Beth peered around the corner. "Her paddleboard. It isn't here."

Lana breathed out. "That's good. She probably just lost track of time in the slough."

"No. We have a deal. She sets her backpack on the table if she's paddling out early. And she has to get to school on time. No excuses, no tardy slips. Otherwise she loses paddle privileges. She'd never risk that."

Lana could hear the worry creeping into her daughter's voice. She peered down at the slough, scanning the gray water. The slough was flat and glassy, crowded with boats and people. Two long hulls of women rowing crew. Three men, barrel-chested, piloting single kayaks upriver. The only paddleboard Lana saw held a paunchy older man, wet suit stripped to his waist, impervious to cold or macho or both. She stared hard at him, willing the stringy hair on his chest to somehow magically transform into a red life vest on a teenage girl.

Beth reappeared beside Lana. "She isn't answering her phone."

"Maybe she left a note?"

"That's not how we do things. Where could she—" Beth reached down and extricated a stone from the edge of her rock labyrinth, squeezing it in her hand.

"Beth, she's a teenager . . ."

"So?"

"She might not tell her mother everything."

Lana braced herself for a tirade. But Beth's face flushed with panic, not anger. Lana awkwardly patted her back, which turned into an even more awkward one-armed hug, Beth leaning her head onto her mother's shoulder. When Beth pulled away, her eyes were pricked with tears.

• • •

When Jack was a toddler, Beth had spent hours memorizing her tiny face, pointed chin, the dark hair that floated around her like a cloud. Beth never slept in those days, rushing from day care to nursing school to work to the house, sitting up late in the patched armchair she'd found on the side of the road while Jack slept and wriggled in her arms. Something about those sleepless hours tattooed itself on Beth's eyelids, keeping Jack always in her sight. She saw Jack peering up at her from patients' deep brown eyes. She saw Jack in report cards and otter posters, bikes and paddleboards, a young Monterey pine holding its own against the wind.

But now, nothing. Had Jack lost track of time, as Lana suggested? Had she deliberately left, paddling away to do God knows what, something Jack had kept from Beth? Or had she been taken, snatched from the slough?

She had to pull herself together. Beth took out her phone and started dialing, calling anyone who might have seen Jack. No one picked up at the Kayak Shack. Same at the yacht club. She texted Kayla, who hadn't seen Jack before school or in the break after first period. She texted Jack again. And then she stopped. She had no one else to call.

She stared at her phone, wondering. How was it possible she didn't know more people in Jack's life? Her connection to Jack suddenly felt paper-thin, the surface of a dark body of water. Jack was paddling out, into the deep, and Beth had no idea where.

CHAPTER THIRTY-THREE

BETH DROVE EAST into the hills, faster than Lana would have liked. Not that she was going to say anything. Beth's mouth was ironed shut, arms locked, her hands about to rip the wheel from the steering column. She careened up and over the train tracks, eyes locked to the window and the reedy bank along the road. The car slowed by the abandoned dairy, and Beth and Lana surveyed the crumbling barns, their doors blown off, big chunks of roof caved in. There was no movement. No Jack.

They kept going, past Kirby Park, to the trestle bridge that separated artichoke fields from the swampy water. They crossed over to the north bank in silence, staring out at the rolling hills of the land trust property and the Rhoads ranch that blocked their view of the slough.

They stopped outside the entrance to the paintball range and got out of the car. Lana handed Beth her binoculars, and Beth looked down toward the water, tracing the curlicued creeks that linked the vernal ponds and irrigation ditches to the slough. A crew in white plastic jumpsuits was spraying rows of future strawberry plants in a low-laying field. Otherwise, it was pickle grass and pelicans as far as the eye could see.

The wind picked up, biting at Lana's flimsy sweater. She felt Beth shift her weight beside her.

"Let's go," Lana said. She put a hand on Beth's forearm, as if to guide her. "There's a lot more places she could be."

By the time Beth's car bumped over the cattle guards at the entrance of the marina, both women were fried. Beth stared at the college boys in Kayak Shack sweatshirts dragging boats from the water to the shop. Her eyes followed each kayak as it disappeared behind the aluminum fence.

"Let's split up," Lana suggested. "You go to the Kayak Shack. I'll take the docks. Maybe I'll find a fisherman who saw her." Lana watched Beth stride over to the boys, then turned, her low heels planting divots in the gravel as she headed in the other direction.

The docks were labeled alphabetically, laid out in rows and right angles like an urban street grid. Each dock held slots for twenty-four boats, a mix of kayaks, fishing skiffs, and small sailboats, their jibs clinking in the breeze.

Lana tackled the rows methodically, starting at *M* and working her way north to *A*. By *F*, her right hip ached. Her toes were curling inside her squared-off mules. And the cutesy names painted on the sides of the sloops—"Seas the Day," "A Wave We Go," "Back That Mast Up"—were starting to piss her off. She met three fishermen on the *E* row who politely looked at the photos of Jack on her phone. One of them took the time to look a little less politely down her braless sweater before lifting his eyes and opening his mouth to tell her he was sorry. They hadn't seen Jack. His buddies broke out giggling as Lana stomped away.

While she was limping along the *C* corridor, Lana heard someone paddle up. A man in a double kayak pulled alongside the *B* dock, loaded down with a cooler, a shovel, and an enormous black duffel bag. The bag was sticking out in front of him, the cooler wedged behind his denim jacket like a high-backed chair.

Lana recognized him as soon as he stepped up onto the dock.

"Paul!" she called out.

"Lana? What are you doing here?"

"Beth left you a message. Jack is missing. We think somewhere out on the slough. Have you seen her?"

"What? I've just been in the marina taking care of a few things . . ." Paul put a proprietary hand on the cooler.

"We've been all over. Beth's probably tearing apart your office right now looking for her."

"No. Let me . . ."

He cast a nervous glance around. There was no one else on the dock.

"Let me help you."

He flung the duffel over one shoulder and threw a ragged sweatshirt on top of the cooler in the kayak. "Dock *L*," he said. "Tell Beth to meet us there."

While Lana texted Beth, Paul took out his phone and turned away from her.

"Scotty, hey." He shot a nervous glance back at Lana. "Listen, I've got a little situation here. Can you pick up the cooler? Dock *B*. I know . . . We'll find a better place soon, bud. Promise. Catch you later."

Lana resisted the urge to take a closer look at the cooler.

"What's on Dock *L*?" she asked.

"I have a motorboat we use for stranded kayakers, tourists who lose a paddle or get caught out too far when the wind picks up. I'll take you out and we can look around."

"We already did that—"

"But you were in a car, right?"

Lana nodded.

"Everything looks different when you're in the water," Paul replied. "Don't worry. I'll keep you safe."

• • •

They peeled out of the marina in a rush of seagull cries and motor oil. Beth watched the water, muttering curses at every bobbing shape that turned out to be a sea lion instead of her daughter. Lana watched Paul.

The boat cut a rippling line up the center of the slough, pushing them past kayaks and clutches of otters. They zipped by Beth's house on the right, Beth's eyes tracing every inch of the narrow beach, praying for a sign of her daughter. The back bedroom window winked at her. But there was no one there.

They kept going, up past Bird Island, past the decrepit shark-hunting blinds and the long spit where harbor seals liked to sleep the day away. There was an old falling-down shack at the end of the spit, and Beth almost asked Paul to stop, to let her out to run toward the slimy, gutted wood and rip the rotted door off its hinges. But it looked too much like a place for a dead girl or a skeleton, a secret long buried. Not a place for Jack with her bright red life jacket over her powerful, thumping heart.

When they passed the mud flats, Lana's voice rose sharply over the whine of the motor.

"There. Stop."

Paul let the boat idle, and Lana pointed north, to a break in the bank where a narrow channel intersected the slough. The channel was edged in tufts of horsetail reeds, a feathery mouth of water that ran perpendicular to the slough for fifteen yards before snaking up to the west in a dizzying swirl of switchbacks and brush.

"Last night, Jack and I were looking at some maps," Lana said. "Those creeks back there, they link the slough to the land trust. Maybe to the ranch as well. Jack and I were wondering . . ." She turned abruptly to Paul. "Can we go in there?"

Paul shook his head. "It's not deep enough for a motorboat. Most of the time, even a kayak would get stuck back there."

"Do you know where it lets out?"

Paul shook his head again, too quickly this time. "It's all private property back in there."

Lana looked at him for a long moment. She knew his leased land for Fruitful LLC was back there somewhere. There had to be more he wasn't telling them. But if his boat couldn't go up the channel, pushing him wasn't going to help them find Jack. They needed him on their side until they found her.

"Do you want to go up farther?" Paul asked, nodding toward the slough, which continued eastward into the Salinas hills.

"Give us a minute, Paul." Lana leaned in close to Beth. "I think she's up that creek somewhere. On the land trust property, maybe. Or the Rhoads ranch."

"We already drove up there."

"I know, but . . . I just have a feeling."

Beth stared at her mother curiously, as if Lana had stolen something from her when her back was turned. Then she nodded.

"I'll call Martin. You call Lady Di and the land trust. We'll find someone who can help us."

While Lana left messages for Diana and Victor, Beth turned and pressed her ear to her phone. "Martin, hi. This is Beth. Sorry to be calling you like this, but, um, my daughter, Jack, is missing, and we think she might be near the ranch somewhere. I'm not sure if you are still down here or not, but if you are, can you take a look around down by the water? We're going to walk up there soon. Jack's five feet tall, brown skin, dark brown hair, maybe you met her at the wake, I don't remember. She has a red life vest and a pink paddleboard. Sorry for the long message. I, uh, hope you're doing well."

"What now?" Lana asked.

"I know another way to get in there," Beth said. "Paul, can you take us back to the marina? We can hike along the bank from there."

The outboard motor roared to life, and they turned back, heading west. Beth kept her eyes closed, telling herself they'd find Jack. She'd be okay. The words filled Beth's head like a mantra, a drumbeat, pushing her terror aside. She'd be okay. Then Lana grabbed her hand and yelled for Paul to stop the boat.

"Jack!"

A figure on a paddleboard was navigating the rotted piers of the public fishing dock, heading south into the slough across white peaks of foam.

"It's her," Beth breathed.

She gave Lana's hand a squeeze.

"She looks okay. Does she look okay?"

Lana nodded. She glanced down at their interwoven hands and squeezed back. Beth stood and started waving, almost losing her balance in the motorboat as she swung both arms high above her head. Paul killed the engine.

"JACK!" Beth shouted. "ARE YOU OKAY?"

The girl looked up toward the skiff. Her backpack and her clothes were soaked and caked with mud. Her life jacket was nowhere to be seen. Jack gave her mom a limp thumbs-up, waggled her paddle in the direction of their house, and started heading across.

The motorboat pulled up to the narrow beach below the house and Beth hopped down into the knee-deep water, still waving to her daughter, watching her every stroke as Jack paddled toward them. The water was freezing, but Beth still felt the adrenaline, the afterburn of fear. It took everything she had not to charge deeper into the slough and drag her daughter to shore herself. Paul was helping Lana step down from the skiff when Jack jumped off her board at the edge of the gravel beach. Beth vaulted toward her and wrapped her in a firm hug.

"I'm sorry, Mom. I lost track of time and—"

"Did you flip your board?" Beth brushed the mud from Jack's sleeves, checking anxiously for blood or broken bones.

"No, I just—I was up in the creeks, following this map I'd made, and I got lost. I screwed up, I know. I tried to call you, but there was this man and—"

"What? Who? Did he . . . hurt you?" Beth pulled back from Jack to study her. Jack looked wet and dirty, but otherwise unharmed. She searched her daughter's eyes for what she couldn't see.

"No. I'm okay, Mom. Really." Jack swallowed, and her voice evened out. She pointed north across the slough. "There was a man back there, an hour ago, digging something up by one of the creeks. He was cursing and grunting, and I couldn't see his face. But he sounded angry, and I didn't want him to know I was there. I took off my life jacket and dropped down behind a bunch of reeds so he couldn't see me." She frowned. "At least I think he couldn't see me. I was lying on my paddleboard, low in the water. That's how I got soaked."

Behind Jack, Beth saw Lana and Paul staring at Jack with questions in their eyes. Beth swallowed her in another hug that blocked out everyone else.

"Shhh," Beth said, feeling her daughter's heart thump through the soaked sweatshirt. "We'll talk about it later."

• • •

Paul lashed his boat to a half-dead oak tree and hoisted Jack's paddleboard above his head. Lana watched as a small avalanche of silt poured off the board's edges and into his coat sleeves. Paul ignored it. They picked their way up the hillside, Paul in front, then Jack, Beth a half step below Lana to make sure she didn't stumble.

When they got to the house, Beth ushered Jack inside, urging her toward a hot shower and warm clothes.

Lana stayed outside with Paul, watching him shake out his jacket. Her nose caught a swirl of wet earth, musk, and motor oil rising off him. Was it the smell of his car? Or whatever he was protecting in that cooler?

"Well, uh, guess I better get back," Paul said.

"To your kayak?" Lana said. "Looked like you had quite a lot to unpack."

"It's just . . . equipment. Kayak Shack stuff."

Paul started half walking, half sliding down the hillside. Lana waited until he was twenty feet down the scree before she spoke again.

"Paul, you should know," she said, "I've been looking into the murder in the mud flats. And the leaseholders near there."

Paul kept moving, picking his way down to the bank.

"Anything you want to tell me, Paul? About Fruitful? Or Ricardo Cruz?"

Paul stopped in front of his motorboat. When he looked up at her, his eyes were cold.

"Lana, I run a kayak rental shop. With a bunch of teenagers. One of whom I just saved. My whole business relies on the slough being safe and open. Why the hell would I do anything to screw that up?"

CHAPTER THIRTY-FOUR

"I'M SORRY. I made a mistake." Jack twisted toward Beth from the passenger seat, willing her mother to look at her.

Beth kept driving.

"I promise I'll never do it again. I was just trying to—I want you to . . ."

Jack twisted her hair around her right fist.

"Mom. Please say something."

Beth made a slow turn into the front lot of North Monterey County High School, pulling into one of the visitor spots beside the basketball court.

"Jack. I know you made a mistake. And you know just one mistake . . ."

"Can change your life forever," Jack sighed.

Her mom gave Jack a curt nod. Then she turned to face her. Beth's hazel eyes were soft and tired, the green flecks peeking through the brown.

"You and me have it pretty good, right?"

Jack nodded.

"Why do you think that is?"

Jack wasn't sure how to respond.

"It's because we trust each other," Beth continued. "You tell me what's going on, and I respect your right to make your own choices. You can't promise me you'll never make a mistake again. You will. Probably even some big ones."

"So?"

"So what you can promise me is that you'll follow the rules. Which are changing. Starting now." Beth looked her daughter in the eye. "No more going out alone on the slough."

"Forever?" Jack's voice cracked.

"Forever's a long time, Jack. Let's just say for now. Until I say otherwise. At least until they figure out what happened to that young man."

"What about working at the Kayak Shack?"

"I need to think about it." Beth reached out and touched her shoulder. "It's not a punishment, honey. There's just a lot going on."

Jack heard the finality in her mother's voice. Her mind raced through the implications, the doors slamming shut in front of her. No morning paddles in the fog. No paycheck. Which meant no sailboat. She'd been looking for the right moment to talk to her mom about the email she'd gotten back from the guy with the used twenty-two-footer, to see if Beth would consider helping advance her the money to buy it. Now she'd probably never set foot on that boat, let alone call it hers.

Jack squeezed her eyes shut, shoving back the tears she felt forming there. "Can I still help Prima with her investigation?"

"*We* can help. But, Jack, you have to be smart. No going off alone. Period."

She swallowed. It all felt heavy and unfair. Except the *we*. The *we* was good.

"Do you want to hear what I found?" Jack asked.

"Was there more than just that man?"

"Well . . . last night, after you and Prima were in bed, I made these maps. They probably got ruined in my backpack in the water, but I think I found—"

Outside the car, the buzzer announced the end of fourth period.

Jack looked up at the school building. "I better go."

"You can tell us more about it at dinner."

Beth leaned over, still buckled in, and gave Jack half a hug. "Now go use those smarts to convince the dragon in the office to let you make up the work you missed this morning."

• • •

Beth returned home drained and ready to reacquaint herself with the pillow from which she'd been so rudely separated three hours earlier. Her mother had other plans. Lana was sitting on the porch swing, knit cap pulled down over her scalp, her body wrapped in a fleece blanket like an oversize poodle. She was holding one of Jack's early Mother's Day presents, a hedgehog carved out of a pine cone, in her lap. When Beth got out of the car, Lana spoke.

"Beth, I—"

"Can we talk about this later?" Beth could feel the weight of every step up to the porch.

Lana reached for her arm. "Beth. Sit down a minute."

Beth stood there, undecided.

"I want to apologize."

Beth plunked herself down on the swing, trapping Lana's blanket under her leg. "I'm listening."

"I never meant to put Jack in danger. You know that, right?"

The older woman seemed genuinely nervous, as if Beth's opinion might matter to her for once.

"This investigation of mine is stupid, I know. Detective Ramirez told me to back off. You told me to be careful. And then I land in the hospital and Jack gets lost up a creek with some maniac with a shovel . . ."

"Ma, Jack's fine. Everything's okay."

"No, it isn't. I knew this would happen."

"That what would happen?"

"That I'd show up here, take over your house, and screw up your life. I'm sorry."

Beth stared at her mother. Even when apologizing, Lana placed herself at the center of the universe. Then again, when was the last time Lana apologized to anyone for anything? This was a woman who had once browbeat a man she rear-ended into apologizing to her. So maybe this was progress. Beth looked at her mother's anxious mouth. The thin collarbones visible through her sweater. And that lavender pom-pom hat hiding what was left of her patchy hair.

"Is that why you never visited us?" Beth said. "You thought you'd mess up my life?"

Lana swallowed. "The day you left, I was so angry. But now . . . I had no right to tell you what to do, Beth. I kept waiting for you to come crawling back to Los Angeles so I could tell you that. So I could look out for you. Instead, you started carving out this impossible little glimmer of a life up here with Jack. And I decided you were better off without me harping on you, trying to control you."

Beth looked down at the hedgehog in her mother's lap. "You decided, huh?"

"It seemed like you were making it work."

Which was true. Once Beth got to know Flora and the other single moms at day care, they'd worked out a patchwork system of babysitting swaps and emergency handoffs, Beth gladly trading medical advice for steaming pots of black beans and tostones. But it took years to build that support network. When they first arrived, Beth had no one. She remembered resurfacing the floors on her own, bone-tired, sawdust everywhere, Jack screaming her head off in the secondhand crib.

"I must have packed up the car fifty times that first year to come back," Beth said.

"But you didn't."

"I didn't. But I needed you, Ma. Every time you sent a package of gold-plated shoes or cashmere baby blankets, I wished it was you instead."

Lana dropped her eyes to the hedgehog, not talking for a long time. "I'm sorry, Beth."

Beth used her foot to gently prompt the porch swing into motion.

Lana blinked out at the dead-end street, rewrapping the fleece blanket around her shoulders.

"You know, I'm glad you started this investigation," Beth said.

Lana looked at her curiously.

"You needed a project," Beth continued. "Something more useful than redecorating the house. And you've clearly lit a fire in Jack . . ."

"She should never have gone out this morning without telling anyone. Completely unacceptable." Lana abruptly stopped the swing with her foot and the hedgehog bounced to the ground.

Beth bent, smiling, and scooped it back up. "Sounds like something you would do."

Lana still looked uncertain.

"Ma, if it's possible Mr. Rhoads was murdered, I want to know too."

"There is something I wanted to ask you about Hal Rhoads," Lana said. "About his medical care."

Without meaning to, Beth stiffened. "The nurses at Bayshore Oaks are very good—"

Lana waved her off. "Of course you are. But listen. I found a notation in Ricardo Cruz's appointment book about a doctor Ricardo was taking Mr. Rhoads to on Wednesdays."

"Okay . . ."

"It started once a month. Then every other week. At first I assumed the appointments were just until he moved into Bayshore Oaks. But the dates kept going, almost every Wednesday, all the way until he died. So I wondered—"

"Almost every Wednesday?" Beth's forehead scrunched into a question mark. "That can't be right."

"What do you mean?"

"Mr. Rhoads had strokes. Three of them. His rehab, all his appointments, happened on-site at Bayshore Oaks. It was one of the reasons his daughter brought him to us. So she wouldn't have to cart him to occupational therapists multiple times per week."

"When he moved into Bayshore Oaks, he didn't go off premises to appointments anymore?"

"Maybe once or twice for neurological exams. But nothing regular. Nothing I knew about. And besides, if Ricardo Cruz was coming to Bayshore Oaks most Wednesdays, I would have recognized him."

"And you didn't."

Beth shook her head.

Lana considered what Beth was telling her. If Ricardo wasn't taking Hal Rhoads to doctor appointments, what was he doing?

"Do you know of any doctors who practice down here in Elkhorn?" Lana asked.

"Practice what? Kayaking?"

"I'm wondering if maybe the appointments were for Ricardo, not Hal."

"There's a shrink with an office near the marina. A dental clinic, the kind you go to if you don't have insurance. And a couple veterinarians who work with farm animals. But that's it."

Beth felt a buzz in her pocket. She pulled out her phone. "It's Martin."

Lana leaned forward eagerly. "Put it on speaker."

Beth stared at her.

"Fine. I'll give you some privacy. But ask him about his father's doctors, okay?"

Lana lifted herself from the porch swing and turned to head back into the house. As she passed, she put a hand to Beth's shoulder. Beth reached up and held it, just for a moment. Then she answered the phone.

"Did you find her?"

"Martin, hello. Yes. Thank you. She's fine. She's safe."

"Thank God." His voice slowed. "I was out all morning with Di at Dad's lawyer's office. I'm sorry I wasn't here to help. Where was she?"

"Oh, she just . . . lost track of time in the slough." Beth wasn't ready to give words to the fleeting terror of the morning.

But he must have heard a kernel of it in her voice. "It must be scary to have your child go missing. Unless you're one of those tough guys like my dad. He'd probably say it builds character."

"In that case, we're building a whole lot of character around here these days."

"What do you mean?"

Before she realized what she was saying, the whole story tumbled out. "Last week, my mom had to go to the hospital, and—"

"Did she have another collapse?"

"Sort of. She was up in Santa Cruz, hunting through papers at the land trust offices, when the building caught on fire. She had to escape through a window." Beth had to admit it sounded pretty hard-core saying it out loud.

"That's horrible! Did she break something in the fall?"

"No, it's a one-story building. She just . . ." Beth swallowed, shoving down another memory of fear. "We got lucky. I think it was more shock than anything. And I don't think anyone else got hurt."

"Do you know how the fire started?"

"I don't—I don't know. She talked with the police on Monday, but I don't think they had clear answers yet. I'm just glad she's okay. That they both are."

There was a pause, and Martin's voice dropped lower. "Are you okay, Beth?"

She considered what he was asking, and what he might be offering. Friendship. Escape. A fast car and a cold beer. It was tempting, but she didn't need any complications in her life right now. Ricardo Cruz had been dead almost three weeks, and the sheriffs still didn't have anyone in custody. Which meant Lana had the capacity to get into more trouble.

"I'm fine. We're good." Beth tried to keep her voice light. "You're still in Elkhorn?"

"For a few more days. Di and I have to review the offer I got to buy the ranch. Hopefully we can sign the papers this weekend so I can get back. Truth is, I should be in the city now. The company's at a pivot point, our burn rate's sky high, and I need to land another investor before . . . I'm sorry. You don't need to hear this."

"Sounds like you're under a lot of pressure." He hadn't mentioned his father, but Beth wondered if the grief was still pressing down on him.

"Nothing a double-malt whiskey can't cure. Di has a function she has to go to tomorrow with her husband. I'll be at the yacht club at seven P.M., toasting my father. You should join me, if you can."

"Tomorrow? Maybe—"

Beth heard a muffled crash from the back bedroom, followed by a hasty "I'm fine!" She said a quick goodbye, then hustled in to help Lana, who was wrestling with the fallen corkboard. A drink didn't sound half-bad.

CHAPTER THIRTY-FIVE

EVERYONE WAS ON THEIR BEST BEHAVIOR during dinner. They ordered Jack's favorite—clam chowder—and laid out mismatched plates and bowls, tearing open the crusty rolls to let the steam rise into their faces before dunking chunks of bread into the soup.

Jack told them about her unsuccessful campaign to retake the morning's chemistry pop quiz and the kid who stuck Cheez Whiz down his pants in the cafeteria.

"But," she added, "I did learn something interesting out on the slough this morning."

Jack and Lana both looked at Beth. Beth took her time folding her paper napkin before responding, relishing a rare moment when the power in the room was tipped in her direction. When her napkin resembled a stubby swan, she spoke. "What is it, honey?"

"Well, I mean, it's interesting to me. I don't know if it's important to the investigation or anything."

Lana and Beth waited.

"So I wanted to follow some of those creeks? On Prima's maps? I was thinking about the tides and where Ricardo's body could have come from. I realized, for him to come down a creek for a day and end up in the mud flats, it would have to be a long one. One with enough twists and turns to get stuck in low tide and get going again in the high."

Lana conjured up a rough image of one of the tidal charts, the water rising and falling every twelve hours. "I see what you mean."

Jack pulled a binder out of her backpack and extracted a printed map covered in intricate marks and topographical lines. "All the creeks I know are short. But I'd noticed one on your land trust map that went up behind the mud flats. And a couple on the Rhoads ranch headed in that same direction."

Lana leaned over. "Where'd you get this map?"

"I texted that grad student I told you about, the one studying ocean navigation. She had this whole database of contour maps of the creeks. This morning, I went out to see if any of them connect to each other."

She looked up for a moment and across the table at Beth. "I know, I know. I should have told you."

Beth stopped buttering a roll to gesture with the knife for Jack to keep talking.

"I found a linkup. It goes from all the way up here"—Jack wiped her hand and put one finger on the map—"to here." Her finger wound from the far end of the mud flats up into the fields, across the land trust property line, and through the ranch, then let out at the public fishing dock. "It runs for at least three miles. You saw me just as I was coming out."

Lana pulled the map to her. "Did you see anything unusual in the creek?"

"Like what?"

"Maybe something to indicate Ricardo had been there? A torn piece of fabric? Muddy boot prints?"

"A giant sign that said 'Man Killed Here'?" Beth suggested.

Lana shot Beth a look. "Perhaps we should discuss this in the bedroom," Lana said to Jack.

"I'll be good," Beth said.

Jack looked back and forth between her mother and grandmother. Were they teasing each other? Or was another war about to start? Was this what it was like to have two parents?

When nothing exploded, Jack continued. "Um, well, no, nothing like that. I was mostly just focused on figuring out if it went through. But then there was that man. I thought he was just some farmer or something, but he spooked me. He was doing something with a shovel for a long time. That's why I was late. I was hiding, waiting for him to leave."

"I know this morning you said you didn't recognize him," Lana said. "But was there anything about him or that spot, anything you remember?"

"It smelled bad, I remember that. Like a dead animal, maybe, or a live skunk. But I didn't see anything. There were these big reeds all around me. I was hidden really well." At least, that's what she hoped. "But here's the weird thing. He didn't go back up into the fields when he was done. He left in a kayak."

"Did you see the kayak?"

"I sort of followed it. That's how I got back out to the slough."

"Jack!"

"Mom, I was way behind him. And I ditched my life jacket. He couldn't see me. I promise."

Beth bit her lip. The crease between her eyebrows was back.

"What did the kayak look like?" Lana asked.

"It was a standard two-seater Tribe, yellow, the same kind pretty much everyone on the slough uses. The guy had a lot of stuff in it. I could barely see him because of it all. He had a big bag covering the bow and a box strapped in behind him on the stern."

"What color was the box?"

"Maybe gray? Or white? It was kind of a blur."

"Could it have been a cooler?"

"Uh . . . I guess so."

Lana tapped her spoon against her bowl of congealing chowder.

Beth eyed her mother. "Ma, what is it?"

"Paul Hanley. Before we met up with you at the motorboat, I saw him paddling into the marina in a kayak. With a huge black bag, a white cooler. And a shovel."

Lana looked back at the map. "Jack, could the man you heard have been doing that digging here?" She pointed to the small wedge of land Paul leased from Mr. Rhoads.

Jack scrunched up her face. "I can't be sure. I passed a gate, and some barbed wire fencing. I don't know how far it was from there to where I was hiding."

"And you couldn't see what he was doing?"

"Just digging, I think. Whatever it was, it sounded like hard work."

Lana tried to recall if Paul had looked fatigued when she'd first seen him. But all she could remember were flashes of her own panic, the spray off the motorboat, the painful searching until they saw Jack and could start breathing again.

Lana's thoughts were interrupted by Beth's voice. "The creek you found let out by the fishing dock?"

Jack nodded.

"There's public access there. From the slough. And a trail. Do you think it'd be possible for someone to head up into that creek from the dock?"

Now Lana and Jack were both looking at Beth.

"Only I was thinking," Beth said, "if that were true, then pretty much anyone could get up into that area."

"Maybe," Jack said. "They'd have to be pretty brave. Or stupid. I spend a lot of time on the slough, and I wouldn't just head up some random creek that I didn't have any idea where it was going." She looked down and blushed. "Not anymore, I mean."

"But someone could do it?"

"I don't know. There was a fast channel here"—Jack ran her finger across the map—"that might be hard to get through going upstream. You'd have to hit the tides right. I'd have to go out there at another time of day to be sure."

Jack looked up at the two older women.

"Not that I would, I mean. I know I can't go out on the slough alone right now. But if you wanted. I could."

There was a long silence.

"You've done quite a lot, Jack," Lana said. She picked up the map. "May I keep this?"

• • •

While Jack did her homework, Lana helped Beth clean up. Or rather, Beth did the dishes and Lana hovered nearby, holding a rag like a fashion accessory.

Jack was on the couch wearing a giant pair of headphones, facing away from them.

"Beth," Lana said.

Her daughter kept doing dishes.

Lana tried again. "Beth, I want to talk to you."

"What?"

Lana glanced over at the couch. Tinny screeches of music leaked out from under Jack's oversize headphones. There was no sign the girl could hear them. "I've been thinking. What if she got it wrong?"

Beth locked eyes with her mother. "What do you mean?"

"What if that man with the shovel did see Jack? What if he was the murderer? Or what if she saw something incriminating? Even if she doesn't know what it is yet?"

"You think it was Paul out there, right?"

Lana nodded.

"Did he have a reason to kill Ricardo Cruz?"

"I don't think so. But he's hiding something about that Fruitful business. Maybe he and Ricardo were secret partners? I think I'd have caught on if Paul was lying about knowing Ricardo. But what if . . . what if I'm wrong?"

Beth stared dumbfounded at her mother. Lana stared back, her eyes wide. Her hands twisted the dishrag into a tight rope, first one direction, then the other.

"It's not like I'm an expert at this," Lana said softly.

Both women looked over to the couch. Jack was bobbing her head to the music.

"Maybe we could just keep an extra eye on her the next few days," Beth said. "Make sure she gets to school and home okay. I already told her I wasn't sure about her going back to work this weekend."

"She won't like that," Lana said.

"I think she understood where I was coming from." Beth shook her head. "We're in this whether we want to be or not, aren't we? Ricardo. Mr. Rhoads. It's like we never had a choice."

Was that true? Lana felt like she'd plunged in headfirst, without thinking about how it might affect her girls. But Beth wasn't looking at her with anger or accusation. Beth didn't even look scared. She looked resigned. Calm.

Lana tried to emulate her daughter. She cleared her throat. "I was thinking tomorrow I could make keftedes," Lana said in a loud, confident voice. "Greek meatballs with yogurt sauce. I remember it was always your favorite."

"When I was eight," Beth said. "The last time you cooked dinner."

"Well. I feel like a thank-you meal from me is overdue."

"Martin Rhoads asked me to meet him for a drink tomorrow." Beth started stacking bowls to take to the sink. "I was wondering if you'd want me to go."

Lana looked at Beth, surprised. "Are you offering to go on a date for me?"

"Ma . . ."

Lana decided not to push it.

"That would be great," Lana said. "And I'm having lunch with Diana tomorrow after my scans. I think she's really starting to trust me. When you talk to Martin, make sure to ask him about the doctor. And the creek. And Paul."

"That's a lot to pack into a beer, Ma."

"Hmpf. I'd give it a try."

Beth smiled. She looked back over at Jack, who was still in her own world on the couch. "Perhaps you could apply your prodigious talents to find out exactly what Paul Hanley's up to."

Lana nodded. It was time to dig deeper on Mr. Fruitful. If her granddaughter was working for a murderer, she'd kill him.

CHAPTER THIRTY-SIX

THERE WAS NOTHING the residents of Bayshore Oaks enjoyed more than pointing out the deficiencies of the facility to which they had been confined. The checkers in the game room were chipped. The strawberry shortcake was served with Cool Whip and yellow cake instead of fresh whipped cream and biscuits. And they never, ever got their packages on time.

On this last issue, they might have had a point. The mail room was managed on a volunteer basis by a rotating group of residents, a mix of nearsighted bureaucrats and busybodies. After a Mother's Day fiasco of bungled deliveries, the group decided each package should be cross-checked by no fewer than three volunteers to ensure it reached the correct destination.

In this case, however, it appeared a volunteer had taken matters into her own home-manicured hands. Beth entered Gigi Montero's room for her infusion and found a manila envelope lying on the bed. It was thick, oversize. And addressed to Hal Rhoads.

"Miss Gigi?" Beth called out.

There was a low grunt from the bathroom.

"All right in there?"

"Beth! The devil is testing me." There was a shuffle, a bonk, and then Gigi threw the door open in triumph. She gave Beth a brilliant smile and waved a bottle of nail polish in the air. "But today is not his day."

The tiny woman's pink hair was perfectly curled. A black sweatsuit hugged her birdlike frame, the words "Auntie Power" looping in silver puff paint across her chest. Beth looked down at her own blue-and-beige scrubs, feeling underdressed for the occasion.

"Where did you get this?" Beth pointed to the envelope.

"Mail room," Miss Gigi said. She settled on a chair, pulled back her sleeve, and presented her arm to Beth. She gave a quick nod of satisfaction when the needle slid in clean on the first attempt. "I have Tuesday shift. And I remember you telling me about Mr. Rhoads's funeral."

"And?"

"And he has a very handsome son." Miss Gigi looked up at her from under a halo of rainbow eye shadow. She pressed two freshly painted fingernails into Beth's forearm. "You like it? Called crackle polish. I can have Cesar bring you some."

"Miss Gigi, you can't just take—" Beth pried the woman's fingers from her arm, with a bit more force than she intended. Then she shook her head. "You know what? It's fine. I'm . . . in touch with Mr. Rhoads's son. I can pass it on to him."

"In touch?"

The expectant look on Miss Gigi's face was accentuated by the rainbows on her eyelids. Beth bent down, suddenly very focused on applying medical tape over the injection site to hold the needle in place.

"We're neighbors," she finally said.

"You bring him pie?"

Beth stared at Miss Gigi. The tiny woman beamed back. "You bring him his dead father's mail, you bring fresh pie, he will look at you differently. You have a nice figure, Beth. Good heart. But you need to—"

"Miss Gigi, I'm not—"

The IV stand started rattling, shaking the infusion bag and giving Beth an escape route.

Beth reached over for her buzzing phone, glanced at the screen, and switched off the ringer. "Sorry about that."

"Maybe it is your neighbor man. You should answer."

"It's my mother."

"Then you should absolutely answer."

"You don't know my mother."

"All mothers are the same. They call, you answer. You want your daughter to ignore when you call?"

Beth started backing out of the room. "Forty-five minutes for this infusion, then I'll be back to set you free."

"God has set me free, Beth! Take the envelope. And promise me you will comb your hair before you bring it to him."

• • •

Lana hadn't really expected Beth to call her back. She had extricated herself from the MRI and PET scanners, upgraded her outfit in the cramped clinic bathroom, and was now driving south into Carmel to hunt for Diana Whitacre's precious country club.

"Is Jack okay?" Lana yelled through the car speaker. The views were incredible on 17-Mile Drive, all windswept Monterey pines and rocky coves and tourists snapping photos from their rental cars. The phone reception, on the other hand, was terrible. All that wealth and no one had figured out how to get decent cell service.

"Ma, Jack's fine. She texted me when she got to school three hours ago. What's up?"

"I was just calling to check. That everything was all right."

The words felt strange coming out of Lana's mouth. But it was true. She didn't have an agenda for calling. It felt . . . embarrassing.

"Well, thank you." Beth sounded as surprised as Lana felt. "How were your scans?"

"Laugh a minute. I'll have the results early next week."

The sound crackled. Lana was about to end the call when Beth's voice came through loud and clear. "Ma, I found something. An architectural firm mailed a package to Mr. Rhoads here."

"That's fantastic! I can swing by on my way back from lunch—"

"Ma, I don't think I can give it to you."

"Why not?"

"Mail fraud."

"Oh, *honestly*." Lana put Beth on mute to blast her horn at a red Mustang full of tourists that had stopped in the middle of the road to gawk at a pod of dolphins leaping out of the ocean.

"Ma, I can tell you're disappointed—"

Actually, Lana was feeling quite pleased with herself. The heads had popped back down into the now-moving convertible, and she could see the sign for the Peninsula Pines Club coming up on the left. She decided to take one more risk.

"Do whatever you think is right, Beth."

She hung up without issuing any suggestion of what that might be.

CHAPTER THIRTY-SEVEN

A TINKLING BELL by the waterfall at the entrance to the Peninsula Pines dining room announced Lana's arrival. The maître d' ran his eyes down from her dark bob to her tasteful skirt suit, his obsequious smile transforming into a genuine grin when he saw the Alexander McQueen boots on her feet. He guided Lana to a table that looked out over the rose garden, where Diana Whitacre was sipping an iced tea.

"I'm sorry it took me a few days to return your call," Diana said. "I've been getting my plans ready to present to my brother." Diana's makeup was understated, her hair combed back under a navy headband that matched her wool suit. Despite being zipped shut, the large leather satchel on the floor beside her bore the unmistakable smell of horse.

Lana stretched out one foot to nudge the bag farther away from her. "I've been busy myself."

"Have I heard correctly? You were in a fire?"

Lana nodded. "At the land trust. The same day I met you at the stables."

"Do they know how it started?"

This struck Lana as an odd question to ask.

"They haven't determined that yet," Lana said slowly. "But they're investigating it as arson. And I'm continuing to learn more about Ricardo Cruz."

Lana watched Diana's face for any reaction. It was as smooth as money and a discreet plastic surgeon could buy.

Finally, the blond woman spoke. "I am sure his loved ones will be grateful when his memory can be put peacefully to rest."

"Have you been in touch with them?"

Diana looked confused.

"Ricardo Cruz's family?" Lana prompted.

"Oh." Diana shook her head. "It wouldn't be appropriate. I barely knew them. And with everything that's been going on, my focus is on the ranch."

"Have your plans progressed?"

Diana reached down for the leather satchel. "Yes. As have my brother's. He's got an all-cash offer from a developer who wants to turn the ranch into a McMansionville. Daddy would have hated it. I've been moving quickly to present my case for an alternative. I was able to get some drawings made, and I've refined the business model. I made a set for you. I was hoping you might be able to offer some feedback."

Lana flipped through the stack of drawings and spreadsheets. Diana had been busy indeed. She paused on a rendering of the main building, a white pine palace with a Hal Rhoads memorial grove planted around it.

"I see you've incorporated your father into the design."

"Yes. Well." Diana blinked, her pale eyelashes catching the sunlight from outside. "I didn't expect him to die so soon."

"You were surprised by his death?"

Diana tilted her head, considering the question. "After his first stroke, I started staying over at the ranch midweek to help. I still do, to maintain the home. When Daddy and I were together those Tuesday and Wednesday nights, I'd see little things, a slip here, a misplaced tool there. But even when he was struggling, he was private about personal matters. And proud. I would have hoped he could confide in me about the extent of his condition, but . . . yes. His death was a shock."

"Did you request an autopsy?"

Diana shook her head. "Daddy was a dignified man. That wouldn't have been to his liking. And the medical director at the nursing home didn't recommend it. He said heart failure is common after multiple strokes. I suppose I was holding an earlier image of him, of a stronger, healthier man. His time had come."

Diana began to dissect her salad, exiling the croutons to the edge of the plate. She cut a single leaf of lettuce, raised it to her mouth, and took a dainty nibble, like a rabbit with a square-cut diamond ring.

"The last time we talked, you mentioned you'd said only a little to your father about this project. Is it possible he heard more than he let on? That he was supporting your project, even before he had the details?"

Diana's fork froze over her salad.

"Whatever do you mean?"

"I found the letter of intent you mentioned, at the land trust." Lana pulled from her purse a printed photograph of the LOI and placed it on the table facing Diana. She held one finger to it, pinning it between them. Then she kept talking. "I spoke with an expert about it. This letter is suggestive, but it isn't binding. Your father might have changed his mind. Look at this."

Lana put the handwritten note on the table next to the legal document, the one addressed to Victor about a project moving forward without the land trust. She watched Diana's eyes shift back and forth across the block printing, taking it in.

"Do you think this note is from your father?" Lana asked. "Is it possible he abandoned his conservation plans to support you instead?"

Diana leaned closer to the scrap of paper, reading aloud the words scrawled there. "'Someone close to my heart has approached me with a bold vision for a project too big to live at the land trust.'"

Lana could see the hunger in her eyes.

Then Diana sat up again, very straight. "I wish I could say yes. But it's not Daddy's handwriting. That kind of flowery language, the idea that he would describe me as someone close to his heart . . . that wasn't him."

"Could it be Ricardo Cruz?"

Diana looked at Lana sharply. "How would I know what his writing looks like?"

"My mistake." Lana folded the papers carefully and slid them back into her purse. "I'm just trying to understand what you might be up against in pursuing your wellness ranch. What we might be up against." Lana took a sip of water. "As I understand it, five years ago, your father promised to donate the development rights to the land trust via a conservation easement. But in the last six months, when Victor assigned Ricardo Cruz to finalize the deal, something changed. Your father and Ricardo were spending a lot of time together. If your father had new intentions for the ranch—"

"I'm not asking you to determine my father's intentions. I'm asking you to help me carry on his legacy." Diana threw back her shoulders and started cutting another small, fussy bite of lettuce. "Look, I know Victor Morales hired the boy and sent him out to the ranch to talk to Daddy about that easement. But clearly nothing came of it."

Or perhaps something different came of it, something Diana didn't know about or didn't want to admit. "Did you ever see him with your father?"

"Ricardo? Only once." Diana looked out the window with a hopeful expression, as if the young man might be outside tending the garden. "Daddy would talk about him sometimes, at the nursing home. It brought him back to old times. I can just imagine them mucking out the stalls together, checking on the swallow boxes."

"What do you mean, old times?"

"Surely you know the story by now," Diana said.

Lana lifted her eyebrows in invitation.

"I was twenty-two when my mother died," Diana said. "There was a terrible fire in the old barn. An accident, of course. My mother was trapped. Alejandro Cruz, Ricardo's father, died as well. But Ricardo's mother, Sofia, she was pregnant at the time—she made it out. Alejandro had just moved her up to the ranch with him from Fresno. When

Ricardo was born, everyone called him the miracle baby. Daddy said he was the only good thing to come out of the fire."

"Did you agree?"

Diana's eyes shot to the window again. "I was overseas when Ricardo was born. But when my fiancé . . . when I came home . . . Ricardo was there. He and Sofia lived in the house. With Daddy and Martin."

"That must have been a surprise," Lana ventured.

"Daddy and Sofia weren't"—Diana laced her fingers together—"but of course people talked. It wasn't right having her in my mother's house. Complicated. But Ricardo was just a toddler, and he had a sweet, rascally way about him. It took a year after Martin left for college for me to convince Daddy they needed to go. Too many whispers. Too many ghosts. Ricardo would have been four when he and his mother moved away. I didn't see him again until that one time last year at the ranch. All grown up, like someone else entirely. A beautiful man."

Lana couldn't decide how much of Diana's story was true. She could sense there were holes. She just didn't know which ones were worth poking.

"When we first met, you gave me the impression you hardly knew Ricardo."

"Surely you're a woman who appreciates the value of keeping some things to yourself."

Lana resisted the urge to adjust her wig.

"And you were meeting with Victor," Diana continued. "I don't believe he knows about Ricardo's history with my family. I'd prefer to keep it that way."

Lana considered what Diana was saying. Was she so uncomfortable about the past rumors about her father and Ricardo's mother that she didn't want them to come to light again? Or was there something else, something more recent, that she was trying to hide?

Lana decided to take a gamble. "I don't believe Ricardo was working for Victor when he died."

"How's that?"

"What if I told you Ricardo and your father had their own plans for the ranch's future? A project that didn't involve the land trust. Or you and your brother."

"I'd tell you you were wrong. Which you are." If Diana's jaw were clenched any tighter, it could double as a vise.

"How can you be so sure?"

"Because he told me."

"Your father told you, or Ricardo told you?"

"I . . ." Diana impaled a piece of lettuce with her fork. "As I said. I've barely seen Ricardo in decades."

"But he mattered to you."

"He mattered to my father," Diana snapped. She chewed in silence, her lips pressed tightly together.

Lana tried a different approach. "Let's suppose for a moment the note I showed you was from Ricardo. That he was leaving the land trust to do something different. Something big. Maybe with your father, or maybe with someone else. How do you think Victor Morales would react if he found out Ricardo was working on a project behind his back?"

"Victor?" Diana looked relieved at the change in subject. Her face resettled into a buffed, placid surface. "Are you asking if I think he is capable of murder?"

It wasn't what Lana had asked, but it was interesting that Diana interpreted it that way.

Diana rotated her fork slowly, hovering above her salad. "I don't know. Victor is a slippery man. He plays in the sandbox of the fortunate, and he thinks he deserves their toys. But he is a man of words. Not one of action."

"What do you think Victor would do with his words if he thought Ricardo betrayed him?"

"He would find a way to play it to his advantage. As would anyone, I imagine."

"A situation you've found yourself in?" Lana asked.

There was a long pause.

"I have, at times, been disappointed by men," Diana said carefully. "But betrayed? The men I involve myself with are far too intelligent to make that mistake."

CHAPTER THIRTY-EIGHT

IT WAS CAREER DAY at North Monterey County High, which meant all the students got herded into the gym after sixth period to begin thinking about their bright futures. As far as Jack could tell from the colorful banners hanging over the booths, there were three options: Silicon Valley if you wanted to get rich; agriculture if you wanted to stay home; or the military if you wanted to get out of town. Jack wanted adventure, but she didn't think it came with a uniform or a gun. She floated around the tables, trying to avoid eye contact with the overcaffeinated recruiters. She spent a few minutes at the Monterey Bay Aquarium's booth, where she picked up a free pen and a pamphlet about their global marine research. But the chipper lady behind the table didn't know anything about the scientists tracking endangered bluefin tuna across the Pacific. She was pushing the glorious opportunity to stand in front of a tank and teach tourists about otters. Jack already had a better gig doing that.

"Jack!"

At the end of the row, at a scratched table with no banner and a few janky xeroxed flyers, Detective Ramirez was calling her name. The detective had on an emerald-green blazer and was standing next to a patrolman so young he practically could be a student.

"Detective Ramirez? You're working the career fair?"

Ramirez pursed her lips at the wobbly folding table. "I was voluntold. Apparently a detective has to put in an appearance."

Then she looked at Jack. "But I am glad to see you. I could use your help with something."

"What kind of something?"

"It's at the marina," Ramirez said. "I'd prefer to tell you about it on-site. How much longer do you have to be here?"

Jack looked at her classmates shuffling around the tables spread throughout the gym. It was last period. No one would miss her.

"I could go now," she said. She felt a twinge of guilt about her promise not to do any investigating on her own. "Should I ask my grandma to meet us there?"

"That's your call."

At this time of day, Lana would probably be taking a nap. And Jack figured a short field trip to the marina with a cop didn't count. "I'm good. I can meet you there in twenty minutes."

"You want to ride with me?"

Jack's eyes flicked to the gun-shaped bulge on the detective's hip. "I'll bike."

JACK ARRIVED TO A sea of cop cars parked at wrong angles around the marina parking lot. A young officer waved her through, and she rolled up to where Ramirez was leaning against a Buick.

"Now can you tell me what's going on?" Jack asked.

"We're taking a thorough look at your boss's operation."

"Paul? Is he here?"

"Mr. Hanley has vanished. But it doesn't matter. We have a search warrant."

They walked over to the fence behind the Kayak Shack and Jack locked up her bike.

"You know this Kayak Shack pretty well, right?" Ramirez asked. "You'd know if something was missing or out of order?"

"Um . . . I guess so? Things can get messy in the back. Still, I probably know it better than anyone."

Ramirez nodded. "I knew you were observant. Listen, when we're inside"—the detective put a hand on Jack's forearm—"just keep calm and tell the truth. That's all I'm asking you to do."

"Is your partner in there?"

Ramirez eyed the girl closely. "He is. But he won't bother you. I promise."

Jack gulped a swallow of air. "Okay. I'm ready."

AS JACK EXPECTED, the back room was a disaster. Or rather, half a disaster. Two officers wearing gloves were picking through a jumble of life jackets and paddles, excavating one layer at a time, while a third photographed each item before stacking it neatly on the other side of the room.

Detective Nicoletti was overseeing the operation from a cleaned-out corner, his linebacker body squeezed into a brown, nubbly suit. He gave a tight nod to Ramirez and Jack, as if their presence in the overstuffed room was just as reasonable as the sixty-four-pack of vegan energy drinks they'd just unearthed.

"Jacqueline runs inventory for Mr. Hanley," Ramirez said. "Anything you'd like her eyes on?"

Nicoletti scanned the room. "I assume this level of disarray is typical?"

Jack grimaced. "I've tried to tell them life would be easier for all of us if we kept it neat. But the guys don't listen. At the end of a long day, it's easier to just throw stuff in here and not think. And I just fix it at the end of the month anyway, so—"

"Anything here you don't recognize?"

Jack scanned the room. First aid kits. Old time cards. A trash bag of empty chip bags and granola bar wrappers, the kind that wreaked havoc on sea turtles. The grungy cot Paul slept on sometimes. A Styrofoam cooler. A stack of boating catalogs, shiny Hobie Cats spraying water off the covers.

Nothing was in place, but everything fit. Except one item, leaned against a wall behind a mountain of life vests.

"That." Jack pointed, and the young officers scrambled to pull the life jackets away. "No one keeps bikes in here. Store policy."

Once unearthed, the bicycle was a nice specimen. It was a road bike, green, with drop handlebars, skinny tires, and the kind of gears you had to lean over the frame to shift. There were cages on the pedals and a black storage bag snapped to the left side of the back wheel. The tires were full of air, and the chain didn't grind when the officer wheeled it into the middle of the room.

"Could it belong to Mr. Hanley?" Nicoletti asked.

"No. He doesn't trust bicycles. Something about his disks. But I think"—Jack walked toward the bike, until the physical bulk of an officer stopped her from proceeding further—"I've seen it before."

She turned back to the detectives. "That Saturday, February fourth. The day before we found Ricardo Cruz."

"You sure?" Nicoletti looked skeptical.

"I biked here early that morning. It was propped up against the fence. I remember thinking it was weird that someone left their nice bike there without a lock or anything."

"What time did you get here that Saturday?"

"Eight. You can check my time card."

"Did you say anything about the bike to anyone?"

"No, I . . . I just assumed it belonged to Travis or maybe someone visiting Paul."

"Paul have a lot of visitors?"

Jack shook her head. "No, I mean, I don't know. I try not to get involved with all the . . ." Jack resettled her focus on Ramirez's warm eyes. "I'm just here for the job."

The two detectives shared a look. Ramirez spoke. "Just a couple more questions, Jack. About the bike. Are you sure the first day you saw it was Saturday? Not Friday?"

"I don't work Fridays. If it was here then, I didn't see it. But it would be seriously weird for a decent bike not to get stolen if it was outside for more than a few hours."

"Can you think of a reason it would end up back here?"

Jack considered the question. It didn't make sense.

"Maybe Paul knew who it belonged to and was holding it for them?" She shook her head. "But it's been almost three weeks. Whoever it was would probably want to get it back right away."

"What makes you say that?"

"Most bikes that get abandoned are total trash. We get them in the marina every once in a while. Flat tires, rusted-over chains, sometimes the seat is missing. This bike isn't like that. Even the pannier—that storage bag. It looks brand-new."

"That's good, Jack. Thanks." Ramirez smiled at her. "Do you have any idea where Paul might be now?"

The girl shook her head. "You think he was involved?"

Nicoletti was still looking at the green bike. "Keep your eye on the local news. We'll inform the public when I get it all buttoned up."

"When *we* get it buttoned up," Ramirez said. "Jack, let's go."

JACK WAITED UNTIL THEY GOT BACK to the fence before she spoke up.

"Your partner's a jerk," she said.

Ramirez said nothing. The detective scanned the chain-link fence, as if there was some secret buried there. But it looked the same as always to Jack.

"You know, there is one place Paul could be." Jack leaned way down over her bike lock and dialed in the combination slowly, one digit at a time. "He leases some land on the north bank of the slough. It's part of the Rhoads ranch, technically."

"What does he use it for?" Ramirez kept her eyes on the fence, her voice low.

"I'm not sure. It's called Fruitful. My grandma—she's the one who discovered it. We think it's close to where Ricardo Cruz went into the water. Maybe. We're still working on it."

"That woman. She does not give up."

Jack could have sworn she heard a hint of admiration in the detective's exasperated voice. She pulled on her helmet. "Well, um, good luck."

She was surprised to find the detective's hand on her shoulder, stopping her from leaving.

"Jack, this isn't a game. If you have information to share, or if you ever need help"—Ramirez fished a business card and a pen out of her pocket, scrawling as she spoke—"here's my cell phone number. Call me anytime. Really."

CHAPTER THIRTY-NINE

WHEN JACK GOT HOME from the marina, she found her grandma at the table, talking on the landline. It was Lana's work voice, but sweeter, as if she'd dipped her vocal cords in honey. And as far as Jack could tell, she was lying her butt off.

"Yes, it is a tragedy. But we hope your wonderful project might live on. In tribute to them."

There was a brief pause.

"More people are involved now with the future of the estate. If you could please send a digital set through . . ."

Lana winked at Jack.

"Now? That's wonderful." Lana spelled out her email address and hung up the phone.

"Who was that?"

"The architectural firm that did the drawings for the Verdadera Libertad project, the ones Hal and Ricardo were planning to review the Friday Ricardo was killed. Apparently no one told them their clients are both dead. They were more than happy to help. And now we'll get to see what all the fuss was about."

"How did you figure out which architect it was?"

"Your mother, of all people. She sent the name to me earlier today, from the return address on a package sent to Mr. Rhoads."

"Did Mom know you were going to lie to them?"

Lana waved it off. "She helped us. Let's focus on that."

• • •

Within minutes, Lana was pulling up the drawings on her laptop. She half expected to see Diana's wellness ranch, or another version of it, women and horses communing on the rolling hills above the slough. But this project was another animal entirely.

Lana zoomed in on the first document, which listed disclosures and notes about the Verdadera Libertad project in a microscopic font. The two men were listed: Hal as the client, Ricardo as project manager. Lana didn't recognize any other names on the lists of contractors. No Diana. No Martin. No Victor.

She scrolled through watercolor sketches of commercial kitchens, a cold storage facility, and a retail operations center, surrounded by a mosaic of five-acre square plots of farmland.

"They're calling it an indigenous farm incubator," Lana said. "Offering below-market leases to women and disadvantaged entrepreneurs."

"Below market?" Jack asked.

Lana nodded. "It means they'll charge less than what a farmer would ordinarily pay."

"Verdadera Libertad," Jack said. She picked up a drawing of two dark-skinned women stripping nopales of their thorns at a stainless-steel counter. "Like, liberating who can have a farm. That's cool."

"Hal and Ricardo certainly thought so," Lana murmured. She scanned the drawings, recalling Lady Di's opulent, exclusive wellness ranch. The two projects couldn't have been more different.

"Do you think someone killed them to stop this project?" Jack asked.

"It's possible," Lana said. "They all want the land, that's for sure. Victor wants it for conservation. Diana wants to build a spa. And Martin wants the money."

"What about Paul?"

"He's the odd man out. Paul doesn't have a claim on the ranch like the others. There's that scrap of land he's leasing. But it can't be worth much. Unless he has a secret out there he's protecting."

"Could it be something else?" Jack said.

"What do you mean?" Lana said.

"It just seems weird that Ricardo got killed first. I mean, if Diana wanted control of the ranch, she could kill her brother and her father and she'd have it. For Martin, it would be his sister and his father. And for Victor, maybe all three Rhoadses. Or just the kids, I don't know. There's got to be a way Ricardo is central to all of this. But I don't see how."

Lana looked up from the drawings, puzzled. "You're right, Jack. Ricardo's death started this whole thing. And we still don't even know where he died."

"Oh!" Jack checked the time on her phone. "I have an idea about that. Can we go for a quick drive? With your binoculars?"

WHEN THEY GOT TO KIRBY PARK, the Lexus bumped up over the train tracks, past the graffitied retaining walls and around the shattered beer bottles. Lana followed Jack out of the car, watching her step. She didn't want to lose another good pair of heels to broken glass.

After sidestepping rusted beer cans and a dead snake, they walked onto the boardwalk flanking the south bank of the slough. Giant fronds of feather grass slapped their legs in the swirling wind, and mud and algae creeped up the outer edges of the wobbly, wood-slatted path.

They followed the boardwalk out to the water, and Jack raised the binoculars. They stood there for ten minutes. Twenty. The wind shot through Lana's jacket, and she longed for her robe and her bed. "I appreciate the nature tour, Jack, but it's getting late, and—"

"Look!" Jack handed the binoculars to Lana and pointed across the slough, toward the mass of mud and otters on the other side. "Left of the big rock."

Lana squinted through the lenses and adjusted the focus. She could see the outline of something boxy, bright red.

"Is that . . ."

"My life jacket." Jack sounded triumphant. She looked at her phone to confirm. "Right where those tourists found Ricardo. Exactly thirty-two hours after I dropped it in the creek where the kayak guy was."

"I thought you did that to stay hidden."

"It was a twofer." Jack shrugged. "It's not conclusive, I mean, I didn't weigh it down, and there could be other spots that would let out to the mud flats in the same way. But still."

"Nice work, Jack." Lana kept her eyes sealed to the binoculars. "Now let's get back in the car before my cheeks freeze off."

THEY SAT IN FRONT, watching the sun descend toward the water, waiting for Lana's seat warmers to kick in. Jack took out her phone and started dialing.

"Who are you calling?"

"Detective Ramirez. She should hear about this."

"Jack, that sheriff's phone tree is where good information goes to die."

"She gave me her cell number today. Said I should call anytime. Oh, shh—Hi, Detective Ramirez? It's Jack Rubicon . . . Yeah . . . Good. Thanks. Listen, I'm out here at Kirby Park with my grandma? Remember how I told you we were . . ."

Lana watched her granddaughter in fascination.

". . . yeah, well, I'm pretty sure the body was dropped at or near that land I told you about that my boss leases. On the Rhoads ranch. Not the land trust . . . What? . . . You should talk to my grandma about that. Hold on."

Jack handed the phone to Lana.

"Hello?" Lana was still getting over the surprise of the detective taking Jack's call.

"What can you tell me about this ranch?" Ramirez's voice sounded serious, focused. Lana tried to match it.

"Hal Rhoads was the longtime owner. In his eighties. He was working with Ricardo Cruz on a project, a vision for the future of his ranch as a nonprofit farming incubator. Ricardo was supposed to visit Hal at his nursing home in Carmel the Friday he died, to bring him the first renderings of their project. I'm not sure if he made it. Have you determined Ricardo's exact time of death?"

Ramirez ignored Lana's question. "How do you know Mr. Cruz was visiting Mr. Rhoads that day?"

Lana hesitated. She wasn't yet ready to tell the detective she had a corkboard full of notes and emails from the land trust.

"My . . . daughter told me," Lana said. "Mr. Rhoads was her patient. He was looking forward to seeing Ricardo." Shit. Now she was lying to a cop.

"Surely Mr. Rhoads would know if Mr. Cruz visited him?"

"Well, yes. But he died, just three days after Ricardo. I actually think it might be connected. That they were both killed because of their shared project."

"There were no other murders that weekend in Monterey County." Ramirez's voice had shifted from curious to brusque, her interest flatlining.

"It's a theory I've been working on," Lana said quickly. "I didn't want to waste your time until I had something concrete, but there's a lot of evidence and—"

"Would your daughter know if Mr. Cruz visited the nursing facility that Friday?"

Lana sighed. This was as far as she was going to get today.

"Of course," Lana said. "I'll ask her. Would that be helpful?"

"Verified information about Mr. Cruz's movements is helpful, Ms. Rubicon. Other theories, well, why don't you just keep those to yourself."

CHAPTER FORTY

AS BETH DROVE AWAY from Bayshore Oaks, her eyes kept sliding to the manila envelope protruding from her messenger bag on the passenger seat. She knew she should bring it to the Rhoads family. She could hand it off to Martin at the yacht club tonight. Easy.

But there was another option too. She could bring the envelope home to Lana first, just for a peek. It would be a prize, an olive branch. A gift to the investigation, which, she had to admit, was getting more comprehensive by the day. It would also be illegal, or at least unethical. Mr. Rhoads had been her patient, and she had responsibilities to him, even in death.

She drove north and west, weighing her options. It was past seven, and the sun had already fallen below the horizon line of the ocean. Ahead of her, the safety lights on the decommissioned power plant outlined two ghostly smokestacks, towering over the water and the artichoke fields. As she got closer to the slough, an enormous flock of seagulls, hundreds of them, rose from the marsh in a dizzying swirl of white against the darkening sky.

She looked one more time at the envelope and made her decision, swinging her wheel to the left to go across the bridge.

The marina was quiet. No boats being washed, no fishermen coming in late. The fluorescent lamps in the parking lot were shot through with salt, casting weak pools of light on the handful of cars outside the yacht club. One lonely cop car idled outside the Kayak Shack. Beth shrugged on her jacket, grabbed her messenger bag, and headed to the club.

From the minute she stepped into the yacht club, she wondered if she'd made a mistake. The dining room was as empty as the lot and twice as gloomy. Three fishermen on their stools were arguing about the Warriors, and in the corner, a sour-faced woman was drinking the harbormaster under the table. Beth scanned the dark-wood tables and spotted Martin at a velvety booth, alone. There was a glass of amber-colored liquid in front of him. From the overlapping, wet halos on the table, it looked like it wasn't his first drink.

She was debating whether to turn and leave when he saw her.

"Beth!" he called, overloud. His smile was broad. He looked younger than she'd seen him in the past, looser. As if the weight of the world had temporarily been relocated to someone else's shoulders. "I'm glad you came."

She ducked under the naval ship bell hanging above the booth and lowered herself onto the bench across from him. He smiled, and she got a whiff of pine needles and granite, laced with scotch.

Scotty walked over, a dish towel in his hand, thick eyebrows raised high above his weathered face.

"Can I have a Corona, please?" Beth asked.

"And another one of these," Martin added.

"You got it, boss."

After Scotty brought their drinks, Martin raised his glass.

"I've learned a lot about my father, these past few days," he said. "The work he did, the things he held on to. But there's still so much I'll never know."

Beth raised her beer bottle, unsure how to pick up his thread. "That's the beauty of the people we love," she finally said. "No matter how well we know them, there's always more to discover."

It wasn't the most graceful toast, but then again, Martin didn't seem sober enough to notice. They clinked, then sat there, sipping in companionable silence. The jukebox flipped from Sammy Davis to the Smiths, and Martin bobbed his head to the music, drumming along with his fingers on the table.

"I wouldn't have pegged you for a New Wave fan," Beth said.

"My mom." He pulled his hands back from the table and smiled again. "She'd sing along to the radio while she was cooking. When I was a kid. She loved those mopey British guys."

"You were close."

"You only get one mother, right?" Martin ran his hand through his hair. "My dad passing, it makes me think of her too. The ranch is full of ghosts these days."

"How's your sister handling it?"

"General Di? Driving me up the wall. I keep telling her she can go home, but she insists on staying at the ranch with me, getting drunk on expensive wine and making wounded noises about every item I put in the pile to give away."

"She must really miss your dad."

"I think she's been using the ranch to get away from her husband. From what I hear, Frank's got girls all over town. I pitched him on an investment once, for my last company, but he said start-ups were too risky for his bank to get involved with. Please. The guy's banging cocktail waitresses and I'm the one taking a risk? No wonder Di was always riding horses in Elkhorn with Dad."

While Beth had never cared for Lady Di, she felt a prickle of discomfort at Martin's drunken revelations. She tried to steer the conversation in a less embarrassing direction. "Were they close?"

Martin sipped his whiskey. "I guess so? They're both horse fanatics. But to be honest, I don't know much about their relationship. Di and I haven't spent a lot of time together as adults. We split up the days down here to help Dad, and it felt like she was always leaving right before I came."

"Weird how tragedy can bring family together. Not always in the ways you want."

"Tragedy." Martin gave her a lopsided smile. "I believe my sister assigned that moniker to an antique wagon wheel this morning."

"My mother would probably agree with her."

"How's she doing? Still recovering from the fire?"

"I'm not sure I'd say that. She's been obsessing over a bunch of old maps and documents she found at the land trust. It's kind of nice to see her working on it." Beth was surprised to hear herself say it out loud. But it was true.

"Has she found the smoking gun yet?"

"I don't think so. When I left this morning, she was on the phone berating someone at the Farm Bureau about a fruit company's business permit. But"—Beth reached into her bag—"I did find something that belongs to you."

Beth scooted around to join Martin on his bench and handed him the manila envelope from the San Francisco architect.

"What's this?" Martin asked.

"I don't know," Beth said. She took a sip of her beer, avoiding his glassy eyes. "It was stuck in the mail room at Bayshore Oaks. For your dad."

Martin tore open the package. For a minute, he was engrossed, leafing through the papers. She snuck some glances, careful not to be obvious. Then Martin swept them back into the envelope.

"Dad never stopped dreaming," he said. "Every couple years, he'd do something like this." Martin patted the envelope on the table. "Come up with a whole new vision, new plans. My mother said his fantasies would be the death of her."

Beth raised her Corona again. "To your father's dreams," she said.

Martin downed the rest of his whiskey and turned to the window, staring into the darkness of the marina.

"What about your dreams?" Beth asked.

"I'm sorry?"

"What are you going to do with the money from the sale?"

He frowned. "I'm not sure there's going to be a sale. Di's dragging her feet. I got us a solid offer, all cash, from a development group that wants to build a bunch of houses there. Could be good for the community, and it could really help my company get over this cash-flow hump. But the offer expires on Monday, and Di's been refusing to discuss it. She's been making noise about family legacies, some dream she has about building a horse spa. We'll probably be holed up at the ranch all weekend battling it out."

When he signaled to Scotty for yet another whiskey, Beth decided to make her exit.

Then the music changed, and Martin's eyes lit up.

"Another one of Mom's favorites," he said.

Beth looked around. Scotty had dimmed the dining room, and Billy Idol was crooning about eyes without a face. She'd always thought the song was kind of creepy, but it clearly had sentimental value for Martin. He was wobbling to his feet, a wistful, lopsided smile on his face.

"What do you think it's about?" she asked.

"Who cares?" Martin said. "Let's dance."

Martin extended a hand to Beth. She smiled but didn't move. Then again, he looked kind of cute with his hand outstretched, his white button-down glowing in the dusky light. Beth let him pull her out into the no-man's-land between the bar and the tables. She swayed back and forth an arm's length from Martin, wary of who might be watching, maybe laughing, from the bar. But Scotty was in the back doing God knows what, and the regulars were all staring deep in their shot glasses like the meaning of life might be drowning down there. She closed her eyes and let the music take her away.

CHAPTER FORTY-ONE

WHEN BETH GOT HOME AT TEN, humming "White Wedding" under her breath, she found her mother and daughter on the sofa in the living room. Lana's head was tipped back, mouth open, sending snores up to the ceiling. Jack was blinking at her phone. There was an empty pill counter and an open laptop on the driftwood side table.

Beth switched off the TV and put her hand on Jack's shoulder.

"Hi, honey," Beth said.

Lana jolted awake at the sound. For a moment her eyes flashed wide, hands grasping the couch cushions. She looked fragile and afraid. Then her eyes focused on her daughter, and her body relaxed.

"Beth." Lana shook away a yawn. "You went to see Martin? Did you give him the envelope?"

"Yeah." Beth decided it wouldn't hurt to tell her mother what she'd seen. "It was a set of plans for some kind of compound, like—"

"Like this?" Lana swung the laptop onto her lap.

"How in the world did you . . . ?" Beth shook her head. "Yes, Ma. Exactly like that. But he didn't seem to think they were a big deal."

"He already knew about the project?" Lana sounded surprised.

"I don't think so." Beth rewound the evening in her head, trying to recall exactly what Martin had said about the plans. All she could remember was his distracted stare out the window, searching the shadows for the parents he'd lost.

"Lady Di acted shocked when I told her about it," Lana said. "I think Hal was keeping the project from both of them."

"I always thought of Mr. Rhoads as a straight arrow," Beth said. "But it sounds like he didn't tell his kids what he was planning, or even how sick he was. Maybe he was hiding other things as well."

"Or he was trying to find the right way to tell them," Lana said. "Maybe he was scared of how it might change their relationship."

Beth looked quizzically at her mother. She wondered if Lana was still talking about the Rhoadses.

"Diana and Martin could be lying," Jack said. "If they killed Ricardo to stop the project, they'd have to know about it."

"I don't think the two of them are close," Beth said. "Martin was talking about Di like he resented her, or pitied her maybe."

"Pitied?" Lana asked.

"I guess her husband cheats on her," Beth said.

"Hm. I'm not surprised. Most men find strong women exhausting—especially when they're married to them."

Again Beth wondered who Lana was talking about. She yawned. "Is there a reason this chat couldn't wait until the morning?"

Lana and Jack looked at each other.

"I think that Verdadera Libertad project is the key to all of this," Lana said. "When Hal and Ricardo died, that project died too. Which would benefit Martin, if he wants to sell the ranch."

"But Martin was in San Francisco when Ricardo was killed. And Diana wants the ranch too, right?"

"With a passion. It might've been her, Beth. I think she's hiding something about Ricardo. But Martin could have been involved in some other way. And you were alone with him."

Beth waved both of them off the couch so she could unlatch the sofa bed. "You don't have to worry about me. I can take care of myself."

"The Rubicon family motto," Lana said. She stepped back and helped pull out the mattress. "We didn't want to meddle, Beth. We just want you to know . . . we care."

Jack got her blanket and fell into the pull-out. Once Jack had nestled in, Beth joined Lana at the door to the back bedroom.

"Do you think it's possible Martin was pretending he hadn't seen those plans before tonight?" Lana whispered.

"Ma, I'm not a mind reader. And the man's a mess. He practically drank his weight in whiskey tonight. He's under pressure at work, and from his sister. Not to mention his grief." Beth looked at her daughter, already conked out on the sofa bed. "It must be hard, to lose a parent."

Lana raised an eyebrow. "Even one who takes over your house and drives you crazy?"

"You're getting stronger every day, Ma. You'll be back running rings around those Beverly Hills bimbos before you know it."

"But what if I . . ." Lana shifted her weight, reaching out to steady herself against the doorframe.

"Yeah?"

Lana looked at her daughter. She squeezed her fingers into the doorjamb. She and Beth had never been close enough to read between each other's lines. The question was pounding inside her head. But she couldn't ask it out loud. Not yet.

"We're close to the killer," Lana said instead. "It has something to do with those plans, that project. I can feel it."

"Maybe it's time to talk to the sheriff, then. Keep everyone safe."

"I will. Once I know what it all means. One way or another, everything will be over soon." She stepped through the dark doorway. "I love you, Beth."

"I love you too," Beth said. But the door to the bedroom was already closed.

CHAPTER FORTY-TWO

LANA ROLLED INTO A VISITOR'S SPOT at Bayshore Oaks the next day at eleven, just as the sun was breaking through the coastal fog. She was finally getting her energy back. Either that, or she'd just hit the time of the month when the chemo took a break from ramming her into a wall on repeat. She'd know more when she got the results from yesterday's MRI and PET scans.

Before leaving the car, Lana straightened her suit. She touched up her lipstick and the heavy concealer she used to cover the fading bruises from the fire. There was no way she'd let anyone clock her for a potential resident of Bayshore Oaks.

Lana clicked her way down the antiseptic hallway to the nursing station, where Beth was listening to a tiny, animated woman with pink hair and a turquoise strapless evening gown. The older woman appeared to be berating her daughter, and Beth was using the Formica counter as a shield.

"Beth, I swear to you, Dr. Ramcharan says I have the heart of a seventeen-year-old! Not joking!"

"You sure he didn't say 'seventy'?" Beth asked.

"No!" Miss Gigi said. "SevenTEEN. It is the candles my Angela lights at Our Lady of Virtues for me every week."

"I am happy for you. But you still need to take your lunchtime pills."

"Why do they make the pills so huge? Why can't they make them easy to swallow, like Tic Tacs?"

"I know it's a pain, but . . ."

"My back is a pain. Left hip is a pain. Giant pills are just stupid."

Lana found herself agreeing with the wrinkled mermaid on this one. She'd often wondered if there was some kind of business opportunity in manufacturing miniature, coated cancer pills. Even taking a handful of small ones would be better than some of the whoppers she choked down every day. Lana stepped up to the counter, careful to stay out of range of the sparkly woman's long press-on nails.

Beth looked up. "Ma?"

"I brought you lunch." Lana put the brown paper bag on the counter, the Moon Valley Café logo stamped on its side.

"I'm sorry, but I don't have coverage today to eat with you—"

"Of course. You're busy. I just wanted to bring you something."

Beth stared dumbfounded at the bag with its twisted hemp handles. Her mother had never brought her lunch. Ever. Beth had started making her own sandwiches in the first grade, graduating from peanut butter and jelly to turkey, lettuce, and tomato when she reached middle school. She kept granola bars in her locker, well aware no one was bringing her a replacement if she forgot her lunch at home.

Miss Gigi used one long fingernail to inspect the bag's contents.

"Moon Valley. Very nice." She nodded. "You get the triple tri-tip sandwich? The best."

Lana looked at Beth. "Are you going to introduce me to your . . . friend?"

"Ma, this is Miss Gigi Montero. Miss Gigi, this is my mother. Lana."

The mermaid beamed at Lana. "Your mother? Ha! More like a sister. Why have I never met you before?"

Lana smiled back. "I live in Los Angeles."

"Very nice. Good market for 7-Elevens, always busy, even three, four A.M."

"Miss Gigi owns convenience stores," Beth said.

Lana's smile turned from vague to appraising. "Tough business," Lana said.

"Not tough. I meet the best people. Sometimes when they are at their worst," Miss Gigi said. "Then I hire them." She turned to Beth. "You know, Cesar has a new store manager in Seaside. Very nice man. Thirty-five. No children. Neck tattoo almost completely removed. I tell Cesar, when the tattoo is one hundred percent gone, he should bring him here. Introduce you."

Beth turned red. "You don't have to fix me up."

"Then who will? Your mother?" Miss Gigi turned to look at Lana. "You tell her. She should not be alone."

Both older women looked at her now. Beth found herself half-worried, half-curious what her mother might say.

"Beth . . . can make her own decisions about men," Lana finally said.

"Like she makes her own decision not to brush her hair?"

"That's a lost cause."

Beth had had enough. "I think I'm fully qualified to manage my dating life. *And* my hair. I'm sorry to disappoint you, Miss Gigi, but I don't think marriage is in the cards for me."

"Marriage? I don't care about you getting married."

Beth looked at the older woman in disbelief. "Miss Gigi," she said, "every time I see you, you are telling me about another man. And how I should put on eye shadow before I meet him."

"Eye shadow is God's highlighter," Miss Gigi said. "But God doesn't want you to get married."

"God doesn't want me to get married?"

Miss Gigi nodded. "God wants you to be happy. How's a husband going to help with that?"

LANA WATCHED THE MERMAID disappear around the corner, her Hello Kitty slippers shuffling along the linoleum floor.

"I like her."

"Uh-huh. Imagine being trapped in a room with her for a forty-five-minute infusion every other day." Beth opened the brown paper bag. Lana had brought a small feast—two sandwiches, two salads, a cup of soup, a kaiser roll, three cookies, and a smoothie that smelled of coconut and kale. Beth laid all the items out on the counter, covering the surface with food.

"I didn't know what you'd like," Lana said.

Beth pulled a Reuben sandwich and a coleslaw toward her, stacking the rest of the food neatly back in the bag. The other nurses would be thrilled. Except whoever ended up with the kale smoothie.

Beth thanked her mother for the unexpected delivery. Then they stood there looking at each other over the paper bag.

"Did you want to watch me eat it?" Beth asked.

"No, I . . . I had a few more questions I wanted to ask you. About Hal Rhoads," Lana said.

"I see."

"What exactly can you tell me about how Hal Rhoads died?" Lana asked.

Beth gave the bag on the counter a small shove. "Ma, I can't talk about that here."

"Really?"

"This is the most sensitive part of my job. How would you feel if I came up to your fancy Century City office asking personal questions about your clients?"

Lana considered the question. She'd drawn a firm line between work and family while Beth was growing up, putting 90 percent of her attention on the work side of the line. She'd never hung up any of Beth's drawings in her office or left work early to see a class play. Not that she had a choice. She'd seen what happened to the careers of women who were foolish enough to show those kinds of weaknesses.

Now Lana looked at her daughter and wondered, not for the first time, if she'd made the right decision.

"I don't want you to jeopardize your work, Beth. I just wanted to bring you a nice lunch. To thank you for your efforts. I'm sorry I asked."

Beth's face softened.

Lana realized it was the second time she'd issued an apology this week, even if this one was halfway disingenuous. She made a mental note not to make a habit of it. Then again, she saw it was a helpful tactic when used sparingly.

Beth threw her a bone. "Is there anything else I can help you with, Ma? Anything that doesn't violate federal health and privacy laws?"

Lana looked up and down the hallway. No one. She leaned in. "Can you tell me about his visitors?"

"Um . . ."

"Just for the week before he died."

"What do you want to know?"

"Ricardo Cruz was supposed to visit Mr. Rhoads on February third. I'm wondering if he made it here before he was murdered."

"Friday, February third? One sec." Beth swiveled the computer monitor in front of her. "Nope. Diana was here that morning, but not Ricardo. The only people who signed in to see Mr. Rhoads the week before he died were Martin, Diana, and Victor."

"Victor Morales?"

Beth nodded. She clicked a few more keys and spoke again. "Interesting. It looks like over the two months Mr. Rhoads was here, there was a consistent pattern. Martin came Friday afternoons and Sunday mornings. Lady Di came Tuesday and Thursday mornings."

"But that final week was different. You said—"

"Right. That last week, Diana came Tuesday and Friday instead. And Martin came on Saturday. He told me that, remember? He was stuck in San Francisco the night before."

"And Victor?"

"It looks like he was less consistent. He came once in December, twice in January. The last time was that Tuesday afternoon, January thirty-first."

"What about Ricardo Cruz? In those two months, did he ever visit?"

Beth squinted back at the screen. "Only once. Seven weeks ago, on January fourth. A Wednesday."

A doctor day.

"Can you write the dates down for me? For that final week?" Lana asked. "Wait. Hal Rhoads died on a Monday. Did anyone visit him that day?"

Beth grabbed a notepad and started scribbling. "There are no visitors allowed on Mondays."

"Why's that?"

"We've been down to one front-desk person for almost a year. Budget cuts. She has to have at least one day off. And since weekends are busy with visitors, Monday made the most sense."

"You usually don't work Mondays either."

Beth nodded. "It's our lightest day."

"What if someone is dying? Can a visitor come in then?"

"If there's an emergency, we make exceptions. But no one knew Mr. Rhoads was going to die that day."

Lana looked around the empty hallway. The fluorescent lights gave the beige walls a bluish cast. "There were so many people at his wake. What a shame to have so few visitors in the final weeks of his life."

Beth looked at Lana. "He was a proud man, Ma. He might not have told many people where he was or what was going on."

Lana felt a brief flash of guilt for not responding to André's last three texts, let alone Gloria's calls.

"Gotta go," Lana said, shaking it off. "See you tonight?"

"I have to cover the first part of Rosa's shift," Beth said. "I'll be home around eleven."

"I'm glad I brought two sandwiches. Have a good day, Beth." Lana put a hand on her daughter's arm. "And thank you."

LANA TURNED AND MARCHED back the way she'd come in, her hips swinging, high heels tapping out precise parallel lines all the way to the double doors.

Once she escaped the building, she reparked under the grove of pines behind Bayshore Oaks and dialed the number she'd copied from Jack's phone. It went straight to voicemail. But at least this time she knew it would reach her intended recipient.

"Detective Ramirez, it's Lana Rubicon. I wanted to tell you right away. I've confirmed that Ricardo Cruz did not make it to Bayshore Oaks on the day he died."

Lana realized it wasn't nearly as impressive a message as she'd imagined.

"I hope your investigation is going well," she improvised. "Okay. Bye."

Lana hung up, feeling deflated and oddly sheepish. She looked down at her lap, at the note Beth had scrawled about Mr. Rhoads's final week of visitors.

> Tues Jan 31—DRW morn, VM aft
> Fri Feb 3—DRW
> Sat Feb 4—MR

DRW. DR. That was it!

Ricardo's standing appointment wasn't with DR, a doctor. It was with Diana Rhoads Whitacre, née Diana Rhoads.

Lana remembered what Diana had said, that she'd first met Ricardo as a toddler, when she came home from England. Before her marriage, when she was still Diana Rhoads. Which would make her DR in Ricardo's book.

The tape ran backward in Lana's head, reviewing everything she knew about Diana Rhoads Whitacre. Her dissatisfying marriage. The children who'd moved on. The spa she wanted to build. At lunch Diana had called Ricardo a beautiful man. And that beautiful man had a standing appointment on Wednesdays, one of the days Diana stayed over at the ranch each week. All by herself in that big old house.

Lana knew enough rich, underappreciated women to know exactly what someone like Diana did with beautiful young men, and why she kept it a secret. Even if her husband was flaunting his own dalliances, a woman like Lady Di would rather be caught dead than be seen as anything less than the perfect Carmel wife.

Lana stared at the slip of paper in her lap, her lips pursing in anger. Diana had been sleeping with Ricardo. Hiding it. Lying about it. Was she lying about other things too? Perhaps Diana's interest in spending time with Lana had less to do with the wellness spa than keeping tabs on Lana's inquiries. Lana felt furious with herself and, more so, at Diana Rhoads Whitacre, for thinking she could pull one over on her.

She pulled out her phone and scrolled through her pictures from the land trust, landing on the photo she'd taken of Ricardo's calendar. As suspected, there was a DR penciled in on February 1, two days before he died. Had something happened at the ranch that night that put him in danger? Or perhaps the following morning? She needed to get more information on Ricardo's final movements from someone who might have talked to him. Someone who wanted to be helpful, who didn't have a reason to lie to her. For that, she knew exactly where to go.

CHAPTER FORTY-THREE

LANA DROVE NORTH, to Santa Cruz. She parked a few spots upwind of the charred land trust building and cautiously opened her door. Men in canvas jackets were carrying in furniture from a panel truck double-parked in front.

Gaby spotted her first. "Ms. Rubicon!"

"Gaby." The girl was standing outside the front door, wearing skin-tight jeans and a frilly, low-cut coral sweater. She had a dust mask dangling from her neck, grazing the swell of her breasts.

"How are you?" The girl clasped both of Lana's arms. "When I heard what happened to you that day, I just couldn't believe it. And now here you are. You look amazing."

Gaby looked around and dropped her voice. "I've told Victor that library door gets stuck. He always just laughed and said I had to put my back into it. It took this horrible . . . incident for him to order a replacement."

Lana regarded the young woman. Gaby was suggesting the door to the library hadn't been locked at all. Could that be true? Lana tried to remember whether she had heard a click when Victor left the room, if she could feel the difference between a thrown bolt and stuck wood. But all she could recall was the siren splitting her ears open. The jagged edges of the window. And the people like Victor and Gaby who left her to burn.

Lana extricated herself from Gaby's embrace. Two well-muscled men gripping a brand-new leather couch moved past them. "I'm glad to see you, Gaby. How's everything here?"

"They finally got the smoke cleared out of the building. Most of our paperwork is destroyed, and it's going to take ages to replace the exterior wall with something permanent. But our donors are helping us refurnish the office. And these restoration guys have been great." Gaby beamed at a man carrying a lamp, causing a near fumble.

"And the police?"

"Detective Choi, he's come a couple times. He said the fire must have been started close to the building. I think they're still trying to track down a couple of the cars parked on the street that day."

Lana wondered what kind of car Diana drove. But she also found herself reconsidering her earlier certainty about Diana's guilt. It was possible Diana knew about the day planner Lana had seen, and she set a fire to try to remove evidence of her meetings with Ricardo. But it didn't seem like her style. It was easier to believe that someone else, someone angrier, someone with more knowledge of the land trust building, might have done it.

"Everyone on staff is okay?" Lana asked.

Gaby nodded. "Did you really break through that window by yourself? I'm just, like . . . wow."

Lana smiled.

"Victor feels terrible about what happened. I'm sure he'd love to see you, but he's out all day at meetings—"

"I know. He's been leaving me messages. But I actually came here to talk with you."

The girl looked confused. "Did you want to make an insurance claim? We found your wig, but it wasn't—"

"It's not about the fire."

"Oh."

"It's about Ricardo Cruz."

"Oh?" Gaby was starting to resemble a very pretty parrot.

"I'm wondering if you can check something for me. Do you know when Ricardo was last here at the office?"

Gaby's eyes went wide. "I'm really not sure I can—"

Lana put her hand on the young woman's forearm. "Please. Victor told me about it when we met, but in all the hubbub, I misplaced my notes. Can you . . . ?"

Gaby pulled her phone out of the embroidered back pocket of her jeans. Her French tips scrolled down the glass surface, her nose scrunched up as she scanned the office calendar for the past month. When she found what she was looking for, Gaby did a tiny hop in place.

"Wednesday, February first," the girl said. "Ricardo was scheduled to go monitor one of our properties that day. But first we had a staff training about condor breeding on Fremont Peak." She gave Lana a tiny grin. "I remember. We had vegan doughnuts."

"And then he went to monitor a property? What does that entail?"

"When someone donates development rights, we have to check on the land from time to time. We don't own it, but we're responsible for making sure no one's running a business or dumping there. Most properties, we do it once a quarter."

"Could it have been the slough property Ricardo was monitoring that Wednesday?"

"Could be. I don't know."

"And then he didn't come in Thursday or Friday?"

Gaby's confident voice began to wobble. "That's right."

"Was that unusual?"

The girl looked pained, as if she had suddenly discovered a pebble in her bra.

"Ricardo often didn't come in on Thursdays until late in the day."

Lana nodded encouragingly. "Do you know why?"

"I think he might have had someone . . . special in his life." The girl looked embarrassed. "Ricardo lived north of here, in Santa Cruz proper. But some Wednesdays, he'd leave the office going south. And the following Thursdays, he'd come in late, from the south too. I think he was staying over somewhere."

"You watched his car?"

Gaby surprised Lana with a giggle, a tinkling glockenspiel of amusement. "Ricardo didn't drive a car. He was against it."

Lana was confused. "Did he use rideshares?"

"He biked. All the time."

"Even to meetings?"

"Everywhere."

"So even if he was meeting with a big donor . . ."

"He'd bike. He had two panniers—bike bags—that were strapped behind the seat. He used one for his laptop, and he carried a change of clothes in the other." Gaby smiled at the appalled look on Lana's face. "Some of our donors? They thought it was cute. Like he was really committed. And he was. To his bike."

"He took good care of it, huh?"

"Have you ever known a guy who loved his truck? Always shining the chrome and rotating the tires and calling it baby?"

Lana gave Gaby a wan smile, along with a silent thanks to God that she had never been intimate with such a man.

"Ricardo was like that with his bike. He even had a drawing of it tattooed on his butt." Gaby blushed. "I mean, that's what I heard."

"Sounds like quite an athlete."

"Oh yeah. A health nut too. He refused to get a smartphone, said it rotted your brain. And he never took a sick day. Ever."

Lana closed her eyes for a moment. She should have known it wasn't a doctor. Just because she had cancer didn't mean the whole world was ailing. She could see the letters *DR* curled on the inside of her eyelids, Ricardo and Diana, on Wednesday nights, rolling around on a bearskin rug in front of the fire at the Rhoads ranch house.

Lana pushed the image out of her mind and refocused on the young woman in front of her. Gaby looked at ease now, watching the tanned, toned gap between the delivery man's T-shirt and his jeans. But Lana had caught a whiff of discomfort earlier. There was something Gaby didn't want to talk about.

"So Ricardo often came in late on Thursdays," Lana said, drawing Gaby's attention reluctantly back to her. "But the week he was killed, he didn't come in Thursday at all?"

"That's . . . right." Gaby's face turned nervous again, like the conversation had careened into a ditch. There was something ugly there. Something about that Thursday, the day before Ricardo died.

"Surely the detectives asked about his absence," Lana said.

"Yes." Gaby was looking at her shoes now.

"What did you tell them?"

The girl traced a tiny circle in the sidewalk with the toe of her shoe.

"Victor told us to say he was out sick," she mumbled.

"But Ricardo didn't take sick days."

"No." Gaby's voice was getting softer, as if she were trying to fade into the asphalt.

"Gaby. Just between us. What happened?"

Gaby looked miserable. She glanced around the sidewalk, but there was no one to overhear them, or to rescue her.

"There was a fight," Gaby whispered. Her words were tumbling out quickly now. "That Thursday. The day after the meeting with the doughnuts. Ricardo and Victor were in the library. At first it was quiet, but then Victor started yelling. When Victor is passionate about something, he can get really intense. Not violent or anything . . ." Gaby shook her head. "But we could hear everything. It was awful."

"What was he saying?"

"He was shouting about honor and betrayal and how Ricardo had taken advantage of him."

"What happened after the argument?"

"Ricardo grabbed his panniers and stormed out. I—I never saw him again."

Gaby raised her eyes to meet Lana's. Tears were running down her cheeks, bringing wet streaks of mascara with them.

"Victor cared about Ricardo. I know he did. He called him hijo, his son. And for that to be the last time they spoke . . ." She broke down again.

Lana dug into her purse and extracted a set of tissues and a compact. She handed them to Gaby and waited, thinking, while the girl pulled herself back together.

She was finally getting somewhere. She knew where Ricardo had been: on Wednesday night, he stayed with Diana. Thursday, he broke the news to Victor about leaving the land trust to work with Hal on Verdadera Libertad. They argued. And then Ricardo went—where?

"Do you remember which direction Ricardo biked when he left? After that fight?"

Gaby still looked miserable. "South."

South. Back to Diana. Lana tried to imagine how Ricardo must have felt that day. Did he bike to the ranch after the fight with Victor to seek comfort from Diana? Did he go there to tell her about the Verdadera Libertad project, only to be murdered by her the next day? Or was it possible Victor had been angry enough to kill Ricardo over his betrayal? Victor could have contacted Ricardo asking to meet at the land trust property by the slough that Friday, to talk things out, to reconcile. Ricardo wouldn't have thought to be afraid, wouldn't have necessarily told anyone or brought someone with him.

Her thoughts were broken by Gaby, pressing Lana's compact back into her hand. When Lana looked up, Gaby's face was back in order. She looked luminous, unbreakable, as confident as Lana felt unsure. Lana knew the look, knew its benefits, the way beauty could serve as armor.

Lana accepted her compact and the unused tissues with a nod. "You've given me a lot to think about, Gaby. And no need to mention our chat to anyone. Women like us have to stick together, right?"

For a moment, Lana saw a fault line open on Gaby's face, a tiny frisson of worry rippling the perfectly smooth surface of her skin. Then the girl breathed out a small sigh. She turned away from Lana, toward the clump of workmen, stretching her back in a way that lengthened her hair and pushed her breasts toward the sun.

"Ms. Rubicon, I've already forgotten we spoke."

LANA SLID BACK INTO HER CAR and checked her watch. There was just enough time to get home and lie down for a bit before Jack got back from school.

As she drove, her mind drifted. She imagined Ricardo biking down to the ranch to see Diana. It had to be at least fifteen miles. Biking. What was the appeal? Lana passed two women in tight floral unitards, pedaling hard on the shoulder of the highway, the ocean glittering off to their right. Sure, their calves looked phenomenal, but the idea of going head-to-head with automobile traffic terrified Lana. Not to mention the damage a helmet could do to your hair.

Not that cardio was a high priority for Lana these days. She thought again about the PET scans from yesterday. She hated waiting for results—waiting for anything, really—but part of her felt safe in this life in Elkhorn, its known aches and pains, balanced with simple pleasures. Lana passed another cyclist by the marina, a wobbly guy in army fatigues with a tiny dog in a basket in front of him. She had a sudden memory of the bike she'd had as a kid. White basket. Red streamers. Lana remembered sailing through the warren of streets behind the synagogue, that sense of freedom, the rush of wind lifting her sticky hair off the back of her neck. She wondered if she'd ever feel that alive again.

Lana parked outside the house and sat in her car, her thoughts turning back to murder. She had to admit it. She'd been wrong. She'd been biased by her professional experience into thinking this whole thing was about land. Who owned it. Who controlled it. What you could and couldn't do with it. Hal and Ricardo had Verdadera Libertad. Victor had his conservation plans. Paul had his mysterious Fruitful company. And the Rhoads children had an entire ranch to fight over. It added up to a hundred different reasons for someone to commit murder.

But love was the trump card. Love was more potent than land. Especially when it got twisted into something ugly by surprise.

What kind of love had led to Ricardo's death? Was it the fatherly love Victor had for Ricardo, and the pain that followed when the older man discovered the younger had betrayed him to pursue his own dream? Or was it lust—an affair gone wrong with Diana?

Lana thought back to Jack's comment about Ricardo being the linchpin, and what Diana had said about not suffering betrayal by men. Perhaps Ricardo was the operations manager she'd mentioned, the one she'd picked out for her wellness ranch. Lana could imagine Diana mapping it all out: Ricardo running the spa by day, then keeping her bed warm at night. Maybe she'd even pitched him on that fantasy. Maybe he'd pretended to go along with it. If Ricardo was promising Diana one thing about her project, stringing along Victor on his, and then making plans behind both their backs with Hal about something entirely different . . . well, that was the best motive for murder she'd heard so far. For either of them.

CHAPTER FORTY-FOUR

JACK SPENT THE BIKE RIDE home from school debating what to write back to the guy with the boat in San Luis Obispo. When she got inside, Lana emerged from the back bedroom with a roll of papers in her hand.

"What are you up to tonight?" Lana asked.

"Um . . . homework? I have to write an essay about early twentieth-century presidents. What about you?"

Lana unfurled the roll onto the table. "Learning what I can about Lady Di's horse spa."

"Ooh . . . can I look?"

"You do your work. I'll do mine. Then we'll talk."

WHILE JACK TACKLED HER ESSAY, Lana marked up the set of plans Diana had given her at lunch the day before. After her discoveries that afternoon, she'd decided to do whatever she could to stay close to Diana. And the plans were interesting. Lana didn't really know whether a wellness spa needed two equine hydrotherapy pools, but the business model looked sound. She had just shot Diana an email with a few bullets on the profitability calculations when she looked up and saw Jack staring at her.

"What?" Lana asked.

"You know how you told me winners never mumble?" Jack held

up the book she was reading about Theodore Roosevelt. "He says you should speak softly and carry a big stick."

Lana scoffed. "You think they let women have sticks?"

NICOLETTI APPEARED on the six o'clock news, after a segment about a despondent lady in Salinas whose winning lottery ticket got shredded in a lettuce harvester. Jack and Lana watched from the couch, sharing a pot of mac and cheese, peas, and corn all mixed together.

The detective stood on the asphalt behind the Kayak Shack, his nubbly brown suit making him look like a bedraggled teddy bear. Nicoletti's droning recitation of the facts of the case was intercut with ominous shots of the slough at night, pickleweed popping out bloodred against the dark water.

"They made the slough look kind of scary with those weird angles," Jack said.

"Someone on the crew thinks they're an artist," Lana replied. "Check out that close-up on the life jacket."

As the camera zoomed out, Nicoletti shared the basics: Ricardo Cruz, twenty-nine, born in Salinas, resident of Santa Cruz, died Friday, February 3, by blunt force trauma, followed by submersion in Elkhorn Slough. Weapon not yet recovered. While the sheriffs anticipated a speedy arrest, anyone with any information about the crime should call the Monterey County sheriff's department tip line.

"Good luck with that," Lana grumbled. She reached for the remote.

"Prima! Look."

The TV screen was flashing the sheriff's department tip line number, under a photograph of Ricardo Cruz smiling and leaning against a green road bike.

"That's the abandoned bike I saw at the Kayak Shack," Jack said. "It must have been Ricardo's."

Both of them leaned forward, Lana reaching out with her phone to take a shaky photo of the TV.

She squinted at the screen, thinking back on what Gaby had told her. "Are there two panniers on the back of that bike, or one?" Lana held up her phone to Jack.

"I can't tell from this picture. But the bike at the Shack only had one."

The newscast flipped to the weather girl. Lana looked at the blurry green-and-black blob she'd captured on her phone for one more second, then shook her head.

"We've got more important things to talk about tonight. Let's go." Lana switched off the TV, grabbed a fresh Diet Coke from the fridge, and headed toward the back bedroom, Jack following behind her.

"I've been thinking about that motive problem you raised," Lana said. "We keep getting stuck because all our suspects have some reason to do it. All of them wanted the ranch. They all had access somewhere along that creek you found. And it didn't take incredible strength or specialized knowledge to kill Ricardo. Or Hal."

Jack frowned. "Is this supposed to be a pep talk? I thought—"

Lana cut her off. "But I realized, there's another way to look at this. BATNA."

"Bat-nuh?"

Lana nodded. "BATNA. Best alternative to a negotiated agreement. It's a term we use in business deals. When you're negotiating with someone over a piece of land or lease terms, you ask yourself: If we can't make a deal here, how bad is it for the other person? What other choices do they have? What's their best alternative if they walk away?"

She could practically see her granddaughter's wheels turning.

"Let me see if I got this right," Jack said. "Let's say I want to buy a boat. The owner wants to sell it now, but I can't buy it yet. I need a few more months."

"That's a very specific example—"

"So maybe I offer him a higher price if he'll wait. Therefore his best alternative to selling it to me in a few months is to sell it now but get less money for it."

"That's right." Lana eyed her granddaughter. "Jack?"

"Yes?"

"Are you interested in buying a boat?"

Jack's eyebrows raised and a small smile appeared on her face. "A sailboat. But, um, I'm not sure my mom will let me."

"Have you asked her?"

Jack shook her head.

"Then your first negotiation is with her. What's her best alternative to letting you buy the boat?"

"Prima . . . I don't think of talking with my mom as a negotiation."

"But you aren't sure she'll say yes," Lana countered. "So maybe you should."

"Um, in that case, I guess her best alternative to saying yes is just saying no."

"And you accepting it?"

"Maybe being grumpy about it. But there's not a lot more I can do."

Lana looked at her. "Jack, that's not true. You could escalate. You could threaten to do something way more reckless if she doesn't let you buy it."

"That seems kind of immature."

"Okay . . . maybe you could show her that the alternative is you being unhappy. Stifled. Not able to be your full self." Lana could see this was starting to click. "Listen, Jack. Life *is* a negotiation. With yourself. With others. You can't sit around waiting for someone else to guess what you want. You have to ask for it, even if it's scary." Lana took a sip of her soda. "But yes, you've got the concept."

"And this BATNA stuff has to do with murder how?"

"Well," said Lana, "all these suspects *could* have killed Ricardo. But who *had* to kill Ricardo? For whom was murder the best alternative to whatever was going on?"

Jack stared at the photographs lined up on the wall. "Martin has an alibi for Ricardo's murder, but he could have killed his dad so he could sell the ranch for money."

"Is that his best alternative to getting money another way?"

Jack scrunched up her face. "Seems extreme. I mean, he's a rich white guy who went to MIT. He could probably get investors in Silicon Valley without having to kill his own family."

Lana nodded, encouraging Jack to keep going.

"But his sister, Lady Di." Jack's voice was more confident now. "If she was hooking up with Ricardo and things got messed up there . . ."

"Exactly," Lana said.

"Couldn't she just dump him?" Jack asked. "Why would she have to murder him?"

Lana was glad her granddaughter had not yet been so thoroughly let down by a man that she wanted to kill him.

"Maybe Ricardo made some kind of demand of her," Lana said. "Or a threat. Maybe the night before he died, he told her about Verdadera Libertad, and he pressed her to support it, to give up her claim to the ranch or else he'd tell her husband. I could see how she could feel trapped, like her best alternative might be to kill him."

Lana looked back at the corkboard. "The same could be true for Victor Morales," she said. "He had to have the Rhoads ranch for his vision of the land trust stretching from the marina to the hills. There wasn't some other property that would accomplish that. If Ricardo and Mr. Rhoads had a project in the works that would stop the land trust from getting it . . ."

"Victor's best alternative would be to kill them both." Jack looked at Lana. "But how could he get the property donated if Mr. Rhoads was dead?"

"He'd need to convince Diana and Martin. Keep waving around that letter of intent and try to pressure them into following through."

"Do you think Victor could do that?"

Lana considered it. Even if Diana and Martin couldn't agree, they at least seemed aligned in their determination to keep the ranch out of the land trust's control. Maybe if Victor knew about Diana and Ricardo's affair, he could lean on her . . . but if he held that trump card, he hadn't pulled it yet. Lana decided she finally had a reason to return one of his many calls.

"I'll find out," Lana said. "Maybe Victor was less driven by his desire for the land than by his anger that Ricardo and Mr. Rhoads betrayed him."

"But that's not about BATNA. That's motive. We're back to where we started."

"We've come a long way from there, Jack. We just have to piece it together, and it will all make sense."

It had to.

• • •

At 7 P.M., Beth was on her way out the back door of Bayshore Oaks for a protein bar break when she was accosted by Miss Gigi.

"Beth! Your mother. She is enchanting. And so young-looking!" Miss Gigi was still in the turquoise evening gown, which she had now accessorized with a flimsy kimono adorned with Disney characters.

"Thank you?" Beth looked uncomfortably at Miss Gigi's press-on nails, which were carving tiny moons into the sleeve of Beth's bomber jacket.

"Beth, there is something I must tell you. I was listening to your conversation with your mother."

"About the sandwiches?"

"About the visitors."

"I see."

The two women stared at each other. Beth squeezed the protein bar, feeling it deform under her sweaty hand. Even under a pound of silver eye shadow, Beth knew Miss Gigi was a force to be reckoned with.

"I can explain—"

The smaller woman waved away Beth's excuses. "You are helping your mother. It is the right thing to do. But what I have done, I am not so sure."

Now it was Miss Gigi who looked nervous.

"What is it?" Beth asked.

"The team in the mail room, we take our jobs very seriously. We are the connection with people on the outside," Miss Gigi said.

"Uh-huh . . ."

"And sometimes, on Mondays, there is someone who needs to connect with someone."

"Like a letter that has to go out?"

Miss Gigi shook her head. "More like someone who wants to come in."

Beth blinked. "Miss Gigi, did someone come into Bayshore Oaks the day Hal Rhoads died? It would have been"—she counted backward in her head—"three Mondays ago."

She had never seen Miss Gigi look so contrite. "I am not sure. I can ask my associates. I was not on duty that Monday, but—"

"On duty? You have shifts for this?"

"At the side door. Just from lunch until dinner." Miss Gigi pulled the kimono tight around her and looked up at Beth anxiously. "Do you think someone came in here to connect with Mr. Rhoads? And murdered him?"

"I . . . don't know." After Lana had left earlier, Beth had looked up Mr. Rhoads's cause of death. All it said was SCD—sudden cardiac death. Without an autopsy or detailed bloodwork, there was no way to get more specific.

"Will we be charged as accessory? Sued for negligée?"

Beth's mind was still reeling, but she found a smile for the tiny woman. "If anyone is going to get sued around here for their nightwear, it would be you."

Miss Gigi puffed out her chest. On the front panels of the kimono, Goofy and Minnie Mouse were posing in yellow bikinis and heels, a sequined tropical beach sprawled out behind them. "These are one hundred percent original. My granddaughter designs, her boyfriend prints them, she sews on sparkles. Cesar sells them at our store in Seaside, big sales last summer, completely sold out. This one is a collector's item."

"You are a lucky woman."

"Maybe not so lucky if I am helping murderers."

"We don't know that. You ask your mail room associates what they remember. I'll look into it as well. And as for any future connections, let's stick to the letters and packages that come in the front door."

Beth waited until Miss Gigi had closed the door to her room before she walked outside. She took a breath, unwrapped the mangled protein bar, and grimaced. The conversation had made her lose her appetite. She felt an urgent desire to go back inside and pull Mr. Rhoads's charts again, to contact the medical director about this. Maybe the EMTs who attended the death as well. But there was someone she had to call first.

CHAPTER FORTY-FIVE

LANA HUNG UP THE PHONE and looked triumphantly at Jack.

"I was right about Hal Rhoads," she said. "He was murdered."

"Whoa," Jack said. "Who were you talking to? Was that Mom?"

Lana nodded. Before she could say more, there was a knock at the door. It was Detectives Nicoletti and Ramirez, looking like sweaty, disheveled versions of the investigators who'd been on television an hour earlier.

"Here to sign autographs?" Lana said.

Nicoletti pulled his shoulders back. "No, ma'am. We need to talk to you."

Lana looked at Ramirez. "Did you get my message?"

The female detective gave her a brief nod.

"Anything I need to know?" Nicoletti asked his partner.

For a moment, Lana had a wild hope that her voicemail had somehow delivered critical evidence.

"It's nothing," Ramirez said. Lana let out a puff of breath, disappointed.

Jack migrated over to the table. "What's going on?"

"The bike we found at the Kayak Shack," Nicoletti said. "We've confirmed—"

"It belonged to Ricardo Cruz," Lana said.

"How did you—"

"Moving on." Ramirez's tone was smooth and authoritative. "We got a warrant to check out the land Paul Hanley was leasing from that Rhoads family. I went out there. No Paul. Nothing except a bunch of dirt all churned up."

Lana had a sudden flash of Paul's loaded-down kayak on the day Jack got stuck in the creek. Whatever he'd been hiding on his leased land, he must have dug it up and brought it to the marina.

"He did a good job clearing out," Ramirez continued. "But he missed one thing—"

She took out a small plastic bag and laid it on the table. Inside, there was a single button, smeared with mud. Nicoletti was watching Ramirez with a forced smile, as if he wished he were the one who'd found it.

"Have you seen this before?"

Lana and Jack shook their heads.

"It's from Ricardo Cruz's jacket. There's trace patterns of his blood on it, which can be roughly dated to the week he died. We believe it came off just before he was dumped in the water."

"Conclusive evidence I was right," Nicoletti broke in. "Ricardo Cruz was on Hanley's leased property. He was killed in the jacket this button came from. And then splash, into the creek."

"You think Paul—"

"We'll be arresting Mr. Hanley for the murder of Ricardo Cruz," Nicoletti said. "Just as soon as we can find him."

Ricardo's bike. Ricardo's button. It was damning evidence, but it didn't make Paul a murderer. There still wasn't a weapon or a motive. As far as Lana could tell, Paul had the least to gain from killing Ricardo, let alone Hal Rhoads. But maybe the sheriffs knew something Lana didn't.

Lana knew how to catch flies with honey. But when time was of the essence, a shot of vinegar to the eyes could be quite effective. She looked straight at Nicoletti and scoffed.

"Paul Hanley, a murderer? Ridiculous. Too obvious. Why would he kill someone and then float him down the slough in a life vest from his own company? Not to mention keeping the bike. Even Paul isn't that stupid. I didn't think you were either."

Nicoletti scoffed right back. "Please. You think you're so clever. Mr. Hanley tried to frame your granddaughter. He knew the tides. He'd know where and when the body might come out. He killed Mr. Cruz and dropped him in a creek Friday night. Then he made a fake booking with Ricardo Cruz's phone for a Saturday kayak tour, tossed the phone, and hid the bike." Nicoletti pointed a meaty finger at Jack. "You guided that Saturday sunset tour."

Jack nodded, her eyes big as plates.

"And Mr. Hanley wasn't around that evening."

"He met a woman," Jack said.

"The lovely Tatiana. His vanishing alibi." Nicoletti had a smug look on his face. "The bastard set you up."

"I don't believe it," Lana said. She looked at her granddaughter. "Paul may be a dope, but he isn't violent, is he?"

Jack nodded. "I just sort of thought he was a loser."

"Exactly," Lana said. "He isn't the type."

Nicoletti barked out a single "Ha!" that echoed in the small kitchen. "Let me tell you something, lady. There is no *type*. I've met nerds who were scared of their own shoelaces but still managed to kill their girlfriends. I've met little old ladies who buried their husbands in their gardens and stood there crying over their peonies. I once collared a gym teacher who hacked up a boy before basketball practice. The only type I've ever run into is the type who is desperate enough to kill someone. Which is everyone, given the right circumstances."

Jack bolted up from the table, her face a mottled gray. "Excuse me," she said, looking at Lana. "I'll be in my room. Your room."

Lana glared at the detective. "You just had to swing your dick around, didn't you."

"What I had to do," Nicoletti said, glaring back, "is impress upon you how serious this situation is. Mr. Hanley is a murderer."

"Allegedly. What's his motive in this fantasy you've cooked up?"

"We think they were in business together, Mr. Hanley and Mr. Cruz, doing something illegal in that valley across the slough."

"Fruitful," Lana said.

"Exactly." Nicoletti waved a meaty hand. "Mr. Hanley leased the land, and Cruz's roommates told us he was spending more time in Elkhorn than he needed for his job, that he had some kind of secret situation going on down here. He wouldn't tell his roommates what, so we're thinking it wasn't aboveboard. They were working together. They had an altercation that Friday. Hanley hit Cruz, hard, with something rounded and metal, maybe a posthole digger or a shovel or that Maglite he wasn't able to produce for us. And then later that night he dumped him in the creek."

Lana kept her face impassive as she considered what he was telling her. Was it possible she'd made an error, and the big project Ricardo had left the land trust to do was not with Hal but with Paul? Or that Ricardo was meeting up with Paul instead of Diana? No. Those ideas were ridiculous. Verdadera Libertad was real, and so were Ricardo's liaisons with Diana. Ricardo's secret activities at the slough were pleasure, not business. Lana was sure of it. Almost.

She was about to open her mouth and wipe the smile off Nicoletti's face when she realized her evidence about the affair was just as circumstantial as his about the illegal business partnership. And despite what she'd boasted to Jack, she didn't yet have conclusive evidence that Hal Rhoads had been murdered. She couldn't tell the detectives her theory. Not until she had rock-solid proof.

Nicoletti appeared to take her nonresponse as noncooperation. He curled his lip into a sneer. "Look, lady, I get it. A younger man pays you some attention, flirts a little, makes you feel—how did my ex-wife put it?—makes you feel *alive*. And reason goes out the window."

Lana glared at him. No way in hell she was going to bring up her theories now.

She caught a whiff of Nicoletti's awful cologne, like rotted apples rolled in pine sap. Strangely, it made her think of Paul, the stink of his car, musky and sweet at the same time. She remembered what Jack had said about the skunk smell at his leased land by the creek, and how the official at the Farm Bureau had told her there was no licensed strawberry farm under Fruitful or Paul Hanley's name. Something was coming together, a vague cloud of an idea that started in her nose and was slowly filtering up to her brain. But before the haze cleared, Ramirez spoke.

"Ms. Rubicon, you've helped us before. We need your help now."

"Meaning?"

"If you know where Paul Hanley is, any idea regarding his whereabouts, we need to know."

"Perhaps I could—"

Nicoletti slapped his notebook down on the table. "Perhaps you could stop playing cute and tell us what you know."

Lana straightened up and fixed the man with a vicious stare. "Detective Nicoletti. I know you are under a great deal of pressure. I know you have not been able to solve this murder, despite having multiple weeks and the full force of your department behind you. I know you have treated me dismissively and bullied my granddaughter. I know you need a goddamned belt to hold up those sagging pants you bought off the discount rack. What else is it that you want to know?"

Nicoletti locked his jaw, his fists, and his hips. After an uneasy pause, Ramirez stepped in front of him.

"Ms. Rubicon," Ramirez said. "I've observed that Paul Hanley seems to have a special relationship with you."

Lana shifted her glare to the younger woman.

"He might have told you about someplace we wouldn't know about. Please."

Lana gave Ramirez a stilted smile. "I'm afraid you've overinterpreted my connection with Mr. Hanley. That day we were all together in his shop, that was the first time we met."

Ramirez persisted. "Even the smallest piece of information could help us find him."

Lana thought for a moment. What she needed now was time. Time to find hard evidence that linked Victor or Diana to the murders. Time to figure out what exactly Paul was hiding.

"He has kayaks," Lana improvised. "Lots of them. He probably knows lots of secret places up in the slough. He might be camping somewhere. He might not even know you're looking for him."

"Have you heard him talk about camping?" Ramirez sounded doubtful, of either Paul or the prospect of sleeping outdoors for fun.

"No," Lana admitted.

"Anyone else we should be talking to? A girlfriend? A business partner?"

There was one person. But Lana wanted to talk to him first. She shook her head. "I really don't know him very well."

"Understood. Well, thank you for your time." Ramirez moved toward the door. Nicoletti unfroze himself and turned to follow her out.

"Oh, and Detective Ramirez?" Lana said.

"Yes?"

"If Paul is the murderer, I'll do everything I can to help you find him."

"I appreciate that. If he contacts you, call me. Lord knows you have my number."

"IS EVERYTHING OKAY?" Jack tiptoed out of the back bedroom and curled up next to Lana on the couch.

"I'm fine. You?"

Jack pulled at the sleeve of her sweatshirt. "It's just a lot. Do you think Paul murdered Ricardo Cruz?"

"No. I had considered him a possibility before, but I honestly doubt if Paul ever even met Ricardo. There's no motive. There's no BATNA. Paul has something going on up by that creek, for sure. But I think someone's setting *him* up to take the fall, the same way the sheriffs say he tried to set you up." Lana looked up at the ceiling. "I wonder how that button got there."

"Maybe someone hiked it down to the creek?"

"Maybe." Lana yawned.

"Did my mom tell you when she's getting home?"

"Eleven, she said." It was only nine, but Lana already felt like it was way past her bedtime.

"I guess we should go to bed."

"I guess so."

Neither of them moved.

"There's a *Law and Order* marathon," Jack said.

"On it." Lana grabbed the remote. "Can you get my legal pad?"

CHAPTER FORTY-SIX

VICTOR SOUNDED DELIGHTED to hear from Lana, or as delighted as a person could be to receive a phone call on a Saturday at eight in the morning. He would love to see her, of course, as soon as possible. He was in Monterey County that morning, conducting a site tour of a heritage apple farm east of Elkhorn with some volunteers. She was welcome to meet him there.

Lana pulled herself out of bed and raided the crate where Beth kept her hiking gear. If Victor really was the murderer, she didn't want to meet him empty-handed. Underneath a lightweight backpack and clunky boots, there was a pocketknife she couldn't get open and a slim bottle of bear spray with a clip on the handle. She attached the bottle to the waistband of her pants, concealing it under an oversize blazer. Perfect.

An hour later, Lana was following the path from Victor's BMW up into the orchard. The morning was crisp, her low heels were more than adequate, and she had a fresh Diet Coke in her hand. If it weren't for the invisible vise squeezing her lungs, Lana might have enjoyed the walk. She passed a gaggle of volunteers in jeans and flannel jackets, hammering what looked like oversize birdhouses to the fence line. Witnesses. She waved. They waved back. Good.

The orchard ran up a long hillside, the apple trees standing in stately rows fifteen feet apart. Their trunks were painted a soft white, as if they were wearing knee socks. Every dozen trees, Lana stopped to catch her breath and look out over the valley from which she'd ascended. She could see for miles. The thin sheet of morning fog was lifting, and below her, cultivated farms gave way to bright, winding estuaries that poured into the bay.

In the third row over, Lana spotted a glimpse of black-and-gold boots on a broad-backed man reaching into the crown of a tree. She straightened her blazer.

"Señor Morales!"

Victor straightened up, and as he turned, Lana got the impression he was fixing his face, cycling rapidly from surprise to concern to something approximating pleasure.

"Ms. Rubicon." His full lips formed an uncertain smile. "You are healed, I hope?" He stood a respectful distance from her, his eyes searching her face for bruises, or answers, or both.

Lana realized the last time she'd seen him, she'd been brandishing a metal-spiked stiletto.

She took a small step toward him, keeping one hand on the bottle of bear spray. "I wanted to thank you for the flowers."

"It was nothing," he said. He gave her a smile, a real one this time. Still, he kept his hand tightly clenched around the small object he had pulled from the tree. "I feel terrible about what happened. If there's anything I can do for you . . ."

"What's that?" Lana asked, pointing at his hand.

Victor opened it to show a green apple with a cratered side. "The birds keep eating them," he said. "That's why volunteers are here."

"Setting off shell crackers?"

"Bird bombs? Those things are dangerous. Perhaps older farms use them, but none of the properties we manage. Our volunteers are putting up nesting boxes for hawks and owls instead. They repopulate predators and control the pests all at once."

"Nature takes care of itself," Lana said.

Victor winked. "With a little help from its friends."

Lana decided this was as warmed up as Victor was going to get.

"I have a confession to make," she said. "I didn't come here to talk birds."

"I hoped as much." His brown eyes twinkled in the dappled light.

Lana gave him an enigmatic smile, inviting him to lean in.

"It's about Ricardo Cruz."

Victor's eyes lost their twinkle.

"I know how much you cared for him," Lana continued, ignoring his stiffened posture. "And since you have so generously offered to do anything you can for me, I'd like to ask a few questions. Please."

Lana smiled again, more girlish this time. She kept her arms by her sides, her eyes wide, in her best attempt to look nonthreatening.

"When I said that, I didn't—"

"It would mean the world to me if you could help."

Victor rolled out his shoulders and neck, like a retired boxer headed back into the ring. "Okay, Ms. Rubicon. I'll give you three questions." His voice was playful, but there was a hint of an edge to it.

"How about five?"

"Three."

"Fine. As far as I understand, Ricardo was not at work the day that he died. May I ask where you were that day?"

Victor eyed her carefully. "I was away that Friday. And Saturday. At a wildlands conservation conference in Santa Barbara."

"You stayed overnight." Lana made sure not to phrase it as a question.

"Yes, I stayed over. It is not so far away that I could not have come home." He kept his eyes steady on Lana. "But a free hotel room by the ocean is nothing to sniff at. You are welcome to call and confirm my reservation. The detectives have already done so."

She nodded. "Question two. When you visited Hal Rhoads earlier that week, that Tuesday afternoon, did he tell you about his change in plans for the ranch?"

"I don't know what you're talking about," Victor said.

"You promised to help me," Lana countered.

They locked eyes, sizing each other up. The experience was not altogether unpleasant. Finally, Victor spoke. "Señor Rhoads had many creative ideas for how we might best preserve the legacy of his land. That last week, he said he and Ricardo hoped to have a more fulsome discussion about the future with me soon. Sadly, that future never came."

"Did you sense he was going to back out of your agreement?"

"This is your final question?"

"Just a clarification."

"I cannot presume to speculate on what he was planning to do."

Victor stepped in, closing the gap between them. Lana could feel his breath on her cheek.

"You have one more question."

Scattered half thoughts floated before her, dancing with the dust motes in the sun. Lana didn't want to ask directly about the fire, or the fight between Victor and Ricardo, or Verdadera Libertad. He'd just lie, or get angry, or tell her what she already knew. But she realized her whole theory rested on one piece of information. Something for which she didn't have ironclad proof.

"Did you know about Ricardo's . . . dealings with Diana Whitacre?"

"You are full of surprises."

Lana waited, holding her ground.

"Before he died, my father told me it takes a man forty years to learn how to listen to women. To take seriously their power, how ruthless they can be. I'm afraid Ricardo didn't grow up with a father to teach him these lessons."

Victor pulled back out of her personal space, as if he had never been there. "You may want to ask Señora Whitacre where she was that Friday. And where she was thirty years ago, when her precious duke fell asleep."

Lana stared at him, hoping he might elaborate. He watched her steadily, his mouth shut, his dark eyes giving away nothing. Then he tipped his hat and strolled away, disappearing into the leafy, outstretched arms of an apple tree.

CHAPTER FORTY-SEVEN

LANA WOKE UP the next morning to her phone buzzing. She rolled over and looked at the clock. Nine fifteen. Too early, especially on a Sunday. But at least somebody wanted to talk to her.

Her phone showed two text messages: one from Diana Whitacre, one from Jack.

The one from Diana was simple: *Need your help. Please call me.*

The message from Jack was not. It was a series of blurry black-and-white images, surrounded by grainy text.

Lana put on her reading glasses and dialed. "Jack?"

"Prima." The girl was whispering. "I'm at the library."

"Is everything okay?"

"Yeah. I only have a minute. I'm doing a research project, going through newspaper databases for primary sources, and I had an idea about that thing you told me last night. About Lady Di. I pulled up the archives for the *Daily Mail*."

"In England?" Lana was either still half-asleep or just not following.

"Yeah," Jack said. "I looked her up. Under her old name, Diana Rhoads. And I found it. When she was young, she had a fiancé in England, a duke of somewhere. He died in his sleep, and she was there."

"Are you serious?"

"I just sent you screenshots. Gotta go."

Lana pulled herself to a seated position and zoomed in on the photograph on her phone. Jack was right. It was a lurid story about a young duke who died mysteriously in the night on his family's estate. There, in the caption of the picture, was Diana Rhoads, age twenty-four, grieving fiancée of the deceased. She was wearing a black veil and everything. The other images were from tabloids that picked up the story, casting it in increasingly scandalous terms.

Adrenaline flooded Lana's body, better than any drug. They'd figured it out. It was Diana. She'd killed a man before. She had access to the victims, the creek, and a life jacket from her daddy's barn. She'd killed Ricardo. Set up Paul. And then she'd used her old playbook to smother her father into silence and secure control of the ranch.

It sounded good. But it was still circumstantial. Lana had to get concrete evidence of the affair, something more than initials on a day planner that had probably burned up in the fire.

Which was why she picked up the phone and dialed Diana.

The call was brief. Diana thanked her for the notes on her financial models, and then issued another request for help, which was something between a demand and an invitation. One Lana was more than happy to accept.

"I'd be delighted to assist you with your presentation to Martin tonight," Lana said. "Anything to help a woman entrepreneur."

SHE HAD EIGHT HOURS to get ready. Lana forced herself to eat a full breakfast, choking down an entire container of cottage cheese with a sorry imposter of a bagel. She planned her outfit carefully, pulling out her best Chanel suit, her Gianvito Rossi black pumps, and the wig that itched, the bob she'd worn to lunch with Diana earlier in the week. She didn't want any reason for the woman to suspect she was sick, to see her as anything less than formidable.

As she lined up her pills for the day, Lana pondered Diana's invitation to dinner. Was it sincere, or was it a trap?

Diana claimed she wanted help negotiating a phased buyout with Martin, and that she hoped Lana could help her play hardball on the numbers. Which could be true. Even if Diana had killed Ricardo and Hal, she might still need Lana's help to get what she wanted.

But the more Lana thought about that, the more it bugged her.

If Diana had willingly killed two men—including her own father—to gain control of the ranch, why hadn't she killed Martin when he stood in her way? What would happen if she couldn't convince him to accept the buyout now?

Lana's mind splintered into possibilities. Maybe Diana didn't want to kill Martin. Maybe he was important to her in some way that other men in her life were not. If Diana could get Martin to see things her way, she wouldn't have to hurt him.

Or maybe she already had her younger brother's support. Maybe Martin had helped her cover up her crimes, and now he and Diana were lying about it, trying to distract Lana from finding out the truth with a fake disagreement about the future of the ranch. Maybe the dinner was a ruse designed to get Lana up to the ranch and put an end to her investigation. In which case, she'd need some backup of her own.

LANA DIALED THE NUMBER, praying this time the woman would pick up.

"Ramirez." The voice popped out at her halfway through the first ring.

"Detective Ramirez, hello. It's Lana. Lana Rubicon."

"Have you found Mr. Hanley?"

"No, but I . . ." She steeled herself. "I think I've found the murderer." Lana quickly explained what she'd figured out about the secret land project, and DR, and Diana's past fiancé, and the timing of it all.

"I see." There was a long pause.

"I'll text you the picture of the old news story right now," Lana said.

"But you don't know where Paul Hanley is?"

"Look at the photograph," Lana urged. "You'll see how it fits together."

"And Mrs. Whitacre is where currently?"

"I'm not sure. Probably at her home in Carmel. But she asked me to have dinner with her tonight at the Rhoads ranch. Six o'clock. I was thinking you could maybe come with me. As my date."

There was silence on the line.

"We're modern women," Lana said. "It's not impossible."

"Ms. Rubicon, I can't go with you to a dinner party."

"Don't you want to talk with these people about their connection with Ricardo Cruz?"

"Maybe at some point. But right now I've got my partner and the chief breathing down my neck to get a certain shaggy-haired kayak shop owner into the station stat."

"But—"

"Look, Ms. Rubicon, I'm not saying your information isn't interesting. But right now the only thing we're focused on is the whereabouts of Paul Hanley. Are you sure you don't know where he is?"

Lana had learned enough to guess what Paul was up to with his Fruitful enterprise. She thought again about his precious cooler, the one he'd asked Scotty to pick up from the docks. She knew what she had to do.

"If I find him, I promise you'll be the first to know."

• • •

Beth was wrapping up her shift when Martin's number came up on her phone. She kept scribbling on the last of the day's charts, letting the call go to voicemail. She'd already gotten two all-caps texts from her mother about Lady Di, and she didn't need any more distractions. Jack had agreed to join her on a sunset treasure hike, and Beth wasn't going to screw it up by being late.

On the drive home, he called again.

"Beth, hi." Martin sounded nervous. "Listen, I'm heading back to the city late tonight. Duty calls. Or rather, my investors do. Seems they've run out of patience for my bereavement leave."

"Did you and your sister work things out?"

"That's what I'm calling about," Martin said. "I thought she was finally on board with the sale, but this morning, she told me she wants to do a formal presentation tonight after dinner about *her* plan for the future and my role in it. And guess who she's bringing to the house to present alongside her?"

"An architect?"

"Your mother."

Beth shook her head at the road in front of her. Of course Lana was involved. Was this her mother's way of getting closer to Lady Di to collect evidence? Or maybe she just couldn't resist the opportunity to nose her way in on a real estate deal.

Martin kept talking. "I thought this was something Di and I could figure out on our own. Keep it in the family." He sighed. "I feel silly asking you this, but could you possibly call your mother off?"

"Call her off?" Beth tried to keep the incredulity out of her voice. "My mother doesn't have an off switch, let alone one I control. And if your sister asked her . . . couldn't you just hear them out?"

"I just feel like I'm going to get blindsided."

"By what?"

"I don't know. That's the problem. I don't know your mother at all."

Beth bit her lip. She knew how formidable a negotiator her mother was. She'd once met a banker at one of her mother's work parties who'd confessed that just hearing the sound of Lana's heels clicking toward his office was enough to lower the interest rate he'd offer her.

"You know her," Martin continued. "And I trust you. Maybe you could come? To balance the scales a bit?"

"I'm sorry. I wish I could help, but I've got plans tonight with my daughter."

"What if you bring her along? There'll be plenty of food. And there's cool stuff for a kid her age to mess around with on the ranch. Please, I—"

Beth scrunched up her forehead. She had no interest in participating in a sparring match over the future of the ranch. But maybe this wasn't about real estate. Maybe it was about murder. And if Jack heard that Lana was gathering evidence at the ranch, she'd probably want to go too.

"What can we bring?"

CHAPTER FORTY-EIGHT

LANA GOT TO THE MARINA just after four. The Kayak Shack looked deserted, strung up with police tape and guarded by a single black-and-white parked head-in to the entrance. Inside the vehicle, Lana could see a young deputy with thick black hair and a clipboard on his lap. He appeared to be logging every vehicle that entered and exited the marina.

Lana waggled her fingers at the officer and continued into the gravel lot, breathing steady. She parked on the far end, by the yacht club, alongside two squat, mustachioed fishermen who were spraying down their boat. Lana touched up her lipstick and added one more bobby pin to her wig. She was just about to go knock on the door of the club when she saw Scotty O'Dell get out of a truck nearby with an awkward bundle in his arms. It was all the confirmation she needed.

"Mr. O'Dell!" Lana clicked her heels a little faster across the gravel.

The man turned around. Dark stubble covered his jaw, and his arms were tangled in a mess of wires and purple-tinted light bulbs. He gave her a short nod and took a step back toward the side of the building. Lana closed the gap between them before he reached the service door.

"Mrs. Rubicon," he said.

"Ms."

"We're closed."

"I'm aware of that."

Lana dropped into silence, watching him juggle the awkward assembly of light bulbs.

"How can I . . . uh . . . help you?" His voice broke over the back half of his sentence, as if the words came out against his own volition.

"Scotty—can I call you Scotty?—I need to talk to your business partner."

A mix of confusion and pride streaked his face. "I own this place myself. Well, me and the bank."

"Not this business," Lana said, gesturing at the building. "That one." She pointed at the heat lamps he was trying not to drop.

"I don't know what you're talking about," Scotty said.

"Scotty." Lana smiled. "Have I ever told you about my friend Gloria?"

He stared back at her. Before this moment, Lana had never told him about anything except a crusty table knife she wanted replaced.

"One day, Gloria was opening her mail," Lana continued, "and she noticed her electrical bill had skyrocketed. It was four times what she expected. So she went on a little hunt for the culprit. Had she been using the jacuzzi too much? Leaving the blow dryer on? Had her boyfriend gone overboard with his beard trimmer? She couldn't figure it out."

Scotty shifted his weight and shot a longing glance at the side door to the yacht club.

"Then one day, she felt warmth coming from the attic. Gloria never went up there, but she wondered if maybe the heating system was out of whack. She pulled down the ladder, which was surprisingly clear of spiders and dust bunnies. And when she got up there, do you know what she found?"

"Ms. Rubicon, I really need to—"

"Plants. Hundreds of them. Her no-good boyfriend was running a clandestine grow operation, right under her own roof. He'd wired up a bunch of fans and a whole string of those"—she nodded at the tinted light bulbs—"and it was chewing through her electrical bill."

Finally, one of the bulbs slid out of Scotty's grasp and hit the ground at his feet, breaking with a sharp snap. When he looked up, stress streaked across his face.

"What do you want?"

"I want to talk to your business partner. Now. Or else I'll do what Gloria didn't have the sense to do. Call the police."

"Growing is legal now," Scotty said.

"With a permit, it is. Without one, it's a federal crime."

Scotty looked around the parking lot for a saving grace. His eyes paused on the black-and-white parked at the Kayak Shack. Lana saw it too.

"Looks like I won't even have to make that call," she said.

"You better come with me," he said.

After an awkward fumble of heat lamps and doorknobs, Scotty begrudgingly handed Lana his key ring. She unlocked the yacht club and held the service door open wide, relishing her newfound proprietorship of the situation. The door opened onto a narrow hallway, made tighter by the crates of onions and toilet paper lining the walls. The smell of fish and old fry grease hung in the air. Lana tried to hold her breath and not touch anything.

They reached a metal door near the end of the hallway, far from the kitchen and the restaurant dining room. Scotty stopped and took a long look at Lana. "You sure you want to peek behind the curtain?"

"It's just the two of you, right?"

Scotty nodded.

"You swear?"

Scotty made an ill-advised attempt to draw the sign of the cross without dropping any more light bulbs.

"Okay, then. Let's go." She dangled his keys. "Got to get those lamps unloaded before another one breaks."

Lana unlocked the door and entered a dank, pungent lair. She clamped one hand over her nose to keep from gagging on the smell. The stench of wet skunk and lemon peels hung in the air, slipping between her fingers to fill her nostrils with an acrid fog.

It was a storeroom. Or it used to be. Boxes were shoved together and stacked in the middle to form a long, uneven table, covered by a large blue tarp. On top of the tarp, a makeshift greenhouse was taking shape. Rows of small, leafy plants had been hastily potted and interspersed with box fans.

Lana's eyes adjusted quickly to the dim light. Her other senses, however, were overwhelmed. The wet-skunk smell had a sweet, fruity underlayer, like berries left to rot in the sun. And then there was the sound, which was almost as bad as the smell. Punk music was pounding from a speaker, harmonizing with the whirring box fans to create the kind of noise Lana imagined you might hear if you ripped the wings off an airplane mid-flight.

Paul was at the far end of the table, bobbing his head to the music, twisting himself over the boxes to rig up a scaffold over the plants, presumably to hold the heat lamps.

"Took you long enough," Paul yelled over the noise, turning toward the open door. Then he saw Lana. "What the hell is she doing here?"

"Gave me no choice," Scotty yelled back. He dumped the electrical equipment onto the tarp and switched off the music, dropping the decibel level into a zone where Lana's ears were no longer in danger of bleeding.

"She knows," Scotty said. "Told me she'd call the cops if I didn't bring her to you."

"And you just rolled over and handed her your keys?" Paul was still shouting. His face was red, and there was a line of sweat that stretched across his chest from one armpit to the other.

"Dude. The sheriffs are looking for you."

"Paul, everything's going to be fine," Lana said.

"Oh, sure. We're all hunky-mc'dory here." He walked over and got right up in Lana's face. She didn't flinch.

"Gimme those." Paul grabbed Scotty's keys out of Lana's hand. She offered no resistance, and Paul's plan apparently ended there. He looked at the key ring in disgust and threw it onto the tarp. Then he kicked a box, causing the half-assembled jungle gym of PVC pipe to clatter to the ground.

"You done?" Lana held herself still, her face a blank wall, while Scotty scrambled across the room to set the rig back into place.

"Why. Are. You. Here." Paul had switched to an imitation of a tough guy, gritting his teeth and standing straight, legs wide, arms folded across the line of sweat on his T-shirt. His gruff appearance was blunted by the box fan blowing in his face, ruffling his hair up like a child who'd woken in the middle of the night with a bad dream.

"You didn't kill that young man," Lana said. "Ricardo Cruz."

"I'm listening."

"I know who did."

Paul said nothing.

"And I need your help to prove it."

"Why should I help you?"

"Well, first of all, it'll get the cops off your back. They think you did it."

Paul waved that off. "I didn't."

"Right. That argument's done you real well so far. Look, Paul, if you don't help me, I'll go to the cops. It'd be a twofer: I'd be turning in a lowlife murder suspect in hiding *and* an illegal marijuana operation."

Paul glared at her. Sweat had started dripping down his shirt toward his navel.

"Oh, and Paul? These plants aren't on your farm anymore. They aren't property of an LLC you set up with an online form. They're in the yacht club. A business owned entirely by your good friend Scotty here. I'm not sure how many laws or health code regulations you're breaking . . . but I'm sure the sheriff's department would be happy to illuminate us."

Paul stared at Lana. Lana and Scotty stared at Paul.

After Paul thought about it for an unreasonably long time, he gave a tight nod. They shut the door on the musky wind tunnel and made an uneasy transition down the hall to the dining room. Paul led the way with the key ring, Lana behind him, Scotty in the rear, stopping by the bar to grab three glasses of water and a bottle of Johnnie Walker Red.

"How do we do this?" Paul asked as they settled at a table in the empty dining room.

Lana still wasn't sure about that.

"First, tell me why you kept the bike," she said.

Paul eyed her over the bottle of whiskey. "I thought you believed me."

"I do. But this is a loose end. It's one of the reasons the sheriffs are looking for you right now. I need to know."

"I saw a bike cluttering the side of my shop. I took it inside. End of story."

"When?"

Paul took a swallow from his glass, then looked up at the decorative fishing nets hanging from the ceiling. "It would have been Saturday. Late morning. The day before he was found."

"Did you know it belonged to Ricardo Cruz?"

"No!"

"Do you have any idea how it got there?"

"No, but . . ." Paul looked reflective. "That Friday night, Scotty and I went out. With those chicks from Seaside, remember?"

Scotty grimaced. "You sang Nickelback at karaoke. Talk about a mood killer."

"Yeah, well, anyway, I got back to the Shack about midnight. I was blitzed, so I crashed on the cot in the back. But then some weird sounds woke me up around two, three A.M. I thought raccoons were raiding the dumpsters again. Then on Saturday morning Jack mentioned the bike when she got here, and I went outside to check it out."

"You think the bike was dumped in the middle of the night?"

"Maybe." Paul shrugged. "It makes as much sense as any of this."

"So Saturday morning you saw this mystery bike, which maybe was dropped on your doorstep in the middle of the night. And you took it inside."

"I thought I was being a Good Samaritan, helping someone who'd come back for it later."

Lana ran it through her head and gave one tight nod of satisfaction. "It fits."

"What do you mean?" Scotty asked.

"The detectives told me this theory they had, that Paul killed Ricardo and then floated him down the slough and made a fake kayak tour booking to pin the death on whoever was leading the tours when, or just before, Ricardo was discovered. I didn't think Paul was smart enough to come up with that. No offense," she said, turning to him.

Paul shrugged. He took another swig of whiskey.

"But there was someone else who's pretty damn smart. Someone I think could have come up with that plan. Someone who could have killed Ricardo, used Ricardo's phone to call in the tour booking, and then dropped the bike down here in the middle of the night to complete the picture."

"And you know who that is?"

She nodded.

"Why don't we just go commando and grab 'em ourselves?" Paul said.

"I don't have enough evidence yet," Lana said. "The cops still think you're the bad guy. I don't think a citizen kidnapping would change their minds."

She picked up a water glass and took a sip.

"Tell me why you moved your grow operation here," she said.

Paul and Scotty exchanged a look.

"Clock is ticking," she said.

Paul sighed. "You gotta understand, this isn't about drugs. It's an entrepreneurial experiment. An innovation. Fruitful. We had this idea of hybridizing marijuana plants with fruit, well, not really hybridize, but we thought if we grew the plants in proximity to strawberries, there might be some interesting ways the leaf would take on the character—"

"Look." Scotty turned to Lana. "It's not complicated. I knew Hal Rhoads from way back. He was always up for a new idea. I pitched him on this one, and he gave us some land."

"Were you growing legally, with a permit?"

Now Scotty took a slug from the bottle.

"It was just an experiment," Paul said. "At first no one ever came down there. It seemed safe enough."

"What changed?"

"A year ago, the land trust took over the farm to the east of Hal's," Scotty said. "They sent that naturalist, Ricardo Cruz, to do an audit of the property. I ran into him when I was out there watering the plants."

"Were you worried he would tell someone what you were doing?"

"Nah. But that's when we added the fence."

"Did you ever see Ricardo again?"

"One time, maybe four months ago, up at the Rhoads house." Scotty looked up. "I told the sheriffs about it when they interviewed me. I was dropping off fresh clams for Hal, and he was there. Just the kind of kid Hal loved. Another dreamer, big into the outdoors. I think his dad herded cattle on Hal's land at one point. But then Hal got shipped down to that nursing home and the vultures started circling. Hal's kids. That big boss from the land trust. We decided to keep our heads down and hope Hal got better. So much for that."

Paul shook his head. "After Ricardo Cruz died, the cops came sniffing around the land trust property. I was out there checking on the plants and saw a bunch of investigators and dogs picking their way along the mud flats. It freaked me out. And then Hal died, and suddenly everyone and his sister was tromping all over the ranch. Our hidden little enterprise didn't feel so hidden anymore, and we didn't want to lose everything we'd built. So, over the past couple weeks, I've been transferring it all here."

"Transferring via kayak? Sometimes at night?"

Paul nodded. "It took a lot of trips."

"Did you use a wheelbarrow?" she asked.

"Nah. Just a shovel, a cooler, and these right here." Paul held up his hands, laced with calluses.

Lana wondered again about the man she'd seen with the wheelbarrow. Could Diana have roped her brother into coming down late Friday night from San Francisco to dump Ricardo's body in the creek? Or did she have another impressionable man to do her bidding?

"Can we ask you some questions now?" Scotty asked.

Lana nodded.

"Who do you think killed Ricardo Cruz?"

"Diana Whitacre, Hal Rhoads's daughter. I'm almost sure of it. She was having an affair with Ricardo Cruz, at the same time as he was secretly working with Hal on a project for the future of the ranch. A project Diana had no idea about. I think Ricardo sprang it on her, maybe even tried to blackmail her into supporting it. Diana's not a woman who takes well to pressure. She whacked him with something heavy, a ranch tool maybe, and dumped him in the creek by your little farm. It wasn't her first time. Look at this."

She held up her phone, showing them the photo of the old newspaper Jack had found.

"She killed two guys she was sleeping with?" Paul said. "That's cold." Lana watched as Paul appeared to run through his list of past dalliances, wondering which of them might come back to attack him. He looked preoccupied. It must have been a long list.

"Lana?" Scotty said. "You got a voicemail. From your daughter."

He handed over the phone, and she turned away from them. Beth's voice leaked out into the empty dining room.

"Hey, Ma, listen, I got a call from Martin. He wants me to come to that dinner at the ranch. He's concerned about you and Lady Di. I don't entirely get what's up, but it sounded like maybe you're onto something, and Jack and I want to help. See you there, I guess."

"Your daughter's still seeing that douchebag?" Scotty said.

Lana squeezed her eyes shut. She could feel her throat constricting, the veins on her neck pressing inward. She'd miscalculated the import of this dinner. This must be Diana's plan. To use Beth and Jack . . . She grabbed her phone off the table and started dialing as fast as she could.

Scotty didn't notice. "Man, that guy with his Maserati and his 'Well, if you don't stock Macallan 25 I suppose I can live with Johnnie Walker Black' and then he leaves this big honking tip like he's doing *me* a favor—"

"She isn't answering." Lana stood up. "Paul." Her voice was steel now, with a hairline crack breaking across it. "We have to go. Now."

Paul was confused. "To the ranch?"

"It went straight to Beth's voicemail," Lana said. "There's lousy reception on the ranch. Beth and Jack must already be up there."

"So?"

"So they're in trouble."

"Should we tell the cops?"

Lana considered it. Not yet. "The only thing the cops care about right now is finding you."

"And my role is what, exactly?"

Lana couldn't tell him what she wanted him to do. There was no way Paul would go for it. She didn't have the time to convince him or the energy to escalate her threats against his precious marijuana business. She decided to appeal to his vanity instead.

"We're going to need some muscle," Lana said. "In case things get heated."

Paul flexed a bicep. "You want me to protect you?"

She looked him in the eye and held a perfectly straight face. "I couldn't imagine anyone better."

CHAPTER FORTY-NINE

ON THE DRIVE UP to the ranch, Jack made her move.

"Mom, I've been thinking."

"Uh-huh?"

"I want to buy a boat." Jack held the marionberry pie tight in her lap to keep it from sliding. And to keep herself from backpedaling.

"What kind of boat?"

"A sailboat. So I can go out in the ocean on my own."

The Camry bounced over a rut in the dirt road.

"Do you even know how to sail?"

"Scotty O'Dell said he'd teach me. I was going to wait to tell you about it until after Prima's investigation was all over, but there's this sweet twenty-two-footer for sale in San Luis Obispo and I've been saving up money and—"

Beth pulled the car to a sudden stop just before the gate to the Rhoads ranch. The cracked sign bearing the upside-down *R* swung in the breeze above them.

"Jack, I appreciate you sharing what's on your mind. To be honest, there is nothing I would like more than to turn this car around, go get some burritos, and hear all about your dream to conquer the high seas. But we agreed to come here and help your Prima. So why don't we try to get through this dinner, and then we can talk?"

"Promise?"

"I promise."

• • •

When Beth turned the final curve, she saw Martin and Diana waiting for them on the driveway. The sun was just starting to set, and warm orange light reflected off the west-facing windows, making the ranch house appear to glow. Beth got out of the car first. She waved at Martin and gave Lady Di a stilted half bow.

Martin smiled, but his eyes didn't soften. He looked stressed. "Thank you for coming."

"Happy to help," Beth said. "Jack too."

The girl emerged from the car with the pie box in her hands. Beth could see the caution in her daughter's eyes, as if she hadn't yet decided how she felt about the meal ahead. Or maybe she was still stewing about the boat.

Martin gave Jack a nod. "You made it just in time for sunset."

"Jack, honey," Beth said, "look."

The four of them stood in a line facing the ocean, Diana and Martin on one side of the Camry, Beth and Jack on the other. Beth reached out and grabbed Jack's hand, giving it a quick squeeze as they watched the sun flatten itself against the horizon. Jack squeezed back. For a moment, they all stood there, their eyes chasing the sun into the water.

Once the last flash of light winked out, the air turned chilly.

"Where's my mother?" Beth asked, looking around.

"Something must have held her up," Diana said. She didn't look happy about it. "Martin, the food's in my car . . ."

She clicked her remote at a green Jaguar parked by a dusty pickup in front of the greenhouses.

Beth and Jack followed Martin to help.

"Do you think Prima's okay?" Jack bit her lip. Lana had been texting her all afternoon about Lady Di and the evidence they still needed to find. It had been exciting when it was just words on the phone. But up on the ranch, it felt different. Isolated. She could hear frogs waking up in the muddy creeks down below, the crickets twitching in the high grass. But there was no light, no movement except their own.

"I'm sure she'll be here soon," Beth said. She looked down the road, squinting at the darkened fields and rolling hills beyond the gate. "A dinner party? Lana wouldn't miss it."

• • •

The parking lot of the yacht club was not so picturesque at sunset. The sun slammed into the ocean at an angle that blinded anyone who was sentimental enough to gaze west.

Paul and Lana were looking north, hunting for supplies in the decrepit boatyard on the far side of the yacht club.

Paul peeled a canvas cover off an upside-down rowboat and pulled out a cardboard box. He dumped it on the gravel beside Lana and began digging through it, tossing aside a sleeping bag and an armful of clothes before wading back in.

"Have you been . . . living under this boat?" Lana stepped between the islands of seagull poop.

"Just the last couple nights." Paul's voice was muffled, his head deep in the box.

"How long did you imagine you could evade the sheriffs here?"

He shrugged. "It's worked so far."

It was disgusting, but also brilliant. With the sheriffs watching everyone coming in and out of the marina, Paul had found the one place he wouldn't be spotted. Even if it did come with the stench of eviscerated fish.

Lana watched with clinical detachment as Paul pulled off his sweat-stained T-shirt, revealing a shark tooth necklace and a blond, furry trail from his navel down to the top of his khaki pants. He put on a black sweatshirt, a leather vest, and a moth-bitten beanie.

"Do I look tough?" he asked.

Lana gave him a curt nod. She felt the slightest twinge of guilt for roping him into this.

"Do you have anything you could use as a weapon?"

He tunneled back into the box and emerged waving an American-flag-coated Maglite.

She stared at it. "The sheriffs are looking for that, you know. They think you used it to kill Ricardo. It could have helped you out a lot if you'd given it to them to test."

"They took all my others," he said. "I needed this one to get my plants."

There was no time to critique Paul's shortsightedness. It might even help her. Lana gave him brief bullet points on his role, telling him where he'd wait and how she'd signal when she needed him. By the time she handed him her backup key fob, it was 6:05.

"We have to go," she said.

"How are we going to get past the cop at the gate?"

"I've got a plan for that."

It took only a little cajoling to get Paul to agree to it.

• • •

Diana stayed out front to wait for Lana while Beth, Jack, and Martin carried the food inside. The ranch house was cavernous and dark, cluttered with farm implements from the ranch's past. They passed a set of massive elk horns in the foyer, a line of spurs mounted above the coat rack, and over every doorway, cattle brands, upside-down *R*s wrought in heavy iron. On the way to the kitchen, Beth peeked left, into a sunken den that was dominated by a leather couch and a fireplace lined with wide, heavy river stones.

After Jack set the pie on the counter, she wandered into the den. Beth and Martin stayed in the kitchen. It was brighter than the rest of the house, all pale wood and windows with frilly curtains. The decor was avian, with wood-framed watercolors and sketches of pheasants, hawks, even a bald eagle.

"It's lovely in here," Beth said.

"This was my mom's domain." Martin poured wine into two glasses, handing one to Beth. "She had a light touch."

Beth leaned in to take a closer look at a framed photograph hanging by the kitchen sink. It was a large group of people, thirty or so, standing in front of the barn. Most of them were holding hand tools, smiling. But not the Rhoadses. Younger versions of Martin and Diana stood on one edge of the doorway, faces solemn, clutching flowers. Hal stood between the open doors, beside a Mexican woman with a toddler. Beth had the feeling she'd seen them before.

"When was this?" she asked.

"Twenty-five years ago, give or take. When the new barn was raised."

Beth looked again. She squinted into the dark mouth of the barn, letting the rest of the crowd go blurry. Then she remembered. Hal, the tired woman, and the baby boy, clipped out and hidden in the back of the picture frame in his room at Bayshore Oaks.

"Who's that?" Beth asked, pointing at the Mexican woman.

Martin leaned closer. "Sofia." His voice was stilted. "She worked here. Her husband, he died in the fire with my mother, in the barn that was here before."

"How awful." Beth looked at the woman with the little boy, imagining how devastated she must have been, knowing the hard path that lay ahead of her.

Her thoughts were interrupted by the low purr of a car approaching outside. A set of headlights swung across the kitchen windows, and Lana's Lexus rolled into view.

Through the kitchen window, Beth watched as Lady Di and her mother greeted each other. Lana was decked out in a sharp black suit and heels. It even looked like she'd had her wig styled. Lady Di was more subdued in her long, camel peacoat, clutching a large folio of papers.

"Martin!" Diana called out. "Come and say hello to Ms. Rubicon."

Martin flinched. But he didn't leave. He pulled back from the window and looked at Beth. "Your mother," he said. "I hear she's quite the real estate shark."

"More of a leopard seal. Cute on the outside, razor-sharp teeth on the inside."

"Is she going to cause problems for me?"

Beth's face froze in a half smile. "I think she's just trying to help—"

"My sister, I know. And Ricardo Cruz. She seems very helpful."

Beth nodded uncomfortably. Maybe bringing their separate family tensions into the same house wasn't such a great idea.

CHAPTER FIFTY

DINNER WAS MORE THAN a little awkward. Diana had bought a salad and fancy pizzas, the kind that came with fussy toppings and no sauce on rosemary-scented crackers. She kept trying to bring up her proposal for the future of the ranch, but Martin refused to talk business until after they'd eaten. They crunched their way through the meal, grasping for something to talk about.

"Jack, I was sorry to hear about your boss," Martin said.

Jack looked at him quizzically.

"What are you talking about?" Beth asked.

"I saw a news alert an hour ago," Martin said. "Apparently the sheriffs have a warrant out for Paul Hanley's arrest. For the murder of Ricardo Cruz. And Hanley appears to be missing."

Lana took a careful sip of her water. "I'm not sure I agree with the sheriffs about who killed Ricardo Cruz." Out of the corner of her eye, she saw Diana's jaw stiffen.

"This is hardly appropriate dinner conversation," Diana said.

"You're right, Di," Martin said easily. He looked almost happy to have contributed to the unsettling of his sister. "So, Lana. I hear you have lung cancer?"

Diana almost choked on her wine.

Lana gazed up at the man neutrally, as if he'd asked her if she had enough salad.

"That's correct, Martin." Lana gave him a thin smile. "And if you'll excuse me, I realize I left my pills in the car."

Lana sauntered to the front door. Once outside, she strode over to Diana's Jaguar. It was a sedan, fairly new, in an understated gray-green. Try as she might, she couldn't recall seeing it before.

But the dusty pickup behind it *did* look familiar. The more she stared at the rusted old Ford, the more certain she was that it was the truck parked behind her at the land trust the day of the fire. It couldn't have been further from Diana's style—which made it perfect if she was trying to hide her tracks.

Finally. Concrete evidence. Lana wanted to shout or jump, but instead she took out her phone and photographed the truck from every angle. Then she headed over to her car to grab an old pill dispenser from the glove compartment and check that the photos were decent. Swiping through them filled her with energy. She was confident there was more to find that linked Diana to Ricardo. Maybe even the murder weapon. She wanted just enough time to get what they could, and then they needed to hand it all over before Diana realized what was happening. She fired off a text to Detective Ramirez.

Meet me at Rhoads ranch. 8 p.m. I promise Paul Hanley will be there.

She got out of the car and put one hand on the trunk to steady herself. She felt a soft flutter, as if the car were pregnant. She looked around. The closest greenhouse was dark, silent, the shadows behind it growing longer. She watched the world slip from twilight to night, hundreds of stars peeking out over the slough.

She was ready. Lana stepped away from the Lexus, considering the presentation ahead. She had to get Diana and Martin talking or arguing or both. She knew how to stretch out the negotiation if she had to. She walked around Beth's Camry and past Martin's Maserati to head back to the house.

Or rather, almost past. Her stride was broken by an aberration, a kind of stop sign slamming in her brain. For a moment, Lana was afraid she was going to have another fall. But then she realized it was something in Martin's car that had caused her to freeze.

The convertible's top was down, the seats packed with suitcases and boxes. It appeared to be a mix of his own personal items and things from the ranch—likely heirlooms Martin wanted to bring back to San Francisco. There was a weathered cane chair sandwiched in the passenger seat upside down, its stiff back creating a kind of cage for a set of antique farm tools laid out on a towel on the floor. A bag stuffed with file folders held the chair in place, settled on the underneath of the seat like an anchor.

It was the bag that stopped her. Glossy and heavy-looking, all black, with two thin plastic grooves running down one side.

She glanced back at the closed door to the house. She'd have to get back in there soon. She pushed aside the images in her mind of Diana Whitacre and Ricardo Cruz and tried to listen with another part of her brain, where a tiny bell was ringing about the bag.

Her concentration was broken by a buzz on her phone. A response from Ramirez:

Where is Hanley now?

Now? Lana hadn't expected the detective to get back to her so quickly. The truck was good, but she needed more evidence. Lana weighed her options. She really didn't want to lie to a sheriff's deputy. Not again. At least, not in text.

She took a deep breath and dialed.

Ramirez picked up right away. The sound quality was terrible, making it seem like the woman was yelling at her. Or maybe she *was* yelling.

"WELL?"

"I don't know."

"You don't know what?"

"I don't know what Paul Hanley's doing at the moment." Lana had some ideas. The possibilities were limited. But technically, she couldn't be sure. "But I know he'll be here at eight."

The detective went into a long speech about the consequences of lying to a sworn officer, wasting government resources, harboring dangerous criminals, and so on. Lana pulled the phone away from her ear and looked at the time: 6:38. She had to get back into the house.

"Reception here is terrible," Lana shouted into the phone. "I can't hear you. I'll see you at eight."

And then, despite her misgivings, Lana hung up.

The front door to the house opened, and Lana hopped sideways, trying to put as much distance as possible between her and the Maserati without it being too obvious. She dropped to the ground, pretending to adjust a nonexistent strap on her high heel. At the same time, she turned the phone in her hand, trying to fashion it into a blunt weapon.

Lana slowly raised her eyes, trying her best to look like a tired, foolish woman who needed her medication.

"Ma, you okay?" Beth asked.

Lana straightened up at the sound of her daughter's voice and gave her a smile. She looked down. Her hand was buzzing with a stream of all-caps texts from the detective. She slid the phone to silent, pocketed it, and followed Beth inside.

BACK IN THE DINING ROOM, Martin was eating the last of his pizza wafer. Diana had pushed aside the plates, making room for a sheaf of papers she pulled out of a slim leather folio.

"Ready?" she asked crisply.

"Almost," Lana said. She held up the pill dispenser. Diana frowned and rocked backward, as if lung cancer might be contagious. "I'll just need a few minutes in the restroom."

Martin stood. "Di, I wonder if we might start this conversation privately. It's clear Lana needs some time to take care of herself. Perhaps we could go into Dad's study?"

Lana looked up. Private was good. Private meant she could search the house. Diana reluctantly stood and walked toward her brother with her stack of paper.

"We'll be out shortly," she said. "To talk through the financials. And the comps we discussed. I sincerely hope you'll be able to participate by then." She raised a hand to Lana, dismissing her, and followed her brother down the hall. A door swung shut beyond the den.

"Well, that was pleasant," Lana said. "Where's Jack?"

"She went exploring," Beth said. "Outside."

Lana nodded.

"Ma, what exactly are you up to?"

"Stay here. Give me a shout if that door opens."

After a quick glance at the closed door of the study, Lana headed up the stairs and along a hallway she hoped led to the bedrooms. And a bathroom, where she could say she wanted privacy if someone came looking for her.

The first door she came to must have been Martin's room. There was a double bed with a dark blue wool coverlet, a scratched-up desk, and a bulky dark-wood bureau with a line of tiny Star Wars figurines marching across it. The walls were adorned with San Francisco 49ers posters, M.C. Escher prints, and an MIT pennant. Despite the personal touches, the room was cleaned out. There were no papers on the desk, no trash in the wastebasket on the floor. The aroma of watered-down bleach hung in the air. Lana took a quick pull at the top drawer of the bureau. Nothing. Not even a dust bunny.

She proceeded to the next door. This room was smaller, more worn. There was a twin bed, a simple dresser, and an antique, heavy-looking crib, the kind someone had probably carried in a wagon over the plains to California generations ago. The closet was stuffed with coats and faded quilts. But it didn't seem to be a storeroom for old furniture. There were small clumps of dried dirt on the floor, and Lana could smell the faint scents of sage and moss on the bed. Someone had stayed here recently, their presence not yet swept away.

Lana crossed the hallway and opened another door. Finally. Diana's room. This one had a more lived-in feel. Diana clearly wasn't rushing home to her husband the instant the land negotiations were over. The queen bed was hastily made, the bureau littered in perfume bottles and creams, plus a wineglass that had yet to make it down to the dishwasher. Lana ran her hand across the silky duvet cover, which had a delicate pattern of roses and thorns around the edge.

Lana moved to Diana's bureau. It was about half-full of clothes, including an entire drawer of lingerie. Lana carefully lifted the flimsy nightgowns in search of something incriminating but found only silk and lace.

In the bedside table, though, she made a discovery. A stack of red envelopes, each sliced open at the top, in the top drawer. Lana didn't have time to paw through months of tawdry love letters. But she couldn't resist a quick peek.

The letters were not the smutfests she expected. They were cards. Generic, store-bought holiday cards with "Merry Christmas" swirling across the front. The stack started in 2000 and went forward from there. Inside each one, someone had written a simple message.

2001 said: "Dear Mr. Rhoads and Miss Diana, thank you for the gift of your friendship."

2005: "Congratulations to Miss Diana on your engagement. May you be as happy as I was with my Alejandro."

2015: "We hold your kindness in our hearts."

The writing in the earlier cards wasn't familiar to Lana. But in the later ones, she recognized the same blocky print from the handwritten note she'd found at the land trust.

As Lana sifted through the cards, a photograph fell out of one dated 2008. It was a snapshot of a tired-looking woman with long black hair, holding hands with a tall young man. They were standing outside an apartment building on a dusty street, somewhere inland maybe, one of those hard, dry towns that swallowed up work and spat out debt. The boy looked twelve or thirteen. His face was spotty, his limbs too big for his thin frame. But his wide smile and bright eyes were unmistakable. It was Ricardo Cruz.

Lana heard her daughter calling her name from the bottom of the stairs. She filed the cards back into their stack and shoved them into the drawer.

"Coming," she called down.

Lana descended the stairs, churning through what she'd found. She knew the Cruz family had worked on the ranch at one point. But she doubted many ranch hands sent heartfelt Christmas cards to their bosses for years after their employment had ended. There was something more there. A relationship with Ricardo and his mother, one that was important to Diana. And try as she might, picturing it now as something sexual felt like a stretch.

"It got quiet. I thought they were coming out." Beth nodded her head down the hall. "But now I'm not so sure."

"Hear anything good?"

"I wouldn't say 'good.'"

Lana listened to the muffled voices. She could make out Martin yelling about how he needed this and Diana lashing back that it was her turn now, that he never took responsibility for anything. It sounded like their dispute was genuine. If not, they were trying to win an Oscar with their performance.

"There is one thing I wanted to show you." Beth gathered up a stack of plates, and Lana followed her to the kitchen.

"This is different," Lana said, taking in the light-colored wood in the bright room. Her eyes swept over the drawings of birds, her mind subconsciously supplying names for all the species she'd gotten to know over the past few months.

"Look at this," Beth said, walking over to the framed photograph by the sink. "Martin told me it's from when they built the new barn after the fire. When I was packing up Mr. Rhoads's room at Bayshore Oaks, I found a cut-up copy, just Hal with that woman and the baby. I wondered if she might be—"

"Sofia Cruz," Lana said.

"Who?"

"Ricardo's mother. And that's Ricardo." Lana pointed at the toddler squirming in the woman's arms. The pieces were falling into place quickly now.

"Do you think it's possible Ricardo was Hal Rhoads's son?" Beth asked.

Lana thought of the cards she'd found upstairs, addressed to both Hal and Diana, their simple messages blending formality and warmth. "I don't think so. I think . . ." Lana rubbed her eyes, rerouting the connections she'd made upstairs to everything they'd mapped on the corkboard in the back bedroom.

"I have to talk to Jack," she said. "I'm going outside."

"Should I come?" Beth asked.

"Stay here," Lana said. "Let's hope they keep fighting."

CHAPTER FIFTY-ONE

WHEN SHE GOT TO THE DRIVEWAY, Lana noticed the barn door was swung open. She headed inside, sure she'd find Jack there, rummaging around. As she entered, Lana noted the fine-grained wood walls and shiny brass hinges. Mr. Rhoads had spared no expense in rebuilding this barn. There were modern copper light fixtures hanging down over each stall, and Jack had turned on the ones in the back row, suffusing the piles of junk in a warm glow. Lana thought back on the photo in the kitchen, the unsmiling Rhoads and Cruz families standing in the newly erected doorway. This barn had been built out of loss. While the structure could be revived, Alejandro Cruz and Cora Rhoads could not.

Jack called to Lana from a stall at the back of the barn. Lana gingerly stepped into a cul-de-sac of tennis rackets, toys, and moldy sleeping bags. She ran a finger over an electronics set, the bright yellow box standing out against the dusty browns and grays of the other items in the stall.

"Look at this." Jack placed a baseball glove in Lana's hand. It was a tiny catcher's mitt, real leather, the kind an optimistic father might get for his baby boy. Lana could barely put three fingers inside of it. But it clearly had been used. The glove was well-worn, a spiderweb of cracks erupting across the faded leather pocket. The bridge was brittle, and one of the ties had been chewed, maybe by a mouse. On the side, along what would have been the back of the thumb, "Ricardo" was written in bold block letters. And under it, fainter, another name: "Martin."

Lana clutched the glove and closed her eyes. She remembered the story Diana had told her about the fire, and what Beth said had happened after. How Martin and Hal had stayed on the ranch but grew apart, while Ricardo, the miracle baby, grew up.

Lana had had it wrong. She'd known Ricardo's murder was about love and betrayal. But it wasn't about Victor's love for Ricardo, or an affair gone wrong between Diana and Ricardo. It was about family love, something that had started decades earlier, something that had burned down and been rebuilt from pain. It was about Hal's son, and Hal's boy, and the distance between them.

"Jack, you were right. It wasn't BATNA at all."

"Do you mean—"

Lana nodded. "Martin." She flashed again to the strange black bag in his car. She didn't have words yet to explain it all, but she could feel it. She could see the excitement in Jack's eyes too.

She looked down at her phone. Seven thirty. There was barely any cell service inside the barn, and she hadn't heard anything more from Ramirez. She looked up at the double kayak lofted in the front corner of the barn, the lone life jacket hanging beneath it.

"Is this the one you saw at the wake?"

Jack nodded.

"Anything different about it?"

"No." Jack looked carefully at the boat. "But a double kayak should have two life jackets . . ."

The girl's voice died, as if she'd been hit by the terrible memory of it: Ricardo Cruz, floating in the mud, a red life jacket strapped around his lifeless body. The timeline leading up to that discovery snapped into focus in Lana's brain. Ricardo was killed midday Friday and dumped in the creek late that night, to be found Sunday morning by the tourists. By Jack. For the first time, Lana considered the significance of that gap on Friday, the hours between the murder and the creek. She considered how long it would take to travel from San Francisco to Elkhorn, back up to the city, and then down again to Elkhorn late that same night. On a bike, it'd be impossible. But in a Maserati, it might even be a pleasure.

That strange black bag in Martin's car. Ricardo's bike with its missing pannier. That was it.

"Jack. Tell me about bike panniers. Are they heavy, like coated canvas?"

The girl nodded, her eyes wide. "Why?"

"Let's get out of here." Lana tucked the catcher's mitt under her arm and picked her way out of the cluttered stall, typing out a quick text to Paul and hoping she had enough of a cell signal to send it.

But before they reached the barn door, Lana heard footsteps. The sound of people talking. Then an angry voice, Diana's, traveling through the darkness.

"Martin, we haven't finished our discussion yet—"

The entrance to the barn was blocked by a tall figure. Which became two figures. Then three.

"Found you," Martin said. His eyes were dark, unreadable in the dim light. "What you got there?"

Lana instinctively stepped in front of Jack and put the baseball glove behind her back. Then she thought better of it. They needed to leave the barn. To get Paul, and Detective Ramirez. She needed to pretend there was nothing worth hiding in here.

She held up the glove, her hand covering the names on the inner edge.

"Jack and I were just playing around." Lana put on a face of nonchalance and tossed the glove into an unlit stall. "It was nothing. Let's go."

Lana advanced toward the door. But no one else moved. Martin blocked the entrance to the barn, Diana catching up to him on his left side. Beth was a few paces behind them, wavering in the darkness beyond the open door.

"Martin, I don't understand this little field trip—" Diana's voice was harsh.

Lana's eyes darted around in the dark. "I apologize, I've kept you waiting. We should go back to the house to discuss the future of the ranch."

"The reason we're all here," Martin said.

"Of course. I just wanted to find Jack first," Lana continued. It came out feebler than she intended.

"What else did you find?" Martin asked.

Lana looked at the man before her. His eyes were fierce. He was tall and athletic. But still, just a man. She could handle him.

"Martin, please, let's go inside the house. Your sister has some good ideas, and with your brilliance, I think we could create something extraordinary. Can't we—"

"We're selling the ranch," Martin said. His voice was loud, hard as iron. It echoed in the drafty barn, bouncing off the metal roof.

"But that's not what your father wanted." Jack's voice shot past Lana, high and unbidden.

Martin took a step toward the teenager. "How do you know that?"

Beth approached him, putting a hand on his shoulder. "Martin—"

"Beth." He turned to look at her, grasping at her fingers and trapping them against his jacket.

Jack looked nervous. "What I mean is—"

"We found the plans," Lana broke in. She didn't like how Martin was looking at her girls. "For the project your father was doing with Ricardo Cruz. Verdadera Libertad."

"I have no idea what you're talking about," Martin said.

Now it was Beth who spoke out in surprise. She pulled her hand away from Martin's. "I gave you those papers," she said. "From the architect."

"So you looked at them? Was it before you gave them to me, or were you snooping over my shoulder?" He shook his head in disgust. "And here I was thinking you didn't play your mother's games. Di, these women have been meddling in our business. In Dad's business."

"Not meddling," Lana said. "Finding the truth."

Lana kept her eyes locked on Diana. If she couldn't get them out, she had to reel them in.

"I told you about it at lunch," Lana said. Her voice was calm and clear. "Your father and Ricardo Cruz had a project together. A vision to turn the ranch into a farm incubator for women and disadvantaged entrepreneurs. Maybe Ricardo talked about it. Your daddy and his big dream."

"That dream is dead," Martin said.

"Dead?" Lana fixed her gaze on Martin. "Because you killed them?"

Martin barked out a laugh. He turned to his sister, a twisted smile on his face. "Is this your negotiating strategy, Di? Get her to make wild threats so I'll let you have the ranch?"

Lana looked squarely at Diana. "Your brother killed Ricardo. Right here at the ranch. He bludgeoned him and dumped his body in the creek. And then he killed your father."

"I don't believe this," Martin scoffed.

"The sheriffs are on their way, Martin," Lana said. "To collect the evidence."

"Evidence?" Diana asked.

"It's here," Lana said, gesturing around the barn. She wasn't sure what was there. But maybe something that could buy time. Something that could keep him away from his car.

Diana's eyes scanned the barn, straining to take in the piles of junk in the dim light. She was questioning. Drawn in.

Martin sneered. "Di, Ricardo Cruz was killed miles from here. And I was in San Francisco day and night. This woman doesn't know what she's talking about. She's nothing but a washed-up snoop."

"You were in San Francisco, Martin," Lana agreed. "But not all day. Not all night."

She absorbed his furious gaze, staring back with what she hoped looked like compassion.

"I know how it feels, Martin." Lana turned her voice into a silk thread, casting out, tugging gently on his name. "When your family doesn't appreciate you. Doesn't respect you." She took a step toward him. "It must have been awful, seeing Ricardo wrap them around his finger again. He disappears for twenty years and now all of a sudden he's swooping in to take over the ranch?"

She saw the slightest flicker of his eyelid, a tiny, involuntary twitch. "You were the only one who saw through him," she said. "The only one willing to protect your family. Your legacy."

Martin said nothing. But his eyes were shining, his head tilting toward her. Lana took another step.

"He was going to steal everything," Lana said. "You had to do something."

"You have no idea what you're talking about." But Martin's words came out fainter this time.

Lana stepped even closer to him. "And then you ran into him here. At the house. Ricardo was staying here, wasn't he? With you, Diana? On Wednesday nights?"

Diana crossed her arms over her chest. Her voice wobbled between uncertainty and defiance. "Ricardo was like my nephew. He slept in his old room, where he and his mom had stayed after . . . It wasn't tawdry. We were just reconnecting about old times."

"Old times. The best ones, right?" Lana said. "When Ricardo was a toddler and you were a young woman with a broken heart. A woman who needed to heal."

"Ricardo was the only good thing at that time." There was a tremble in Diana's voice. "Our little angel. Our little boy."

Lana nodded. Then she took a guess. "That last week, you both stayed Thursday night as well. To talk about the future."

Diana looked back, into the night, as if Ricardo were standing on the other side of the barn door. "I wanted to ask him to join me in developing the wellness center. I thought it could be a way for us both to honor our parents, to build something beautiful together." Diana's face flushed, and her voice sharpened. "Then I discovered he and Daddy had other plans."

"You argued."

"Thursday night, yes. We had words. I left early Friday morning, before Ricardo was up. To go to Bayshore Oaks to talk to Daddy. To work things out. I would never have hurt Ricardo."

Lana nodded. "You would never have hurt him. But you did keep him a secret."

"I had to protect myself," Diana said stiffly. "Once I heard about his death, I realized I might have been the last person to see him alive. He stayed over with me at the ranch, and then he died. It was horrible. I've lived that nightmare before, in England. The authorities would pounce, the rumors would spread. Even if I didn't get charged with killing him, my reputation would have been ruined."

Lana felt a sudden shot of compassion for Diana, who had loved Ricardo and lost him. But she had to keep the focus on Martin. "What about before then, all those times you met up with him? I understand keeping it from your husband, but your own brother? Didn't you want to invite Martin to catch up on old times with Ricardo? To dream together about the future?"

Diana cast a nervous glance toward Martin. "I didn't think he would be interested."

Lana caught a flinch from Martin's direction. A small wound, one she could pry open. Lana looked up at Martin with wide eyes. "You see what I mean? Your own sister, lying to you for months. Protecting her little angel Ricardo."

Lana held up a hand to quell a flutter of protest from Diana's direction and took one last step toward Martin. She didn't have all the details, but he knew what he'd done. She just had to speak to his heart.

"I know what it's like to be pushed outside your family, Martin. The inside jokes, their little secrets. It started when you were a teenager, didn't it? When they began leaving you out of things. Your mother died. You were mourning. But everyone only had eyes for Ricardo. It must have been quite a shock, seeing him in the house after all those years."

"You're wrong. I didn't care about Ricardo," Martin said. His voice was flat, unconvincing. "He was just a baby who grew up. So he was back at the house again, having pajama parties with Di. So what? I couldn't have cared less."

"Like your dad did, Martin? Like he cared less about you than he did about Ricardo?" Lana was just an arm's length away from Martin now.

"You don't know what you're—"

Lana remembered something Beth had told her, way back when Mr. Rhoads had died. It felt like a lifetime ago. "Even at the nursing home, they knew. Your father talked about him to the nurses. You were his son. But Ricardo was his boy, his golden boy who returned."

Martin turned to Beth, his eyes full of hurt and questions. She stared back at him with a steady gaze.

"It's not your fault, Martin," Lana said, pulling his attention toward her again. "He shouldn't have abandoned you like that." She reached out a hand to him. He wavered.

"You're making something out of nothing," he mumbled.

"Giving Ricardo your old baseball glove? Giving him the ranch? It wasn't nothing, Martin. You deserved more." Lana clasped his left hand in both of hers. He didn't pull away.

She had him. She knew she did. "You deserved your father's love. You deserved to know what he was planning. As a mother, I know what you were due."

His hand went stiff between her fingers. She hauled him in with one last tug on the line.

"If your mother were here, she would have stood by you. She would have protected you. If only she hadn't—"

A deafening smack cut off Lana's speech.

Despite all her experience sparring with men, Lana had never been in a situation that had turned truly violent. There had been shouting. There had been smashed vases. Once, there was hot coffee poured into her favorite white patent-leather pumps. But Lana's adversaries tended to draw the line at hitting women.

Which is why Lana was woefully unprepared when Martin's open hand reached her cheekbone. There was a crack of stinging pressure. The room started to spin. She felt herself slide away from him, away from all of them, toward the cold dirt floor.

It was impossible to think clearly over the ocean of hurt, impossible to contemplate where precisely she'd gone wrong in her attempt to trap him. But she knew one glorious thing. Above the pain, riding the crest of the shock waves ricocheting through her body, was a feeling of triumph. Lana's final thought was simple: she'd gotten it right.

CHAPTER FIFTY-TWO

BETH STARED IN HORROR at the pile of linen and high heels on the ground where her mother had been. Her medical training told her that Lana wasn't likely to die from a single slap. But her eyes and her heart were shouting something different. Lana wasn't moving. Wasn't groaning. Her wig had shaken loose, lying next to her like a dead animal, exposing her wiry hair and tender scalp. Even in the darkness, the mark on her cheek blazed bright red.

Beth was too focused on Lana to have a clear view of what happened next. There was a burst of motion, and then, in the corner of her eye, she saw Jack launch herself at Martin, running headfirst toward his stomach like a bull. He stepped to the side, and Jack's momentum pulled her past him. She tripped, pitching forward, then banged into the sidewall of the barn with a sickening thud.

"Martin!" Diana's voice reverberated with anger, and a thin sliver of fear.

He brushed off his sleeve, clenched and opened his fist. "She can't talk about Mom that way," he spat. "She doesn't know what we . . ."

Beth covered Lana's body protectively, using her arms to try to block out his look of disgust. She wanted to go to Jack, who was now staggering to a crouch, holding her right knee, but Lana needed her more. Beth could see the adrenaline pumping in her daughter's flushed face. Jack looked bruised. But not broken.

Lana was another story. She made no movement, no reaction to Beth's warm hands or whispered words.

Martin turned to his sister. "Let's go."

Diana looked at her brother. "Lana needs medical attention," she said. Her face looked hot, and her British accent had disappeared. "And you, you need . . ."

"What?" He scowled at her.

"You need to explain what the hell just happened."

Beth turned her head at a rustle of movement from outside the barn. Was it possible Lana had been telling the truth, and the sheriffs were on their way? She peered out into the darkness, praying it was a human, not a raccoon or coyote. But there was no one. No more sounds. Nothing.

Martin grunted. "Why don't you explain, huh?" He stepped up to his sister, towering over her. "Why you let that rat, that boy, back into our home. Why I found him lording it up at the dining room table that Friday morning, all pleased with himself, while I'm busting my ass to keep the ranch from falling apart and find a buyer so we don't have to break our backs the way Dad did all those years. You know Ricardo told me he was happy to see me? He told me about his precious Verdadera Libertad. Big grin on his face, couldn't wait to show me the drawings, all these small plots with priority for Mexicans and Filipinos and Natives and everyone who ever got their land stolen. He's going on and on with this bleeding-heart bullshit, even suggested that he and I go to Bayshore Oaks to talk to Dad about it together. Please. I couldn't wait to wipe the smile off that shit-eater's face."

"So you killed him?" Diana's voice was low, her face ashen.

"I protected what's ours. I took out the trash. Like our father should have done thirty years ago."

Beth didn't know what Martin was talking about. But it didn't matter. Not compared to her family getting out of there. Jack was leaning against the wall near the door, which was good, but she was still clutching her knee, and Beth wasn't sure whether she could walk. While Martin and his sister argued, Beth scanned the barn, looking for something useful, something within reach. All she saw were shadows.

"What about Daddy?" Diana asked. Her voice was a broken whisper.

Martin's eyes went dark. "I went to see him the next day. I asked him about the project."

"And?"

"He was going to take away the ranch from us, Di. Our inheritance. Your children's inheritance. I tried to talk sense into him, but you know how he gets when he's set on something—"

Some part of Beth knew that if Martin confessed to killing his own father, he'd never let them out of there. She imagined Mr. Rhoads in his little room at Bayshore Oaks facing his wild-eyed son, his aggrieved, furious son, with stubborn calm. With kindness. And it not being enough.

She looked toward the open door of the barn. Toward freedom, blocked by Martin. Then she looked at Jack in the corner, slumped against the wall below the lofted kayak. And she had an idea.

"Martin," she called out. Her voice sounded scared, but she had to try. "Let's just put this behind us, okay? I'm going to help Lana get to the hospital. You and your sister can sell the ranch. Like you wanted. And Jack's going to get her boat." Beth looked at her injured daughter, trying by sheer force of will to make her words sink in. "Just breathe, Jack. Focus on the boat. We're all going to move past this."

"No one's going anywhere," Martin growled. It was as if he'd barely registered her words. He was fixated on Diana, she on him, each of them searching the other for answers.

But Jack was the one Beth was counting on to hear her. To understand.

Jack nodded slightly and pulled herself away from the wall slowly, holding her hands out in front of her.

Martin turned toward her. "What are you doing?"

"I'm just getting the life jacket," Jack said. "As a pillow, for my grandma's head."

Beth watched as Jack half limped, half crept to the life jacket hanging on the wall. She tossed it back to Beth.

"Stay there," Martin barked.

Jack shrank back, as if pinned to the wall. She shifted her weight. She stayed.

Beth wedged the life jacket under Lana's head. Lana let out a low, gravelly wheeze, somewhere between a breath and a moan.

"This is crazy," Diana said. "I'm calling the cops."

"Like hell you are," Martin said. He grabbed his sister by the wrist and dragged her into the darkness of a stall, reemerging with a strange, plasticky gun. It was black and orange, small in his hand. Was it a toy? Beth couldn't be sure. Diana looked terrified. And the twelve-gauge shell he loaded into it certainly looked real.

"Get out here, Di," he said. "On the floor."

His sister shuffled out of the stall and knelt, shaking, in the middle of the barn.

He waved the gun around, pointing it in Beth and Lana's direction. "None of you move," he said. "I'd hate to see someone get hurt."

• • •

The first thing Lana saw when she woke up was the gun. Two guns, three maybe, floating in the air in a ghostly flurry of hands. Her left eye didn't seem to be working properly. And her head was pounding. Not her forehead, like she was used to, from the medicine and fatigue and too-tight wig caps. This pain was in the back, deep-seated, where her skull met her neck.

She tried to sit up. No luck. For a terrifying moment, she was afraid she'd somehow landed back on the kitchen floor of her Santa Monica condo, that she'd fallen into some kind of cosmic wormhole and would have to relive the past five months all over again. But that didn't make sense. There was only the chilly barn, the amber light, and the raging figure who was rapidly resolving from four men to two, to one.

She heard his voice and she remembered. Martin Rhoads. Murderer. She rolled the word around in her head, satisfaction pushing aside the blistering pain for a moment. She'd found him out. He'd made mistakes. Ricardo's bike bag. The truck he'd driven to the land trust. He wasn't going to get away with it.

What was it he was saying now? Something about this time not being an accident?

Lana opened her eyes another millimeter and saw him swinging around a large canister. She heard splashing, and then she felt it, cold and wet, slapping at her thighs. The smell was strong, sweet, with a chemical underlayer. It made her think of Paul. Not his swamp-grass marijuana plants. Something else, something earlier, that time she'd slid into his car outside Beth's house, that first ride that set this whole investigation into motion.

• • •

"Paul . . ." Lana groaned.

Beth looked down at her mother, dumbfounded. Was this really the first word Lana was going to say at this moment?

"Paul." It came out in a strangled croak, almost like Lana was trying to shout.

"Paul's not here, Ma," Beth whispered. "We have to do this ourselves."

Beth tried to shift her mother's weight off her lap. Her careful movements were rewarded with another groan, which drew Martin's attention, and the gun, in their direction.

"She's going to be okay!" Beth said nervously.

"I don't think so," Martin said. He shook out the last drops of gasoline onto Lana's shoes.

"Martin. Don't do this." Diana rose slowly to her feet, her hands up, her voice low and desperate.

"It's a shame you came out here, Di. While I was washing up from dinner. That the gasoline spilled. And these old bird bombs"—he looked almost lovingly at the strange gun—"they can be so unreliable. It can all blow up so quickly. You shoulda seen the damage the one I set up behind the land trust did . . ." He looked down at Lana. "Oh, wait. She saw it."

He let out a spasm of laughter that died as soon as it had started.

"Don't laugh at her," Jack said. She was still in the shadowed corner, clutching her knee.

Beth had to keep him from turning in Jack's direction. "This isn't who you are, Martin," she called out. "Not really."

"You think you know me? You don't." He practically spat the words at her. "You don't know what I'm capable of. None of you do." He rotated slowly toward his sister, holding the gun level. "Not even you."

Beth watched, confused, as Martin and Di locked eyes again.

"Thirty years I've been hiding, Di," he said. "Thirty years since Mom died."

Diana's voice came out slowly, cautious. "The fire chief said that was a freak accident. High winds and dry grass on a hot day."

"Did you believe him?" Martin sounded sulky, like a petulant teenager. "Because you left, Di. You put six thousand miles between us."

"I . . . I was grieving. That wasn't about you."

It was as if Martin hadn't heard his sister. His voice was getting louder, wilder. "You left, and then it got worse. Dad turned his back on me. He replaced me. He gave everything he had to Ricardo."

"That's not what happened." Diana took a careful step toward him.

"Stay back!" Martin pulled a plastic lighter from his pocket and held it out in front of him, like he was warding off vampires.

"Martin." Diana's voice softened, shifting from anger to sadness. "Daddy and I. We loved you. I still do."

"You wouldn't love me if you knew what really happened—"

"I knew."

Martin stared at her.

"I knew right away, Martin. You were always messing with those model rockets behind the barn. I was up on the cow pasture when Daddy found you down by the creek after the fire, sobbing and scrubbing your arms in the freezing mud. I saw him comforting you there."

The picture was starting to become clear to Beth. The barn fire. The deaths. The painful secrets families hang on to for decades. She imagined a teenage Martin, terrified and ashamed of what he'd done. The man in front of her retained some of that fear. But none of the shame. It had twisted into something else, something that had festered and seethed within him for thirty years. He looked swollen with it now, like there was a wasp's nest behind his eyes, anxious to get out.

Diana was still trying to get through to him. "Daddy took care of you, Martin. He cleaned up the evidence. He convinced the detectives no one was involved. He protected you."

"You don't know what he told me." Martin's voice was heavy, dark. "You left—"

There were tears in Diana's eyes now. "Daddy said I should give you space. That you'd tell me about it when you could. Maybe that was wrong. Maybe I should have told you right away that I knew. It doesn't matter. Whether it was dry grass or model rockets, it was an accident, Martin. A horrible accident. And we loved you. Daddy loved you."

Her voice got louder, more confident. "He wouldn't stop talking about you. Even now. That's probably why Ricardo wanted to take you along to show him the drawings. It would have been Daddy's greatest dream, the three of you building something together."

For a moment, Beth thought Diana might have succeeded. Martin's eyes were filmed over, as if he were rewatching his own history, searching for a different story in the tape. A story where his father cared for him. Where his family protected him. Where he had been a young man with a terrible secret, and they loved him anyway.

He dropped his head, directing his words to the gun and lighter in his hands.

"You know what he told me, Di? That day by the creek, while he was—how did you put it—*comforting* me? He said he would always love me . . ."

"Yes—" Diana took a step closer to him.

"But he would never forgive me." Martin whipped his tortured face up to hers, his eyes glittering. "Will you forgive me, Di?"

He stepped to the open door of the barn and flicked the lighter into flame.

CHAPTER FIFTY-THREE

"JACK! BOAT!"

No one could ever accuse Paul Hanley of running a tight ship. But there was one thing he insisted on all his employees doing properly: carrying a kayak. If he ever caught someone dragging when they should be lifting, or using their back instead of their knees, he'd rip up their time card. Jack had often heard Paul muse that it would be the perfect Olympic sport: synchronized kayak lifting. From the ground. From the water. From the racks. He trained his staff to do it all.

And so, on her mother's command, Jack Rubicon, at 105 pounds, with a messed-up knee, lifted the double kayak from its hook, swung it around, and slammed it into Martin Rhoads.

The fiberglass hull made contact below his shoulder blades, driving through his jacket and lifting him off his feet. The gun and the lighter shot out of his hands, and Martin tumbled to a landing face-first by Lana's side.

Jack watched as her mother scrambled to grab the gun, which skittered sideways toward the open door.

But it must have hit something. She heard a bang, and a scream.

Jack whirled around to see the barn wall behind Lana explode in a sea of fire.

It was fast, it was big, and it was everywhere. There was no dim copper glow anymore. Bright yellow-orange flames cartwheeled across the barn. Fire danced up the wall. The hay bales in the stall behind Lana were crackling, shooting sparks and jets of steam into the air. Her mom was screaming at her to get to the door. But her grandma was lying there in the middle of the chaos, the smoke and flames racing toward her.

Jack ran to Lana, ignoring the fire, ignoring her mother, ignoring the pain in her knee. Before she got there, though, she was thrown forward by a blast of pressure. A tremendous hiss filled the air and everything went white.

CHAPTER FIFTY-FOUR

"PAUL?"

Lana coughed, expelling smoke from her lungs. There was white dust everywhere, floating in the air, covering the stalls, as if someone had sprinkled the inside of the barn with powdered sugar.

"Not Paul." It was a woman's voice. Low. "You told me you were the one who had Paul, remember?"

Lana blinked, trying to clear the grit from her eyes so she could see.

"Ms. Rubicon. You can lower the shoe now."

Lana looked down. Her field of vision was slowly expanding to encompass her body. She was half sitting, half lying on the ground, holding one of her spike heels to Martin Rhoads's throat.

"Is he dead?" Lana blinked again, searching the smoky air for her daughter and granddaughter. She kept her grip tight on the shoe.

"He'll be fine," Beth said. Lana looked up.

"Jack knocked the wind out of him. With the kayak. She saved us all."

Through the smoke, Lana could now see her daughter and granddaughter on either side of her, covered in white and gray dust.

There were two other figures in the middle of the barn. On the ground, Diana was bent over, her blond hair turned fully white. She looked broken, cracked, as if she'd aged a lifetime in an evening. The second person was standing, a red fire extinguisher in her hand.

"You came," Lana said to Detective Ramirez. She dropped her arm, the one with the shoe, which poked into Martin Rhoads's larynx. The man coughed, and Lana jolted back from him, letting his head bonk onto the dirt floor.

Martin clutched his head and groaned. He rolled onto his hands and knees, turning his head from side to side to shake the powder loose from his face.

Ramirez strode over and stood directly above him. "Martin Rhoads. You are under arrest for murder. Attempted murder. Arson. And a few other crimes."

Lana watched the detective put handcuffs on him with a practiced snap of her manicured hands. She couldn't have been prouder if she'd done it herself.

SOON, THE RANCH was lit up with a flotilla of cop cars and ambulances. Lana sat in the back of a fire truck, a metallic blanket around her shoulders, and watched, squinting, as Jack walked the sheriffs through the importance of the catcher's mitt, the lone life jacket, and the black bag. They pulled five shovels, seven cattle brands, and two wheelbarrows out of the barn to test them for human blood.

Overseeing all the activity was Teresa Ramirez. The young detective stood in the center of the asphalt in tall black leather boots, spotlighted by the high beams from the trucks. The other officers, even Nicoletti, looked small in comparison. They scurried around like ants, approaching her with information and dashing off to do what she commanded.

After the first hour, there was a lull in the excitement. Diana was on her way to a private hospital. Martin was handcuffed in an ambulance, awaiting his fate. The Maserati and the barn were being meticulously picked over. The left side of Lana's face was now completely numb from an ice pack, and the cold had sunk through to her bones. Even Beth and Jack looked exhausted, their adrenaline shot through. They were leaning up against each other, engaged in a slow, sleepy discussion about whether sailboats were more or less dangerous than murder investigations.

Lana glanced at her phone. It was time.

She walked up to the young detective, who was sipping from a coffee cup an officer had delivered to her a few minutes before.

"Can you help me with something?"

Ramirez looked at Lana. Lana could only imagine what she saw. Her wig was a mess, and the left side of her face was blossoming into a purple bruise. The old stitches on her cheek had broken open as well. But Lana's eyes were bright, her voice clear.

"What is it?" Ramirez asked.

"Paul Hanley."

"Oh. Right. He's not a priority now that—"

"I just want to confirm that. He's no longer a suspect? Not wanted for anything?"

The detective shook her head.

"And I wouldn't be in trouble anymore for harboring a dangerous criminal?"

Ramirez looked at Lana, perplexed, as if she hadn't just lived through the past two hours.

"No."

"Good," Lana said. "Then could you help me get him out of my trunk?"

CHAPTER FIFTY-FIVE

LANA WALKED INTO THE YACHT CLUB three weeks later in a new tailored suit, with a large gift-wrapped box under her arm. Her face had finally healed. The only evidence of what had happened was a thin yellow halo under her eye, one she easily covered up with concealer.

At the door, Lana paused to run her hand across her scalp, checking that everything was in place. Her real hair was growing in, and she had paid a tattooed girl in Santa Cruz a small fortune to shape it into a chic pixie buzz cut. Lana was still undecided about the wigless look, despite Jack's repeated assurances that she didn't look like a Chia pet.

She found Paul and Scotty at the bar, deep in conversation about a new business scheme involving giant inflatable hamster balls you could rent and take out on the water. Scotty gave her a friendly nod. Paul shrank back, as if he was still afraid of her. Not as if—he *was* still afraid of her. Which was ridiculous. It wasn't her fault the key fob had slipped out of his pocket in the trunk.

Lana fluttered her hand at Fredo and his compatriots at the bar before making her way to the booth in the corner, where her date was waiting.

Even in the shadows cast by the brocade curtains, Teresa Ramirez shone. She was wearing a long, canary-yellow blazer over a white V-neck. Her fingernails were a deep cerulean, with metallic gold tips.

Scotty materialized just as Lana was sitting down.

"Corona, please," Ramirez said.

"Make it two," Lana said.

"Congratulations on your arraignment," Lana said. She tipped her beer toward the younger woman. "I hear he pled guilty on all charges?"

"Pretty much." The detective ticked them off on her fingers. "Murder of Ricardo Cruz. Murder of Hal Rhoads. Arson at the land trust. He pled to everything except the last fire. He says that was caused when your granddaughter threw him across the barn."

Lana smiled. "I've been in touch with Diana Whitacre. I don't think she'll be pressing charges against Jack."

"Do you know what she's going to do with the ranch?"

"A hybrid. She'll have her luxury spa, plus a smaller version of the farm incubator her father and Ricardo had envisioned. Supplying her wellness center with organic, hyperlocal produce. A win-win." Diana was handling the situation extraordinarily well, all things considered.

"So Verdadera Libertad lives on."

"Renamed. La Reina de la Libertad."

"The queen of liberty," Ramirez said. "Very modest."

"Indeed." Lana took a tentative sip of beer and shot a glance over at the men congregated by the bar. "Did you really think Paul was the murderer?"

Ramirez smoothed her hair back, the gold tips of her fingernails turning it into a glittering stream.

"I don't have the luxury of operating solely on my own judgment. But I never entirely agreed with Detective Nicoletti about Paul Hanley. There was too much that didn't fit. There was no meaningful connection between him and Ricardo. And according to the records on Ricardo's phone, that kayak tour booking was made near a cell tower in San Francisco. I was curious about other possibilities."

Suddenly, Lana remembered something Gaby had told her. "Ricardo used a flip phone. It probably didn't have a pass code. So Martin wouldn't have had trouble using it to make that call."

Ramirez nodded. "He was very careful about covering his tracks.

Dumping the body in the creek confused the evidence, and running up and back to San Francisco was pretty clever. But he also took stupid risks. Like holding on to that pannier and setting the fire at the land trust. He told us he didn't know if Ricardo had other hard copies of the plans for Verdadera Libertad or notes in his files. So he went up there in his dad's truck to obliterate any potential materials related to the project, just in case."

Lana brushed a finger over the memory of the stitches on her cheekbone. "But if I had seen him in that truck . . ."

"Exactly. Risky."

"Did you suspect him right away?"

"No. When you first told me about the Rhoadses, I was playing catch-up, processing the information you gave me about Diana and Ricardo. I tracked down that story about that suspicious death in England. But that young duke? His death certificate was kept from the press, but I was able to get a coroner's report. He died of a brain aneurysm. There was no foul play."

Lana felt a twinge of sheepishness for her mistaken casting of Lady Di as a black widow.

"So?"

"So you had it wrong about Diana Whitacre. But I was still interested in the Rhoads family. I found some old pictures of the ranch in the county archives. That cattle brand—I had a feeling it might be our missing murder weapon. The way Ricardo Cruz was struck, the pattern in his skull was more complicated than an arc. The coroner thought he was hit twice with the same object, a shovel maybe, but the pressure was identical for both impressions, which would be hard for someone to do, especially in the heat of the moment. I thought it was one blow, from one weapon with an unusual shape. And the corner of an *R*, of the right size, swung in the right direction—that would fit."

"Why didn't you go up to the ranch earlier to check it out?"

Ramirez sniffed. "No way some rich ranching family lets me in without a warrant. And Nicoletti was fixated on Paul Hanley. The longer Paul was MIA, the more intent Nicoletti became. He made me swear I wouldn't do anything that didn't have a straight line to finding Paul. So when you texted me about Paul, I saw my opportunity to check out the ranch."

"A shame you couldn't get there a little bit sooner."

"Oh, I did. But the house was empty. You all must have been in the barn already."

"Why didn't you come in?"

"I didn't know what I was walking into. I did a quick survey of the cars. Trying to guess how many I might be up against. And that's when I saw it."

"Ricardo's bike pannier."

Ramirez nodded. "It clicked. Of course we had to test it later. But I knew."

"Me too," Lana said.

"Great minds think alike."

Lana breathed the words in. Held them.

"It was stupid of him to keep all that evidence," Lana said.

Ramirez shrugged. "He might have felt safer that way. Or he was arrogant enough to think he was in the clear. Lots of criminals would rather hold on to evidence, keep it under their control. It certainly made life easier for us. Ricardo's bike bag. The cattle brand. We also found traces of Ricardo's blood and Martin's skin cells on one of the wheelbarrows in the barn. That initial tip you gave us about a strange farmer dumping something in the middle of the night? We're pretty sure you saw Martin, dropping Ricardo in the creek by Paul's land. And then there was the car."

"The car?"

"That's how we nailed him for his father. Your daughter introduced me to a group of vigilante nursing home residents who were running their own visiting service on Mondays at Bayshore Oaks. The day Hal Rhoads died, a tall man made an unauthorized fifteen-minute visit via a side door. The old lady who manned the door wasn't sure it was

Martin—he was wearing a hat and gave her a fake name. But she identified the Maserati with one hundred percent certainty."

"And that was enough to prove he did it?"

"The lady spent the entire time Martin was inside taking photos of his car for her grandson. We've got time stamps and everything. As soon as we showed those to Martin, he folded."

"I still can't believe he killed his own father."

"I'm not sure he could either. The whole time he was confessing, he talked about it as if he was forced to do it. I think he killed Ricardo in a jealous rage, and then that fury dragged him like a runaway train through the rest of it. He *had* to hit Ricardo with the cattle brand to save his family. He *had* to smother his father with a pillow to keep control of the ranch. He *had* to set the land trust on fire to destroy any paperwork about the project. That's what he kept saying, that he had to."

Lana remembered the desperation on Martin's face in those final moments in the barn, his twisted attempts to justify his actions, to cast himself as the victim even as he threatened them. It wasn't his strength that had made him dangerous. It was his self-loathing, and his fear.

"Why didn't you storm into the barn as soon as you saw the bike pannier?" Lana asked.

"I was on my own, remember? And by the time I got to the barn, Martin already had that gun. He was waving it around, erratic. It wasn't safe. I had to pick my moment."

"So you could snowblow us with chemicals. My pores were unbalanced for a week."

Ramirez put her hands up in a conciliatory gesture. "Next time I'll consider the consequences," she said. "Before I save your life."

Lana leaned down and pulled the enormous box off the bench beside her. She slid it across the table. "I got this for you. As a token of thanks."

"Ms. Rubicon, I can't accept gifts—"

"Just open it."

Teresa Ramirez lifted the top off the box to reveal a pale blue skirt suit. She pulled out the jacket. The label was in Italian. She ran her hand over the baby-soft wool, admiring the flecks of peach and cream woven into the blue.

"I heard about your promotion," Lana said. "I figured a senior investigator deserves a wardrobe upgrade."

Ramirez folded the jacket carefully, placing it back in the box.

"I can't accept this," she said.

"What if it's a gift from a friend?"

"Are we friends now?"

Lana stretched an arm out across the table.

"Call me Lana," she said.

"Teresa." The younger woman shook her hand. "But I can't take it."

"Why not? You're a terrific detective, Teresa"—Lana looked up to make sure the name was well received—"but your choice of apparel doesn't quite match your skills."

Teresa laughed. It was a warm, throaty sound. "Do you know why I dress the way I do?"

The older woman shook her head.

"You have a lot going for you, Lana. You've got money. Class. People listen to you."

"Right. Because I dress like this."

"Wrong." Teresa looked her in the eye. "There are things about you that will never be true about me. If I show up in gray and lilac, you know what happens? I become invisible. The disappearing good girl, assigned to get coffee and not much more. But when I wear this"—Teresa stepped out of the booth and turned a lazy circle that flared her yellow blazer out around her tight black jeans—"everyone pays attention."

The fishermen at the bar certainly were. Poor Fredo looked about to slide off his stool, taking his bourbon with him.

"Not for the right reason," Lana countered.

"The reason doesn't matter. They make up their own reasons. You did, even. I can't control that. All I can do is make you see me. If you see me, I can't be invisible."

Teresa Ramirez was still standing, blue fingernails pressed to the table, face flushed. Serious.

Lana thought about what she saw. A great detective. In a yellow blazer.

"Fair enough," Lana said. She slid the box back onto the bench. "I guess you know what you're doing."

Teresa tucked herself back into the booth. "And you, Lana? What are you doing next?"

"I . . . had a good scan last month." The words were out of her mouth before Lana knew what she was saying. "The tumors are shrinking faster than expected. The doctors say I can stop doing chemotherapy, that I can switch to immunotherapy only now. One infusion every six weeks. And fewer side effects."

"That's incredible."

Lana nodded. "I'm cleared to go back to Los Angeles, to my condo. To work, if I want." She looked out the grimy window toward the sailboats.

"And?"

"I'm not sure I want to go back." Lana hadn't said this out loud yet, not even to herself.

"No?"

"No."

"They must miss you in the big city," Ramirez said.

"They might have forgotten about me."

"I don't think that's likely."

The two women stared at each other across the table. Teresa Ramirez raised her Corona.

"To being underestimated," she said.

"To being seen." Lana clinked her bottle.

CHAPTER FIFTY-SIX

IT TOOK THREE MORE WEEKS for Lana to finally make her move.

She woke up early that Wednesday to the sound of an animal shuffling outside her window. When she sat up and peeked through the blinds, she shook her head. It was Beth messing with her rock garden again. Lana got up, pulled on her robe, and went into the kitchen to brew a pot of coffee.

Lana opened the back door and handed her daughter a steaming mug. "What's bothering you, Beth?"

"Nothing." Beth accepted the cup of coffee, pocketing the piece of shale in her hand. "It's just . . . you're all packed up."

It was true. Lana had spent the past ten days working like a demon, taking down the bulletin board, sorting out shoeboxes, and bagging clothes. She'd convinced Beth it wouldn't hurt to get the bedroom painted, and Jack chose a steely blue that mirrored the slough at sunrise so perfectly you could wake up thinking you were already outside with the plovers diving for fish for their breakfast. Later today, Esteban and Max were coming to deal with the last of the junk in the garage. Lana had left a biography of Eleanor Roosevelt and a fresh legal pad on Jack's desk, and she'd convinced Beth to take a vintage suede trench coat. Everything else was moving.

Lana joined her daughter in the swirling river of stones beyond the concrete step. She picked up a yellowed hunk of sandstone, the grainy surface rough against her cold fingers. It had rained on and off all March, and Lana could see grass and thistle peeking up between the curling stone paths. By May, the whole labyrinth might be hidden in foxtails.

"Beth, we made this decision together," she said.

"I know," Beth said.

"Jack needs her own room."

"I know." Beth kept winding through the stone maze, replacing a flat black oval with a quartz-veined cube. She didn't alter the overall shape of it anymore, but she kept making adjustments. Tiny choices, made slowly over time, building something beautiful.

"Beth, we're going to make this work."

There was a shout from below, and the two women looked down the gravel hillside to the beach. Jack was down there, her back to them, paddle in hand, yelling goodbyes to a lean, muscular figure paddling farther up into the slough.

"Who's that?" Beth asked.

Lana shook her head. "Want me to get the binoculars?"

Jack bounded up the hill, her pink paddleboard on top of her head. "Mom, so I met this guy at school who's interning with the harbormaster? He's older, a senior, and he went to Semester at Sea in the fall. He was telling me all about how they lived on this ship and cataloged wildlife and I was thinking, maybe instead of buying my own boat, I could—"

Jack suddenly noticed Lana behind her mother. "Oh, hi. Heard you're coming with us to the drive-in tonight."

Lana had agreed to join Beth and Jack for date night, on one condition. "We're dressing up to celebrate, right? You'll brush your hair?"

Jack grinned and pulled a slimy rope of seaweed off her life jacket. "We're not heathens, you know."

LANA SPENT THE REST of the day directing traffic in the garage. By six that evening, she was at the front door in a new burgundy skirt suit and her dented metallic Jimmy Choos. Jack had on a pair of dark jeans with no rips in them and an old blazer of Lana's that made her look like she'd already gotten her PhD. But Beth was the real surprise. She was a vision in a forest-green knee-length dress and black square-toed boots Lana had snapped up on a trip to a nearby Nordstrom that was shutting down. If only she'd ditch that bomber jacket.

Beth handed out new homemade earrings to everyone: miniature snail shells for Jack, coral for herself, sea glass for Lana. Lana marveled at the tiny treasures in her palm, using a finger to trace the silver wire her daughter had coiled around the pale teardrops of light.

"Oh! I have a present for you too," Jack said. She disappeared behind the house, coming back with a redwood branch that had been sanded into an uneven staff.

"What's this?" Lana asked.

"A big stick." Jack grinned. "For your new office, when you find one."

"Thank you." Lana hefted the stick in her hands. "I'm looking at a potential sublet in the marina tomorrow. It could be the new headquarters for Lana Rubicon and Associates."

"Associates, Ma?" Beth raised an eyebrow.

Lana smiled. "It has a nice ring to it."

They piled into Beth's car, and twenty minutes later, they rolled into the Hot Diggity, thoroughly surprising the owner, Lolo, who was accustomed to seeing the two younger Rubicon women in scrubs and sweats. He dropped a vat of relish on his right foot, causing him to shot-put the wiener in his left hand out the service window of the little red hut. Once his foot stopped throbbing, Lolo apologized for swearing, handed them three foot-longs with onions on the house, and offered to take their picture. Even Lana had to admit that the hot dogs were delicious.

When they got to the drive-in in Salinas, Lana talked the farmer into letting them park in the middle of the front row, in a space Beth was pretty sure the farmer reserved for his own wife. Lana opened a cooler and passed out sodas to all of them—Coke for Jack, Sprite for her and Beth. Beth looked at the Sprite bottle, confused. She'd never seen Lana drink any soda other than Diet Coke. But Lana was already mid-swig. Beth opened her own bottle and took a sip. It was some kind of sparkling wine. Not bad.

The movie was a whodunit. It might have been a good one, but Lana and Jack's loud, premature conclusions about the murderer made it impossible for Beth to follow the story. By her second bottle of Sprite, it didn't really matter to Beth either.

Beth looked at Lana. Her mother's eyes were shining in the reflected light from the screen, her new suit hidden under the patchwork quilt she was sharing with Jack in the back seat. Beth didn't know, couldn't know, all the ways it would prove insufferable to have Monterey County's newest land consultant living in what had once been her garage. She didn't know the disasters would start the very next day, when she'd come home to find a massive hole punched in her roof to install skylights she hadn't ordered. All Beth knew was that they were together, they were safe, and they were laughing. And that was enough.

ACKNOWLEDGMENTS

THIS BOOK WAS BORN out of desperation and love. Four years ago, my mother—my smart, energetic, independent mother—was diagnosed with metastatic lung cancer. I changed my life and quit my job to care for her. We were grateful to be together, but as the surgeries and treatments mounted, we started to lose hope. We needed a distraction, a project that could connect us in joy instead of anxiety. This book was that project.

My mom and I have always enjoyed reading mysteries, so we started imagining one that featured characters a bit like us—hardworking California women trying to balance professional ambition and motherhood. We sat in hospital waiting rooms discussing the main characters and debating potential victims, suspects, and motives. While my mom rested, I sat next to her on the bed, writing. When she woke up, I'd hand her a cup of tea and a rough chapter to read. We kept building the story—me writing, her reading, us discussing—until the first draft was complete.

The world of the Rubicons was a world we chose, a world we leaned into, the way a houseplant stretches toward the sun. I wrote and my mom read, and we immersed ourselves in the world of the Rubicons. This book is dedicated to my mother, Sarina, who continues to bring strength, love, and humor into the world.

While this story started with me and my mom, it didn't end with us. The business of inventing a story is terrifying, and I hit about a million moments when I wondered if I should give up. Each time, a kind word from a loved one kept me going. It was my mom texting me to ask what would happen next, my best friend cooking me dinner, my husband reassuring me this was a good use of time. Henri Matisse once said that creativity takes courage. It does. But it also takes encouragement. Thank you to all the family, friends, and generous humans who read early drafts and gave valuable feedback, including Sibley Simon, Morgan Simon, Carson Nicodemus, Beck Tench, Elise Granata, Meg Watt, Scott Simon, Debbie Richetta Simon, Kay Sibley, Mike Sibley, Paul Dichter, Susan Dichter, Abby Saul, Jessica BrodeFrank, Katherine Caldwell, Kate Coltun, Maria Daversa, Will Delhagen, Jo Dwyer, Elaine Heumann Gurian, Chloe Jones, Allison Kraft, Erin Leary, Taylor Lilley, Lilia Marotta, Kiera Peacock, Serena Rivera, Kate Roberts, Sierra Van Ryck DeGroot, and Susan Walter. Your suggestions made this book stronger, and I was buoyed by your support.

Thank you to those who contributed to the research for this book. I've lived in the Monterey Bay for fifteen years, but this project helped me grow closer to the place I call home. I acknowledge and honor the longstanding care for this land by the Amah Mutsun Tribal Band and Ohlone Native people, whose stewardship continues despite waves of oppression and dislocation. Thank you to the many agencies that protect and conserve Elkhorn Slough. Thank you to my daughter Rocket for being my trusty research buddy, kneeling on the front of my paddleboard and pointing out potential murder sites along the banks. Thank you to Robert Stephens for sharing historical documents, touring me through the real Roadhouse ranch, and patiently spelling the name of every plant and bird we encountered on the rolling hills above the slough. Thank you to Jess Grigsby and Kayak Connection for teaching me about the art and business of kayak touring. Thank you to Eileen Campbell, Mark Silberstein, and the Monterey Bay Aquarium for your illustrated guide to the flora and fauna of Elkhorn Slough. Thank you to Terry Corwin for explaining the legal intricacies of land trusts, and thanks to Doctors Rachel Abrams and Bill Skinner for always being up for a gruesome medical question. Despite all this excellent advice, I'm sure I made some mistakes. All errors and exaggerations are mine.

Everyone I've thanked so far got involved before we ever imagined this book would be published. But here it is! Real! Which is only possible because of the brilliant efforts of my agent, Stefanie Lieberman, ably assisted by Molly Steinblatt and Adam Hobbins. Stefanie, Molly, and Adam taught me so much about good writing, and they challenged me to keep adding depth and layers to this story.

Thank you to Stefanie for bringing this story to Liz Stein, my editor at William Morrow. I first met Liz by phone while I was laid up with COVID-19. Even through my fevered haze, I heard Liz's vision for this book loud and clear. Thank you to Liz for steering me down creeks I might not have visited. Thank you for pushing me to put my whole heart into the Rubicon women—their goals, desires, conflicts, and most of all, the love they have for each other. I hope that love shines through.

The whole team at William Morrow has been wonderful to work with. As a debut novelist, I often felt I was stumbling into someone else's serious business. Thank you to sensitivity readers Cath Liao and Alejandra Oliva for helping me realize the full potential of these characters. Thank you to Stephanie Evans, a wonderful copy editor, and to Kim Glyder and Nancy Singer for the stylish cover art and interior design. Thank you to marketing and publicity superstars Rachel Berquist, Danielle Bartlett, and Kathleen Carter for helping readers find and connect with the Rubicons. Huge thanks to Reese Witherspoon and the Reese's Book Club team for sharing this story with millions of book lovers. And thank you to all the hardworking folks at William Morrow and HarperCollins who helped bring this book to life.

Finally, I'd like to thank you for reading this book. I wrote it to carve out a den of creative comfort for me and my mother. The idea that it might also bring some pleasure to you is beyond my wildest dreams. Wherever you are, whatever you're dealing with, I hope this story reaches out and gives you a fierce little hug in the wilderness. I'm rooting for you, and for love.

QUESTIONS FOR DISCUSSION

1. The Rubicon women embody strength in different ways: Lana, the warrior; Beth, the caregiver; and Jack, the explorer. What traits do you associate with those of a "strong woman"? How do the Rubicon women demonstrate those qualities differently from or similarly to one another?
2. Lana Rubicon is brand new to investigating crimes. What do you feel is her most effective skill as an amateur detective? What do you believe is her greatest weakness?
3. All the primary suspects—and the murder victims—have different visions for the future of the ranch. If you had the power to decide what should happen to the Rhoads ranch at the end of the story, what would you do and why?
4. Lana and Beth disagree about why the sheriffs focus on Jack as a potential suspect. As Lana puts it on page 50, "Not everything is about racism or discrimination. This is just good old-fashioned incompetence." Do you agree with Lana? What role, if any, do you see discrimination playing in the investigation of Ricardo Cruz's and Hal Rhoads's deaths?
5. Lana Rubicon and Hal Rhoads are both tough, exacting single parents. What differences do you see in their parenting styles, and how do you think those differences impact the relationships they've built with their adult children?

6. Self-love and family love are important themes throughout *Mother-Daughter Murder Night*. On page 122, Lana tells Jack, "You have to love yourself the most. No one else can do that for you." How do you feel about this advice and Jack's response to it? In what other moments of the book do these themes appear?
7. Lana Rubicon and Teresa Ramirez both use their appearance to command attention in a world that tries to render them invisible. How else do the women in the novel assert themselves? If you've had experiences of feeling invisible and wanting to assert yourself, how did you do it?
8. The whole story begins when the iron grip Lana holds on her life is suddenly knocked loose. How did this experience reverberate throughout the novel? Have you ever experienced a sudden loss of power or agency? If so, how did you deal with it?
9. Jack is hungry to go on adventures beyond her small town. On page 20, she thinks about the fact that it's not that she doesn't love the slough, she just isn't "surprised by its secrets anymore." Do you remember a time when you thought you knew everything about your community and then were surprised by a shift in your understanding?
10. The Rhoads family is full of secrets that lead to pain, emotional distance, and murder. Do you think there are times when keeping secrets from family members can be good or even compassionate? Do you agree with the Rhoadses that keeping their secrets was a necessity?
11. Lana Rubicon and Gigi Montero both offer the young women in their lives unfiltered and unsolicited advice. Have you ever received an audacious piece of advice from an elder that has stuck with you (whether you agreed with it or not)?

ABOUT THE AUTHOR

Nina Simon writes crime fiction about strong women. She is the author of the *New York Times* bestseller *Mother-Daughter Murder Night,* which she wrote for her mother as a way to entertain, comfort, and connect with her during a major health crisis. This debut novel was a Reese's Book Club pick, a Golden Poppy Award winner, and a "Best of 2023" selection for Amazon, Barnes & Noble, CrimeReads, and *Library Journal.*

Before turning to fiction, Nina wore many hats: NASA engineer, slam poet, game designer, museum director, and nonprofit CEO. Her work on community participation in museums, libraries, parks, and theaters has been featured in the *Wall Street Journal* and the *New York Times,* as well as on NPR and the TEDx stage. Born and raised in Los Angeles, Nina now lives off the grid in the Santa Cruz Mountains with her family. More information can be found on her website, ninaksimon.com.